Zenescope Entertainment Presents:

Grimm
Fairy Tales

Different Seasons

GRIMM FAIRY TALES
DIFFERENT SEASONS

CREATED AND STORY BY
JOE BRUSHA
RALPH TEDESCO

TRADE DESIGN BY
CHRISTOPHER COTE

TRADE EDITED BY
RALPH TEDESCO

THIS VOLUME REPRINTS THE FOLLOWING COMIC BOOK ISSUES PUBLISHED BY ZENESCOPE ENTERTAINMENT: GRIMM FAIRY TALES GIANT-SIZED #1, GRIMM FAIRY TALES 2009 HALLOWEEN EDITION, GRIMM FAIRY TALES 2009 HOLIDAY EDITION AND GRIMM FAIRY TALES 2009 LAS VEGAS ANNUAL.

WWW.ZENESCOPE.COM

FIRST EDITION, FEBRUARY 2011
ISBN: 978-0-9830404-0-8

zenescope
WWW.ZENESCOPE.COM
ZENESCOPE ENTERTAINMENT, INC.

Grimm Fairy Tales: Different Seasons trade paperback, February, 2011. First Printing. Published by Zenescope Entertainment Inc., 433 Caredean Drive, Ste. C, Horsham, Pennsylvania 19044.

Grimm Fairy Tales
Different Seasons

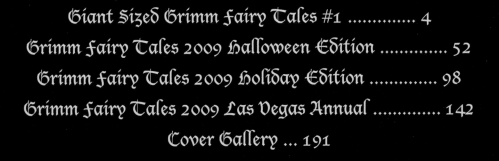

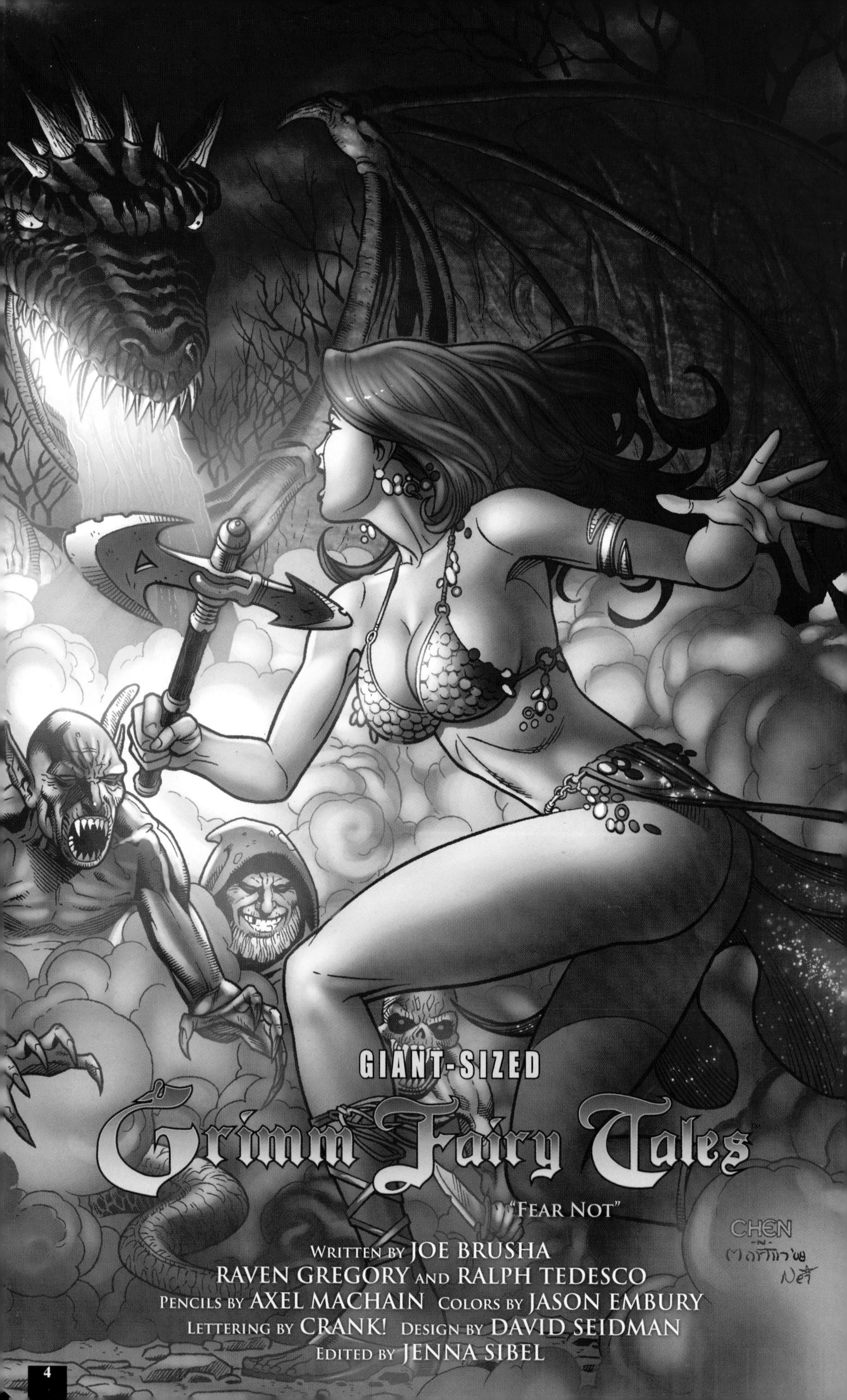

GIANT-SIZED

Grimm Fairy Tales™

"Fear Not"

Written by JOE BRUSHA
RAVEN GREGORY and RALPH TEDESCO
Pencils by AXEL MACHAIN Colors by JASON EMBURY
Lettering by CRANK! Design by DAVID SEIDMAN
Edited by JENNA SIBEL

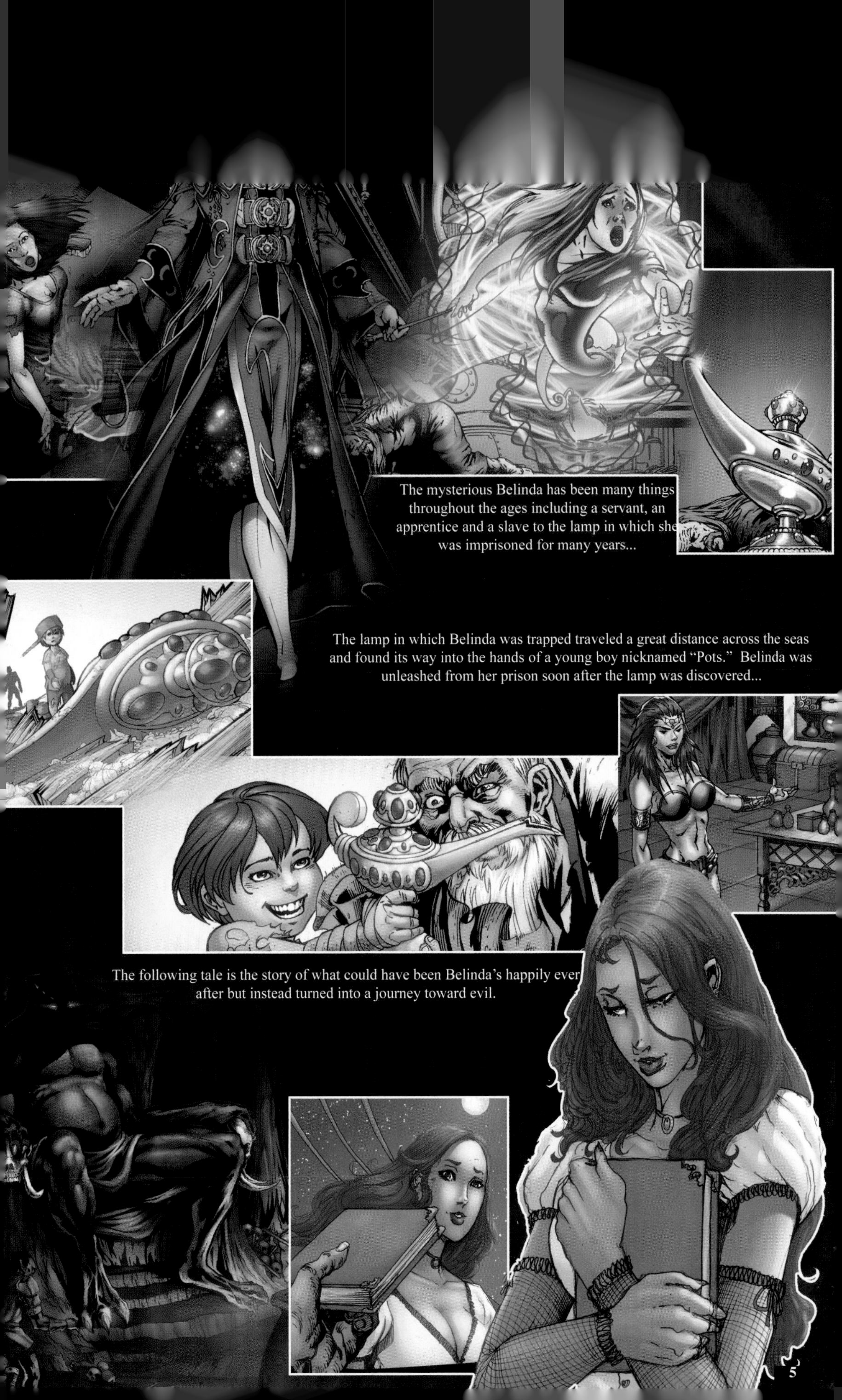
The mysterious Belinda has been many things throughout the ages including a servant, an apprentice and a slave to the lamp in which she was imprisoned for many years...
The lamp in which Belinda was trapped traveled a great distance across the seas and found its way into the hands of a young boy nicknamed "Pots." Belinda was unleashed from her prison soon after the lamp was discovered...
The following tale is the story of what could have been Belinda's happily ever after but instead turned into a journey toward evil.

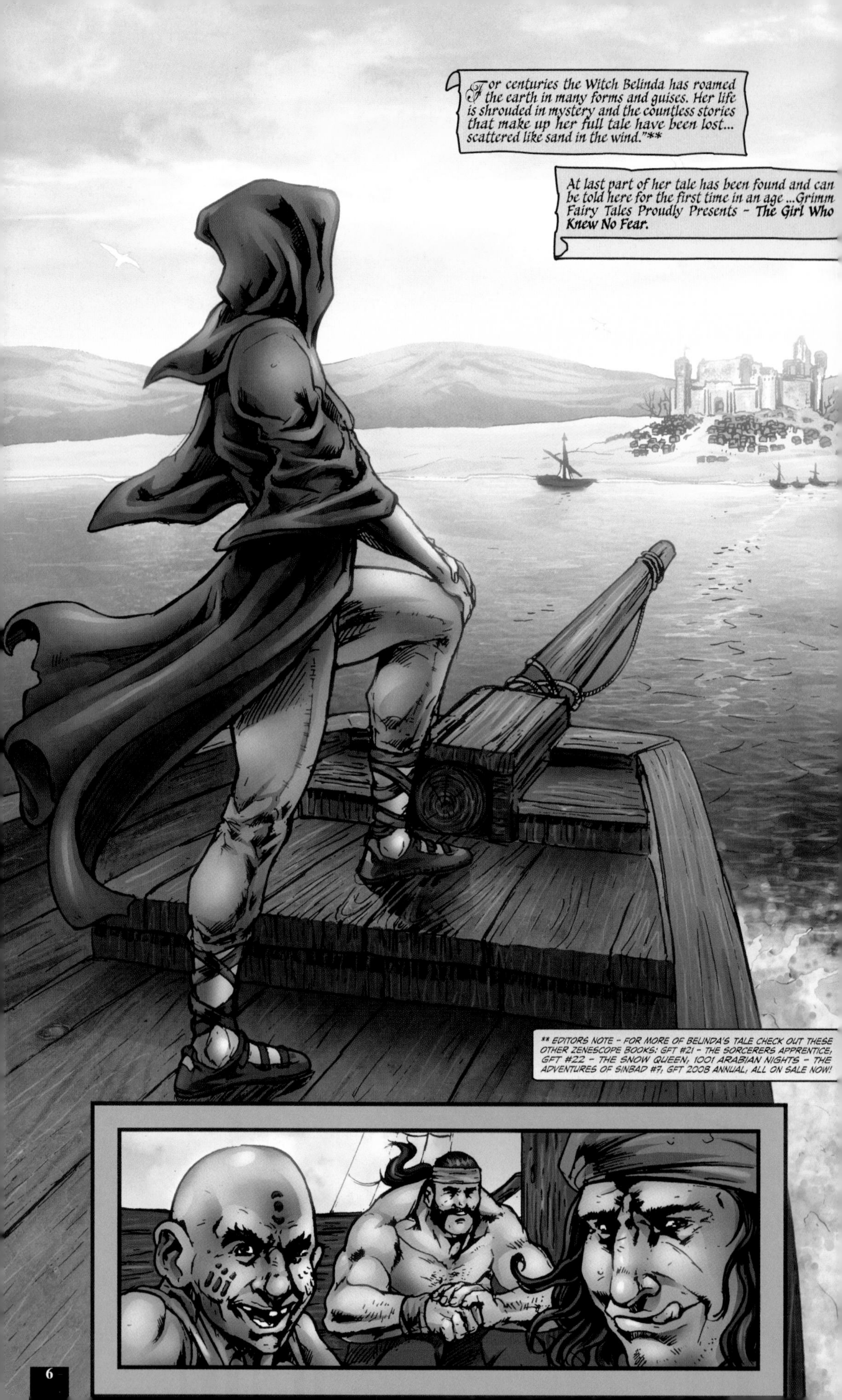
For centuries the Witch Belinda has roamed the earth in many forms and guises. Her life is shrouded in mystery and the countless stories that make up her full tale have been lost... scattered like sand in the wind."**
At last part of her tale has been found and can be told here for the first time in an age ...Grimm Fairy Tales Proudly Presents - The Girl Who Knew No Fear.
** EDITORS NOTE - FOR MORE OF BELINDA'S TALE CHECK OUT THESE OTHER ZENESCOPE BOOKS: GFT #21 - THE SORCERERS APPRENTICE, GFT #22 - THE SNOW QUEEN, 1001 ARABIAN NIGHTS - THE ADVENTURES OF SINBAD #7, GFT 2008 ANNUAL; ALL ON SALE NOW!

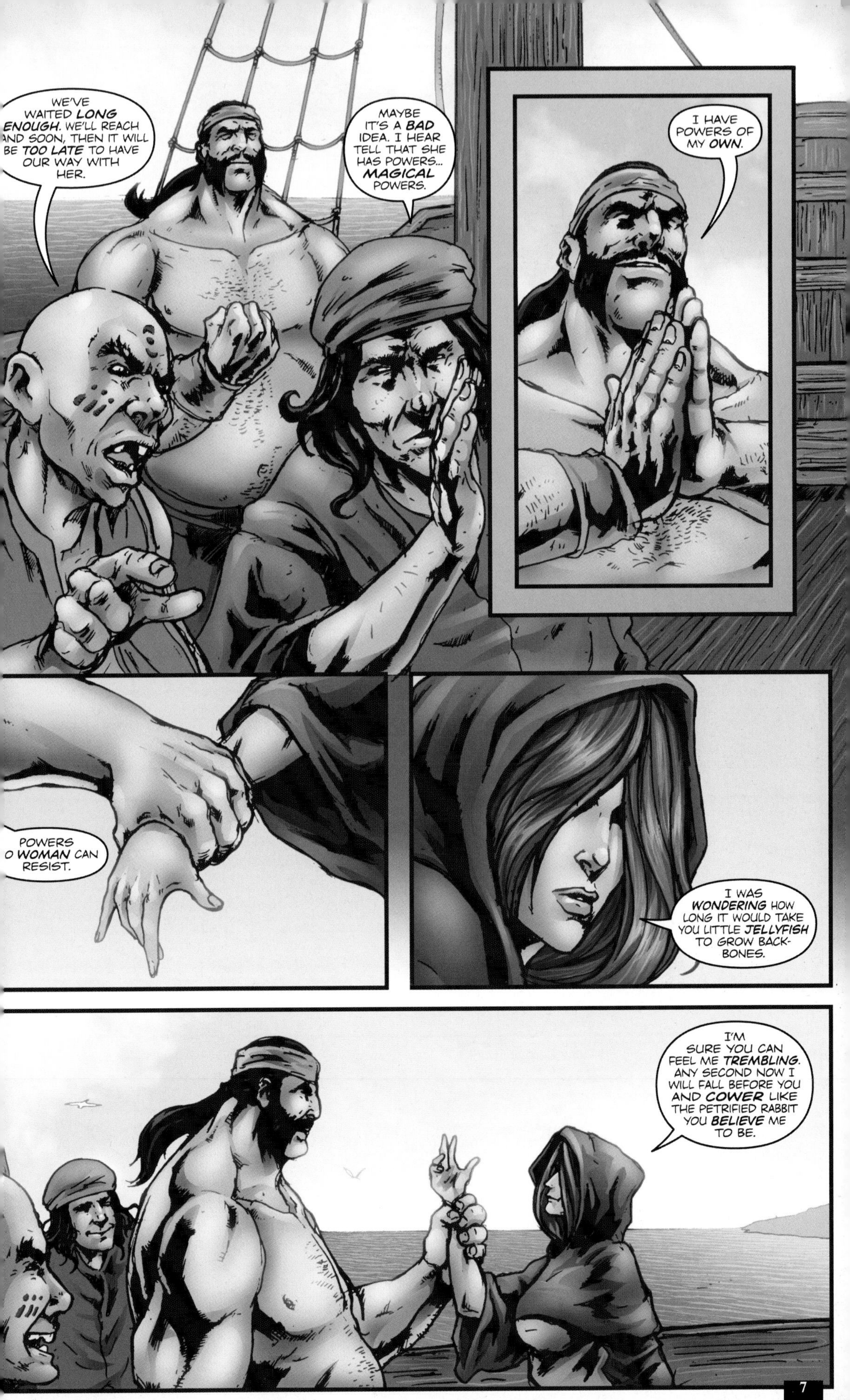
WE'VE WAITED LONG ENOUGH. WE'LL REACH AND SOON, THEN IT WILL BE TOO LATE TO HAVE OUR WAY WITH HER.
MAYBE IT'S A BAD IDEA. I HEAR TELL THAT SHE HAS POWERS... MAGICAL POWERS.
I HAVE POWERS OF MY OWN.
POWERS O WOMAN CAN RESIST.
I WAS WONDERING HOW LONG IT WOULD TAKE YOU LITTLE JELLYFISH TO GROW BACK-BONES.
I'M SURE YOU CAN FEEL ME TREMBLING. ANY SECOND NOW I WILL FALL BEFORE YOU AND COWER LIKE THE PETRIFIED RABBIT YOU BELIEVE ME TO BE.

AS SOON AS I LEARN WHAT IT IS TO *FEEL* FEAR...

BUT I *DOUBT* THAT WILL HAPPEN BEFORE YOU *LOSE* YOUR ARM.

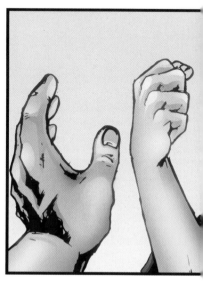

I HATE THIS CONSTANT ROAMING FROM PLACE TO PLACE... SEARCHING FOR A HOME THAT SUITS MY NEEDS. HOW I LONG FOR MY PALACE BACK IN BAGHDAD. *

*EDITORS NOTE: SEE '1001 ARABIAN NIGHTS – THE ADVENTURES OF SINBAD #7', ON SALE NOW, & '1001 ARABIAN NIGHTS/GRIMM FAIRY TALES - ALADDIN', COMING SOON!

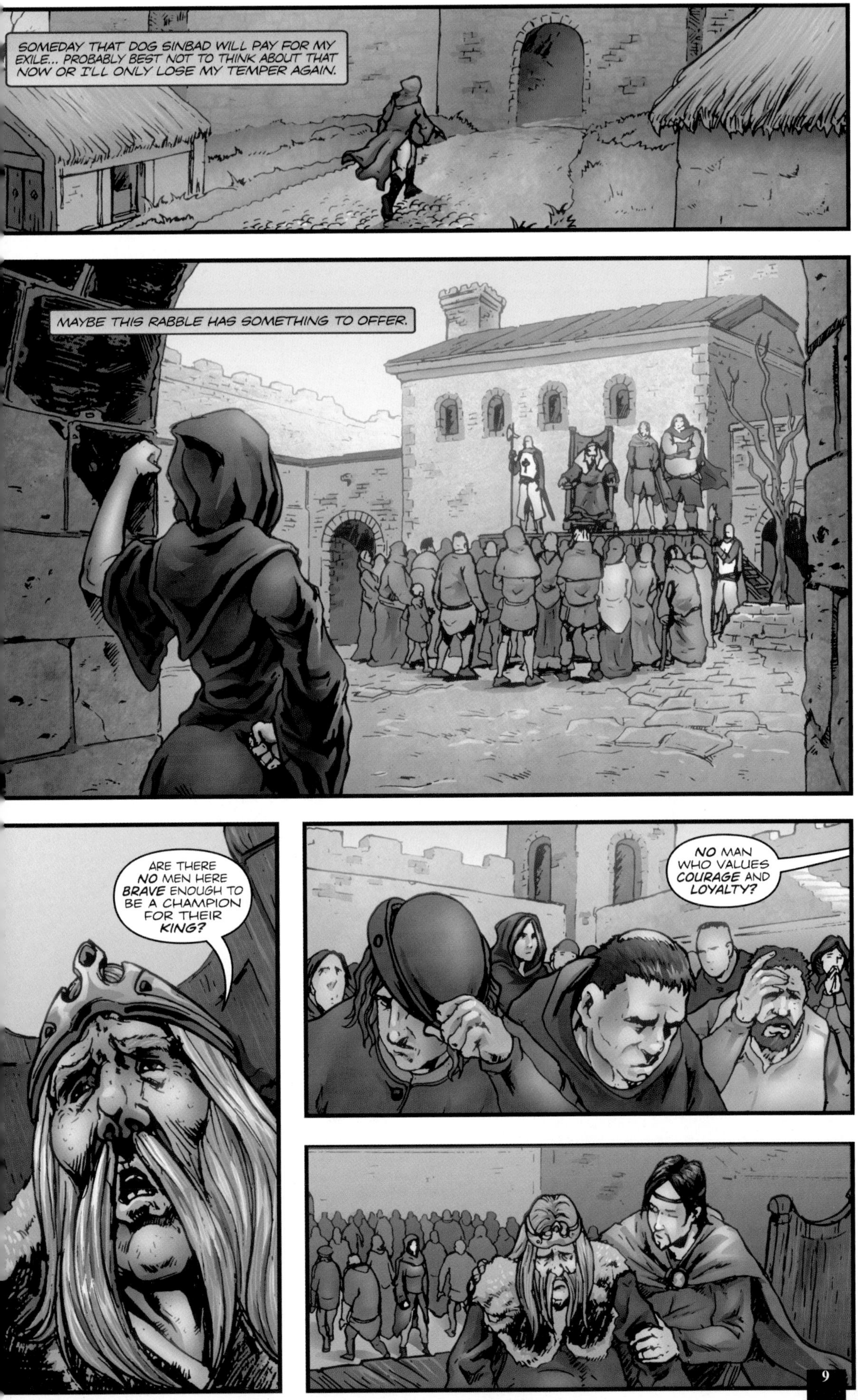

SOMEDAY THAT DOG SINBAD WILL PAY FOR MY EXILE... PROBABLY BEST NOT TO THINK ABOUT THAT NOW OR I'LL ONLY LOSE MY TEMPER AGAIN.
MAYBE THIS RABBLE HAS SOMETHING TO OFFER.
ARE THERE NO MEN HERE BRAVE ENOUGH TO BE A CHAMPION FOR THEIR KING?
NO MAN WHO VALUES COURAGE AND LOYALTY?

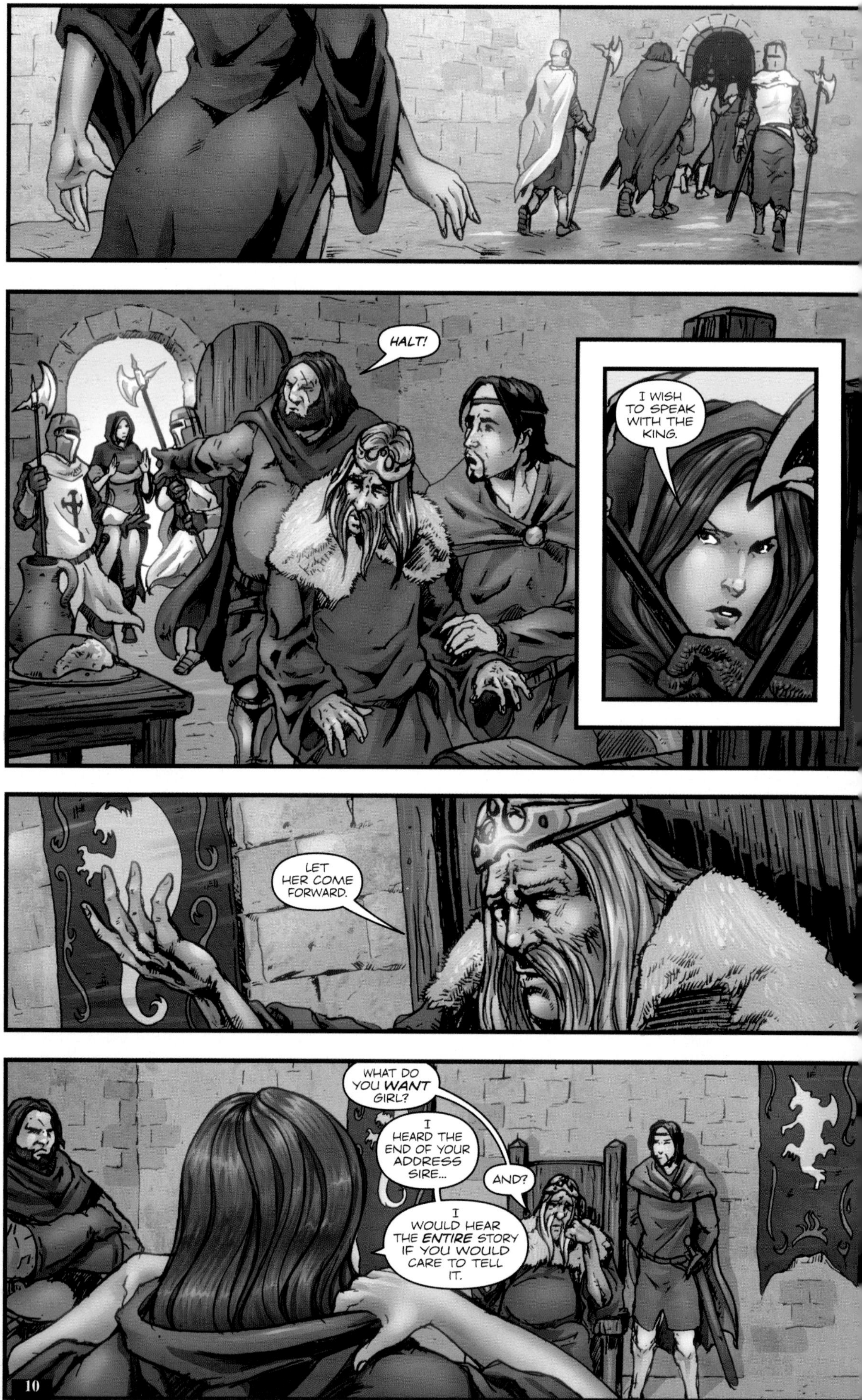
HALT!
I WISH TO SPEAK WITH THE KING.
LET HER COME FORWARD.
WHAT DO YOU WANT GIRL?
I HEARD THE END OF YOUR ADDRESS SIRE...
AND?
I WOULD HEAR THE ENTIRE STORY IF YOU WOULD CARE TO TELL IT.

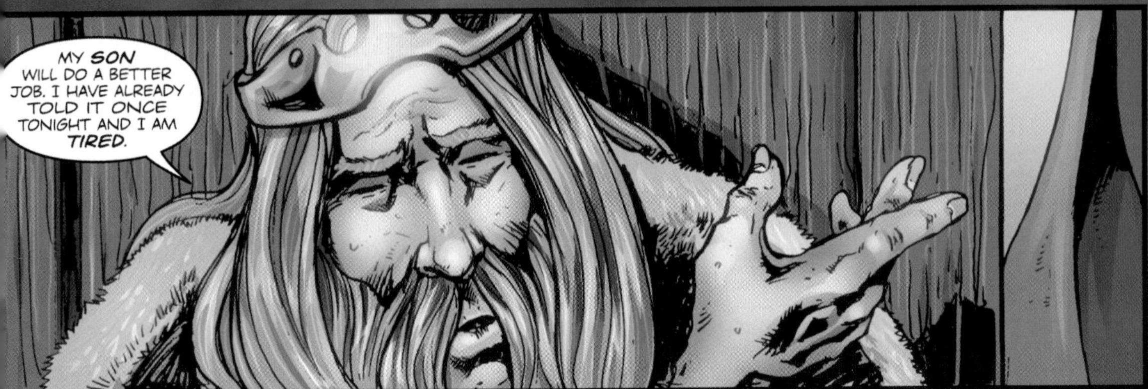
MY SON WILL DO A BETTER JOB. I HAVE ALREADY TOLD IT ONCE TONIGHT AND I AM TIRED.

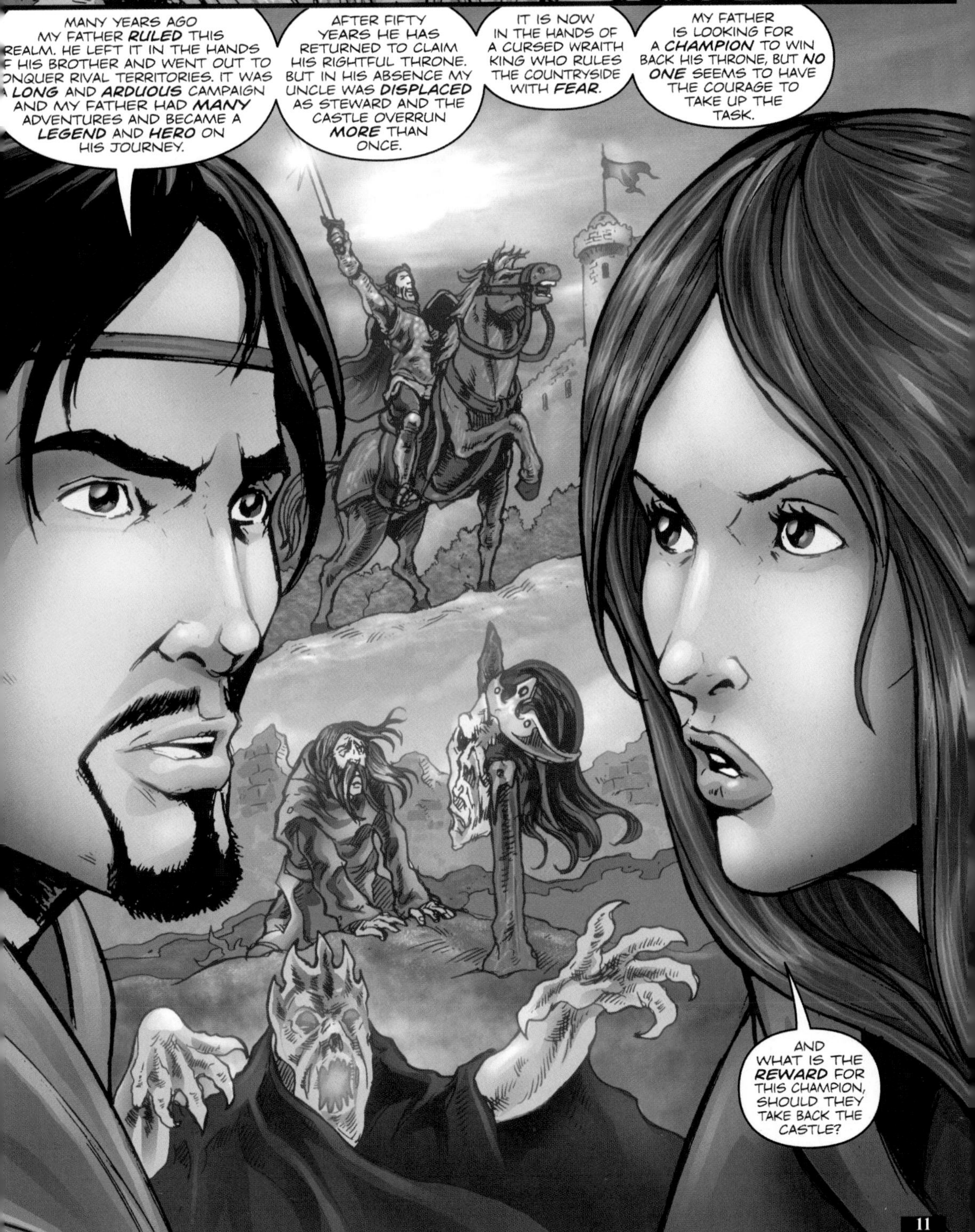
MANY YEARS AGO MY FATHER RULED THIS REALM. HE LEFT IT IN THE HANDS OF HIS BROTHER AND WENT OUT TO CONQUER RIVAL TERRITORIES. IT WAS A LONG AND ARDUOUS CAMPAIGN AND MY FATHER HAD MANY ADVENTURES AND BECAME A LEGEND AND HERO ON HIS JOURNEY.
AFTER FIFTY YEARS HE HAS RETURNED TO CLAIM HIS RIGHTFUL THRONE. BUT IN HIS ABSENCE MY UNCLE WAS DISPLACED AS STEWARD AND THE CASTLE OVERRUN MORE THAN ONCE.
IT IS NOW IN THE HANDS OF A CURSED WRAITH KING WHO RULES THE COUNTRYSIDE WITH FEAR.
MY FATHER IS LOOKING FOR A CHAMPION TO WIN BACK HIS THRONE, BUT NO ONE SEEMS TO HAVE THE COURAGE TO TAKE UP THE TASK.
AND WHAT IS THE REWARD FOR THIS CHAMPION, SHOULD THEY TAKE BACK THE CASTLE?

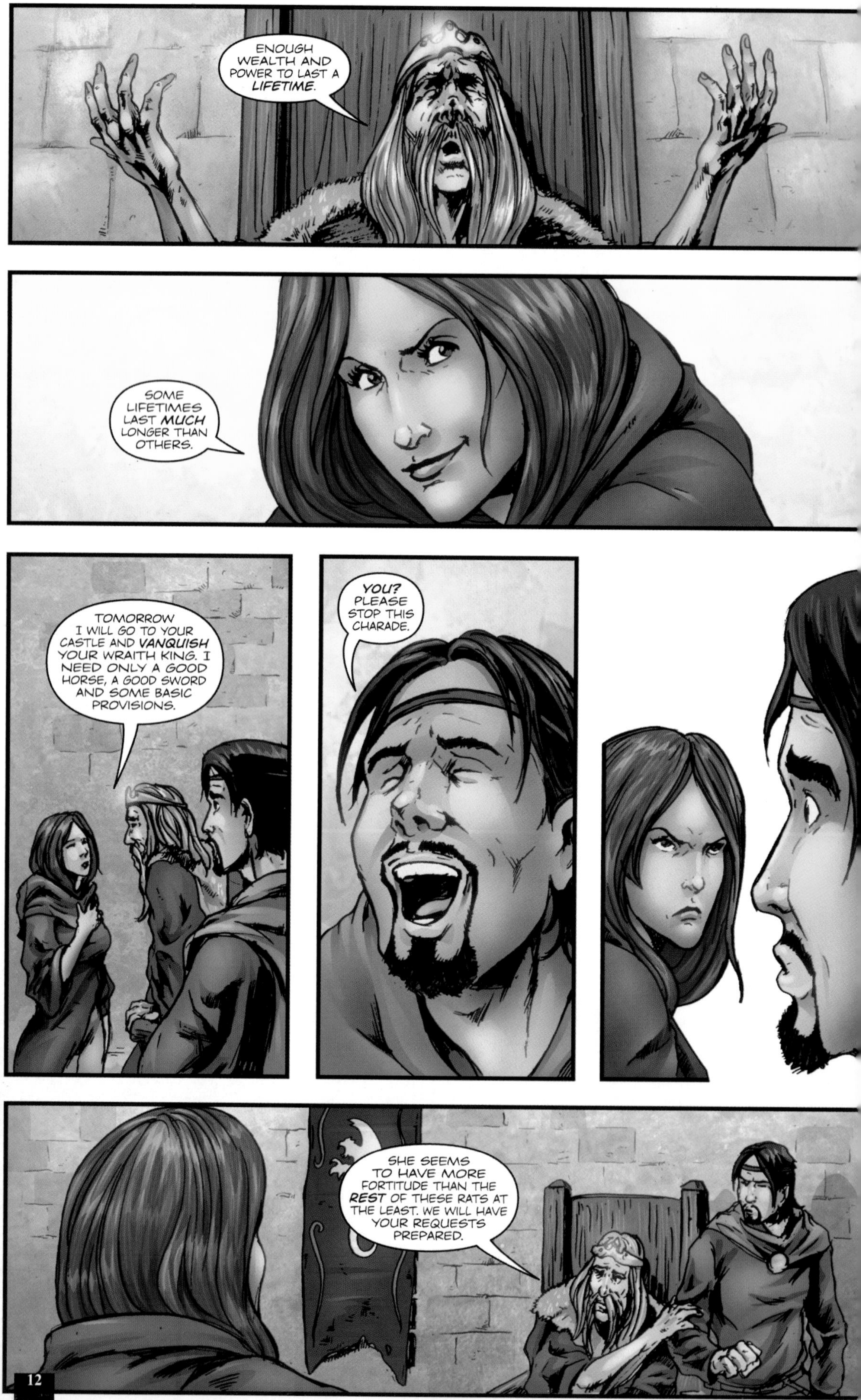
ENOUGH WEALTH AND POWER TO LAST A LIFETIME.
SOME LIFETIMES LAST MUCH LONGER THAN OTHERS.
TOMORROW I WILL GO TO YOUR CASTLE AND VANQUISH YOUR WRAITH KING. I NEED ONLY A GOOD HORSE, A GOOD SWORD AND SOME BASIC PROVISIONS.
YOU? PLEASE STOP THIS CHARADE.
SHE SEEMS TO HAVE MORE FORTITUDE THAN THE REST OF THESE RATS AT THE LEAST. WE WILL HAVE YOUR REQUESTS PREPARED.

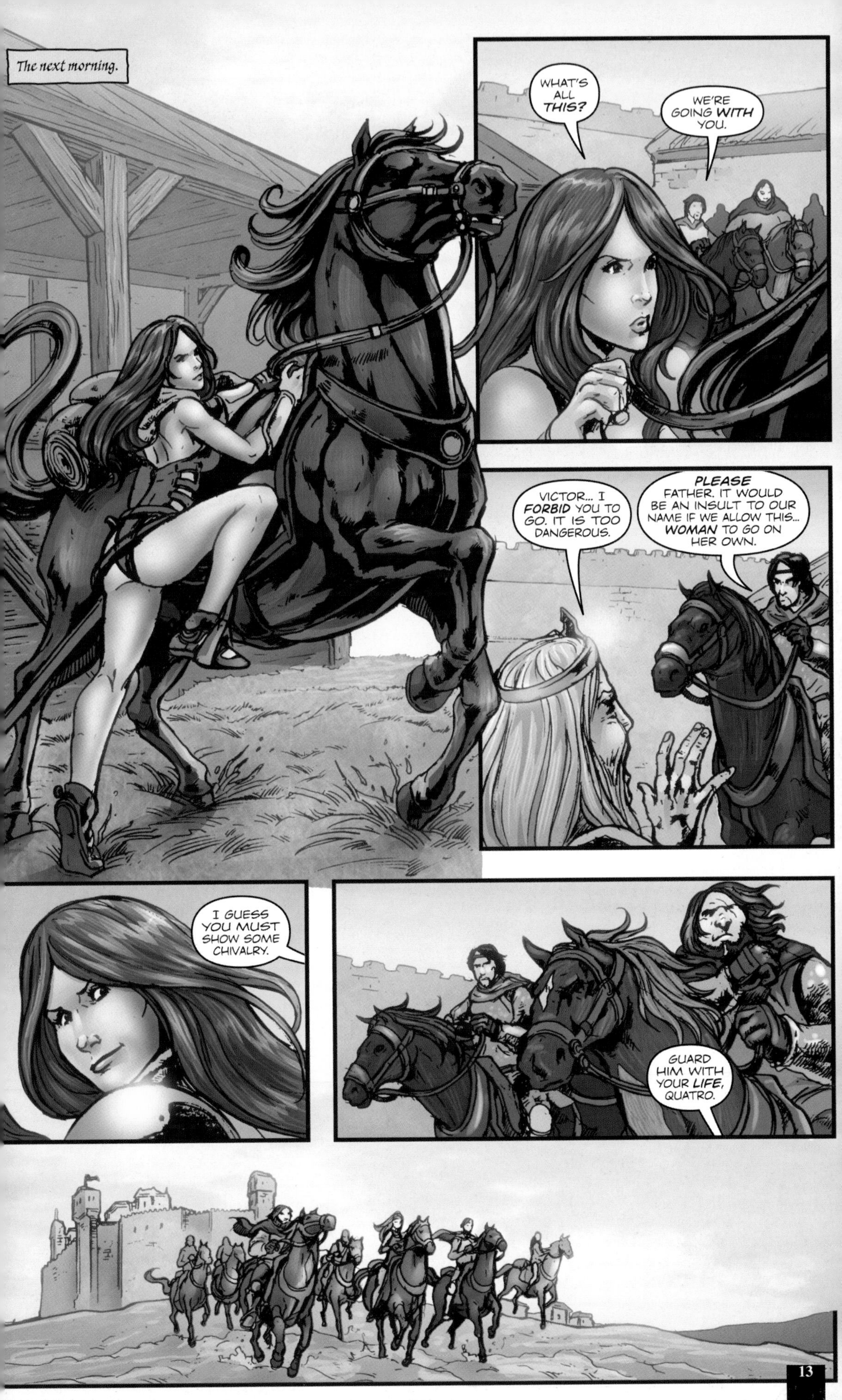
The next morning.
WHAT'S ALL THIS?
WE'RE GOING WITH YOU.
VICTOR... I FORBID YOU TO GO. IT IS TOO DANGEROUS.
PLEASE FATHER. IT WOULD BE AN INSULT TO OUR NAME IF WE ALLOW THIS... WOMAN TO GO ON HER OWN.
I GUESS YOU MUST SHOW SOME CHIVALRY.
GUARD HIM WITH YOUR LIFE, QUATRO.

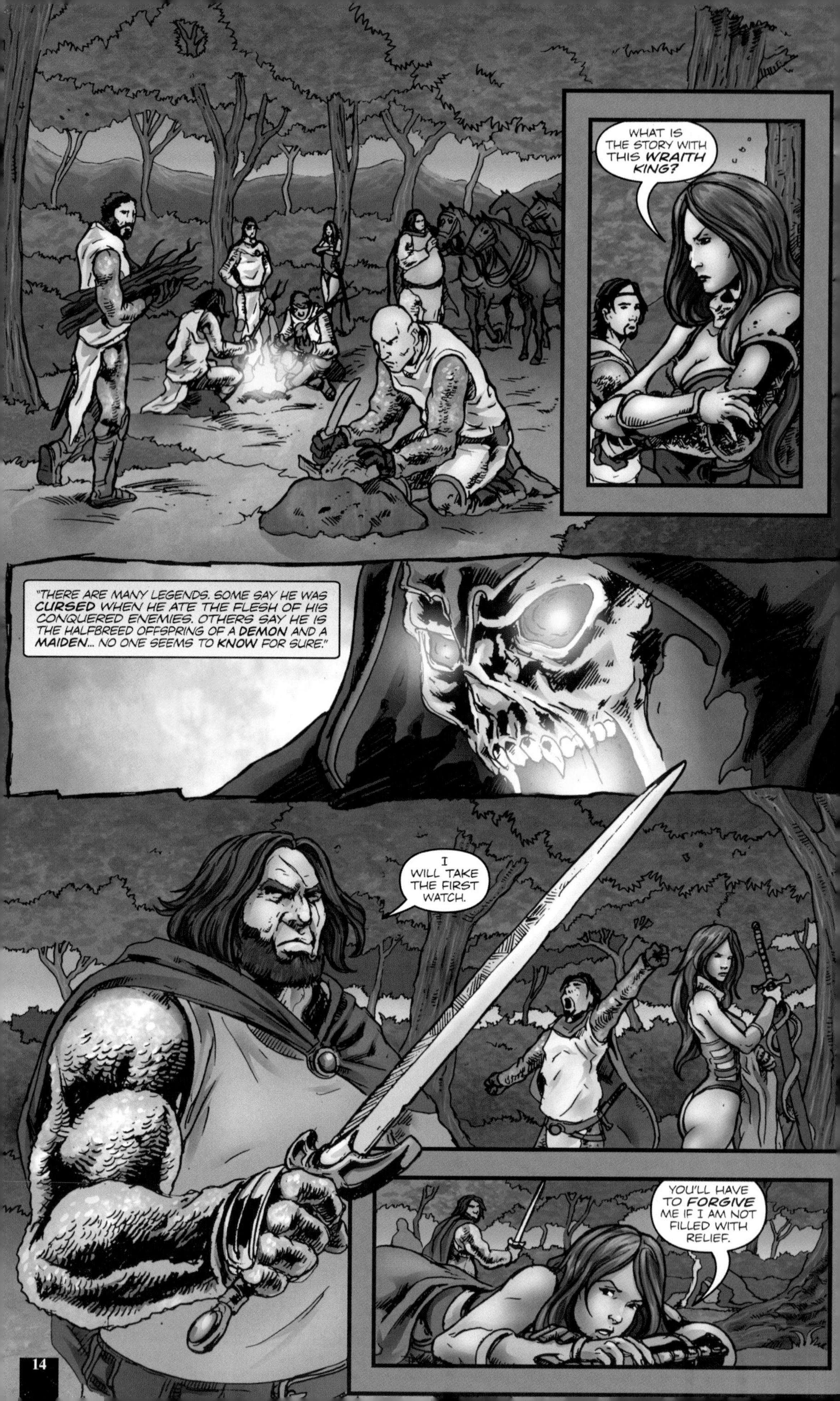

WHAT IS THE STORY WITH THIS WRAITH KING?
"THERE ARE MANY LEGENDS. SOME SAY HE WAS CURSED WHEN HE ATE THE FLESH OF HIS CONQUERED ENEMIES. OTHERS SAY HE IS THE HALFBREED OFFSPRING OF A DEMON AND A MAIDEN... NO ONE SEEMS TO KNOW FOR SURE."
I WILL TAKE THE FIRST WATCH.
YOU'LL HAVE TO FORGIVE ME IF I AM NOT FILLED WITH RELIEF.

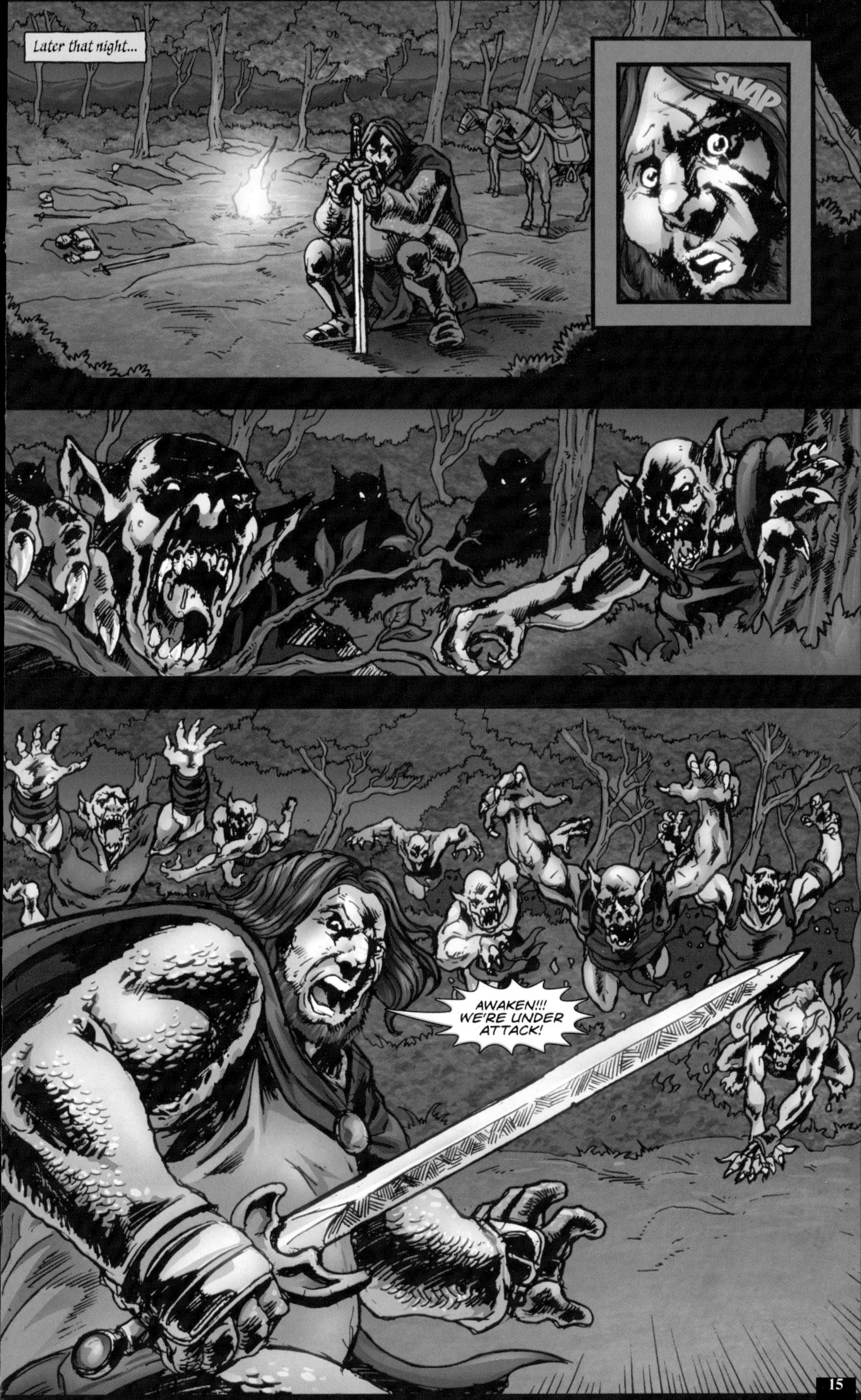
Later that night...
SNAP
AWAKEN!!! WE'RE UNDER ATTACK!

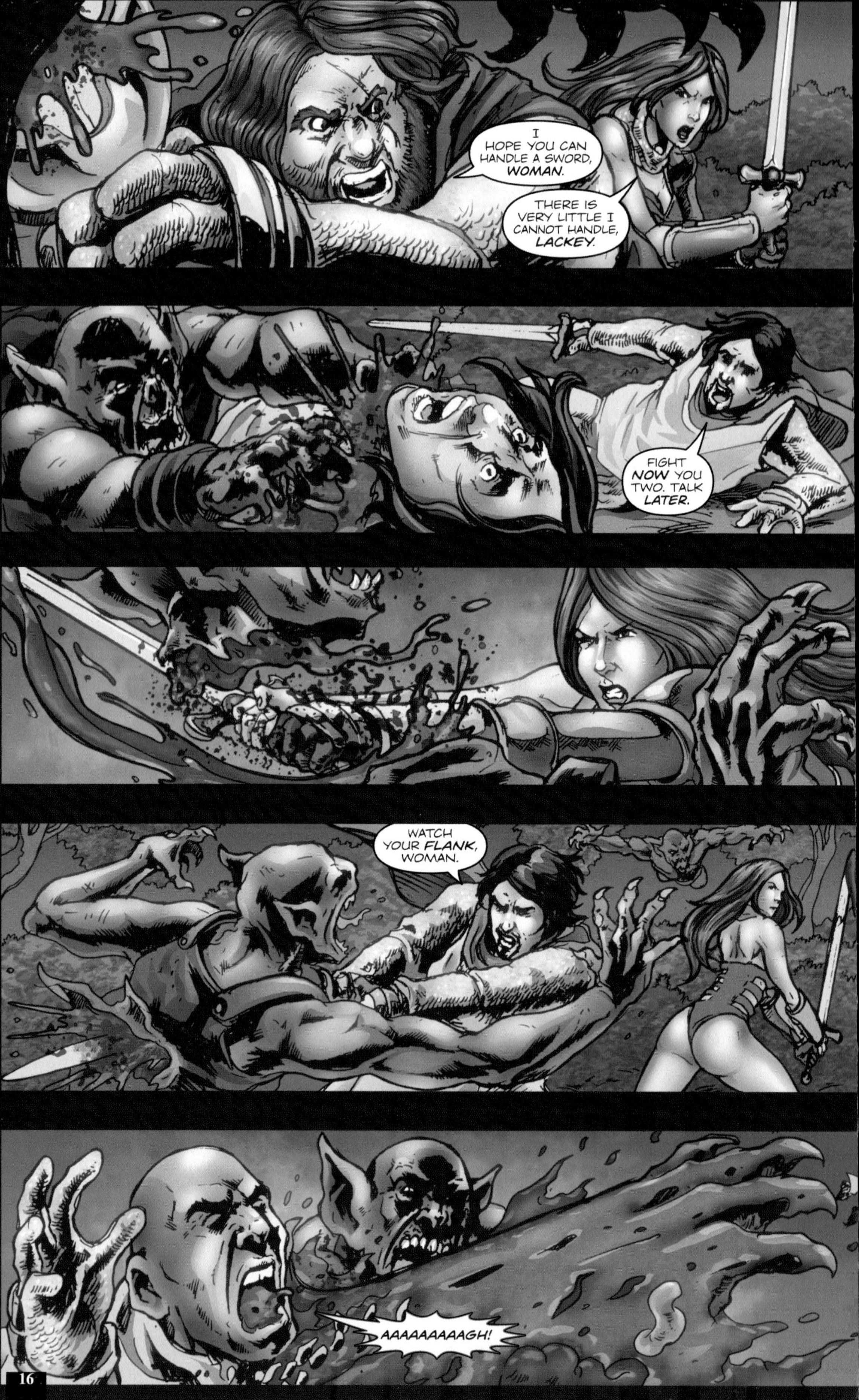
I HOPE YOU CAN HANDLE A SWORD, WOMAN.
THERE IS VERY LITTLE I CANNOT HANDLE, LACKEY.
FIGHT NOW YOU TWO. TALK LATER.
WATCH YOUR FLANK, WOMAN.
AAAAAAAAAGH!

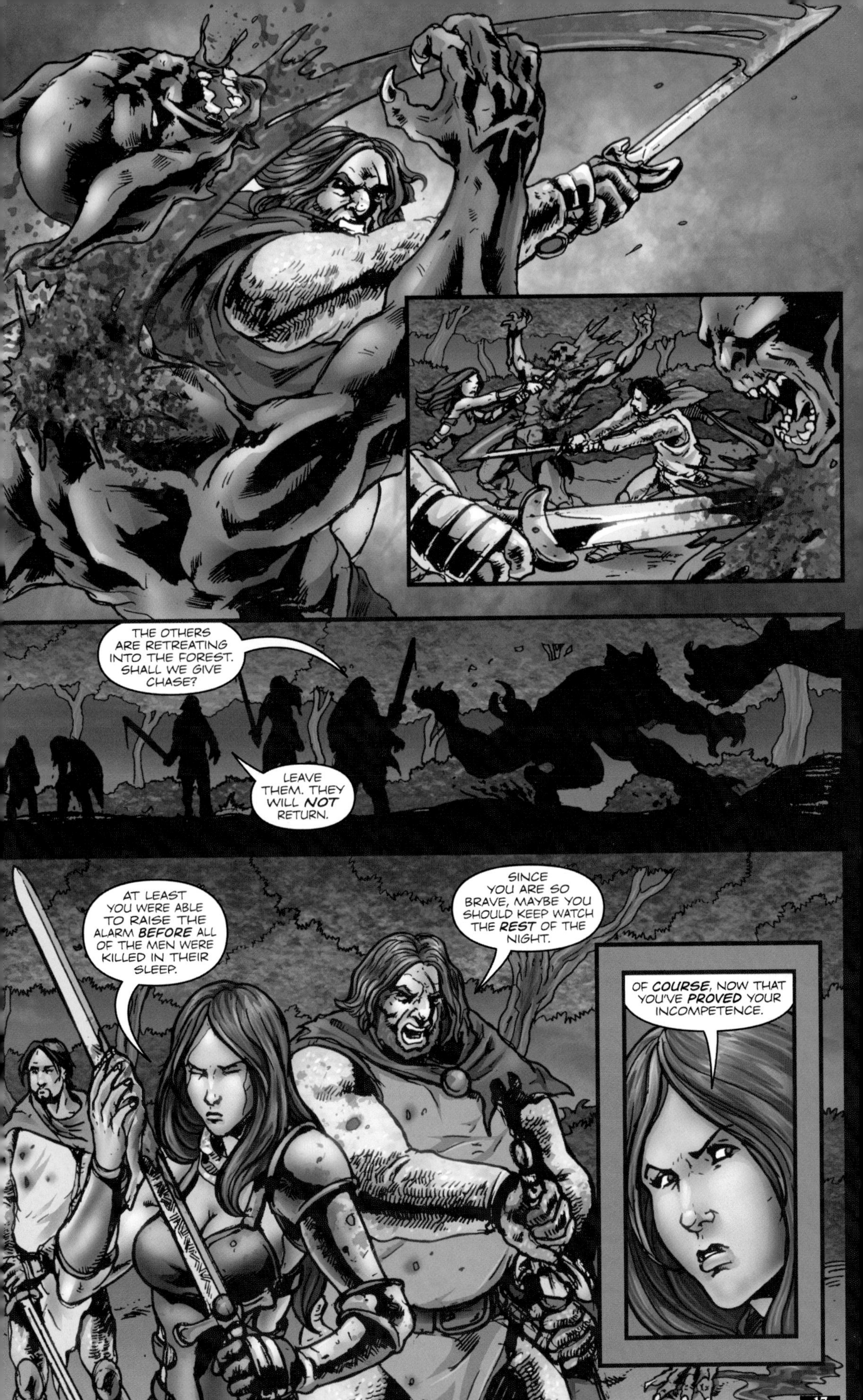
THE OTHERS ARE RETREATING INTO THE FOREST. SHALL WE GIVE CHASE?
LEAVE THEM. THEY WILL NOT RETURN.
AT LEAST YOU WERE ABLE TO RAISE THE ALARM BEFORE ALL OF THE MEN WERE KILLED IN THEIR SLEEP.
SINCE YOU ARE SO BRAVE, MAYBE YOU SHOULD KEEP WATCH THE REST OF THE NIGHT.
OF COURSE, NOW THAT YOU'VE PROVED YOUR INCOMPETENCE.

I WANT TO APOLOGIZE.

FOR...

I MISJUDGED YOU.

ONE FIGHT AND YOU ARE READY TO CHANGE YOUR OPINION OF ME?

I HAVE NEVER SEEN A WOMAN FIGHT LIKE YOU. IN FACT I HAVE SEEN VERY FEW MEN FIGHT LIKE YOU.

TELL ME, WHERE DID YOU COME FROM AND WHERE DID YOU LEARN TO FIGHT LIKE THAT?

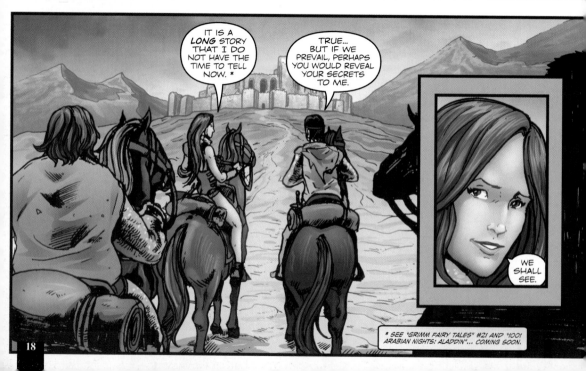

IT IS A LONG STORY THAT I DO NOT HAVE THE TIME TO TELL NOW. *

TRUE... BUT IF WE PREVAIL, PERHAPS YOU WOULD REVEAL YOUR SECRETS TO ME.

WE SHALL SEE.

* SEE "GRIMM FAIRY TALES" #21 AND "1001 ARABIAN NIGHTS: ALADDIN"... COMING SOON.

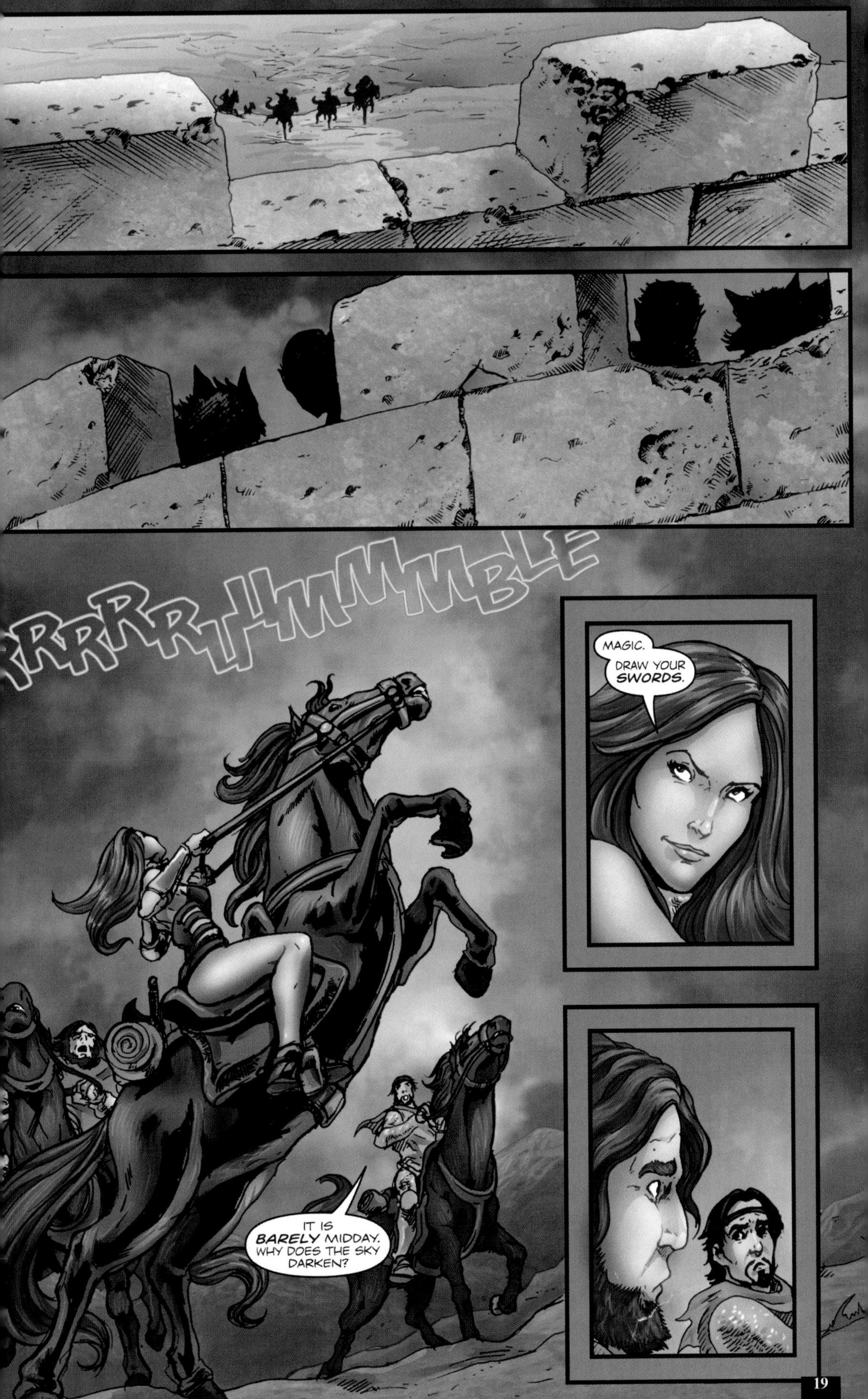

RRRRUMMMBLE
MAGIC.
DRAW YOUR SWORDS.
IT IS BARELY MIDDAY. WHY DOES THE SKY DARKEN?

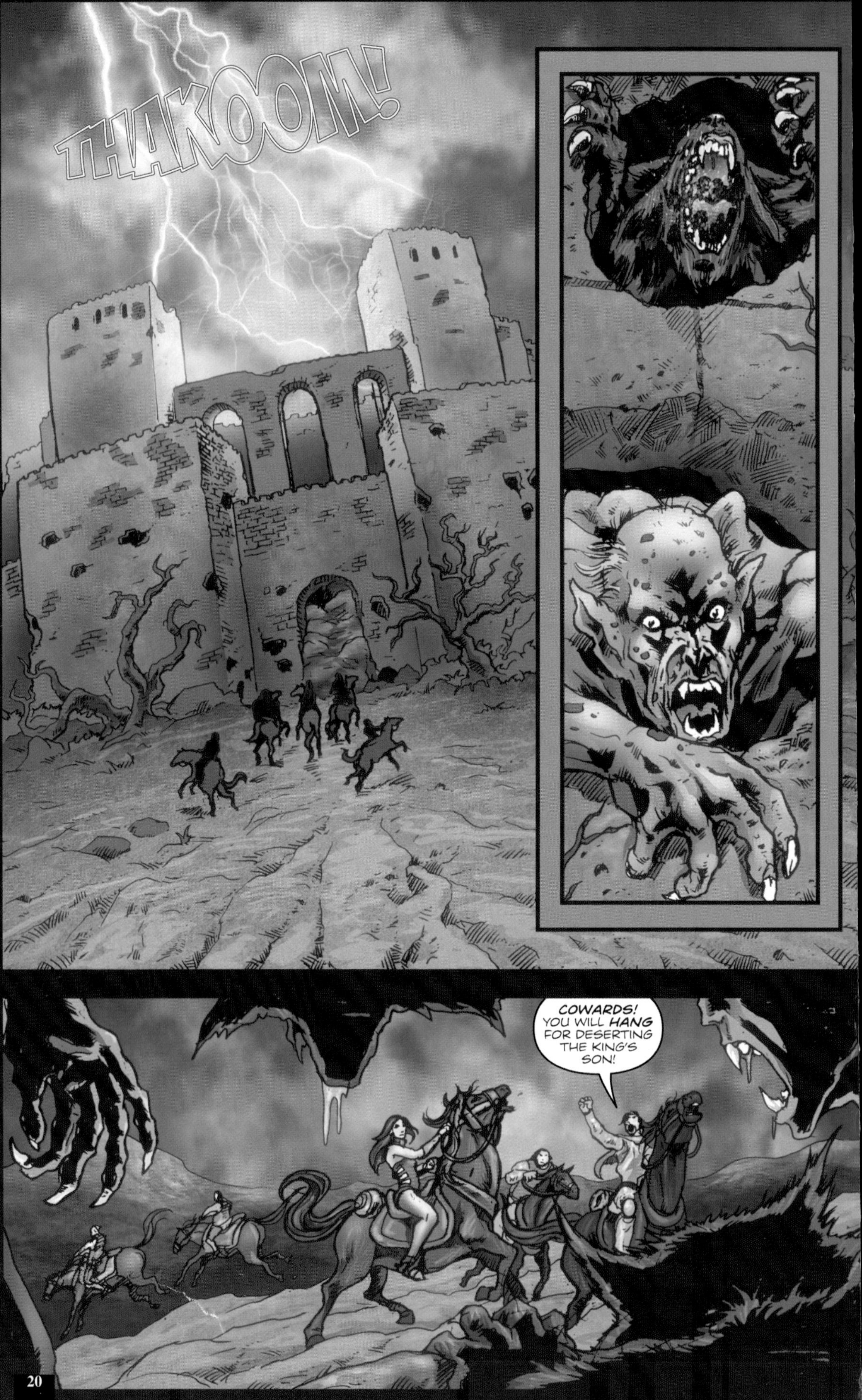
THAKOOM!
COWARDS! YOU WILL HANG FOR DESERTING THE KING'S SON!

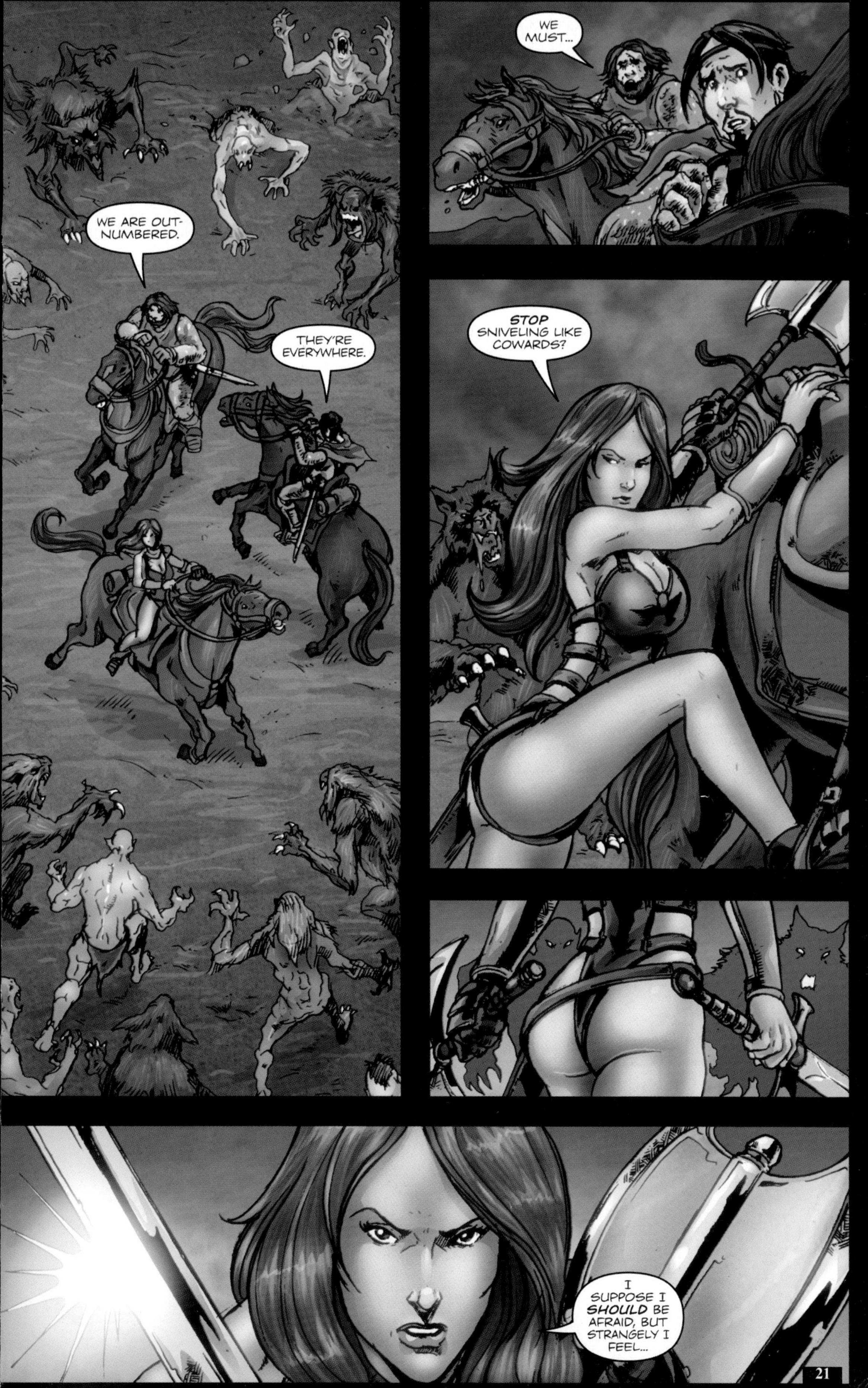
WE ARE OUT-NUMBERED.
THEY'RE EVERYWHERE.
WE MUST...
STOP SNIVELING LIKE COWARDS?
I SUPPOSE I SHOULD BE AFRAID, BUT STRANGELY I FEEL...

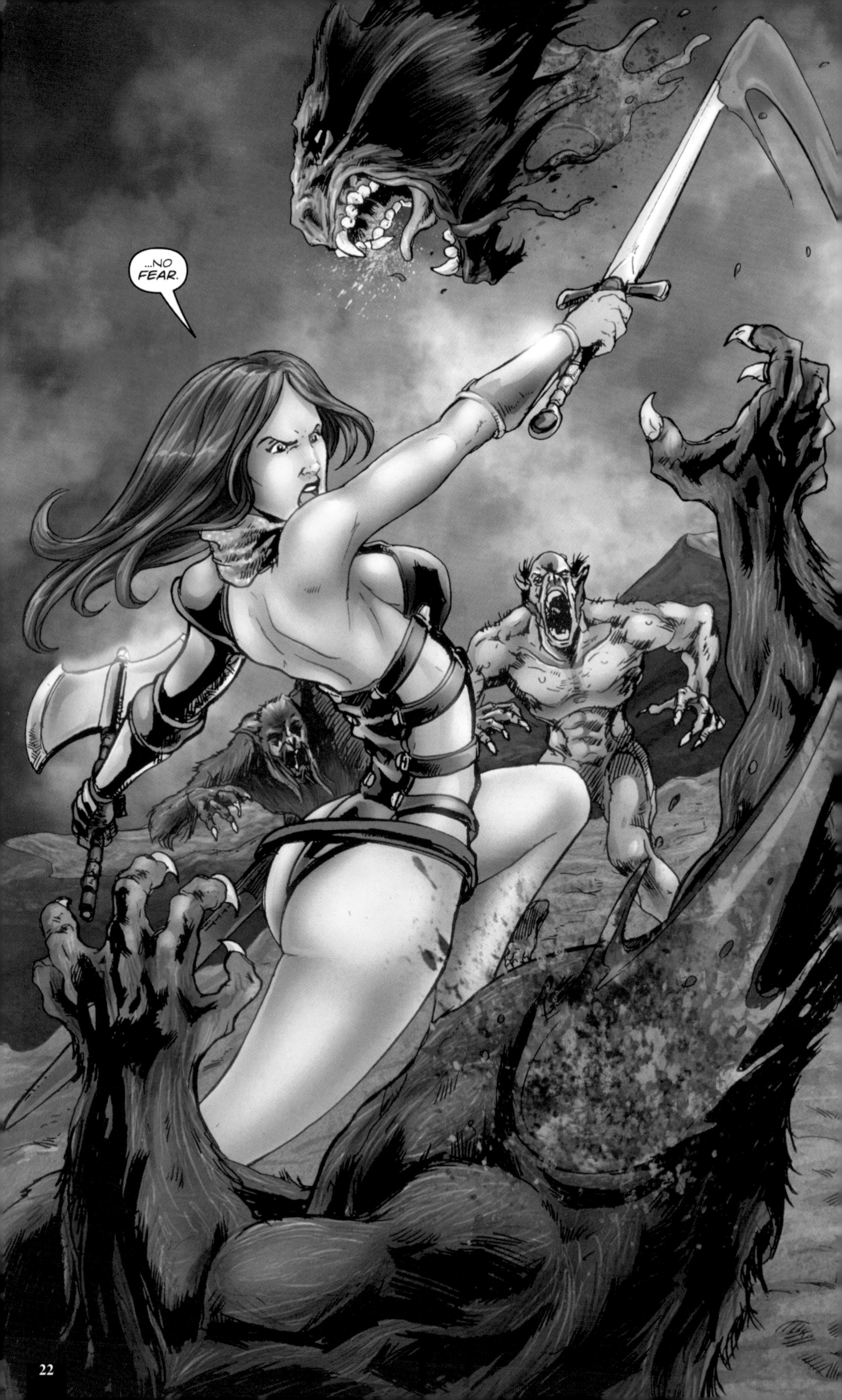
...NO FEAR.

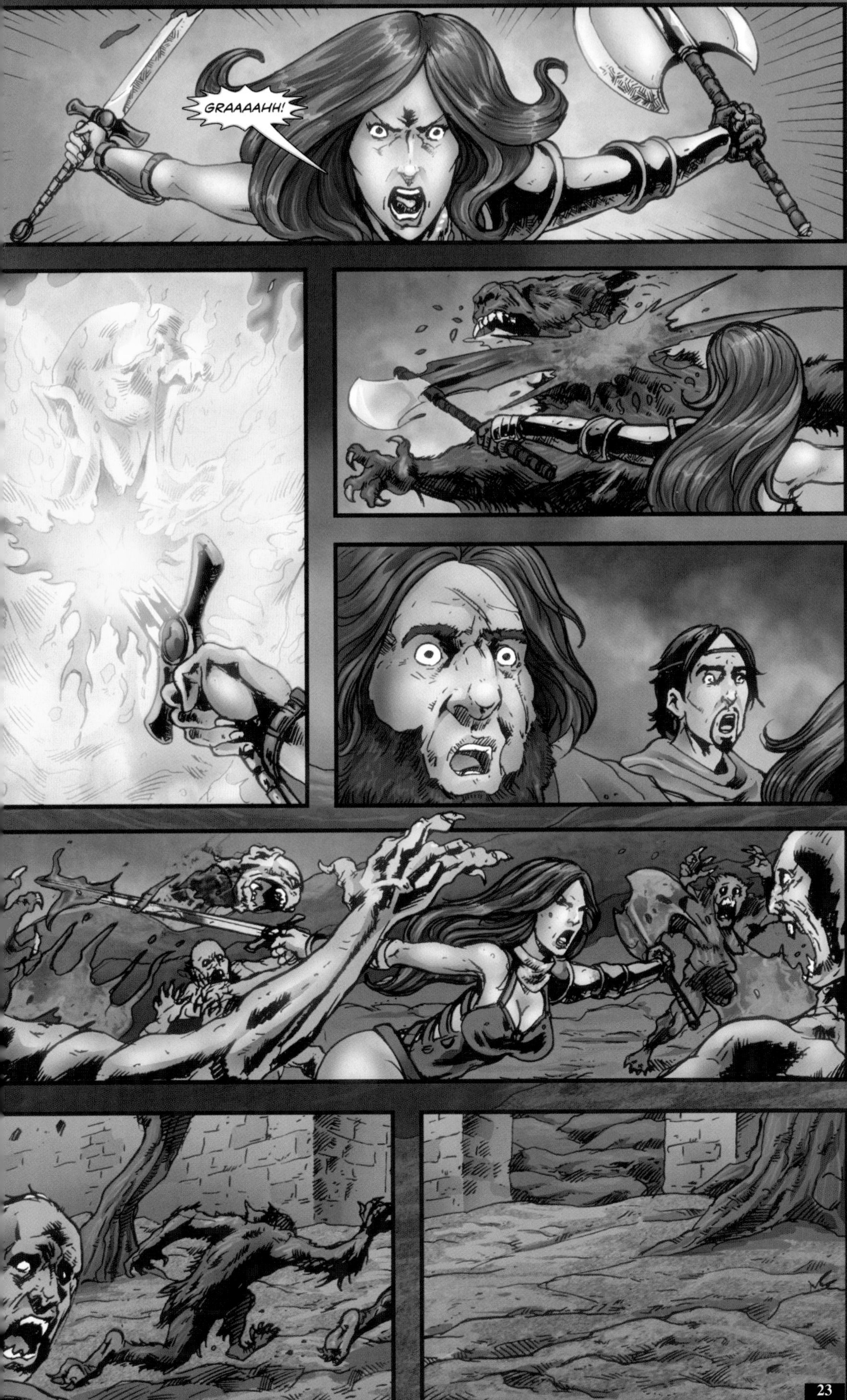
GRAAAAHH!

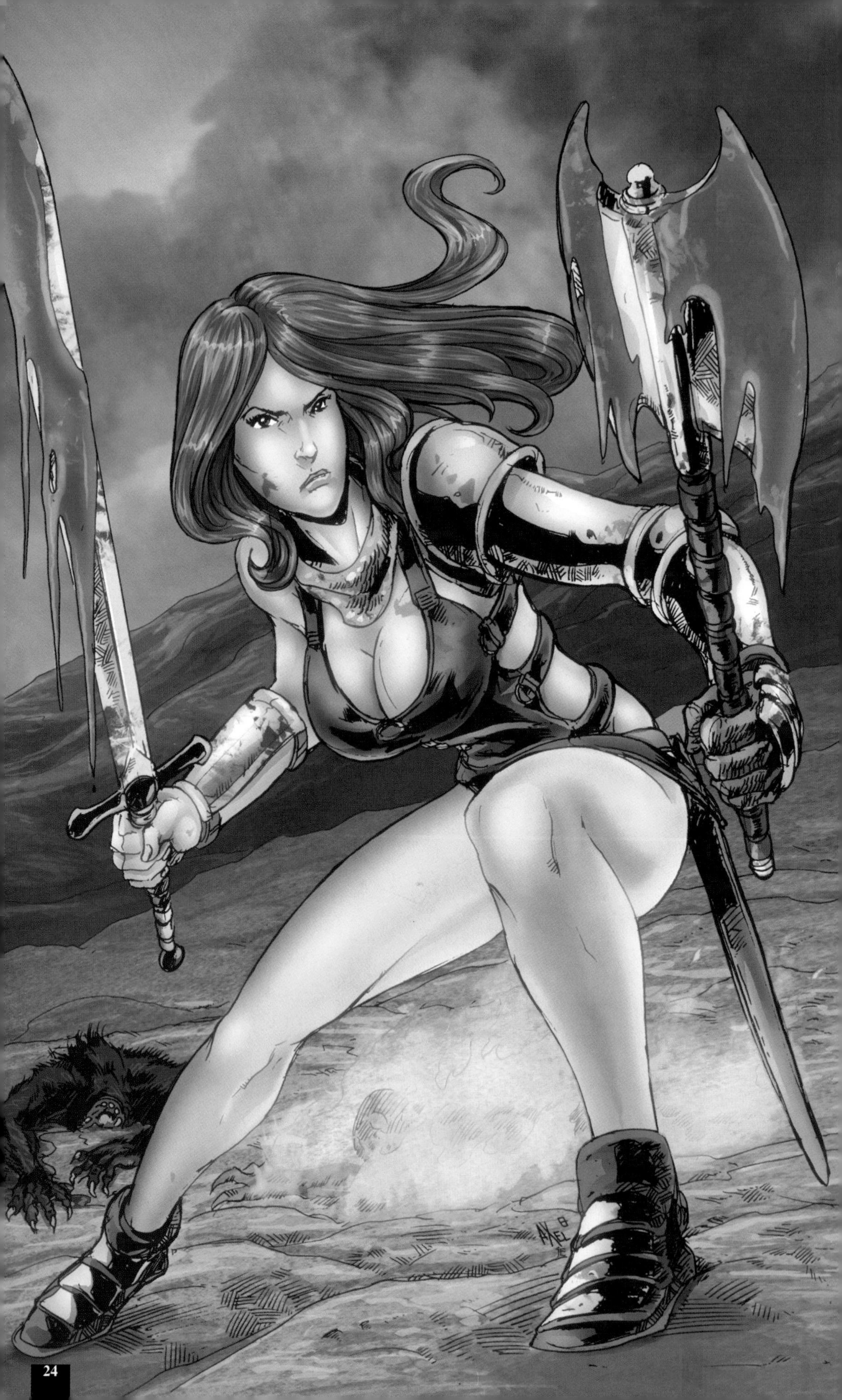

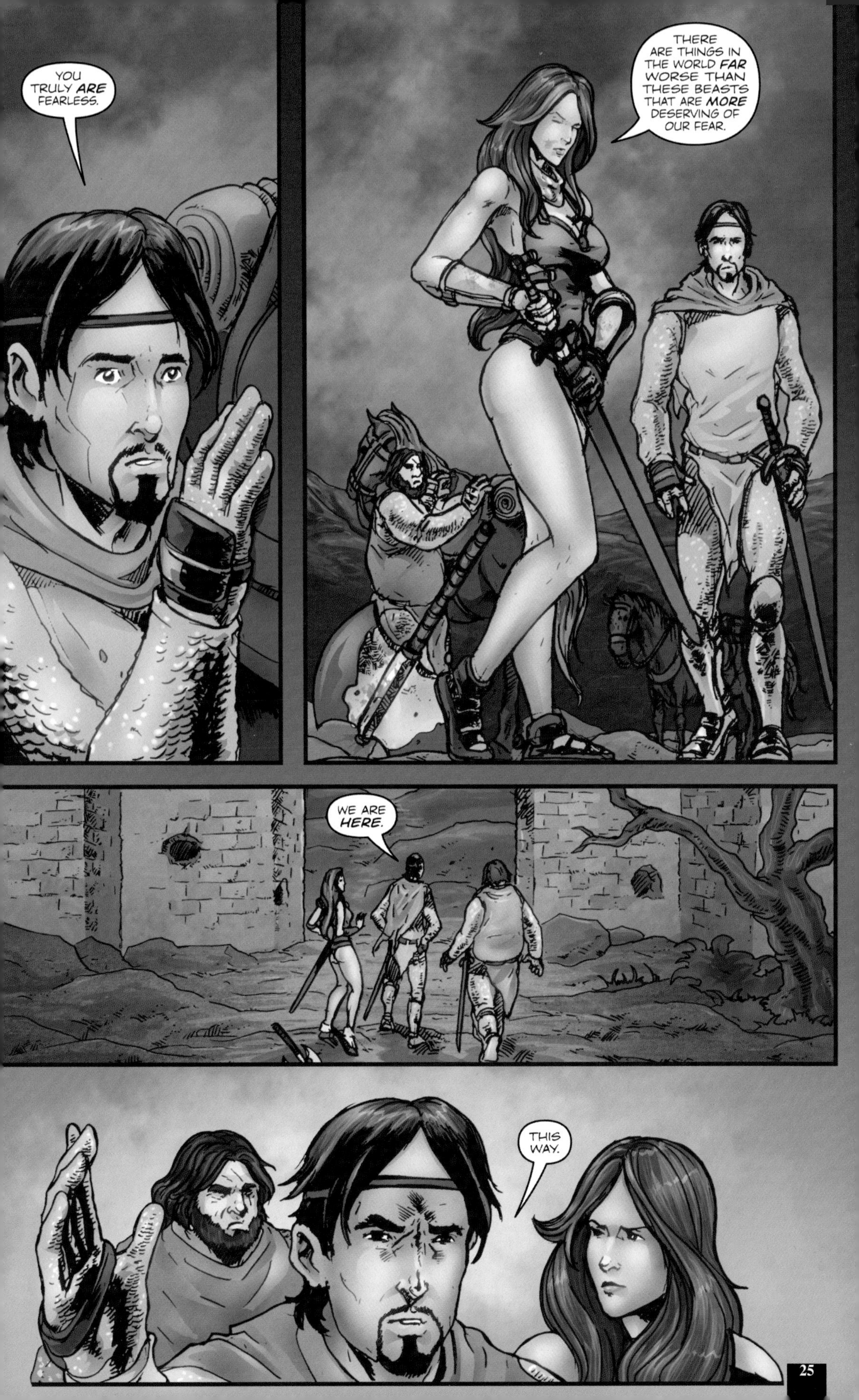
YOU TRULY **ARE** FEARLESS.
THERE ARE THINGS IN THE WORLD **FAR** WORSE THAN THESE BEASTS THAT ARE **MORE** DESERVING OF OUR FEAR.
WE ARE **HERE**.
THIS WAY.

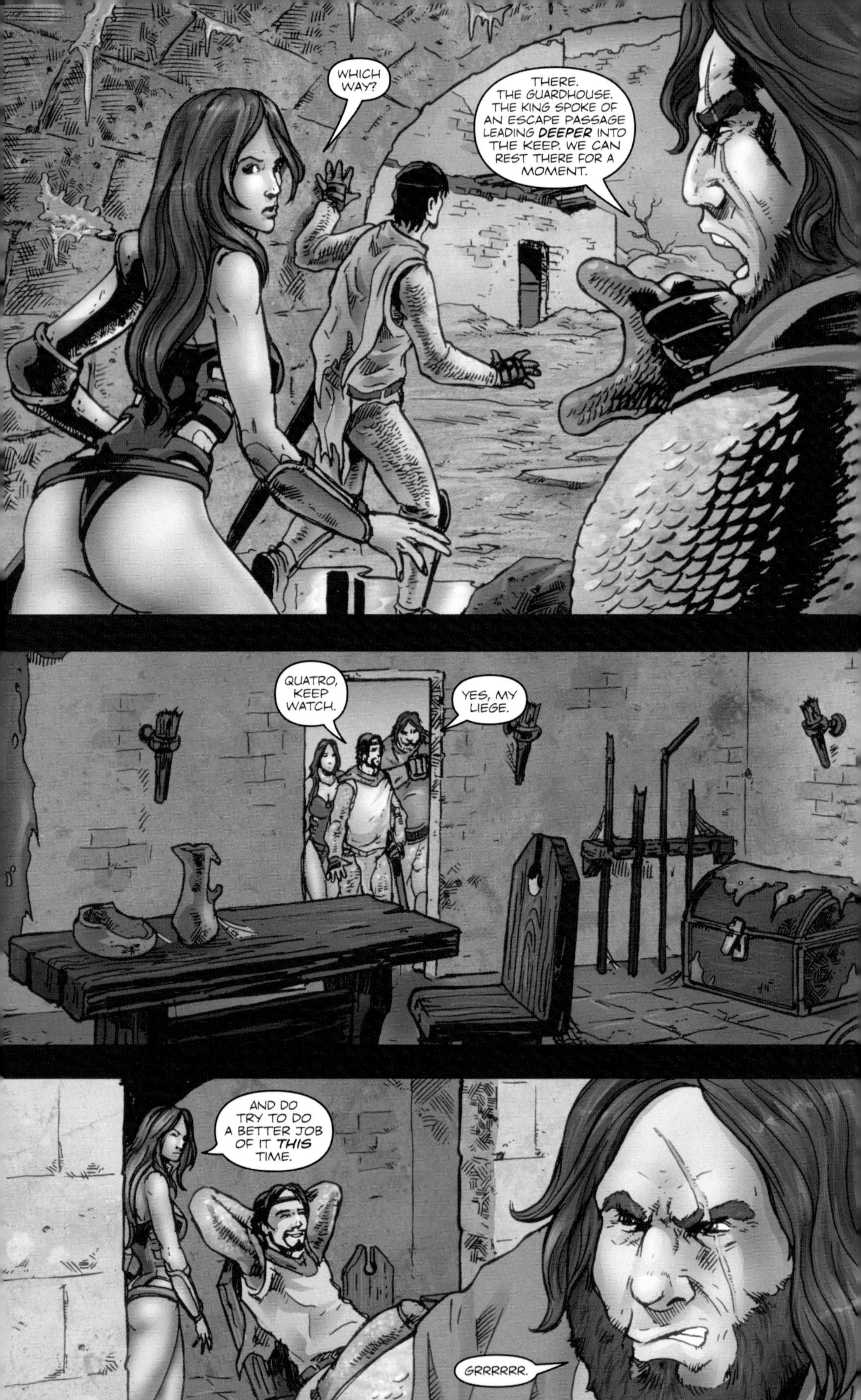
WHICH WAY?
THERE. THE GUARDHOUSE. THE KING SPOKE OF AN ESCAPE PASSAGE LEADING **DEEPER** INTO THE KEEP. WE CAN REST THERE FOR A MOMENT.
QUATRO, KEEP WATCH.
YES, MY LIEGE.
AND DO TRY TO DO A BETTER JOB OF IT **THIS** TIME.
GRRRRRR.

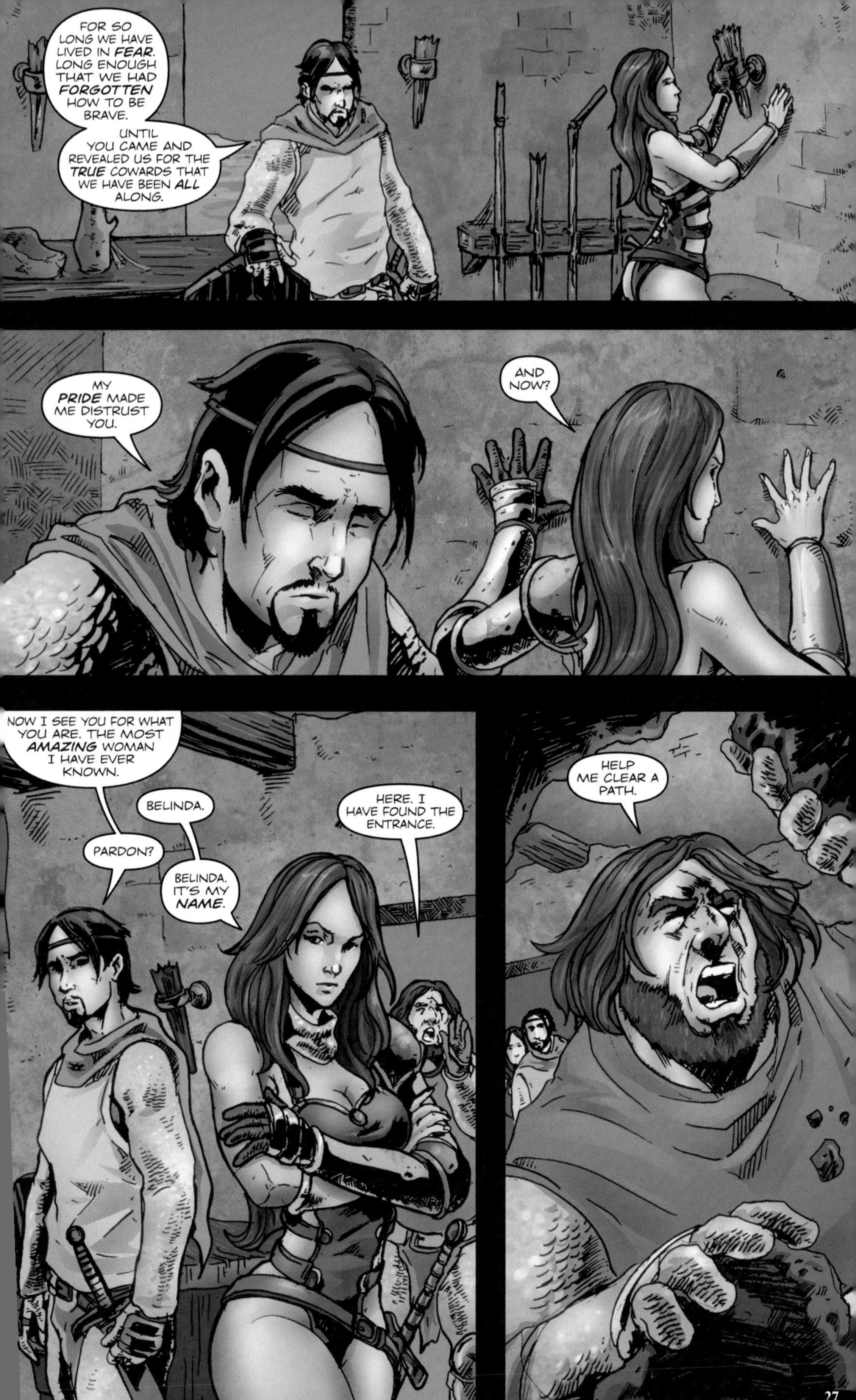
FOR SO LONG WE HAVE LIVED IN FEAR. LONG ENOUGH THAT WE HAD FORGOTTEN HOW TO BE BRAVE.
UNTIL YOU CAME AND REVEALED US FOR THE TRUE COWARDS THAT WE HAVE BEEN ALL ALONG.
MY PRIDE MADE ME DISTRUST YOU.
AND NOW?
NOW I SEE YOU FOR WHAT YOU ARE. THE MOST AMAZING WOMAN I HAVE EVER KNOWN.
BELINDA.
PARDON?
BELINDA. IT'S MY NAME.
HERE. I HAVE FOUND THE ENTRANCE.
HELP ME CLEAR A PATH.

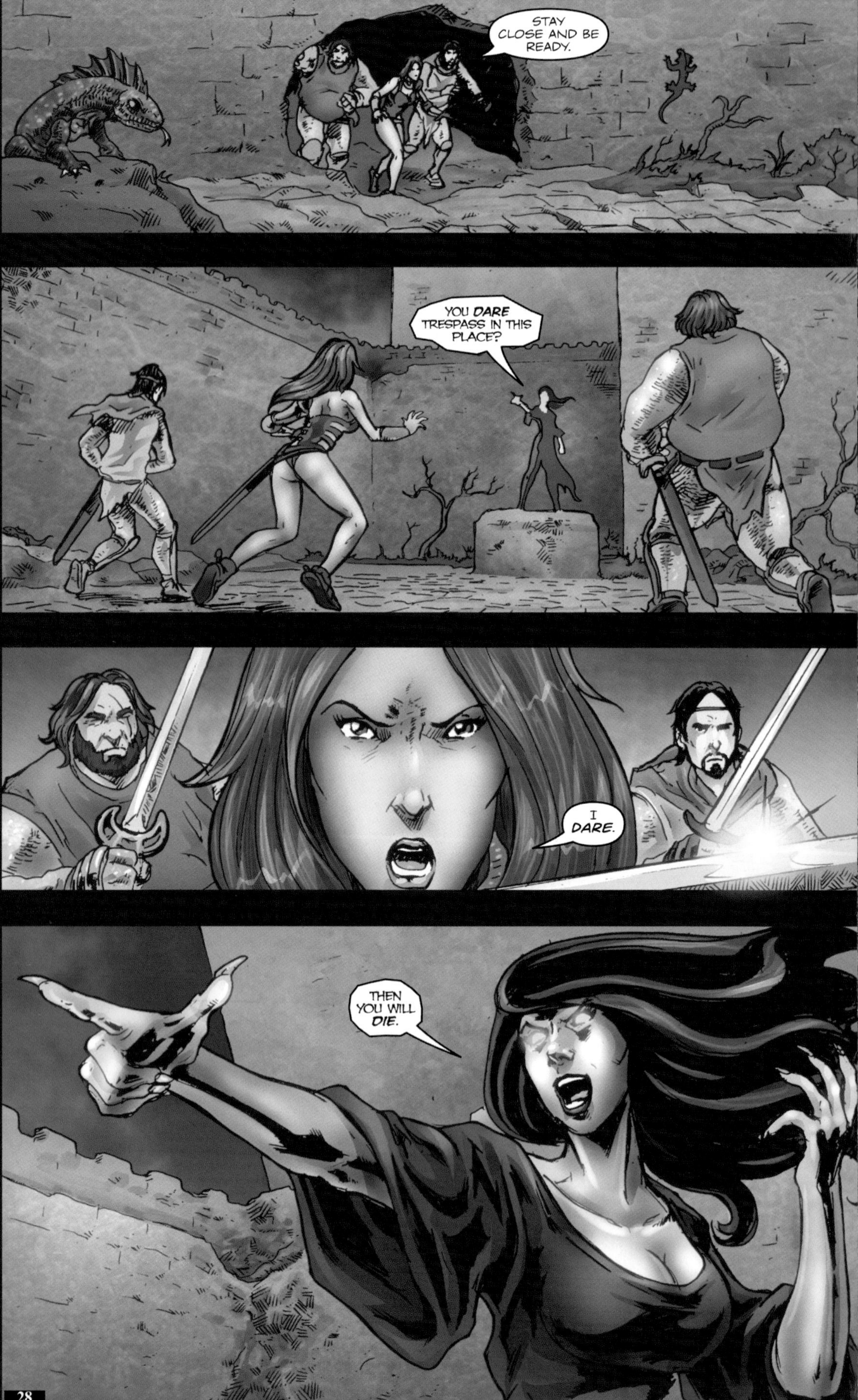

STAY CLOSE AND BE READY.
YOU DARE TRESPASS IN THIS PLACE?
I DARE.
THEN YOU WILL DIE.

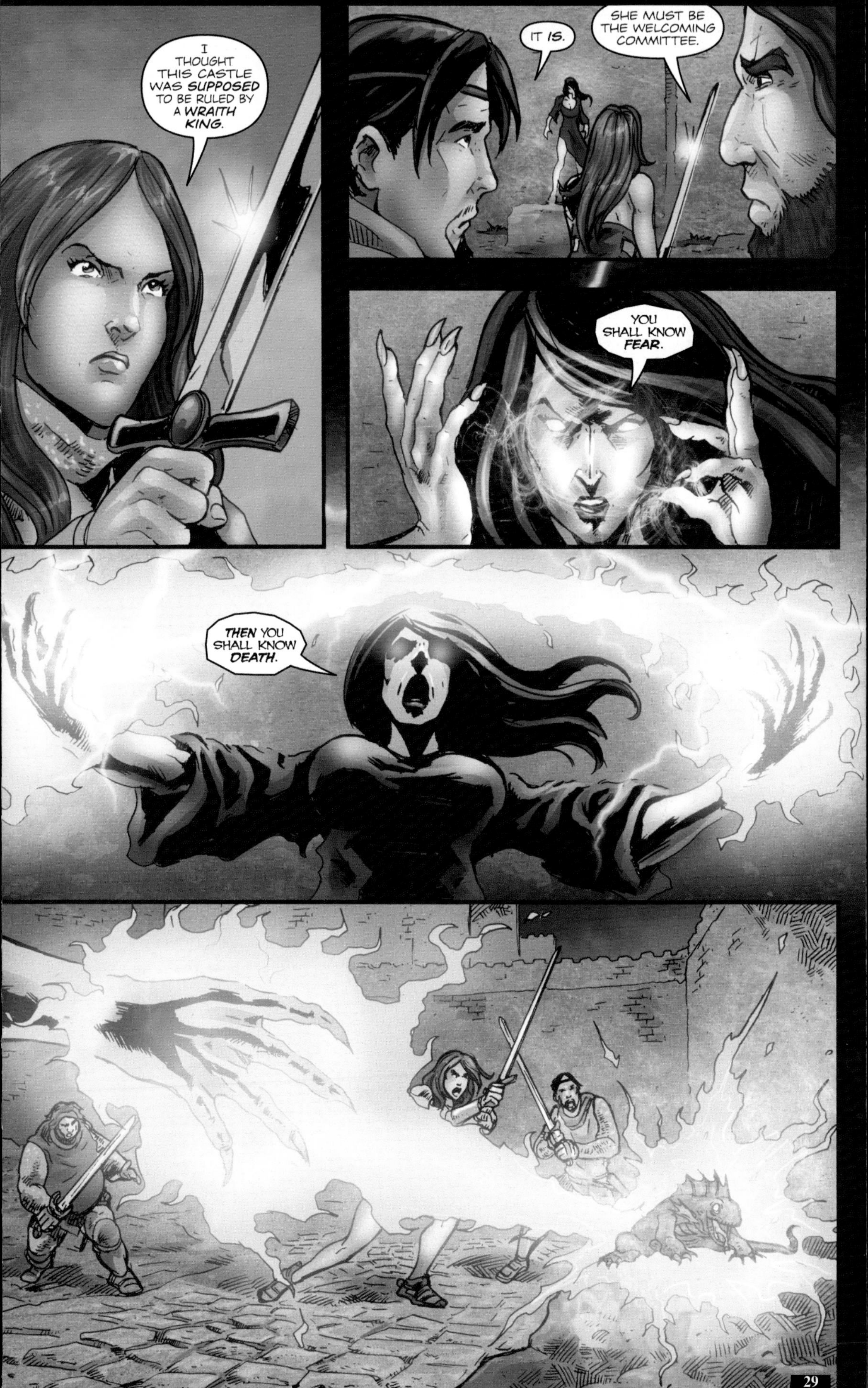
I THOUGHT THIS CASTLE WAS SUPPOSED TO BE RULED BY A WRAITH KING.
IT IS.
SHE MUST BE THE WELCOMING COMMITTEE.
YOU SHALL KNOW FEAR.
THEN YOU SHALL KNOW DEATH.

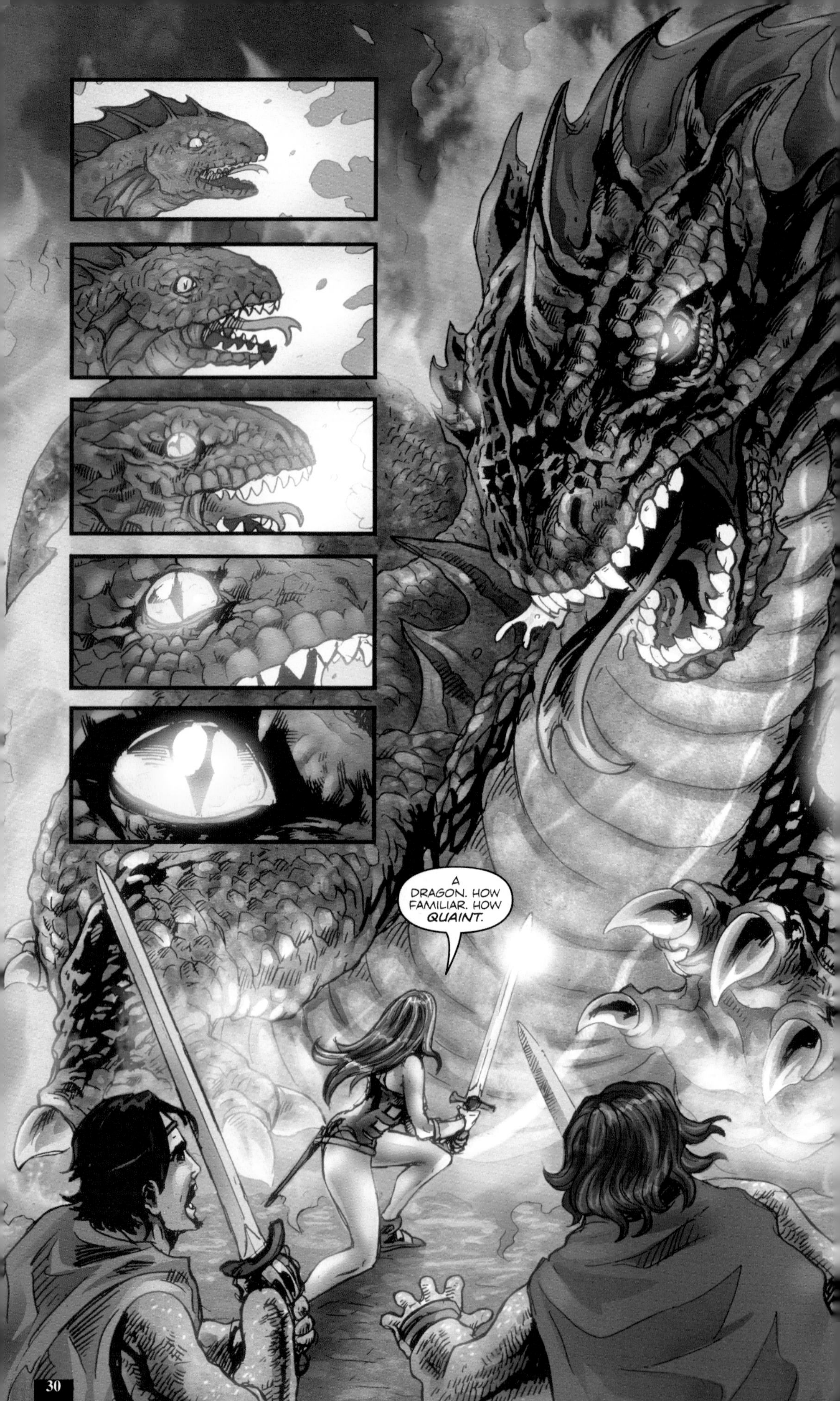
A DRAGON. HOW FAMILIAR. HOW *QUAINT*.

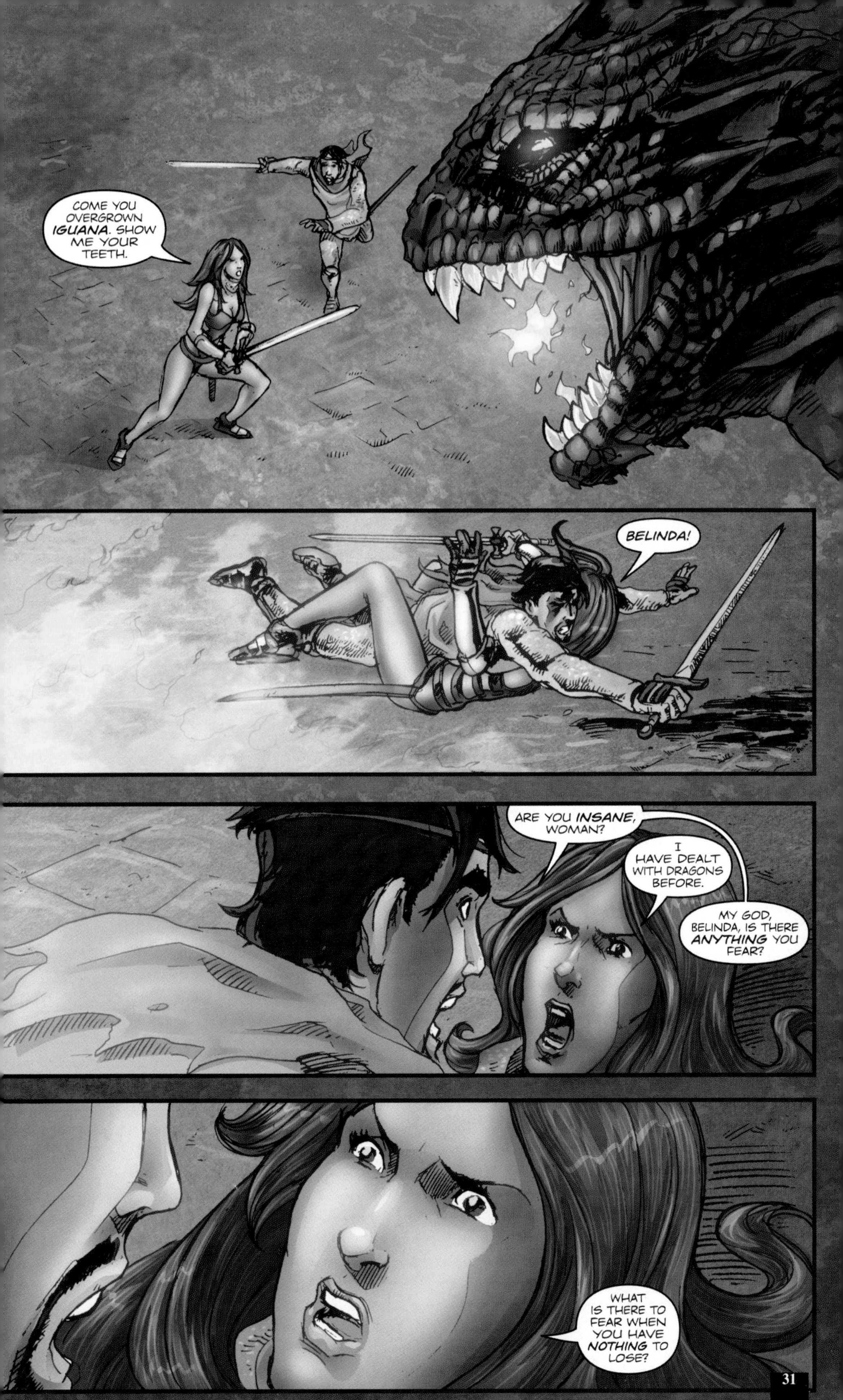
COME YOU OVERGROWN IGUANA. SHOW ME YOUR TEETH.
BELINDA!
ARE YOU INSANE, WOMAN?
I HAVE DEALT WITH DRAGONS BEFORE.
MY GOD, BELINDA, IS THERE ANYTHING YOU FEAR?
WHAT IS THERE TO FEAR WHEN YOU HAVE NOTHING TO LOSE?

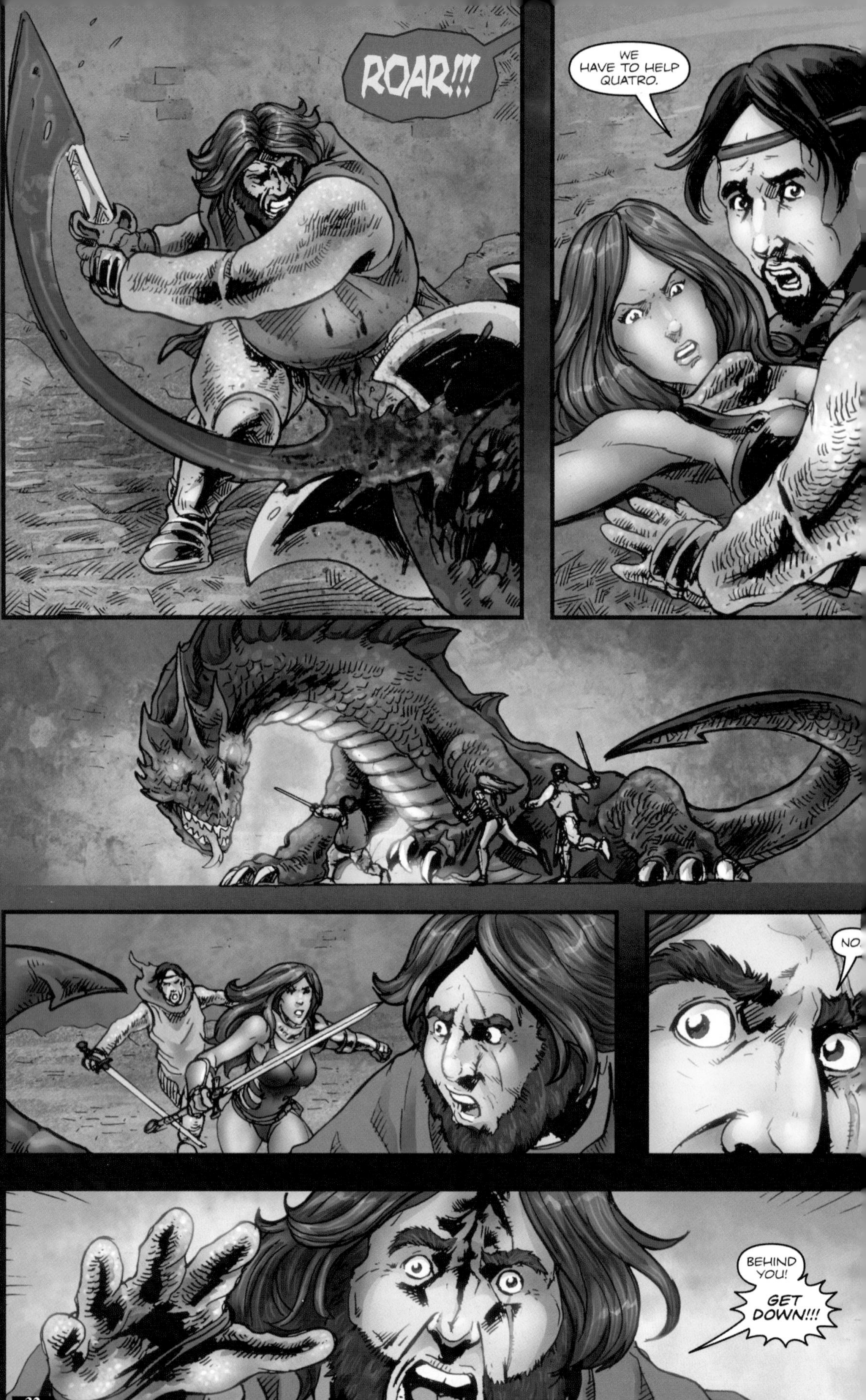
ROAR!!!
WE HAVE TO HELP QUATRO.
NO.
BEHIND YOU! GET DOWN!!!

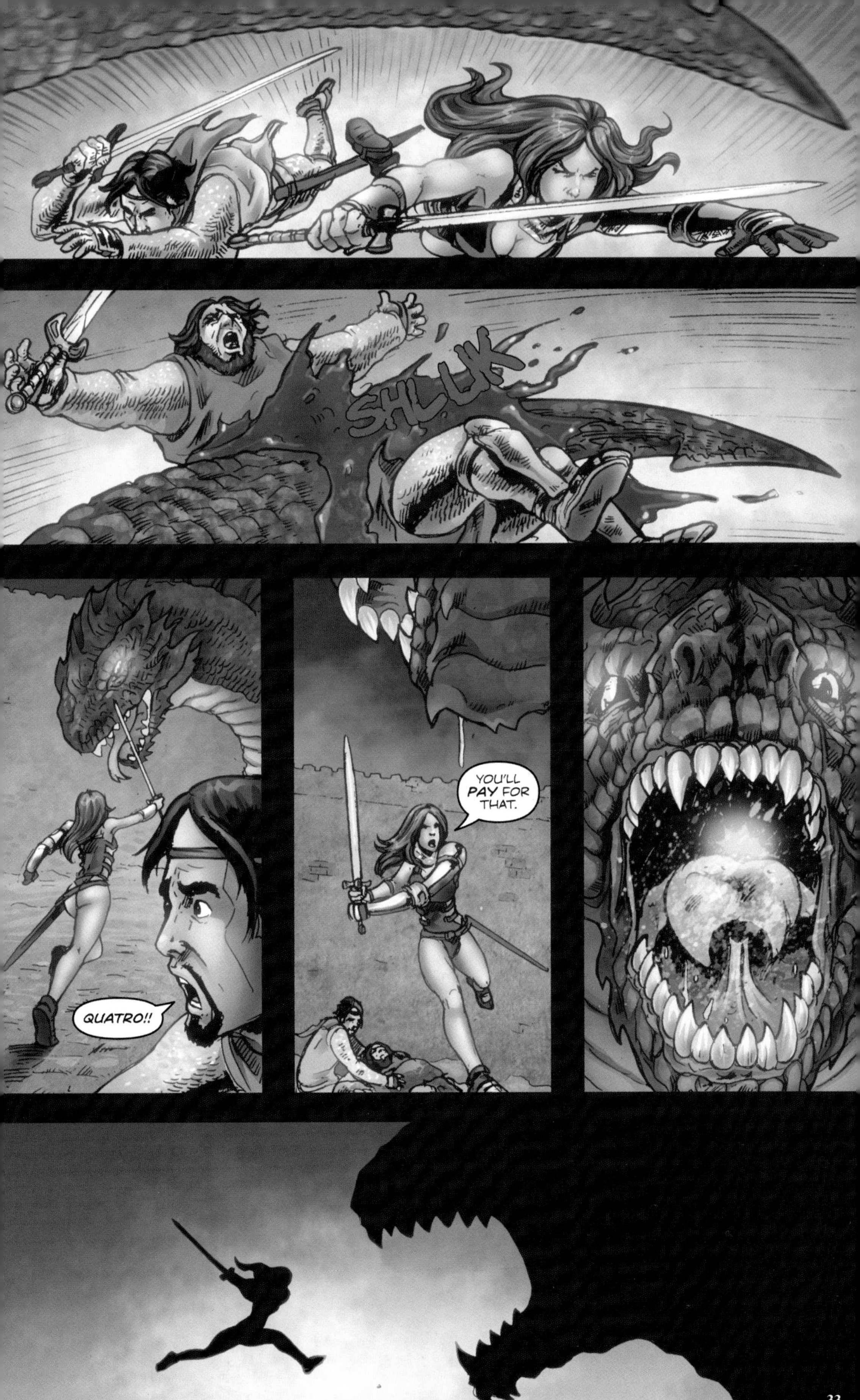
SHLUK
QUATRO!!
YOU'LL PAY FOR THAT.

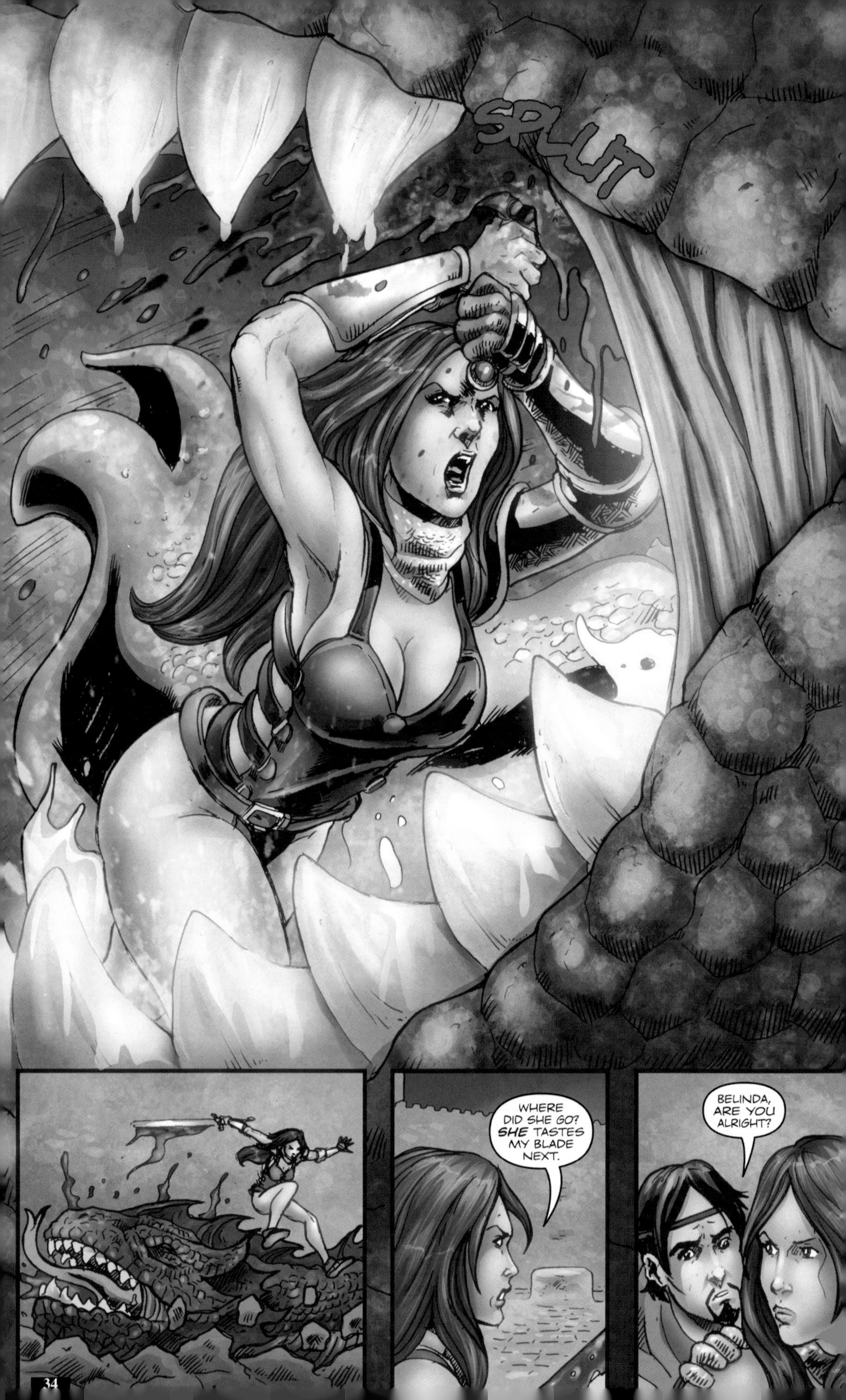
SPLUT
WHERE DID SHE GO? SHE TASTES MY BLADE NEXT.
BELINDA, ARE YOU ALRIGHT?

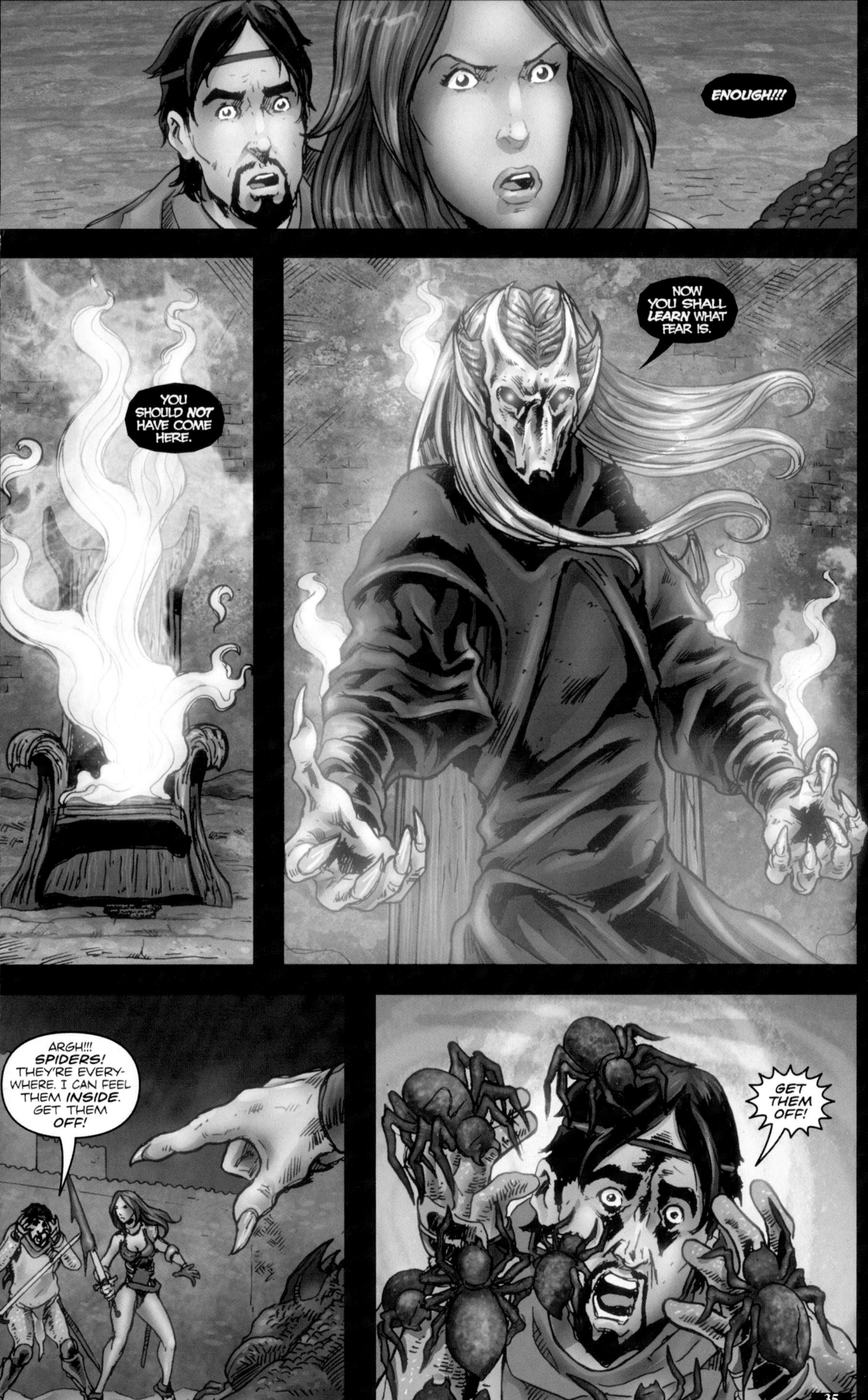
ENOUGH!!!
YOU SHOULD NOT HAVE COME HERE.
NOW YOU SHALL LEARN WHAT FEAR IS.
ARGH!!! SPIDERS! THEY'RE EVERY-WHERE. I CAN FEEL THEM INSIDE. GET THEM OFF!
GET THEM OFF!

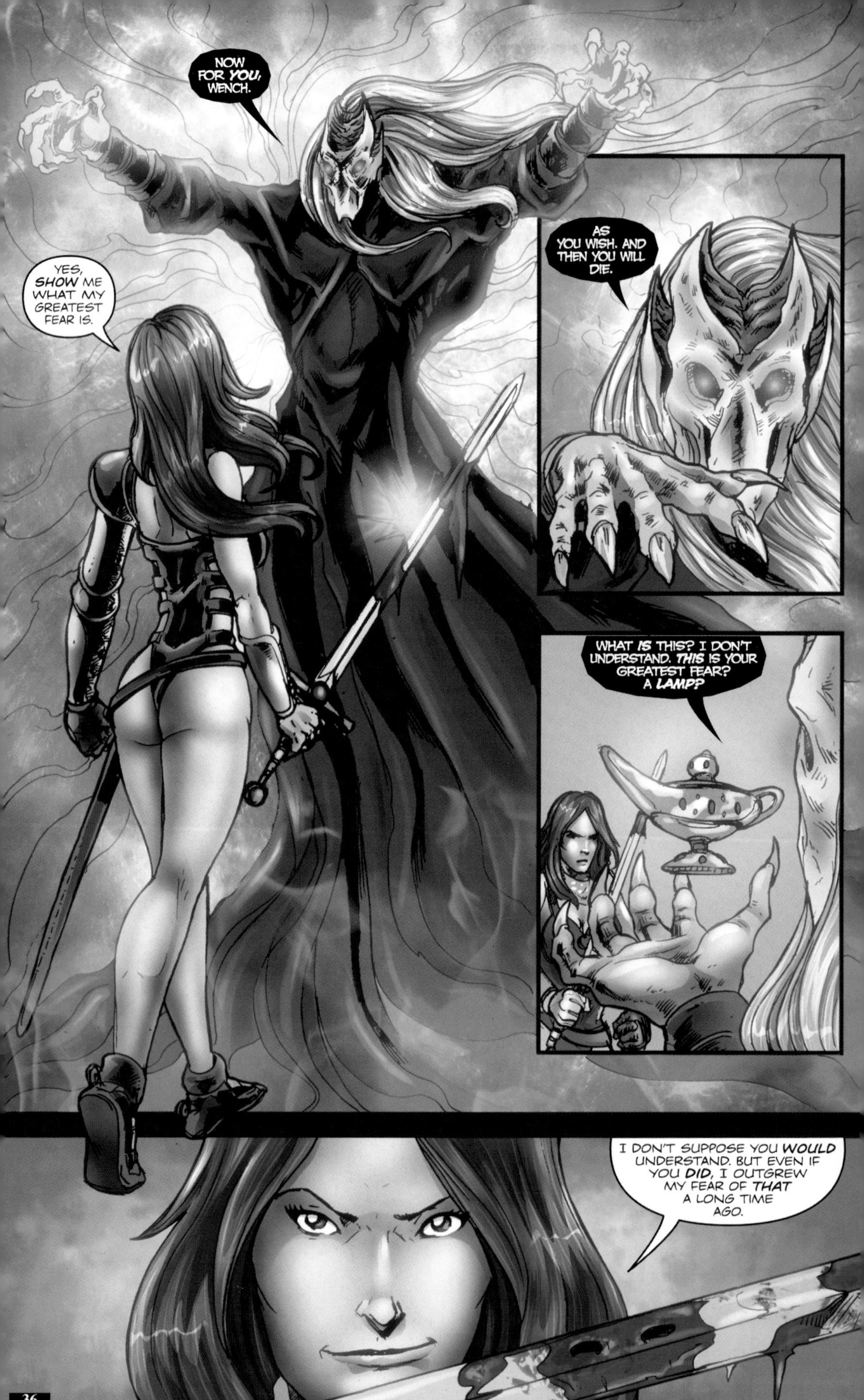
NOW FOR YOU, WENCH.
YES, SHOW ME WHAT MY GREATEST FEAR IS.
AS YOU WISH. AND THEN YOU WILL DIE.
WHAT IS THIS? I DON'T UNDERSTAND. THIS IS YOUR GREATEST FEAR? A LAMP?
I DON'T SUPPOSE YOU WOULD UNDERSTAND. BUT EVEN IF YOU DID, I OUTGREW MY FEAR OF THAT A LONG TIME AGO.

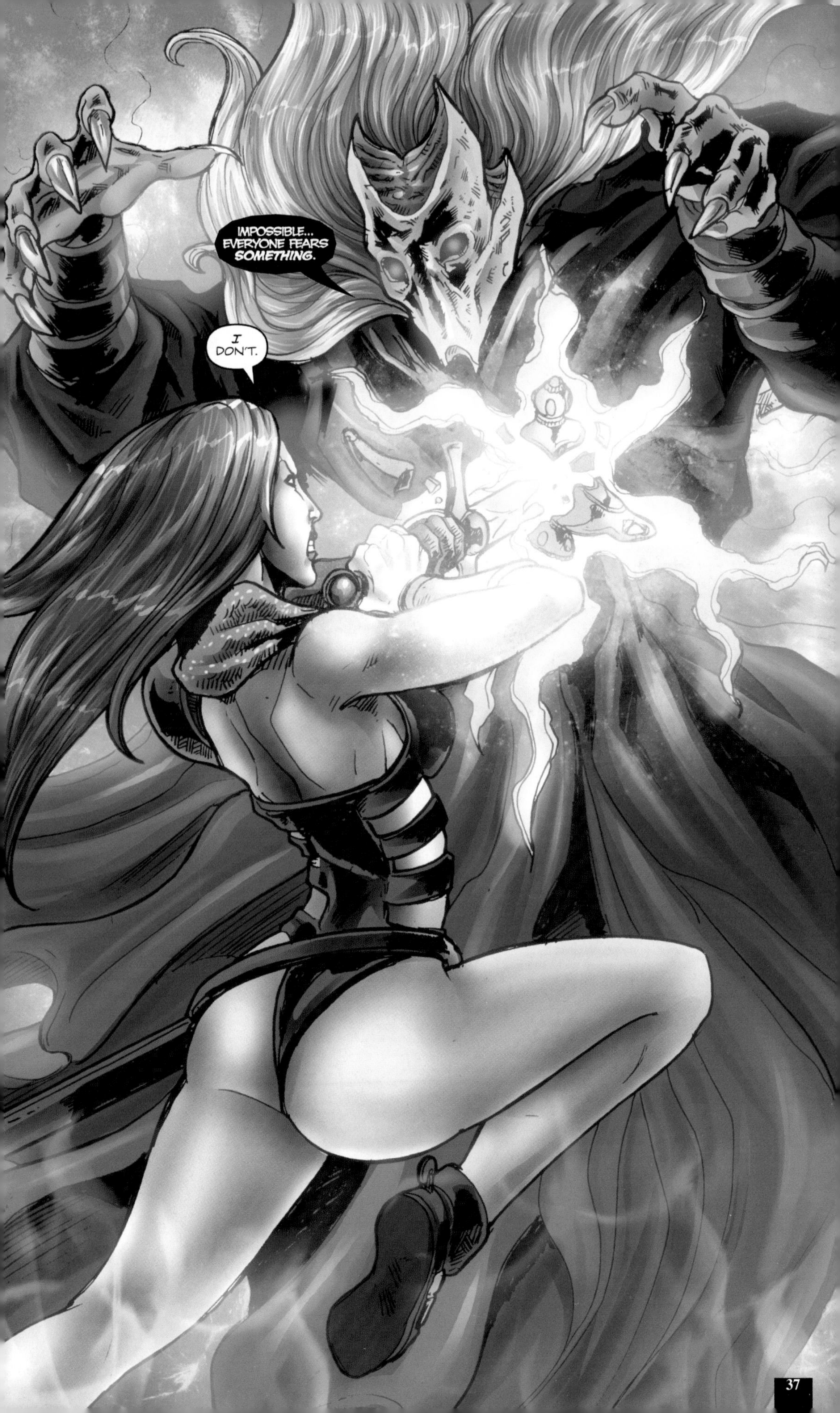
IMPOSSIBLE... EVERYONE FEARS SOMETHING.
I DON'T.

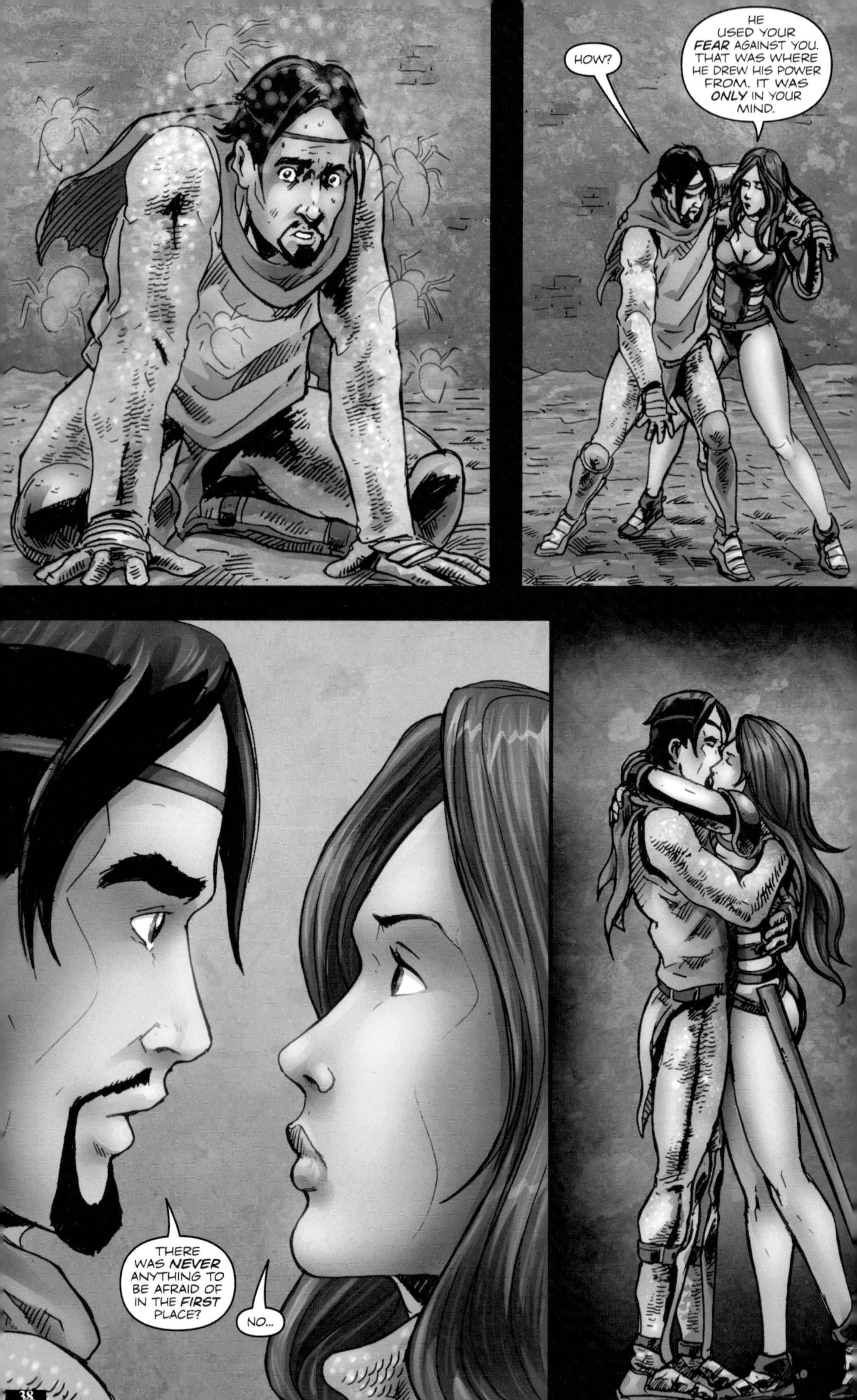
HOW?
HE USED YOUR FEAR AGAINST YOU. THAT WAS WHERE HE DREW HIS POWER FROM. IT WAS ONLY IN YOUR MIND.
THERE WAS NEVER ANYTHING TO BE AFRAID OF IN THE FIRST PLACE?
NO...

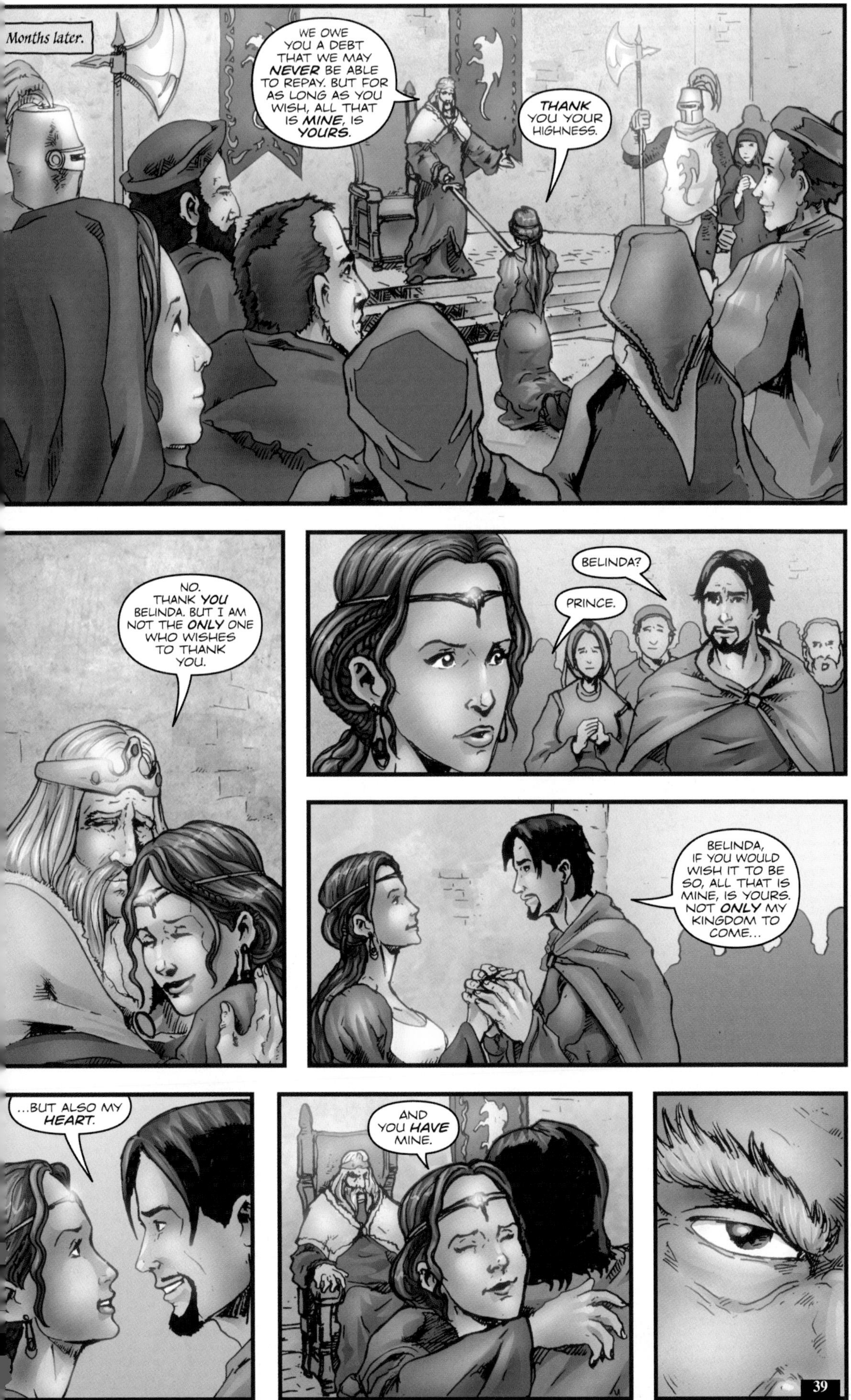

Months later.
WE OWE YOU A DEBT THAT WE MAY NEVER BE ABLE TO REPAY. BUT FOR AS LONG AS YOU WISH, ALL THAT IS MINE, IS YOURS.
THANK YOU YOUR HIGHNESS.
NO. THANK YOU BELINDA. BUT I AM NOT THE ONLY ONE WHO WISHES TO THANK YOU.
BELINDA?
PRINCE.
BELINDA, IF YOU WOULD WISH IT TO BE SO, ALL THAT IS MINE, IS YOURS. NOT ONLY MY KINGDOM TO COME...
...BUT ALSO MY HEART.
AND YOU HAVE MINE.

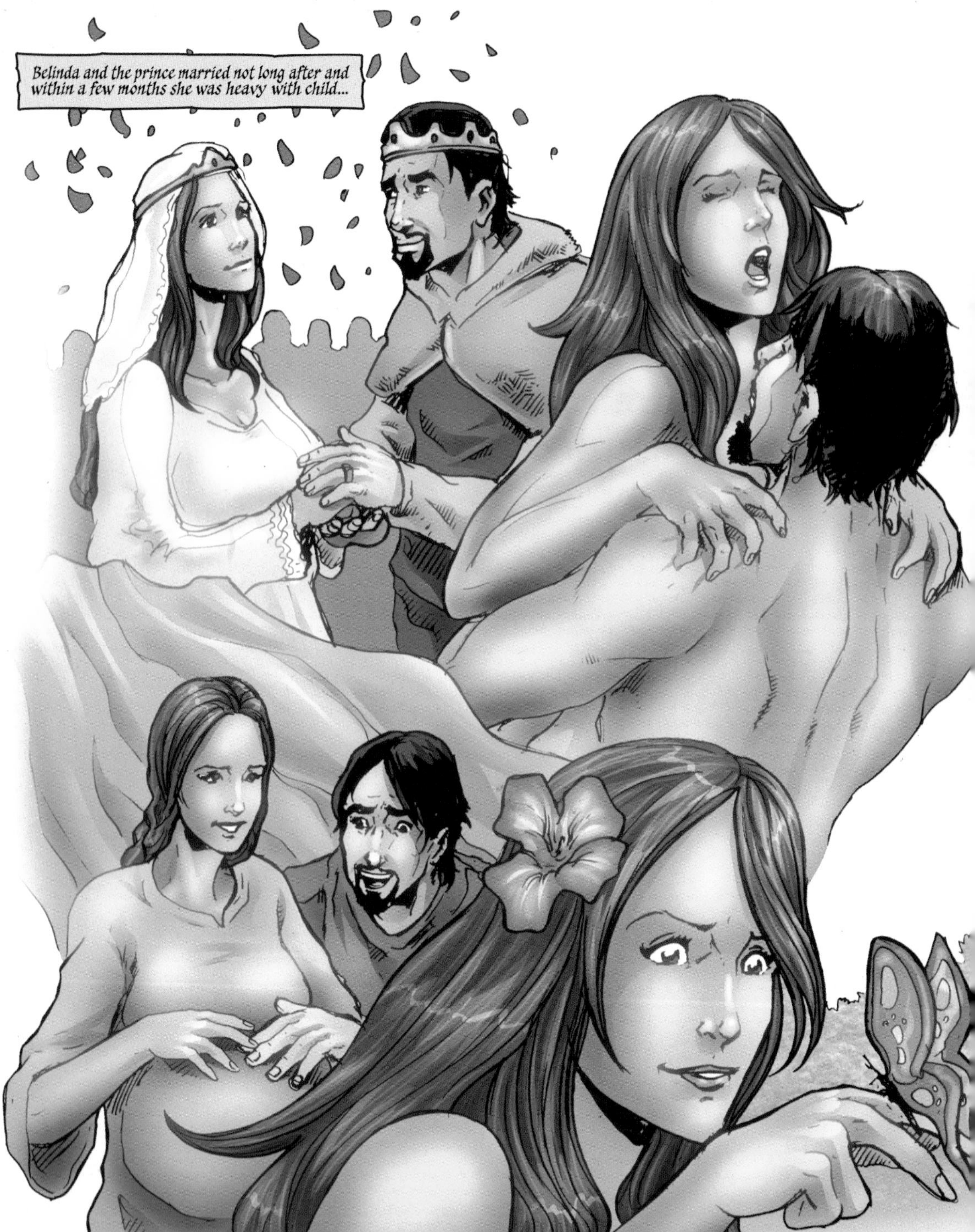
Belinda and the prince married not long after and within a few months she was heavy with child...

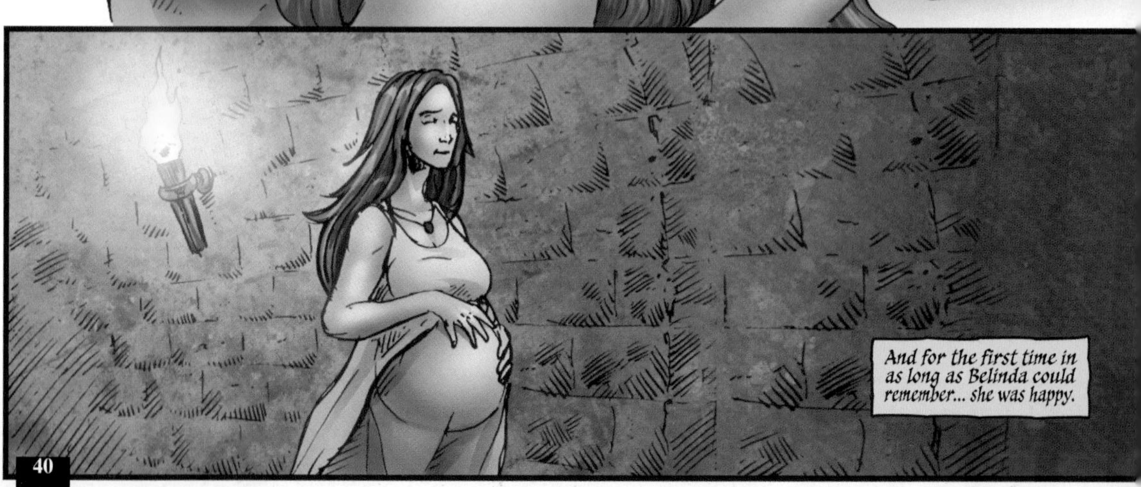
And for the first time in as long as Belinda could remember... she was happy.

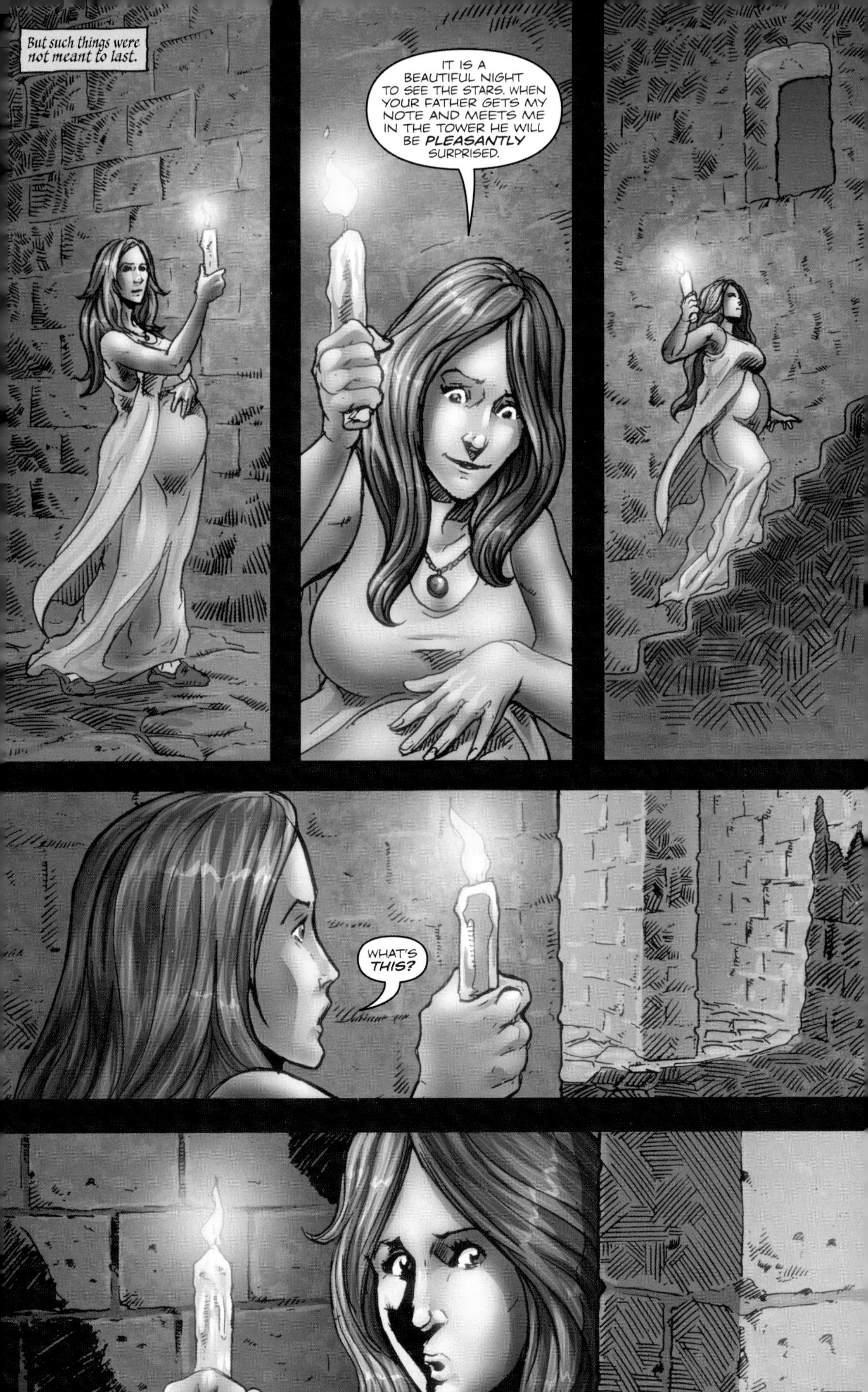
But such things were not meant to last.
IT IS A BEAUTIFUL NIGHT TO SEE THE STARS. WHEN YOUR FATHER GETS MY NOTE AND MEETS ME IN THE TOWER HE WILL BE PLEASANTLY SURPRISED.
WHAT'S THIS?

THE TIME IS ALMOST UPON US.

SOON THE *CHILD* WILL BE BORN...

...AND THE DEMON WILL HAVE ITS *SACRIFICE.* MY SON MUST *NEVER* KNOW THE TRUTH OF WHAT IS TO COME.

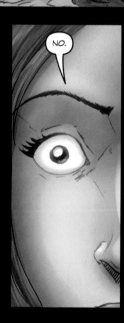

NO.

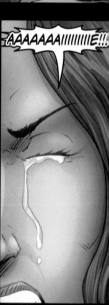

AAAAAAAIIIIIIIE!!!

NO. NOT *NOW.*

And for the first time in what seemed like an eternity, Belinda felt fear.

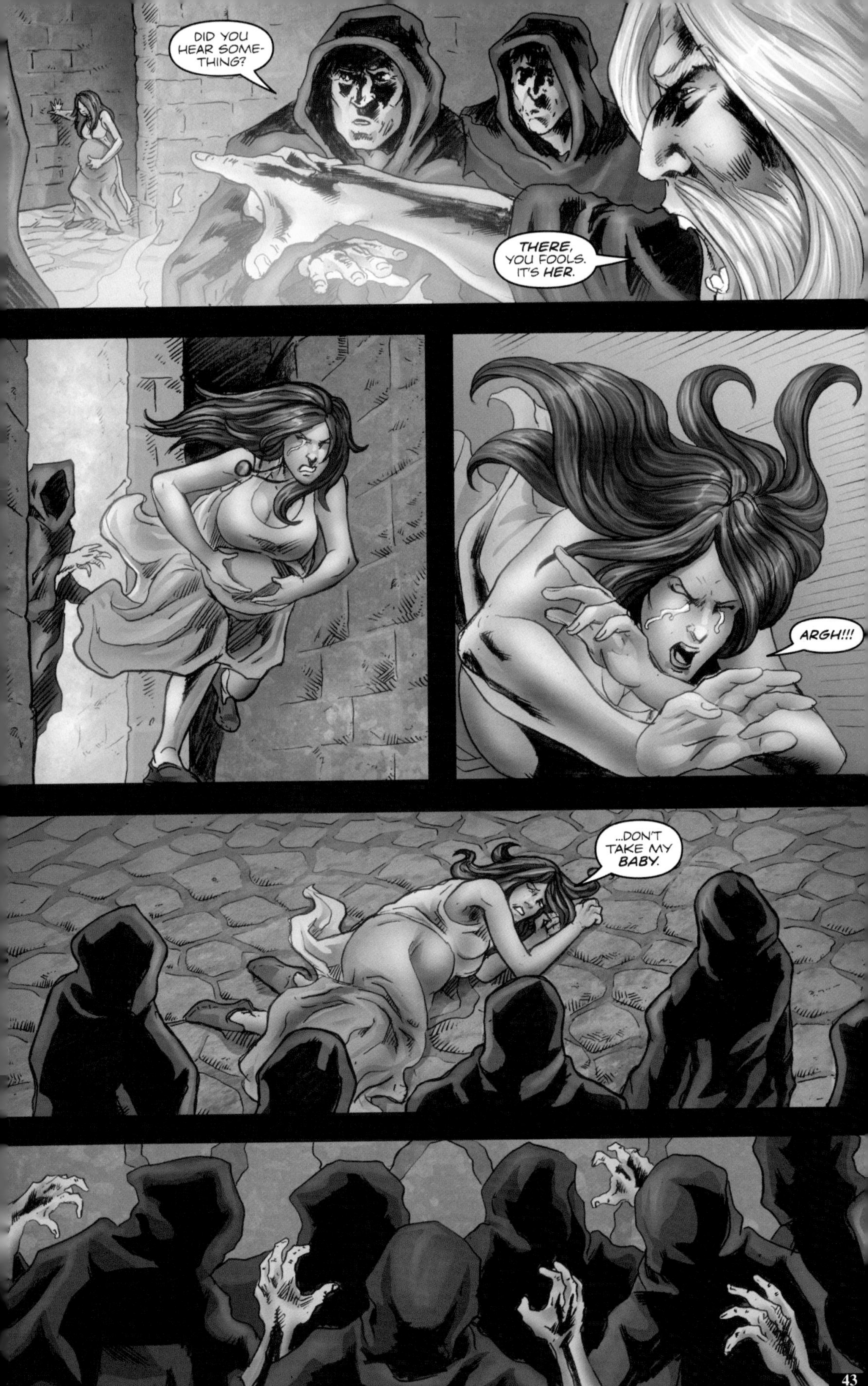
DID YOU HEAR SOME-THING?
THERE, YOU FOOLS. IT'S HER.
ARGH!!!
...DON'T TAKE MY BABY.

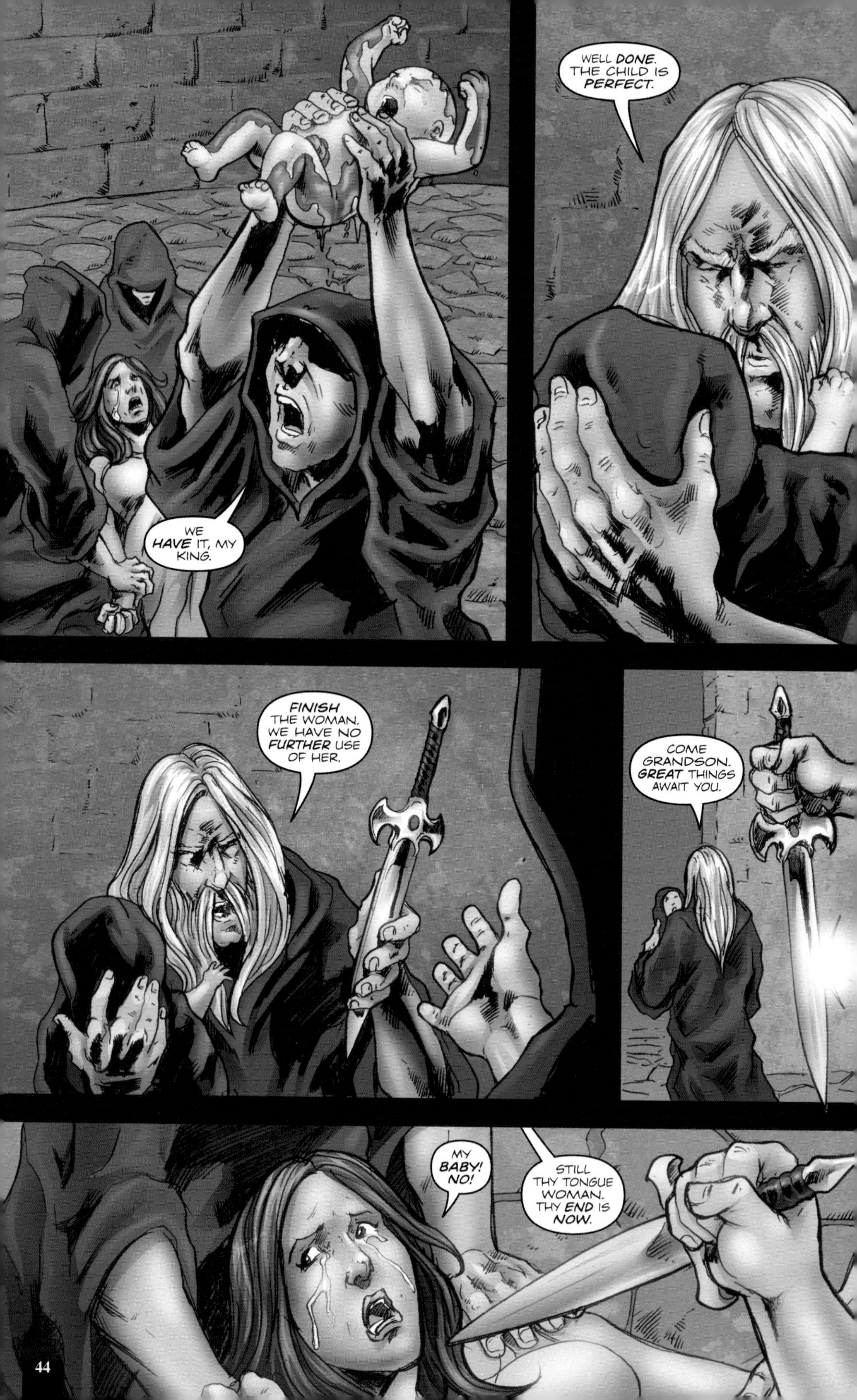
WE HAVE IT, MY KING.
WELL DONE. THE CHILD IS PERFECT.
FINISH THE WOMAN. WE HAVE NO FURTHER USE OF HER.
COME GRANDSON. GREAT THINGS AWAIT YOU.
MY BABY! NO!
STILL THY TONGUE WOMAN. THY END IS NOW.

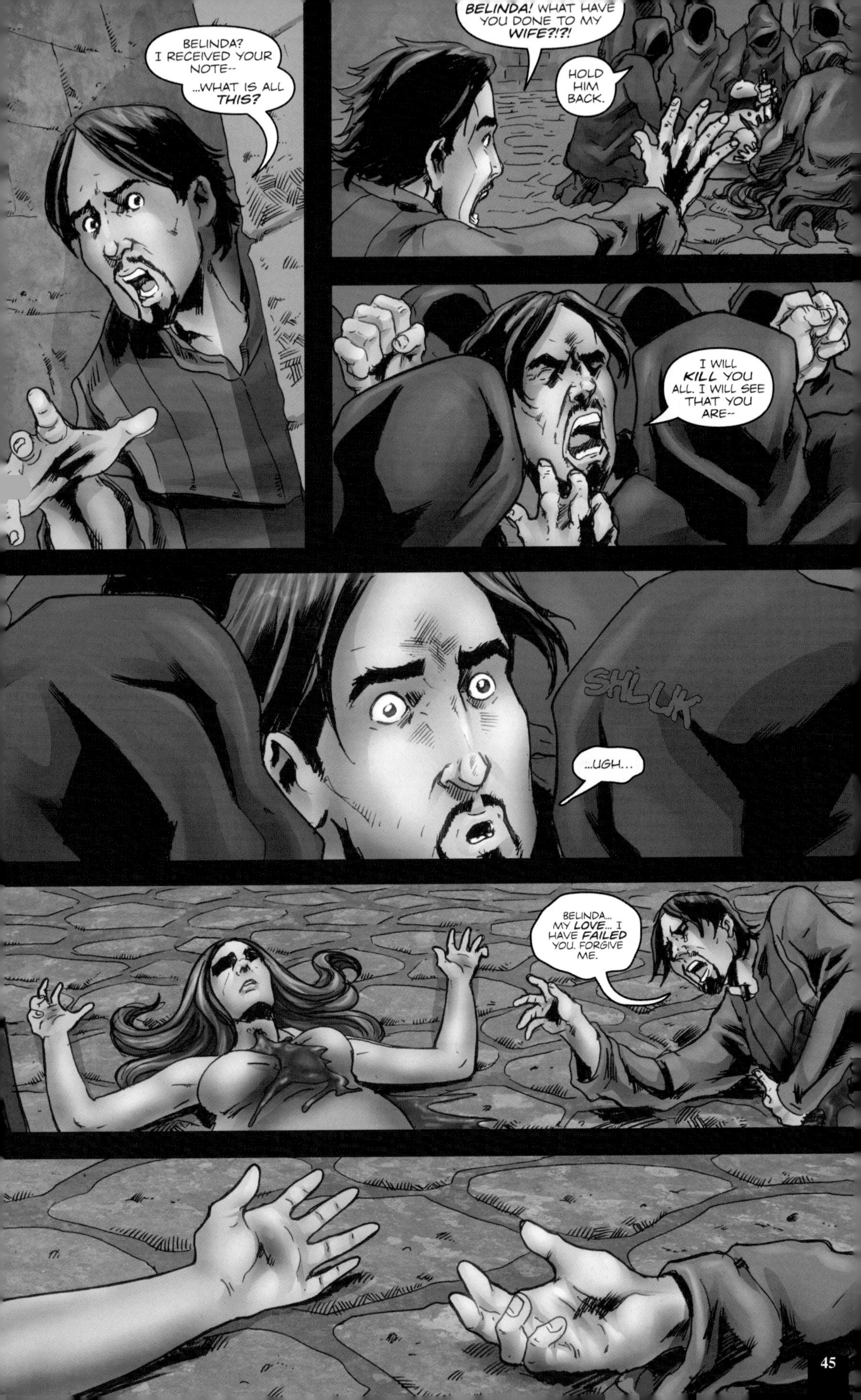
BELINDA? I RECEIVED YOUR NOTE--
...WHAT IS ALL THIS?
BELINDA! WHAT HAVE YOU DONE TO MY WIFE?!?!
HOLD HIM BACK.
I WILL KILL YOU ALL. I WILL SEE THAT YOU ARE--
SHLUK
...UGH...
BELINDA... MY LOVE... I HAVE FAILED YOU. FORGIVE ME.

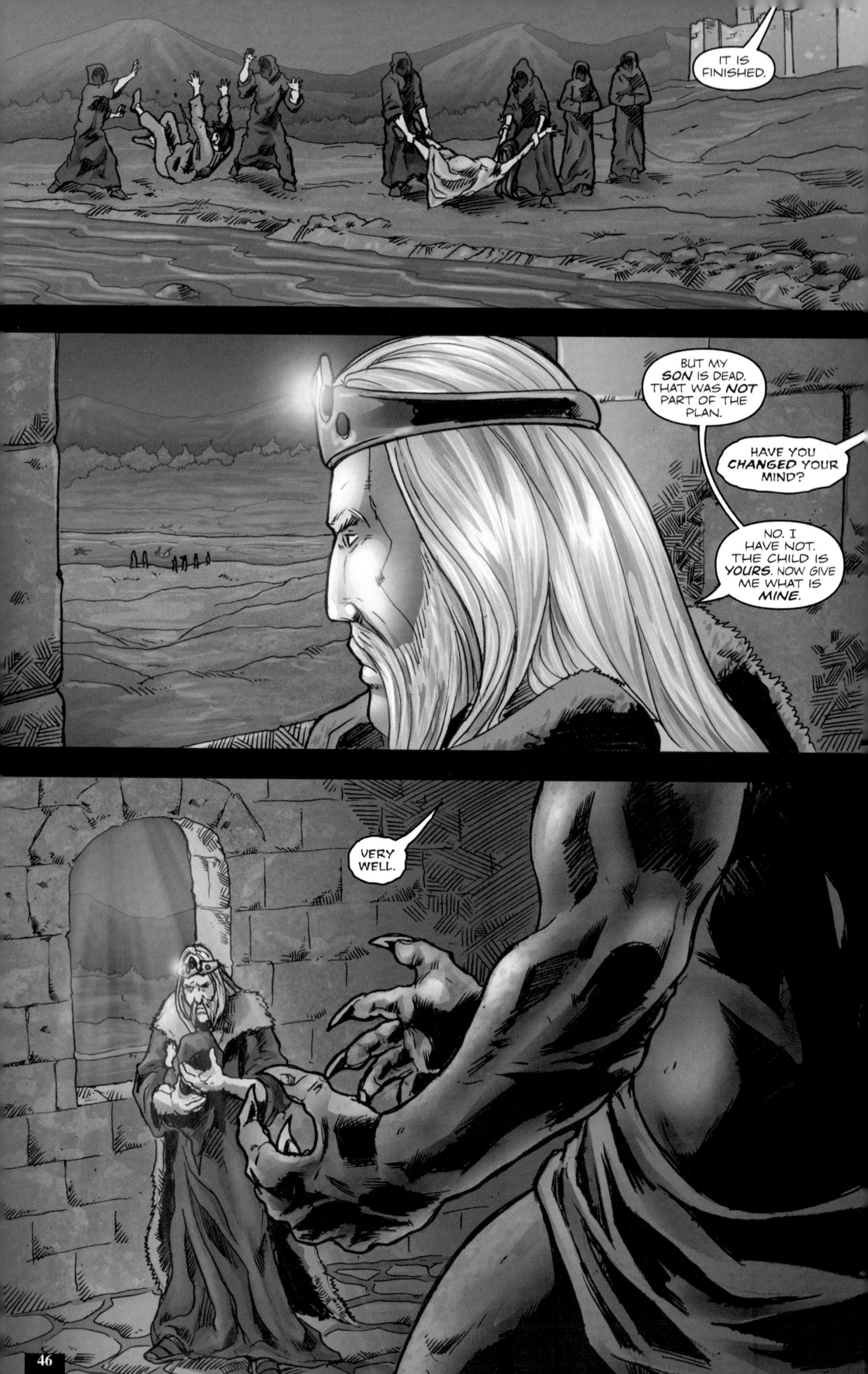
IT IS FINISHED.
BUT MY SON IS DEAD. THAT WAS NOT PART OF THE PLAN.
HAVE YOU CHANGED YOUR MIND?
NO. I HAVE NOT. THE CHILD IS YOURS. NOW GIVE ME WHAT IS MINE.
VERY WELL.

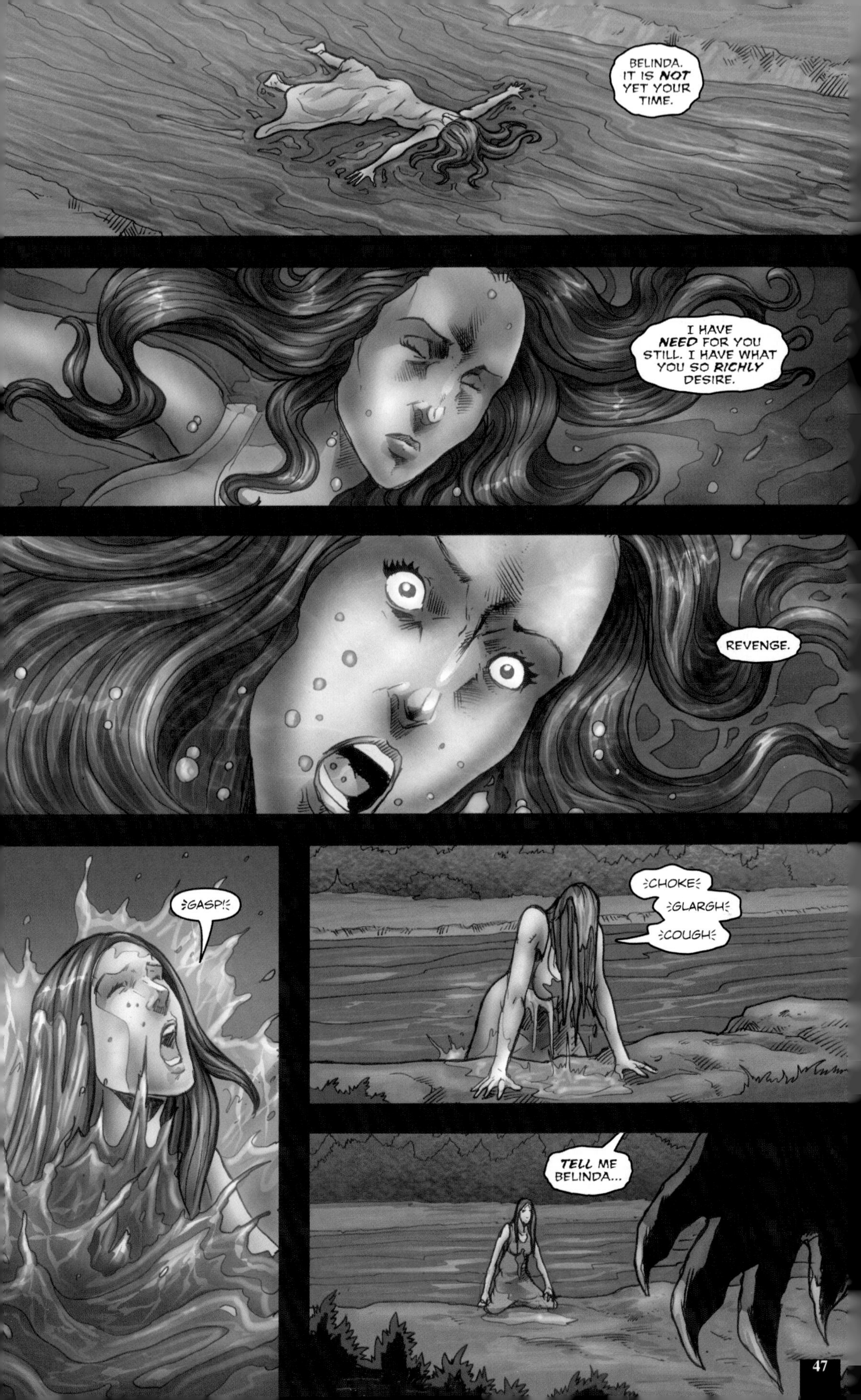
BELINDA. IT IS NOT YET YOUR TIME.
I HAVE NEED FOR YOU STILL. I HAVE WHAT YOU SO RICHLY DESIRE.
REVENGE.
GASP!
CHOKE
GLARGH
COUGH
TELL ME BELINDA...

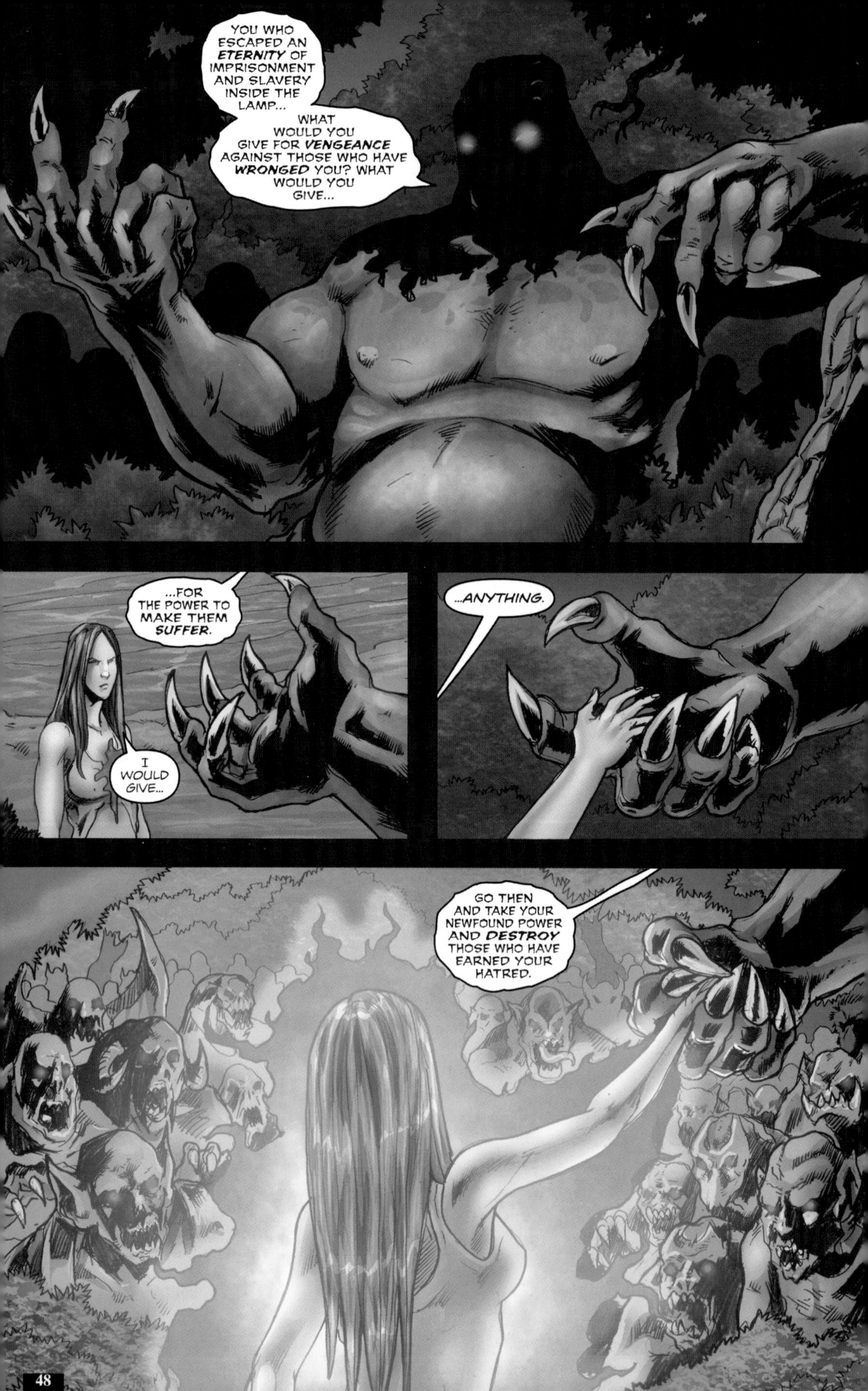
YOU WHO ESCAPED AN ETERNITY OF IMPRISONMENT AND SLAVERY INSIDE THE LAMP...
WHAT WOULD YOU GIVE FOR VENGEANCE AGAINST THOSE WHO HAVE WRONGED YOU? WHAT WOULD YOU GIVE...
...FOR THE POWER TO MAKE THEM SUFFER.
I WOULD GIVE...
...ANYTHING.
GO THEN AND TAKE YOUR NEWFOUND POWER AND DESTROY THOSE WHO HAVE EARNED YOUR HATRED.

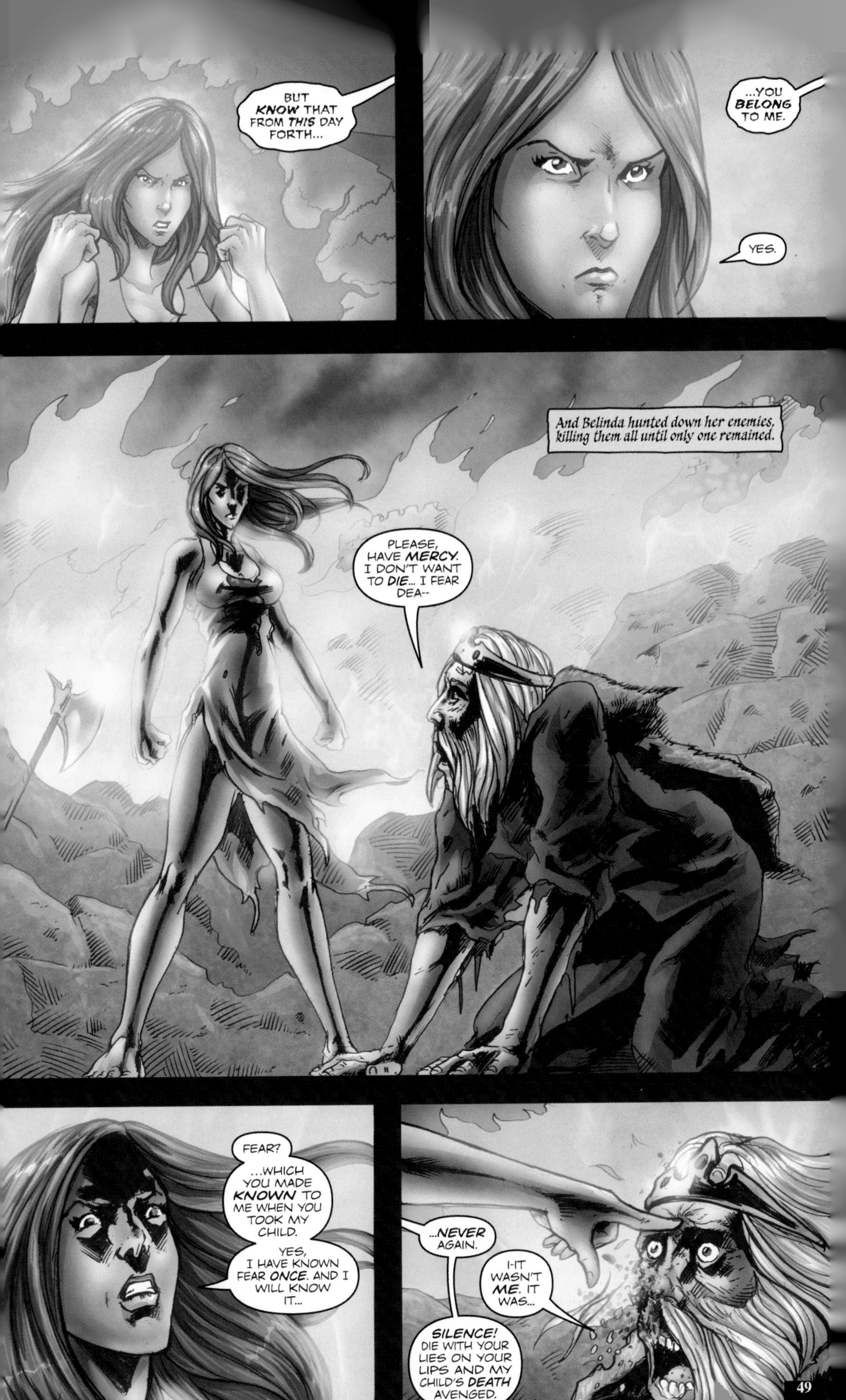

BUT KNOW THAT FROM THIS DAY FORTH...
...YOU BELONG TO ME.
YES.
And Belinda hunted down her enemies, killing them all until only one remained.
PLEASE, HAVE MERCY. I DON'T WANT TO DIE... I FEAR DEA--
FEAR?
...WHICH YOU MADE KNOWN TO ME WHEN YOU TOOK MY CHILD.
YES, I HAVE KNOWN FEAR ONCE. AND I WILL KNOW IT...
...NEVER AGAIN.
I-IT WASN'T ME. IT WAS...
SILENCE! DIE WITH YOUR LIES ON YOUR LIPS AND MY CHILD'S DEATH AVENGED.

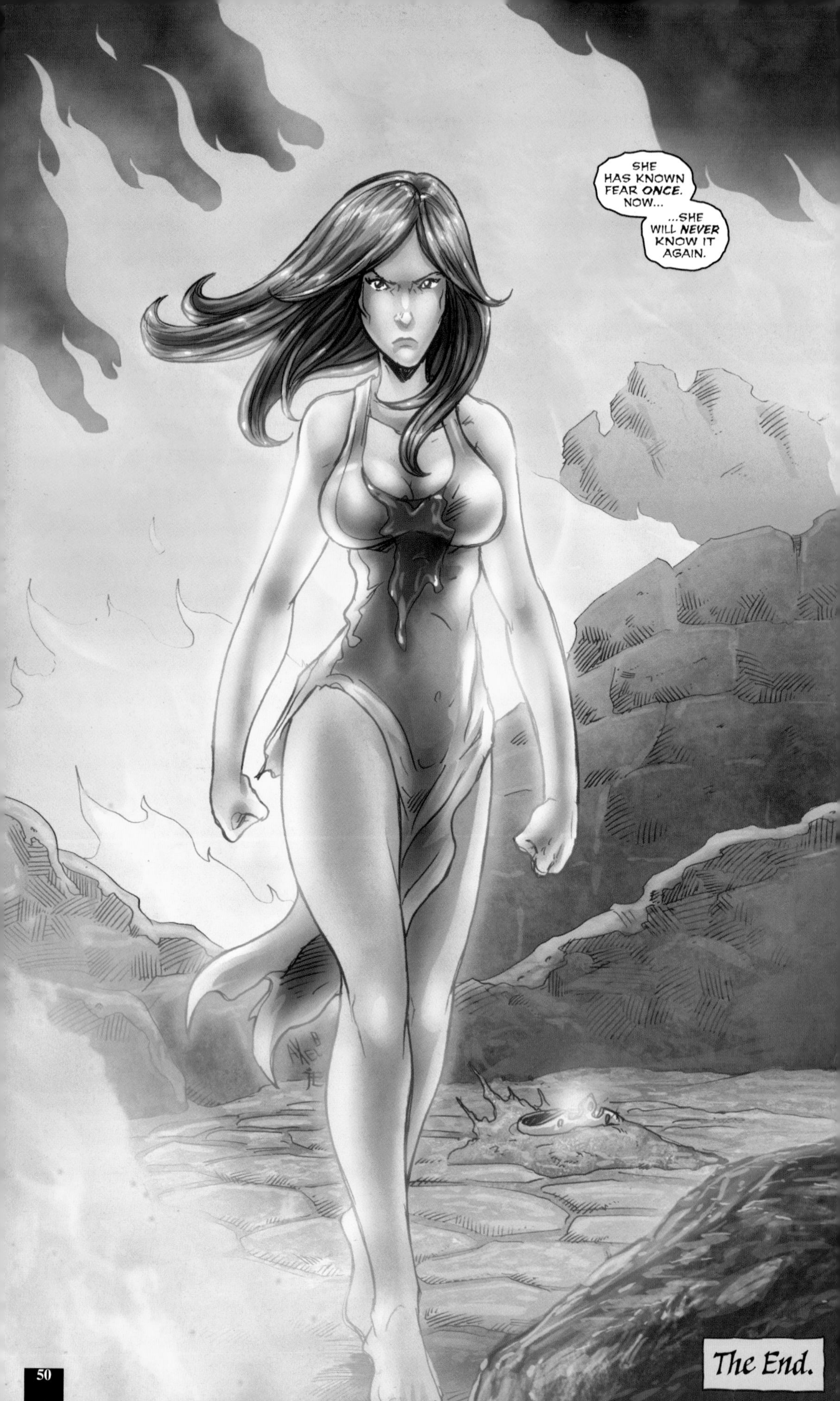
SHE HAS KNOWN FEAR *ONCE*. NOW...
...SHE WILL ***NEVER*** KNOW IT AGAIN.
The End.

Grimm Fairy Tales

Different Seasons

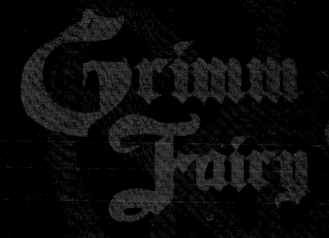

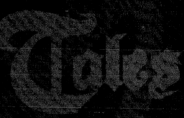

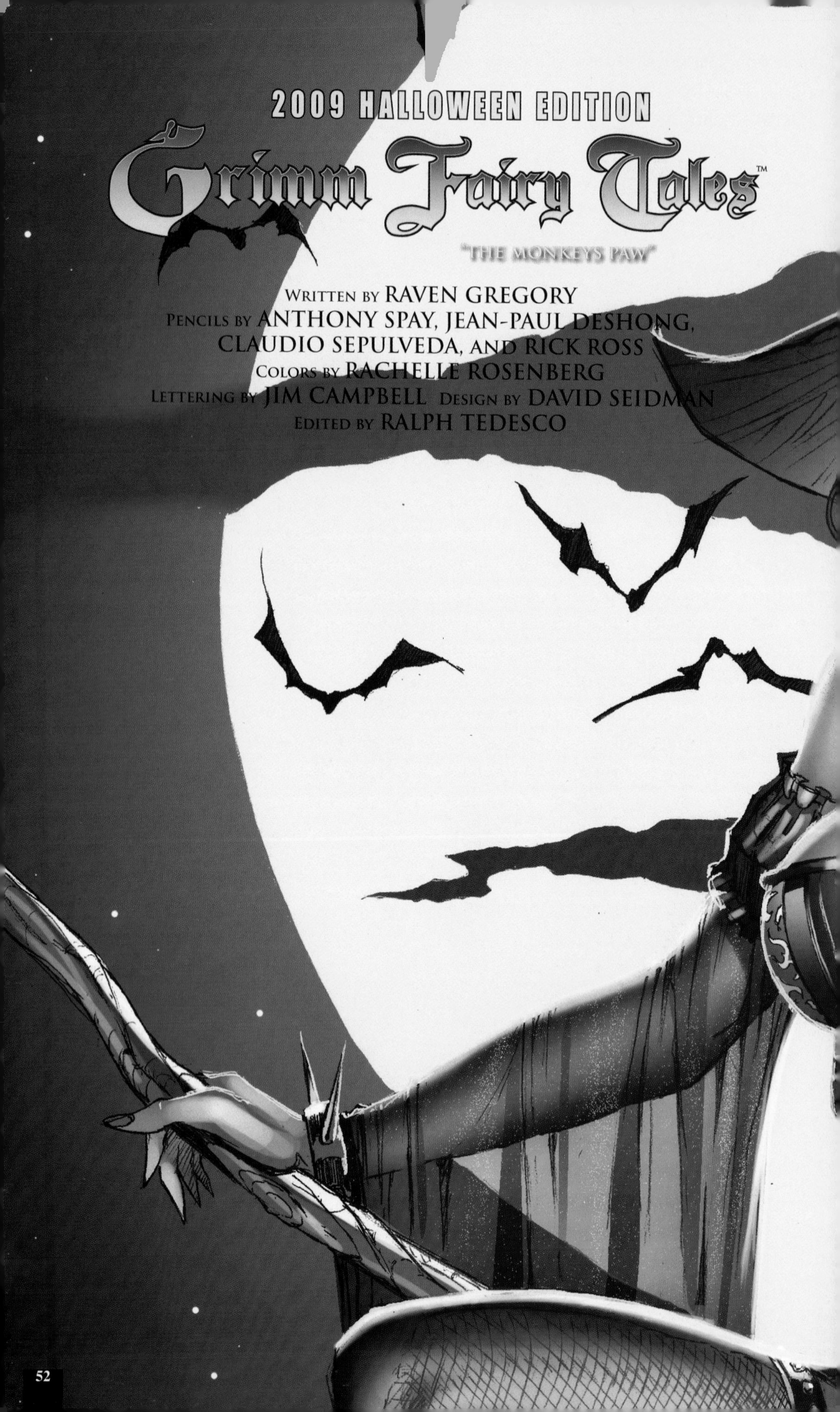
2009 HALLOWEEN EDITION
Grimm Fairy Tales™
"THE MONKEYS PAW"
WRITTEN BY RAVEN GREGORY
PENCILS BY ANTHONY SPAY, JEAN-PAUL DESHONG,
CLAUDIO SEPULVEDA, AND RICK ROSS
COLORS BY RACHELLE ROSENBERG
LETTERING BY JIM CAMPBELL DESIGN BY DAVID SEIDMAN
EDITED BY RALPH TEDESCO

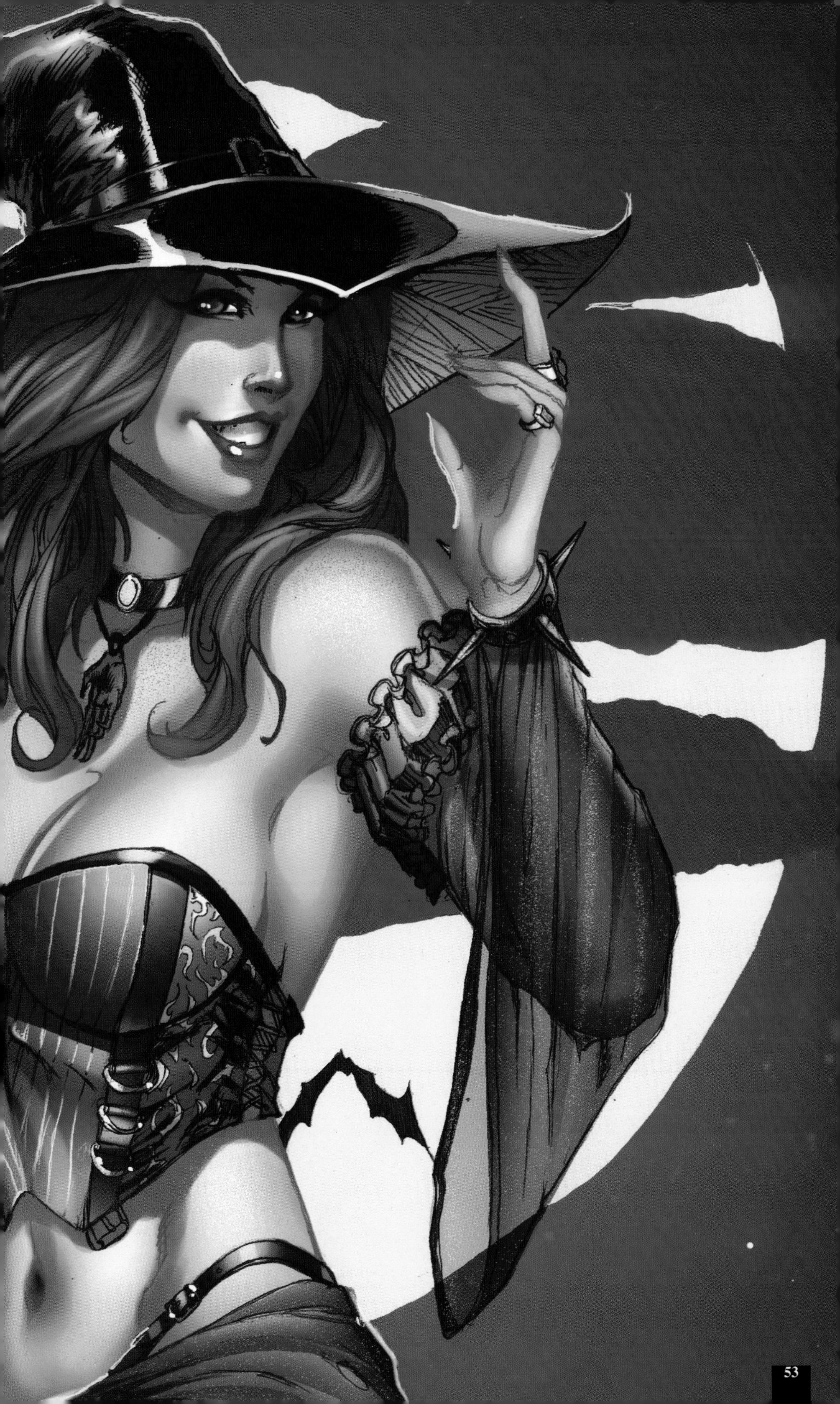

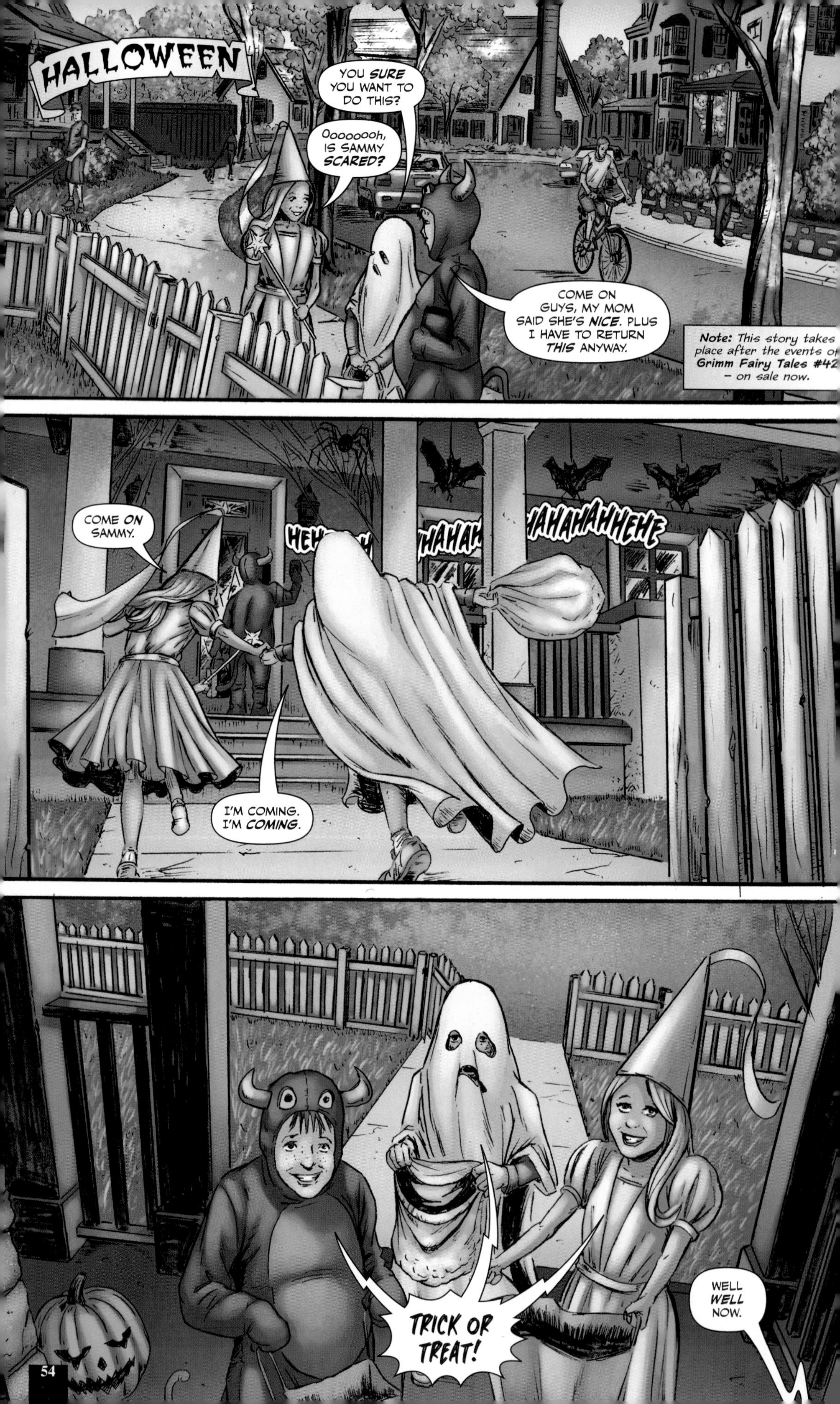

HALLOWEEN
YOU SURE YOU WANT TO DO THIS?
Ooooooh, IS SAMMY SCARED?
COME ON GUYS, MY MOM SAID SHE'S NICE. PLUS I HAVE TO RETURN THIS ANYWAY.
Note: This story takes place after the events of Grimm Fairy Tales #42 – on sale now.
COME ON SAMMY.
HAHAHAHHEHE
I'M COMING. I'M COMING.
TRICK OR TREAT!
WELL WELL NOW.

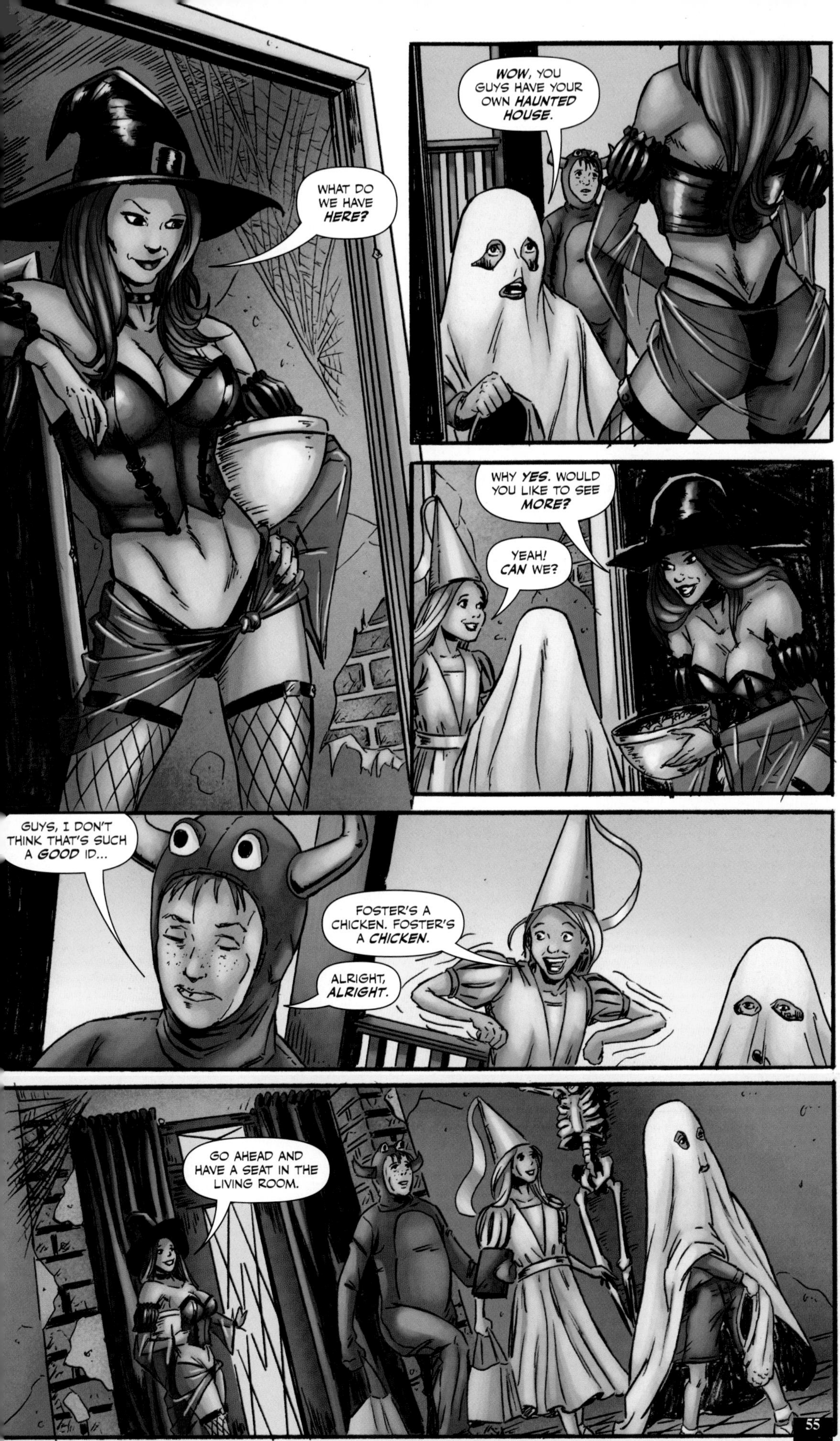
WHAT DO WE HAVE *HERE?*
WOW, YOU GUYS HAVE YOUR OWN *HAUNTED HOUSE*.
WHY *YES*. WOULD YOU LIKE TO SEE *MORE?*
YEAH! *CAN* WE?
GUYS, I DON'T THINK THAT'S SUCH A *GOOD* ID...
FOSTER'S A CHICKEN. FOSTER'S A *CHICKEN*.
ALRIGHT, *ALRIGHT*.
GO AHEAD AND HAVE A SEAT IN THE LIVING ROOM.

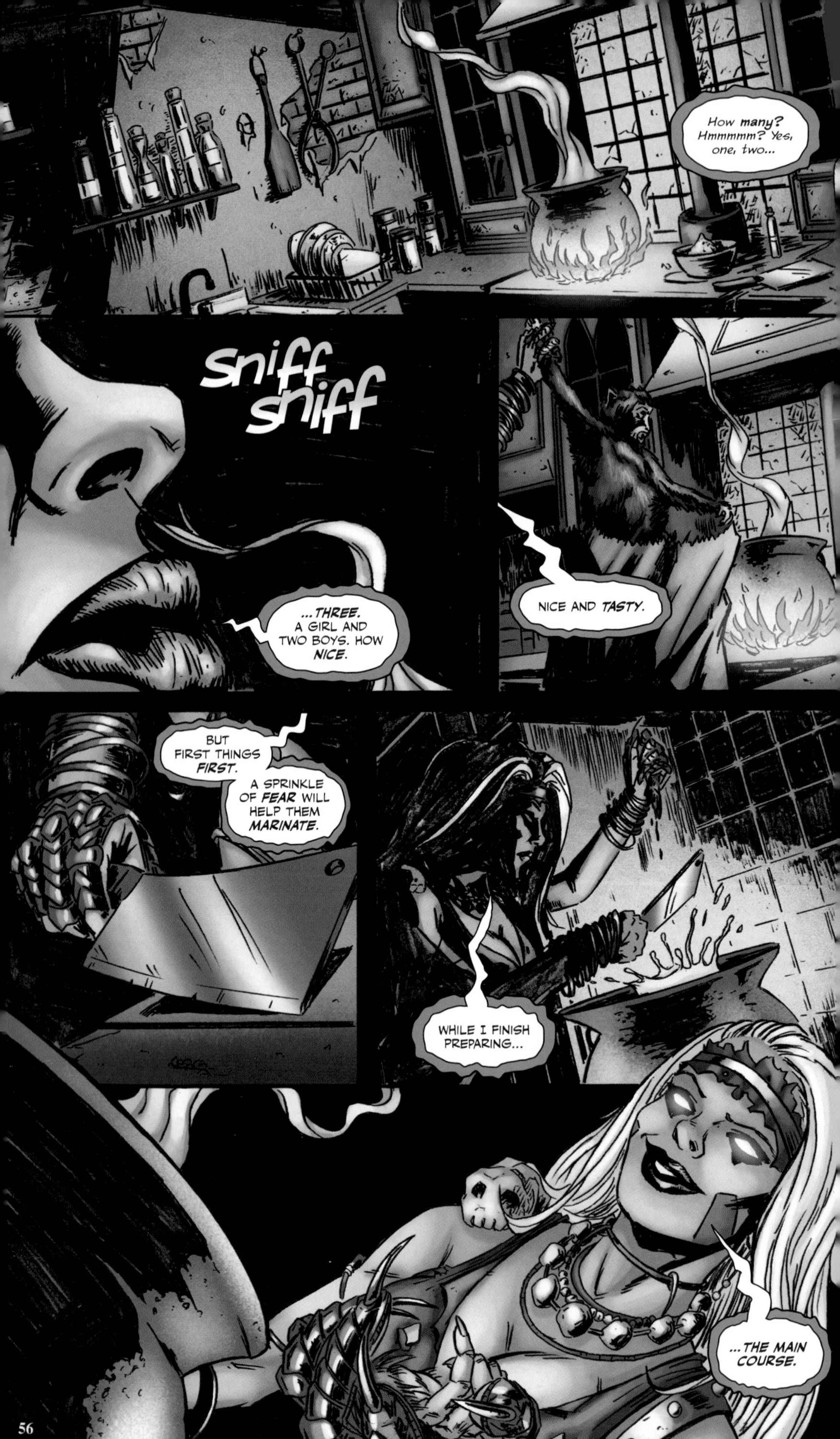
How many? Hmmmmm? Yes, one, two...
sniff sniff
...THREE. A GIRL AND TWO BOYS. HOW NICE.
NICE AND TASTY.
BUT FIRST THINGS FIRST.
A SPRINKLE OF FEAR WILL HELP THEM MARINATE.
WHILE I FINISH PREPARING...
...THE MAIN COURSE.

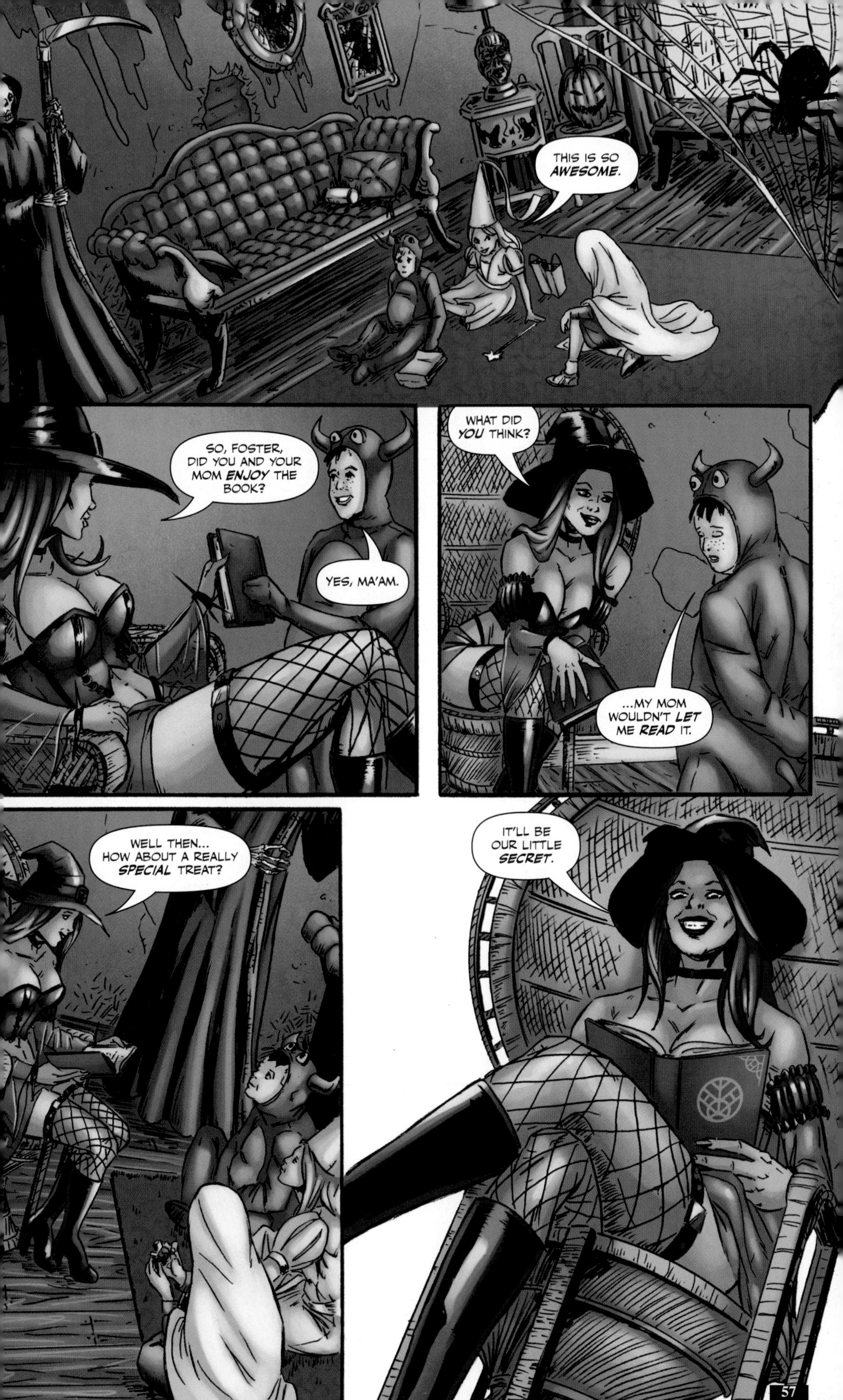
THIS IS SO AWESOME.
SO, FOSTER, DID YOU AND YOUR MOM ENJOY THE BOOK?
YES, MA'AM.
WHAT DID YOU THINK?
...MY MOM WOULDN'T LET ME READ IT.
WELL THEN... HOW ABOUT A REALLY SPECIAL TREAT?
IT'LL BE OUR LITTLE SECRET.

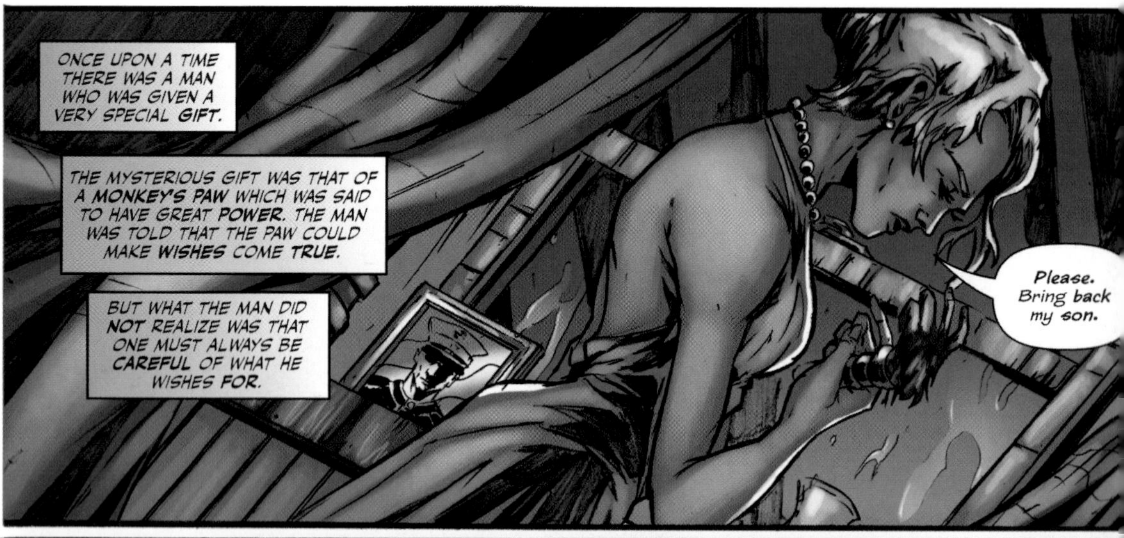
ONCE UPON A TIME THERE WAS A MAN WHO WAS GIVEN A VERY SPECIAL GIFT.
THE MYSTERIOUS GIFT WAS THAT OF A MONKEY'S PAW WHICH WAS SAID TO HAVE GREAT POWER. THE MAN WAS TOLD THAT THE PAW COULD MAKE WISHES COME TRUE.
BUT WHAT THE MAN DID NOT REALIZE WAS THAT ONE MUST ALWAYS BE CAREFUL OF WHAT HE WISHES FOR.
Please. Bring back my son.

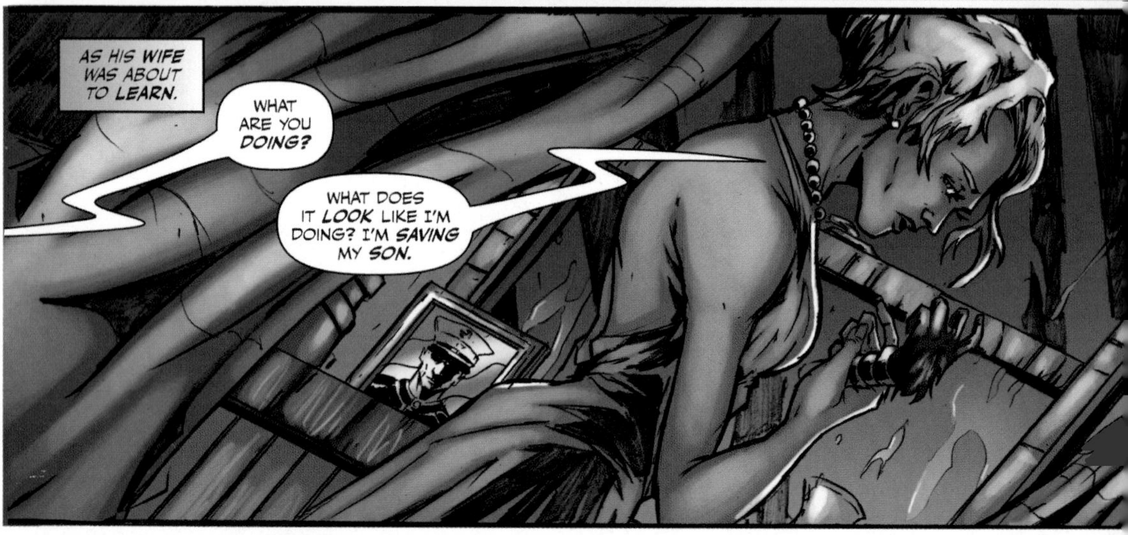
AS HIS WIFE WAS ABOUT TO LEARN.
WHAT ARE YOU DOING?
WHAT DOES IT LOOK LIKE I'M DOING? I'M SAVING MY SON.

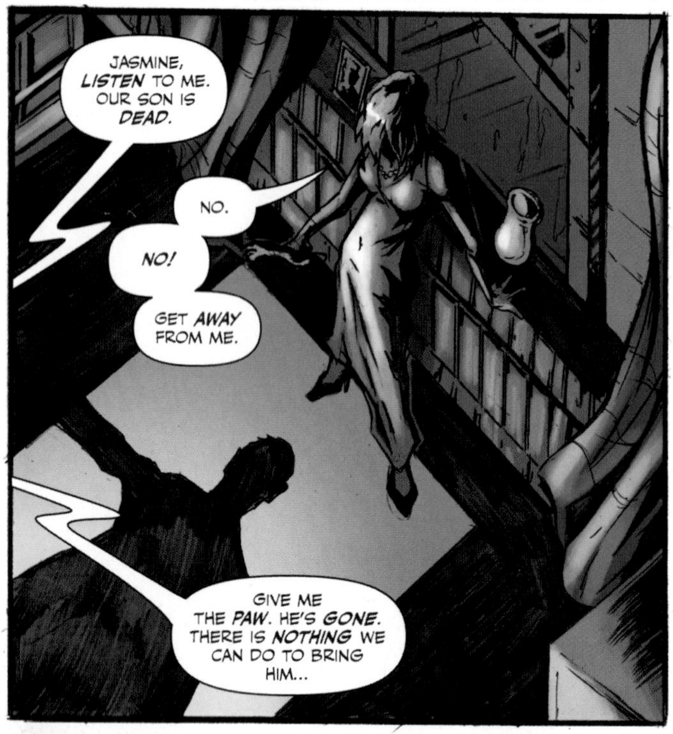
JASMINE, LISTEN TO ME. OUR SON IS DEAD.
NO.
NO!
GET AWAY FROM ME.
GIVE ME THE PAW. HE'S GONE. THERE IS NOTHING WE CAN DO TO BRING HIM...

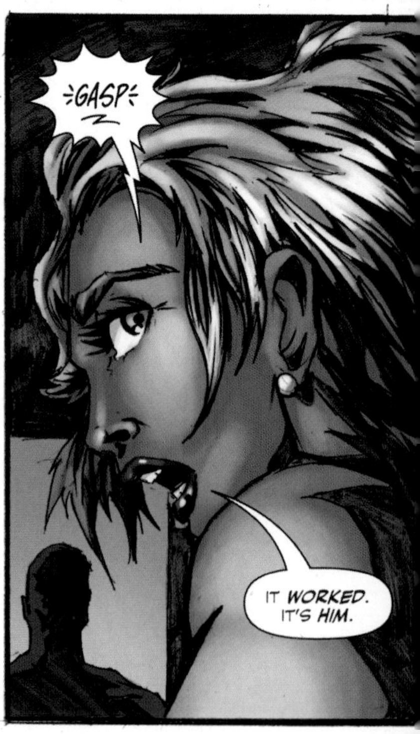
GASP
IT WORKED. IT'S HIM.

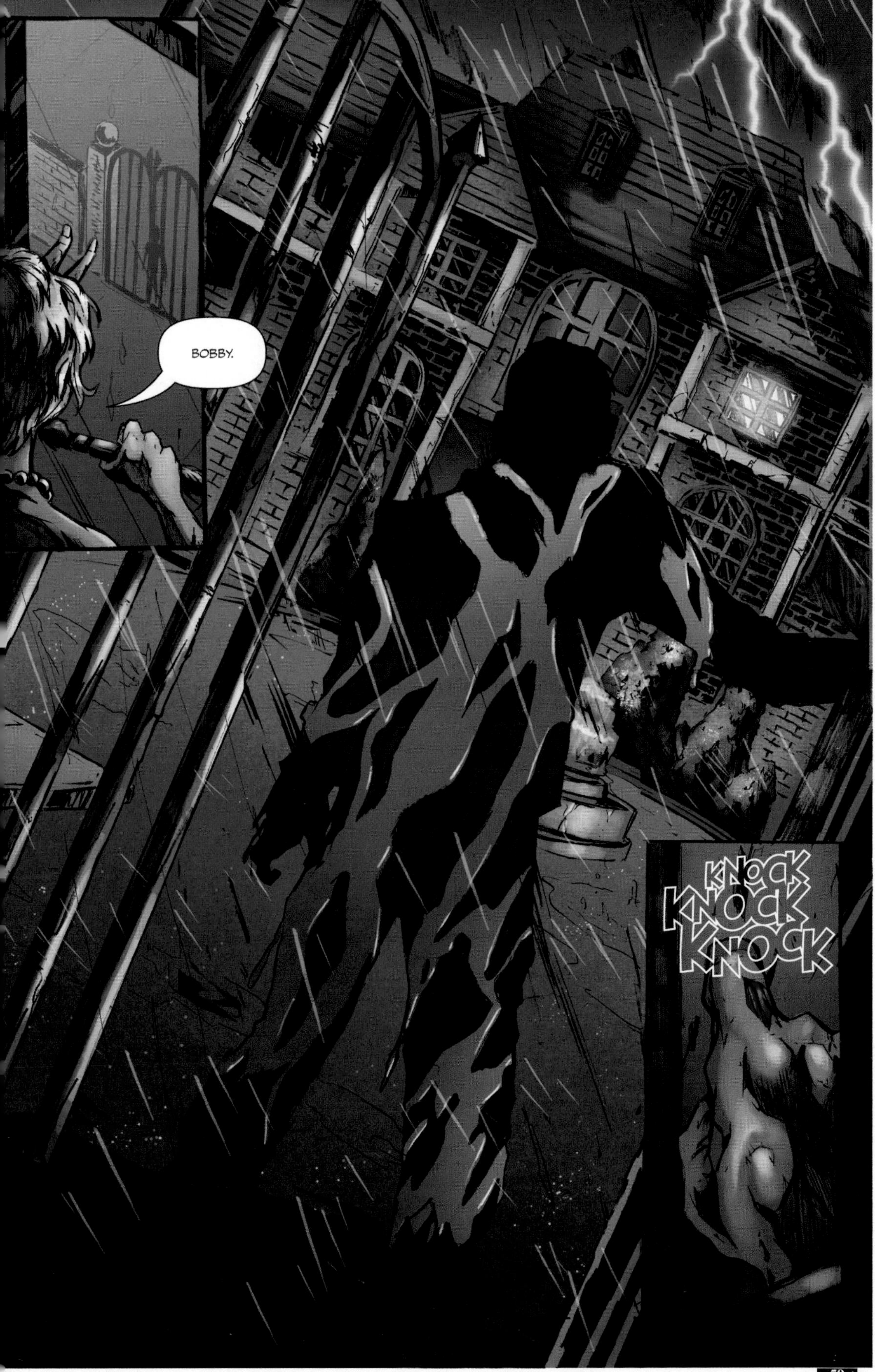
BOBBY.
KNOCK
KNOCK
KNOCK

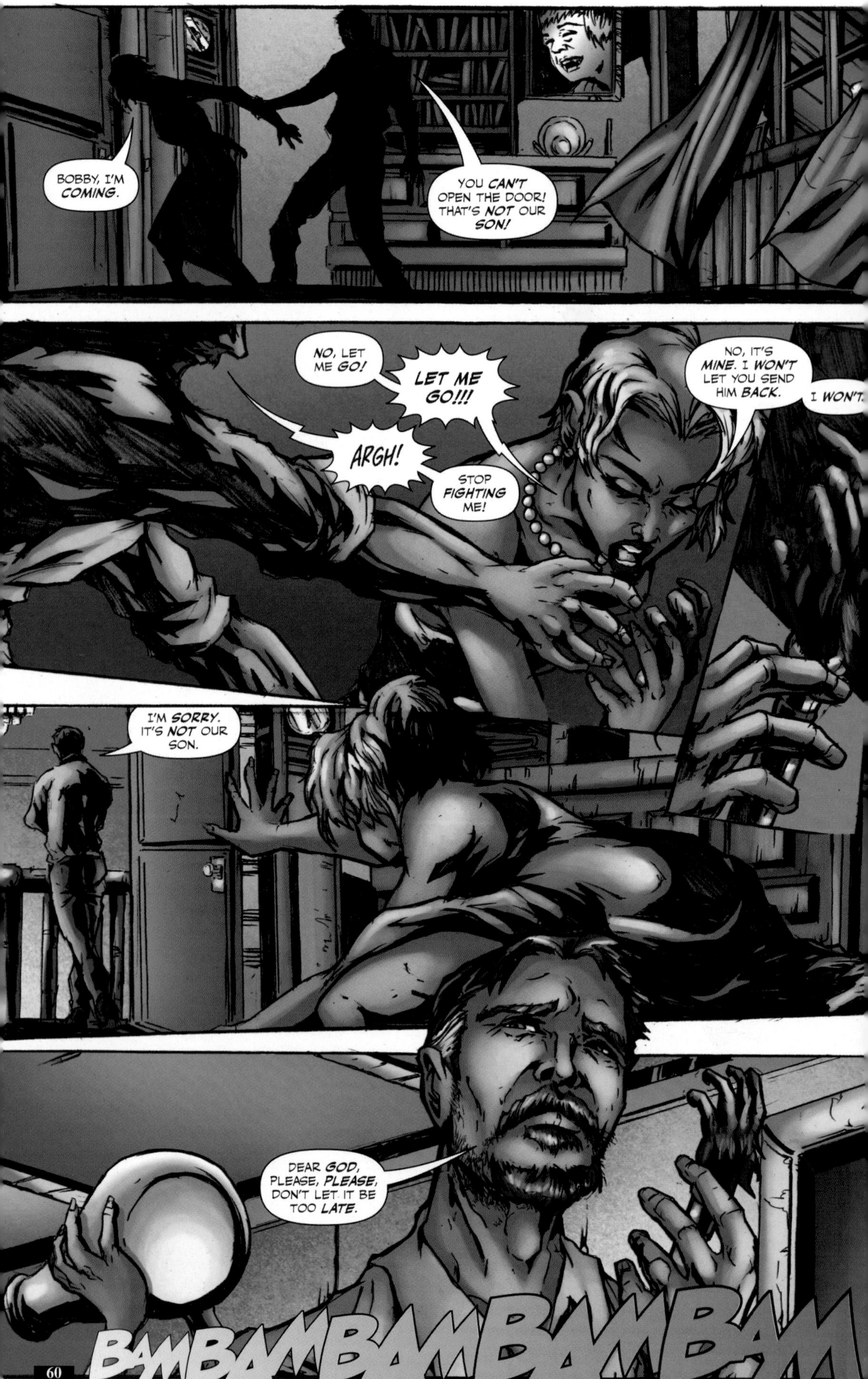
BOBBY, I'M COMING.
YOU CAN'T OPEN THE DOOR! THAT'S NOT OUR SON!
NO, LET ME GO!
LET ME GO!!!
ARGH!
STOP FIGHTING ME!
NO, IT'S MINE. I WON'T LET YOU SEND HIM BACK.
I WON'T.
I'M SORRY. IT'S NOT OUR SON.
DEAR GOD, PLEASE, PLEASE, DON'T LET IT BE TOO LATE.
BAMBAMBAMBAMBAM

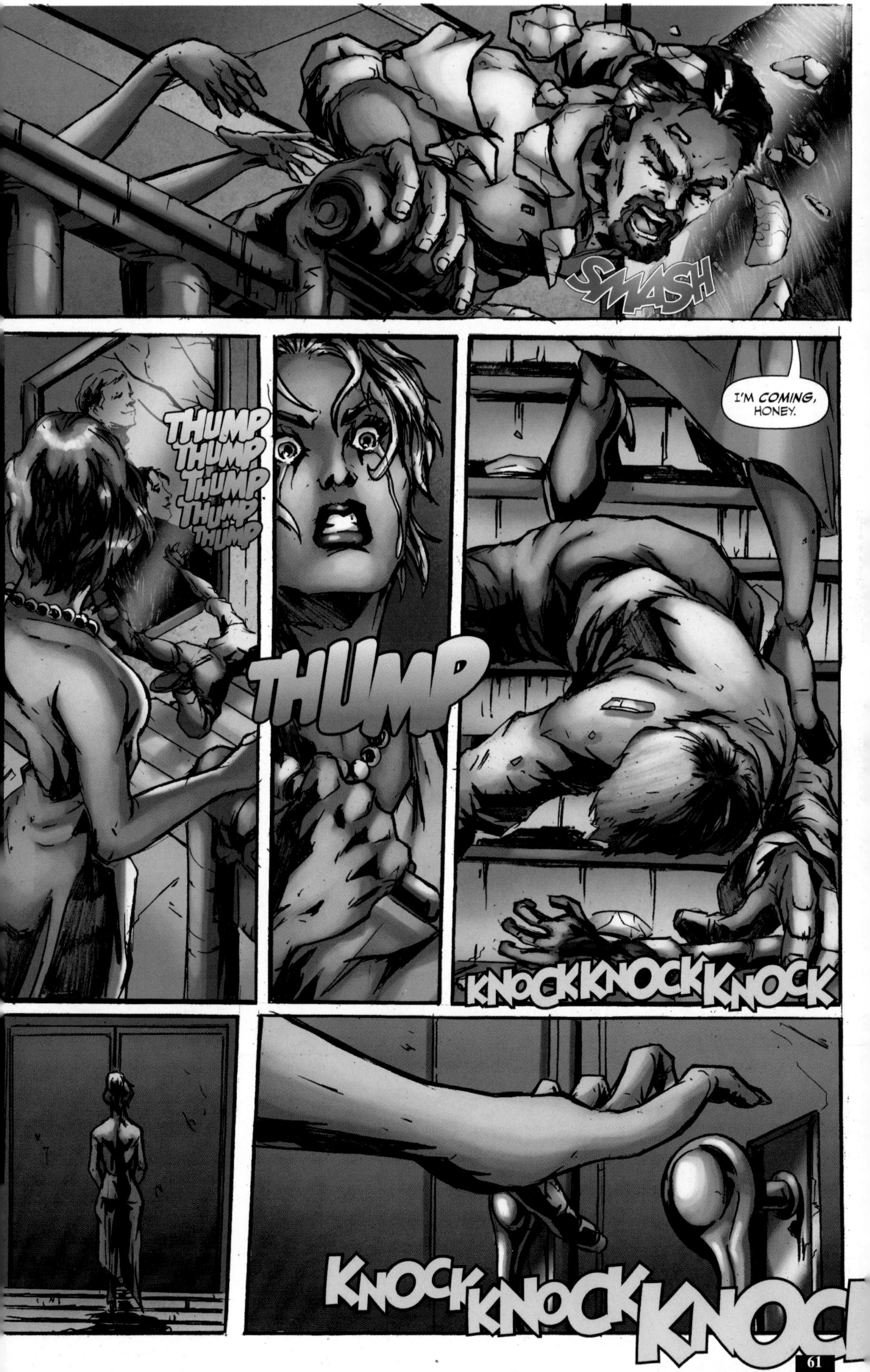
SMASH
THUMP
THUMP
THUMP
THUMP
THUMP
THUMP
I'M COMING, HONEY.
KNOCK KNOCK KNOCK
KNOCK KNOCK KNOC

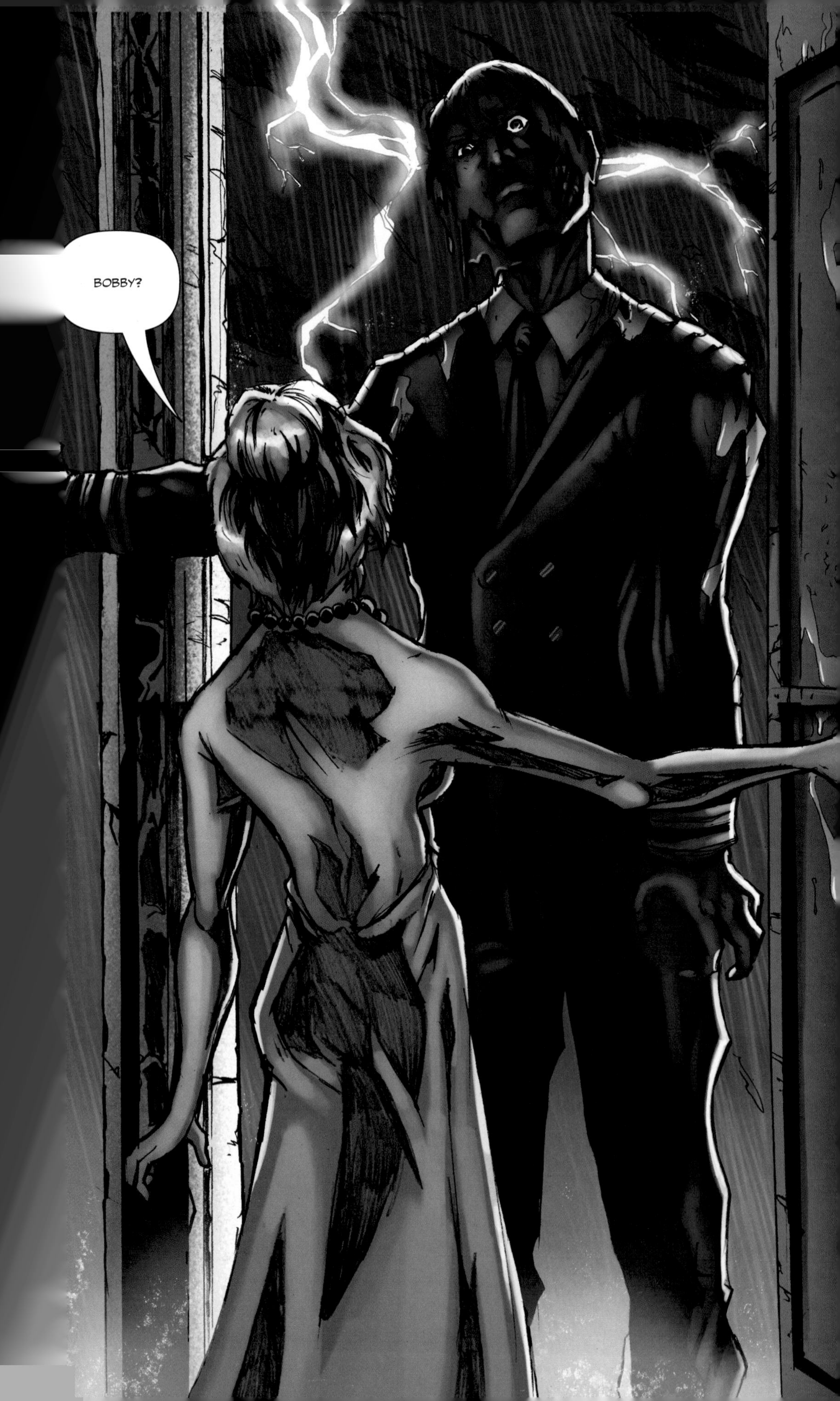
BOBBY?

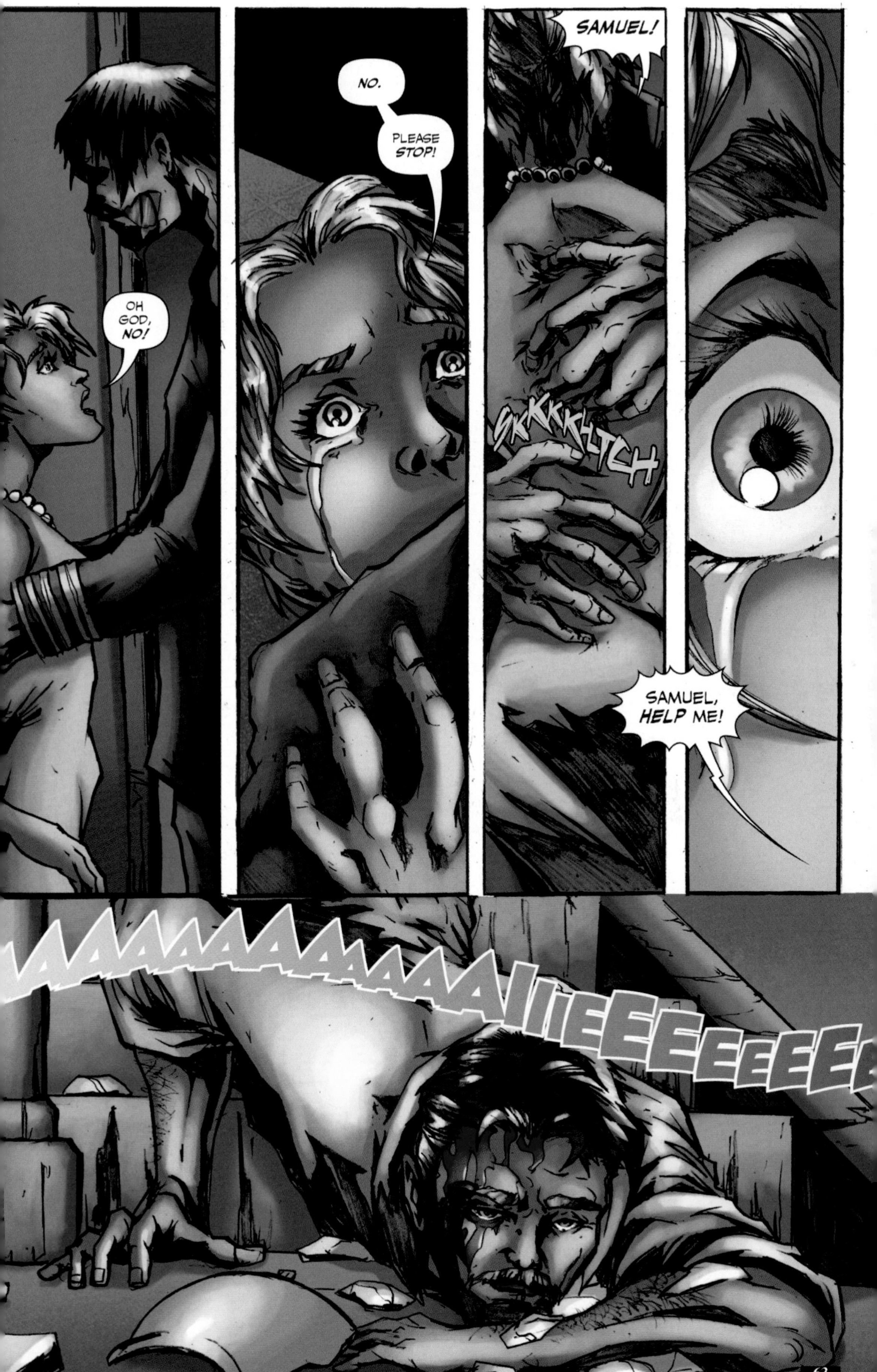
OH GOD, NO!
NO.
PLEASE STOP!
SAMUEL!
SKKKHTCH
SAMUEL, HELP ME!
AAAAAAAAAAAAAIIIEEEEEEEE

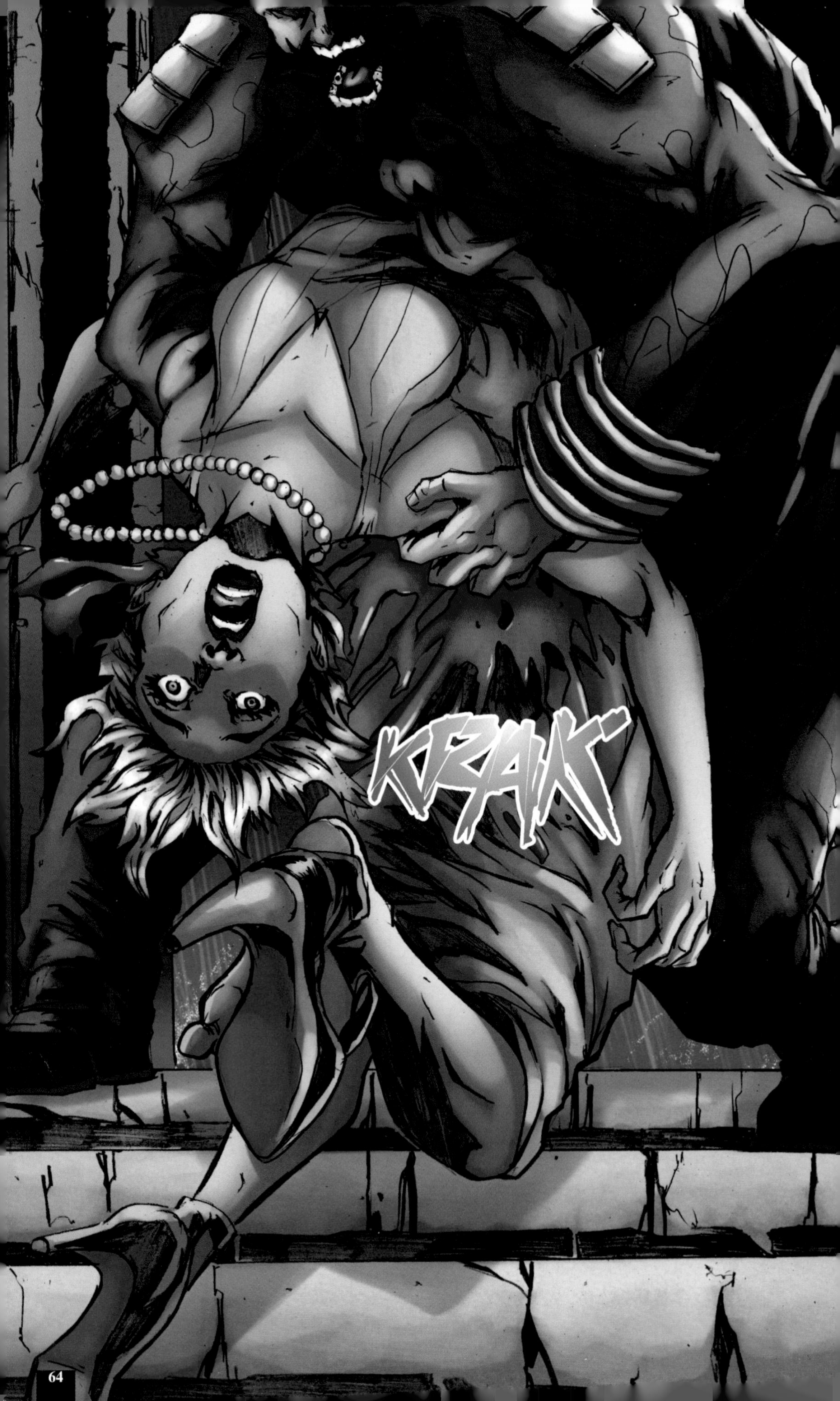
KRAK

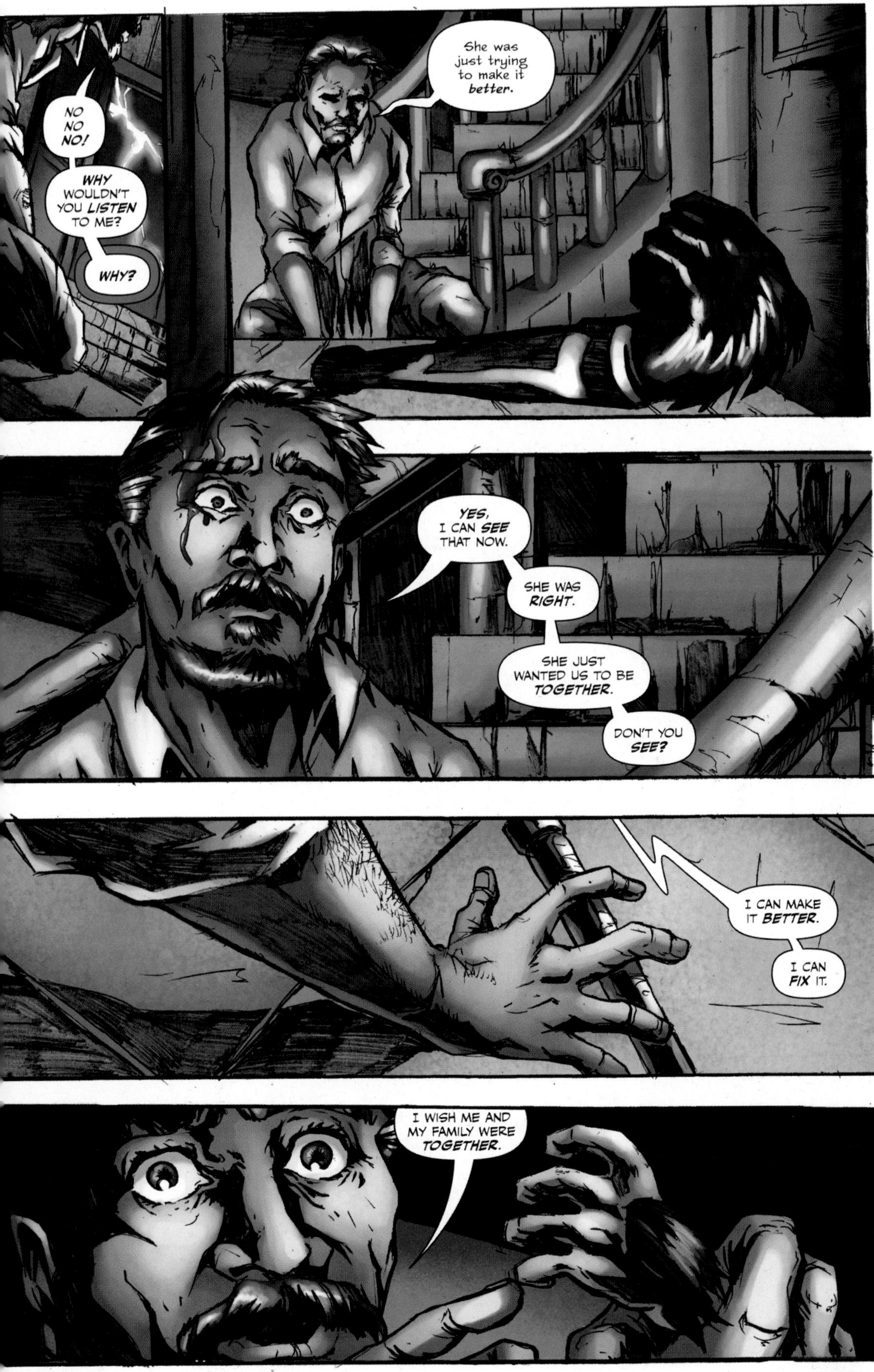
NO NO NO!
WHY WOULDN'T YOU LISTEN TO ME?
WHY?
She was just trying to make it better.
YES, I CAN SEE THAT NOW.
SHE WAS RIGHT.
SHE JUST WANTED US TO BE TOGETHER.
DON'T YOU SEE?
I CAN MAKE IT BETTER.
I CAN FIX IT.
I WISH ME AND MY FAMILY WERE TOGETHER.

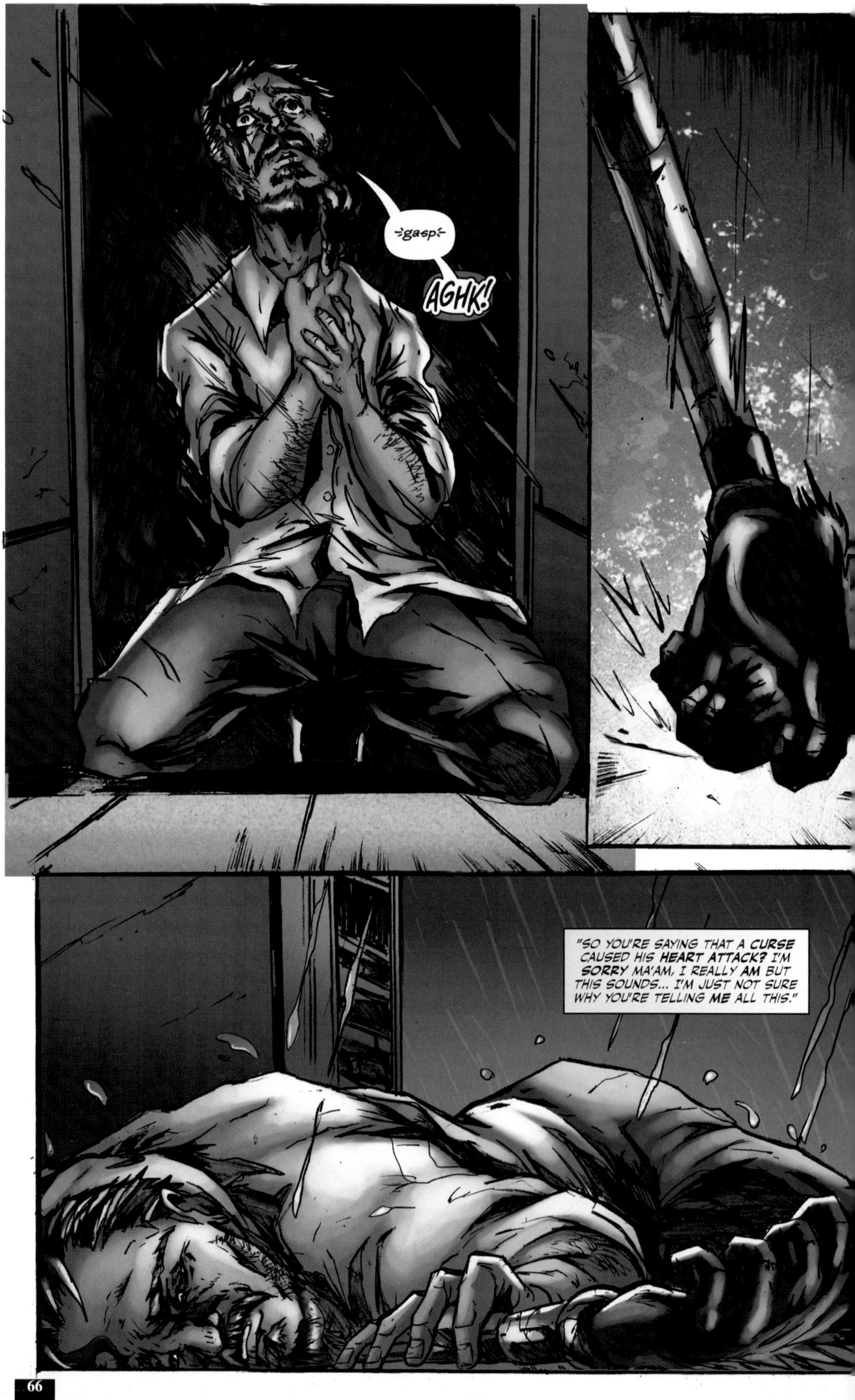

-gasp-
AGHK!
"SO YOU'RE SAYING THAT A CURSE CAUSED HIS HEART ATTACK? I'M SORRY MA'AM, I REALLY AM BUT THIS SOUNDS... I'M JUST NOT SURE WHY YOU'RE TELLING ME ALL THIS."

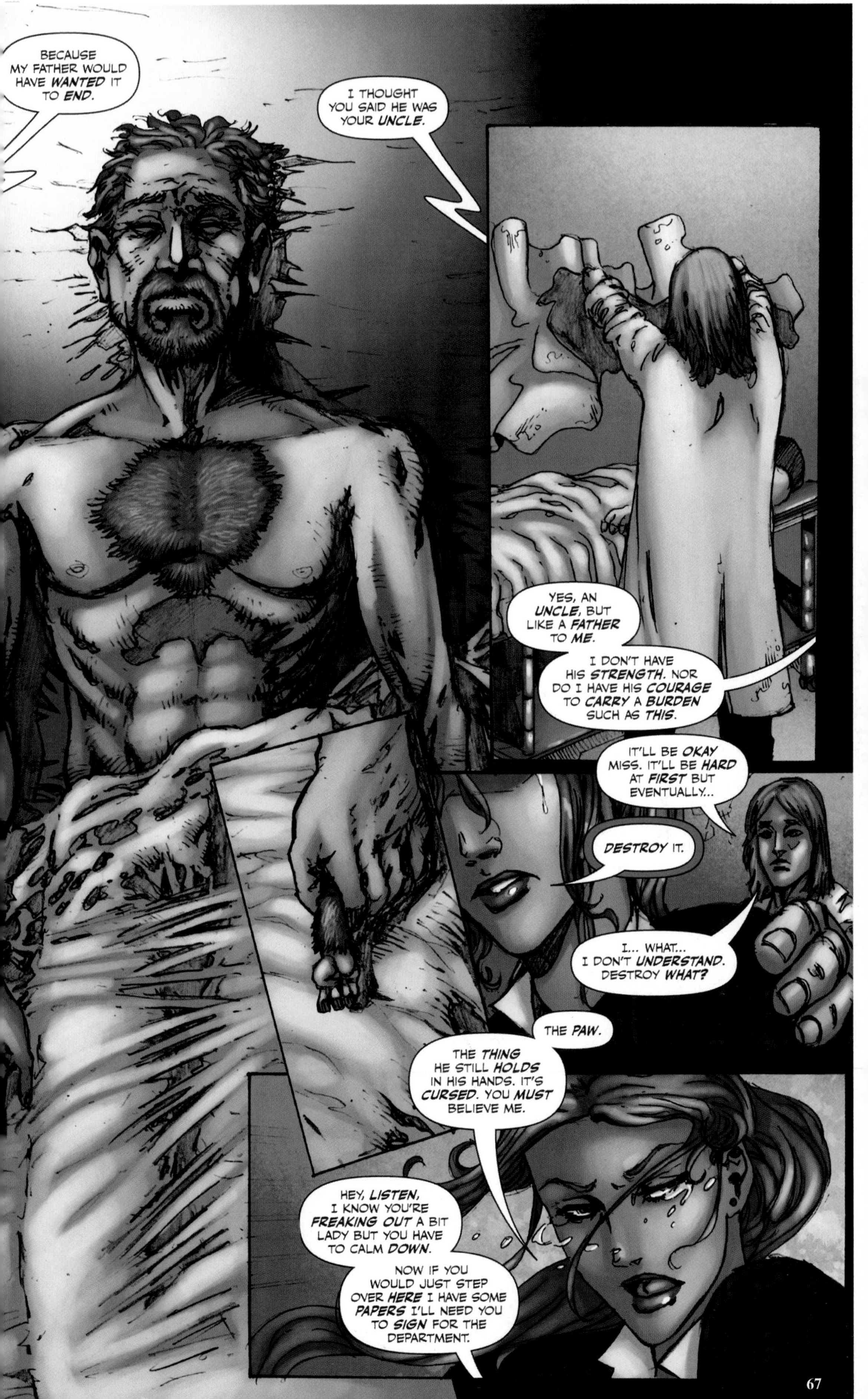
BECAUSE MY FATHER WOULD HAVE *WANTED* IT TO *END*.
I THOUGHT YOU SAID HE WAS YOUR *UNCLE*.
YES, AN *UNCLE*, BUT LIKE A *FATHER* TO *ME*.
I DON'T HAVE HIS *STRENGTH*. NOR DO I HAVE HIS *COURAGE* TO *CARRY* A *BURDEN* SUCH AS *THIS*.
IT'LL BE *OKAY* MISS. IT'LL BE *HARD* AT *FIRST* BUT EVENTUALLY...
DESTROY IT.
I... WHAT... I DON'T *UNDERSTAND*. DESTROY *WHAT?*
THE *PAW*.
THE *THING* HE STILL *HOLDS* IN HIS HANDS. IT'S *CURSED*. YOU *MUST* BELIEVE ME.
HEY, *LISTEN*, I KNOW YOU'RE *FREAKING OUT* A BIT LADY BUT YOU HAVE TO CALM *DOWN*.
NOW IF YOU WOULD JUST STEP OVER *HERE* I HAVE SOME *PAPERS* I'LL NEED YOU TO *SIGN* FOR THE DEPARTMENT.

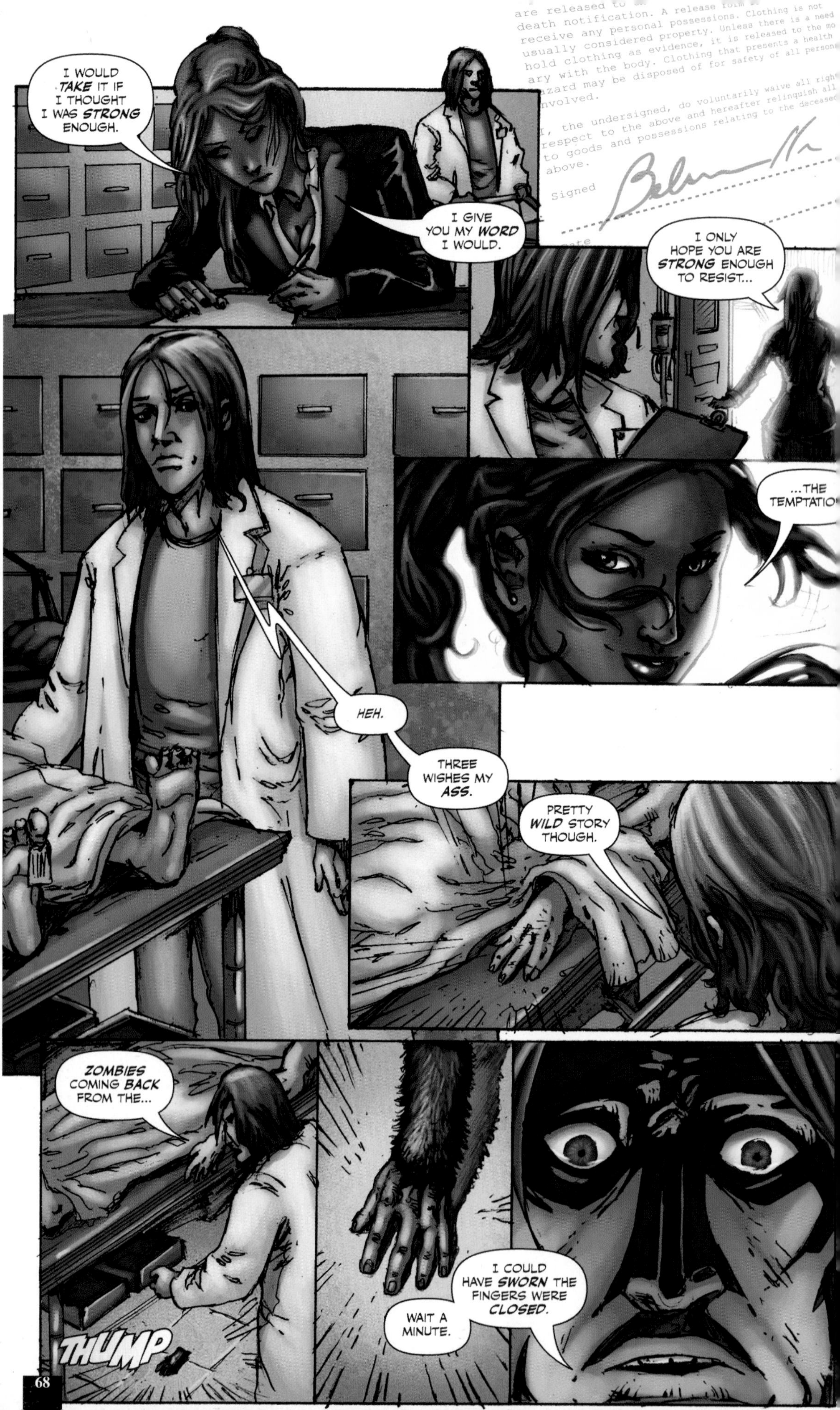
are released to
death notification. A release form
receive any personal possessions. Clothing is not
usually considered property. Unless there is a need
hold clothing as evidence, it is released to the mo
ary with the body. Clothing that presents a health
azard may be disposed of for safety of all person
nvolved.
I, the undersigned, do voluntarily waive all righ
respect to the above and hereafter relinquish all
to goods and possessions relating to the deceased
above.
Signed
I WOULD TAKE IT IF I THOUGHT I WAS STRONG ENOUGH.
I GIVE YOU MY WORD I WOULD.
I ONLY HOPE YOU ARE STRONG ENOUGH TO RESIST...
...THE TEMPTATIO
HEH.
THREE WISHES MY ASS.
PRETTY WILD STORY THOUGH.
ZOMBIES COMING BACK FROM THE...
THUMP
WAIT A MINUTE.
I COULD HAVE SWORN THE FINGERS WERE CLOSED.

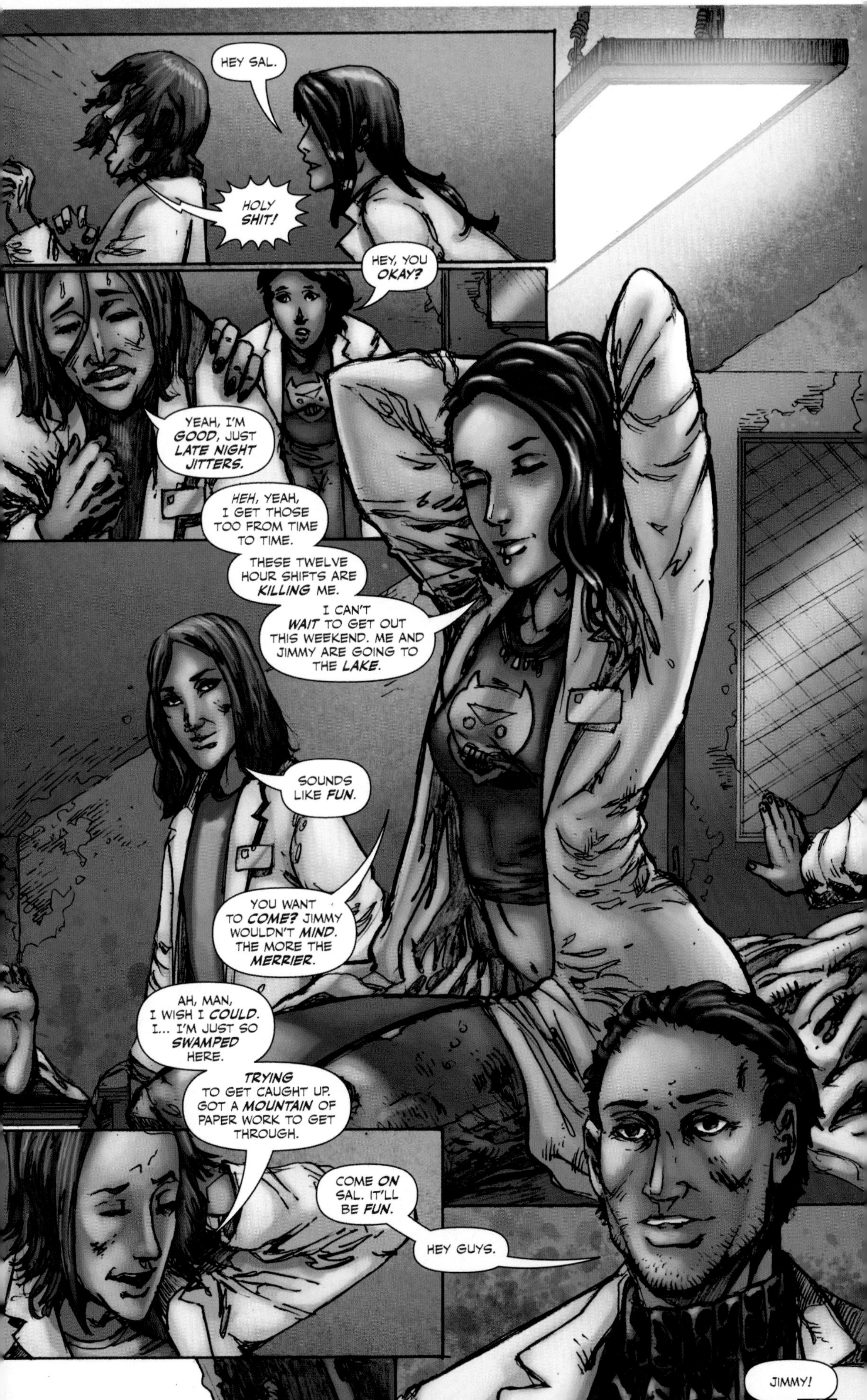

HEY SAL.
HOLY SHIT!
HEY, YOU OKAY?
YEAH, I'M GOOD, JUST LATE NIGHT JITTERS.
HEH, YEAH, I GET THOSE TOO FROM TIME TO TIME.
THESE TWELVE HOUR SHIFTS ARE KILLING ME.
I CAN'T WAIT TO GET OUT THIS WEEKEND. ME AND JIMMY ARE GOING TO THE LAKE.
SOUNDS LIKE FUN.
YOU WANT TO COME? JIMMY WOULDN'T MIND. THE MORE THE MERRIER.
AH, MAN, I WISH I COULD. I... I'M JUST SO SWAMPED HERE.
TRYING TO GET CAUGHT UP. GOT A MOUNTAIN OF PAPER WORK TO GET THROUGH.
COME ON SAL. IT'LL BE FUN.
HEY GUYS.
JIMMY!

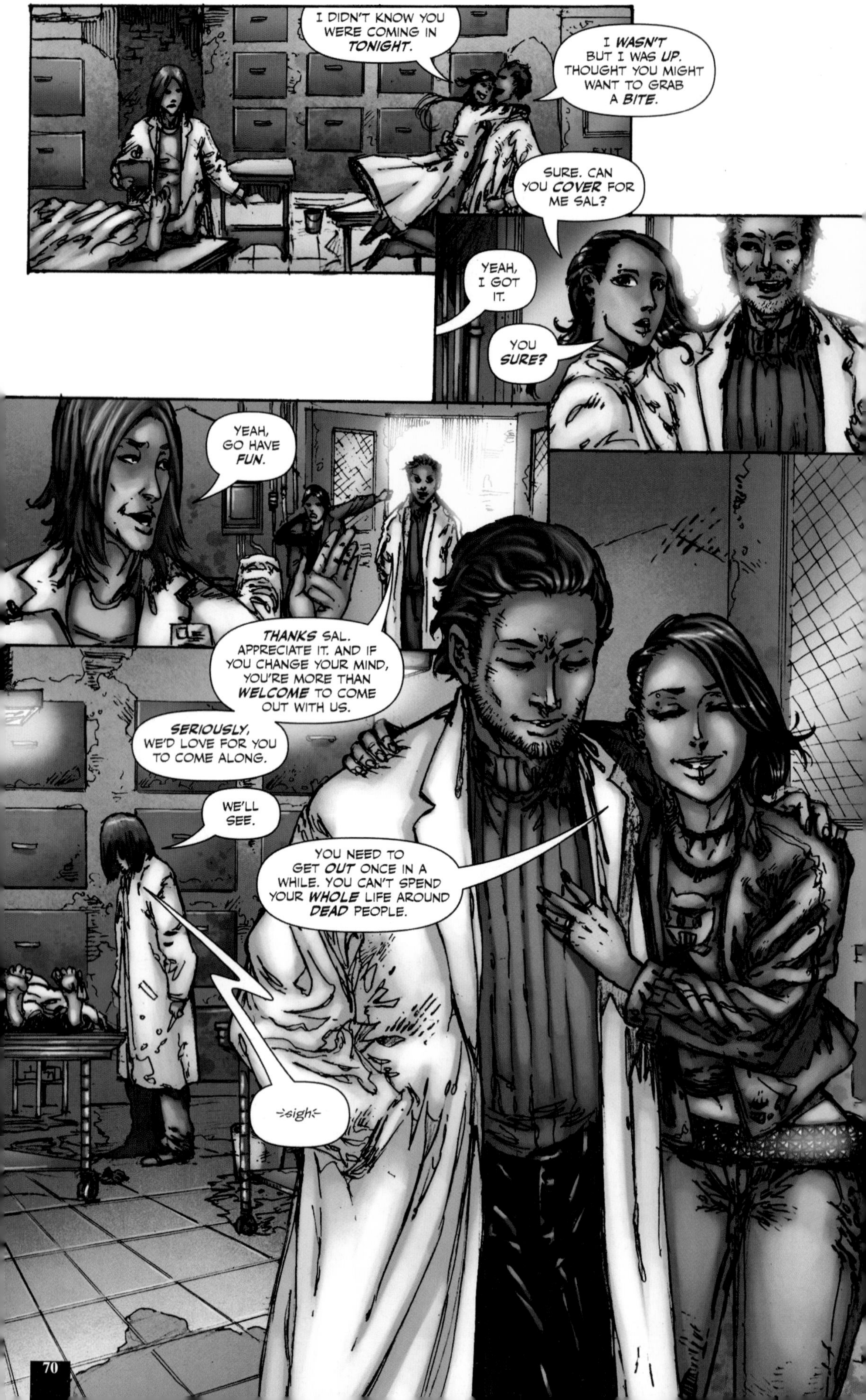
I DIDN'T KNOW YOU WERE COMING IN TONIGHT.
I WASN'T BUT I WAS UP. THOUGHT YOU MIGHT WANT TO GRAB A BITE.
EXIT
SURE. CAN YOU COVER FOR ME SAL?
YEAH, I GOT IT.
YOU SURE?
YEAH, GO HAVE FUN.
THANKS SAL. APPRECIATE IT. AND IF YOU CHANGE YOUR MIND, YOU'RE MORE THAN WELCOME TO COME OUT WITH US.
SERIOUSLY, WE'D LOVE FOR YOU TO COME ALONG.
WE'LL SEE.
YOU NEED TO GET OUT ONCE IN A WHILE. YOU CAN'T SPEND YOUR WHOLE LIFE AROUND DEAD PEOPLE.
-sigh-

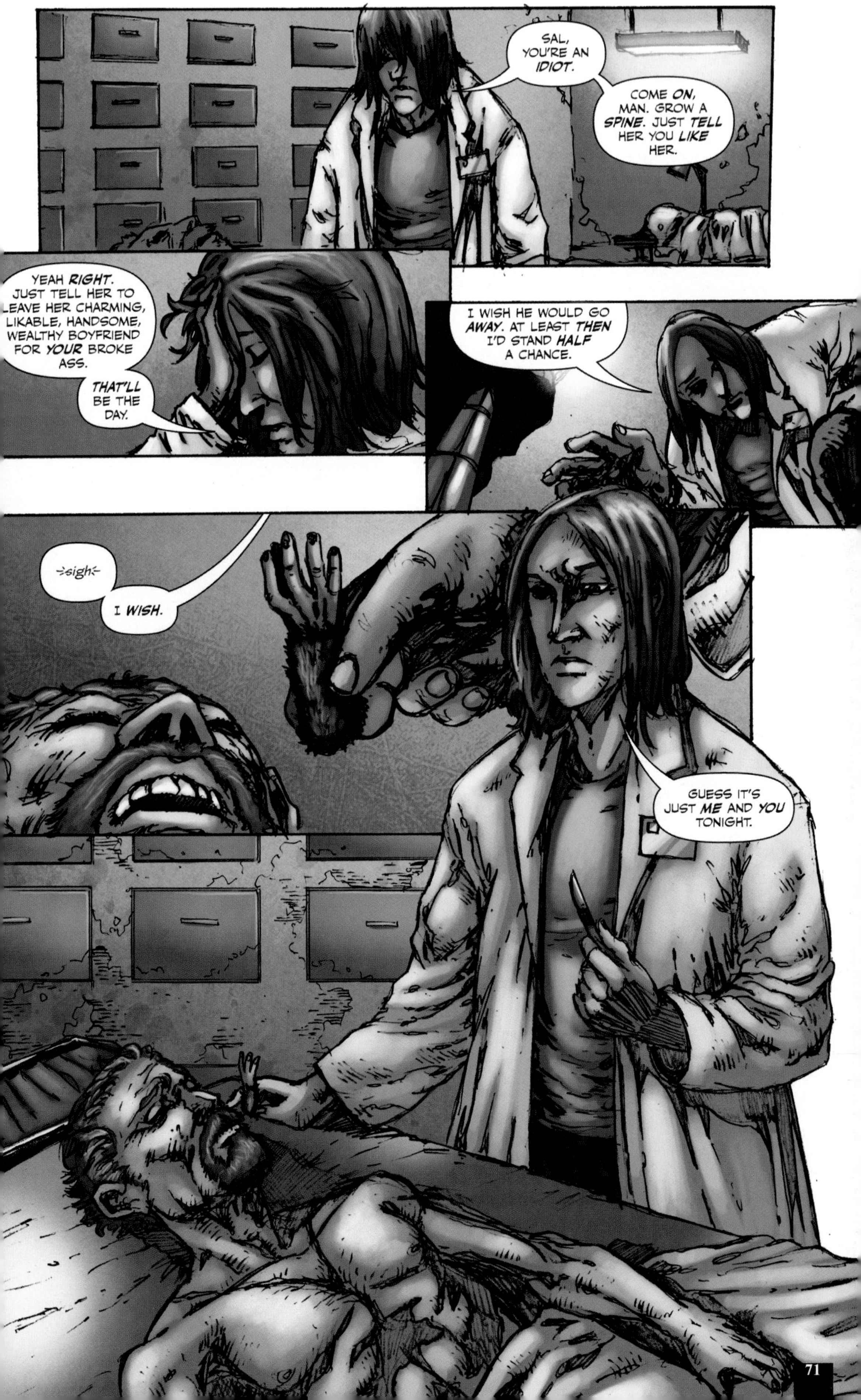

SAL, YOU'RE AN IDIOT.
COME ON, MAN. GROW A SPINE. JUST TELL HER YOU LIKE HER.
YEAH RIGHT. JUST TELL HER TO LEAVE HER CHARMING, LIKABLE, HANDSOME, WEALTHY BOYFRIEND FOR YOUR BROKE ASS.
THAT'LL BE THE DAY.
I WISH HE WOULD GO AWAY. AT LEAST THEN I'D STAND HALF A CHANCE.
~sigh~
I WISH.
GUESS IT'S JUST ME AND YOU TONIGHT.

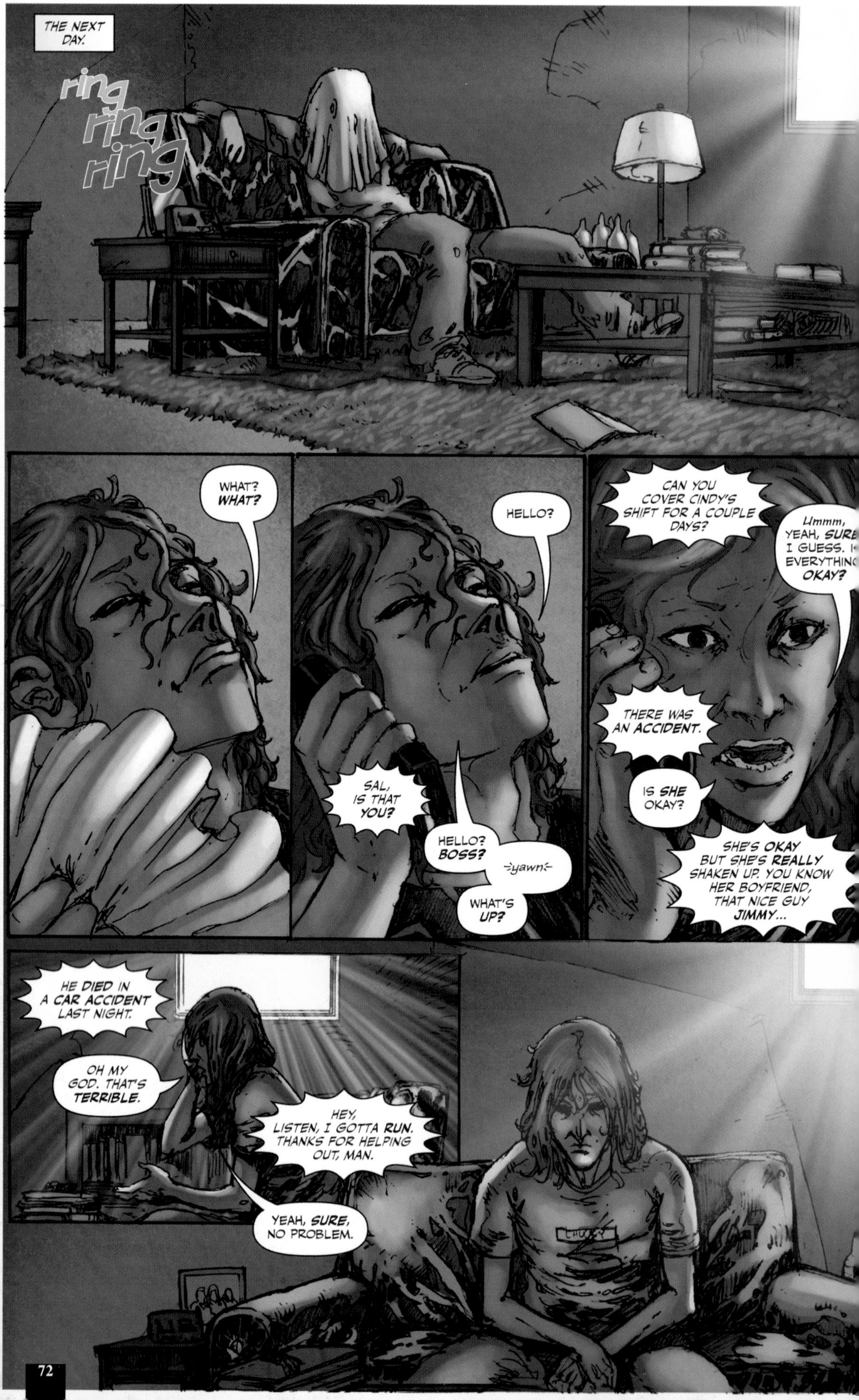

THE NEXT DAY.
ring ring ring
WHAT? WHAT?
HELLO?
SAL, IS THAT YOU?
HELLO? BOSS?
-yawn-
WHAT'S UP?
CAN YOU COVER CINDY'S SHIFT FOR A COUPLE DAYS?
Ummm, YEAH, SURE I GUESS. IS EVERYTHING OKAY?
THERE WAS AN ACCIDENT.
IS SHE OKAY?
SHE'S OKAY BUT SHE'S REALLY SHAKEN UP. YOU KNOW HER BOYFRIEND, THAT NICE GUY JIMMY...
HE DIED IN A CAR ACCIDENT LAST NIGHT.
OH MY GOD. THAT'S TERRIBLE.
HEY, LISTEN, I GOTTA RUN. THANKS FOR HELPING OUT, MAN.
YEAH, SURE, NO PROBLEM.

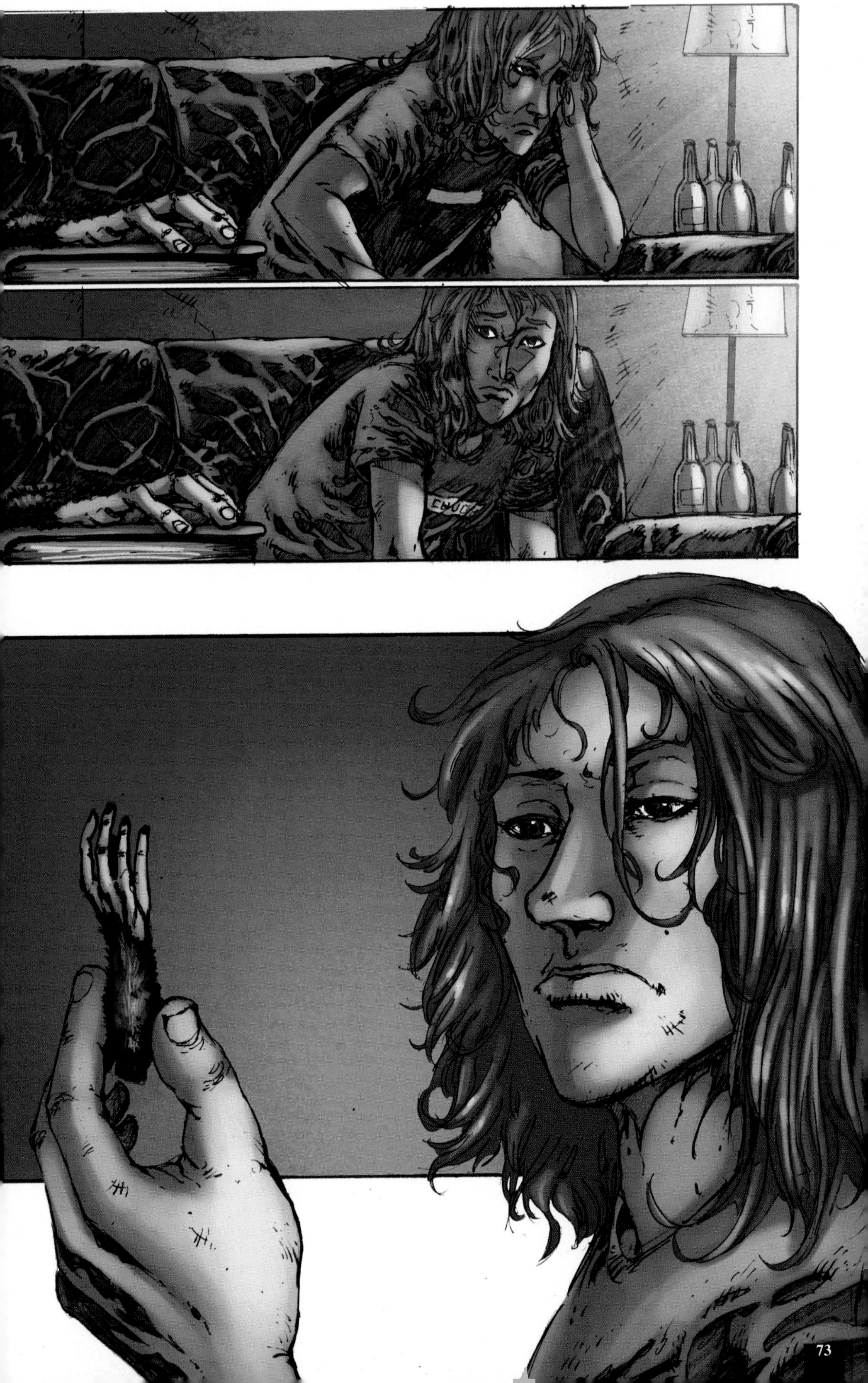

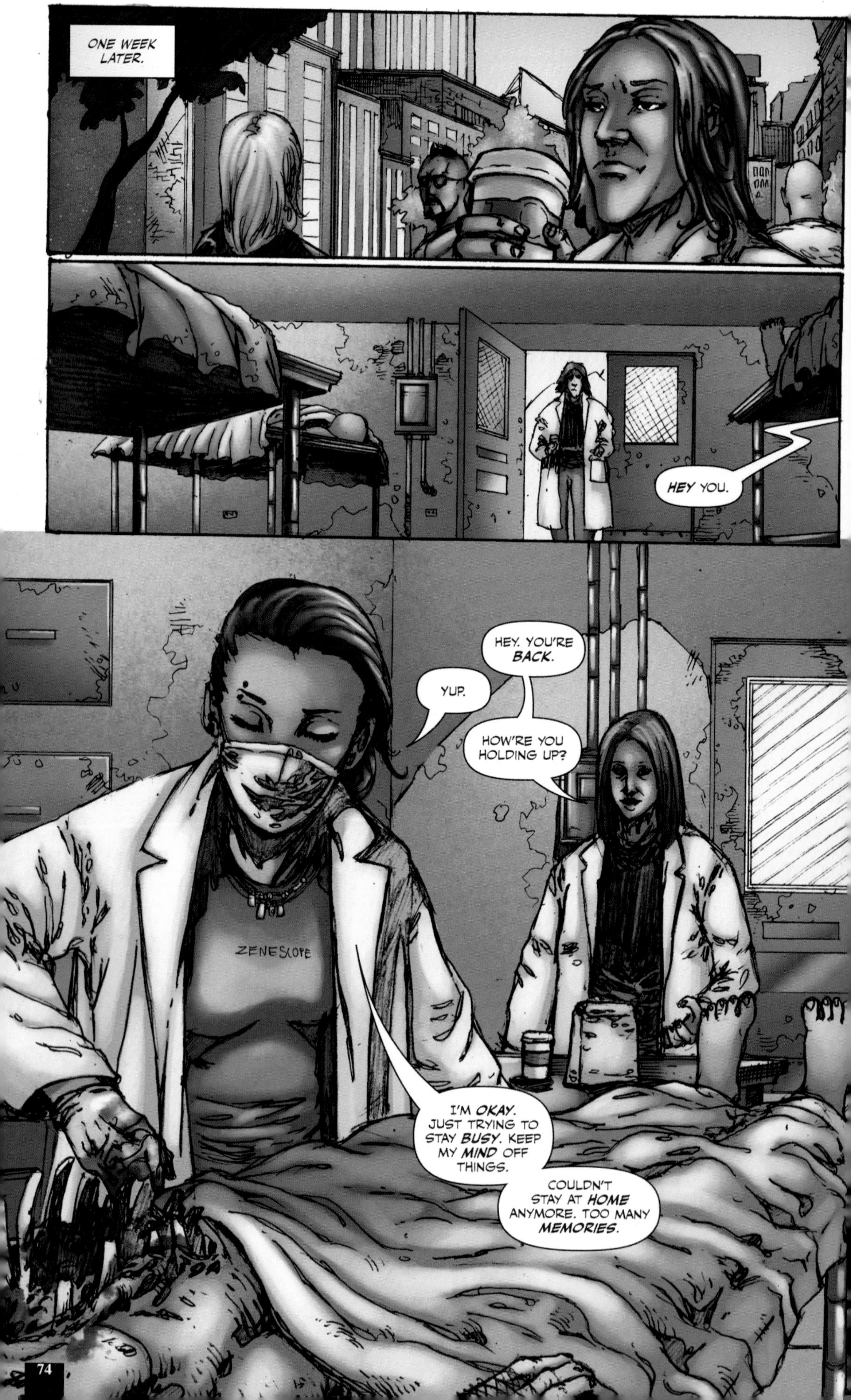
ONE WEEK LATER.
HEY YOU.
HEY. YOU'RE BACK.
YUP.
HOW'RE YOU HOLDING UP?
ZENESCOPE
I'M OKAY. JUST TRYING TO STAY BUSY. KEEP MY MIND OFF THINGS.
COULDN'T STAY AT HOME ANYMORE. TOO MANY MEMORIES.

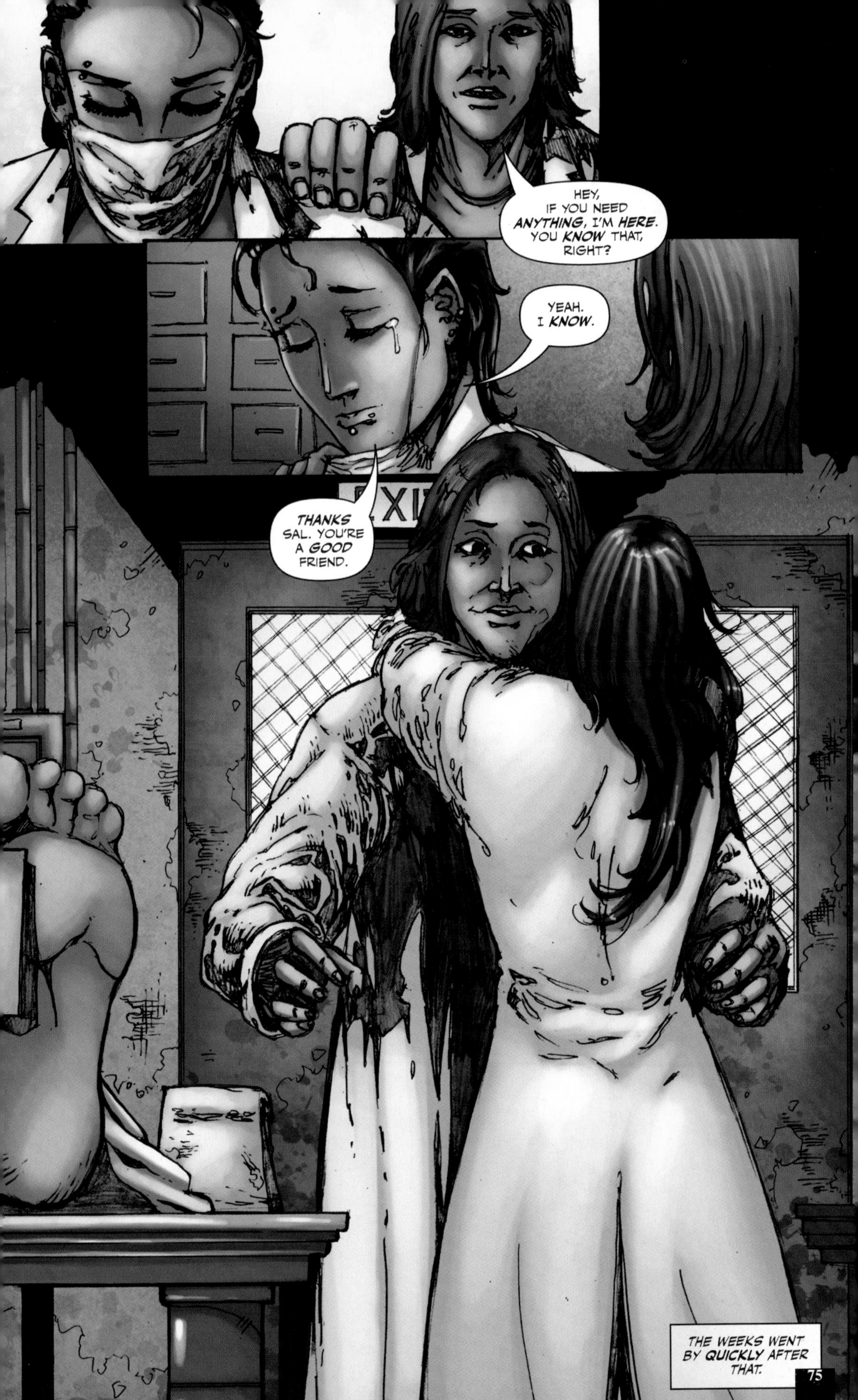
HEY, IF YOU NEED ANYTHING, I'M HERE. YOU KNOW THAT, RIGHT?
YEAH. I KNOW.
THANKS SAL. YOU'RE A GOOD FRIEND.
EXIT
THE WEEKS WENT BY QUICKLY AFTER THAT.

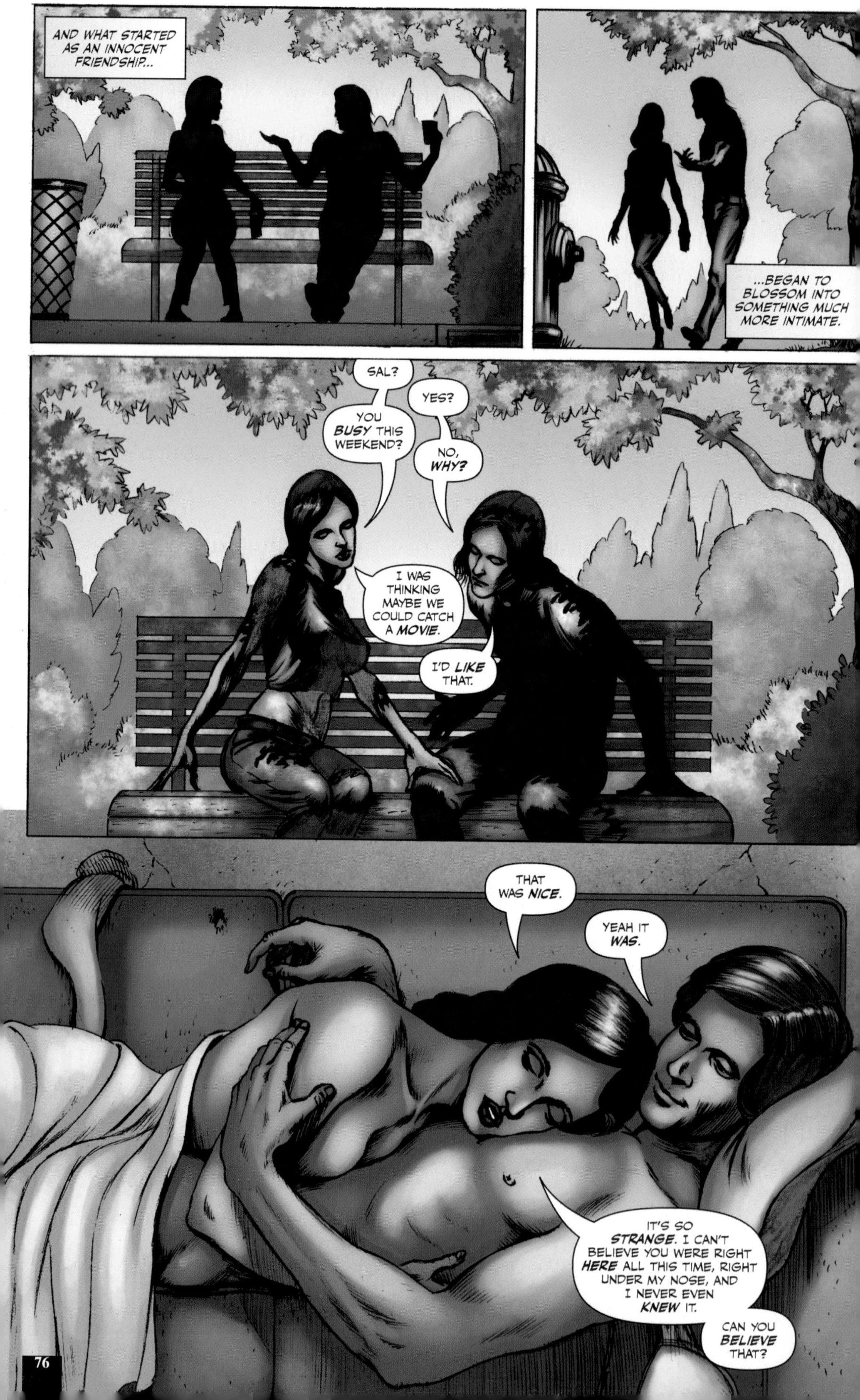
AND WHAT STARTED AS AN INNOCENT FRIENDSHIP...
...BEGAN TO BLOSSOM INTO SOMETHING MUCH MORE INTIMATE.
SAL?
YES?
YOU BUSY THIS WEEKEND?
NO, WHY?
I WAS THINKING MAYBE WE COULD CATCH A MOVIE.
I'D LIKE THAT.
THAT WAS NICE.
YEAH IT WAS.
IT'S SO STRANGE. I CAN'T BELIEVE YOU WERE RIGHT HERE ALL THIS TIME, RIGHT UNDER MY NOSE, AND I NEVER EVEN KNEW IT.
CAN YOU BELIEVE THAT?

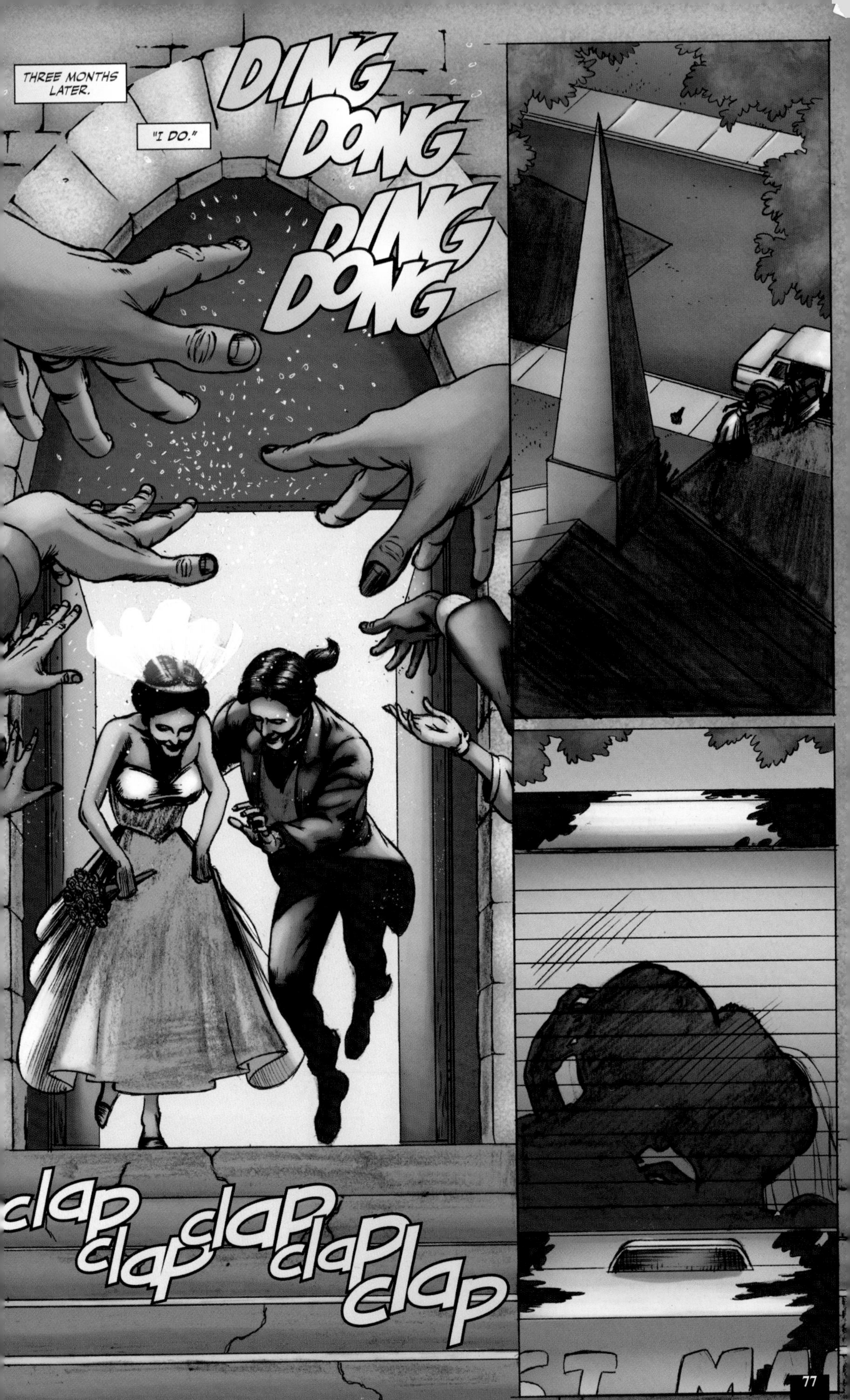

THREE MONTHS LATER.
"I DO."
DING DONG DING DONG
clap clap clap clap clap clap

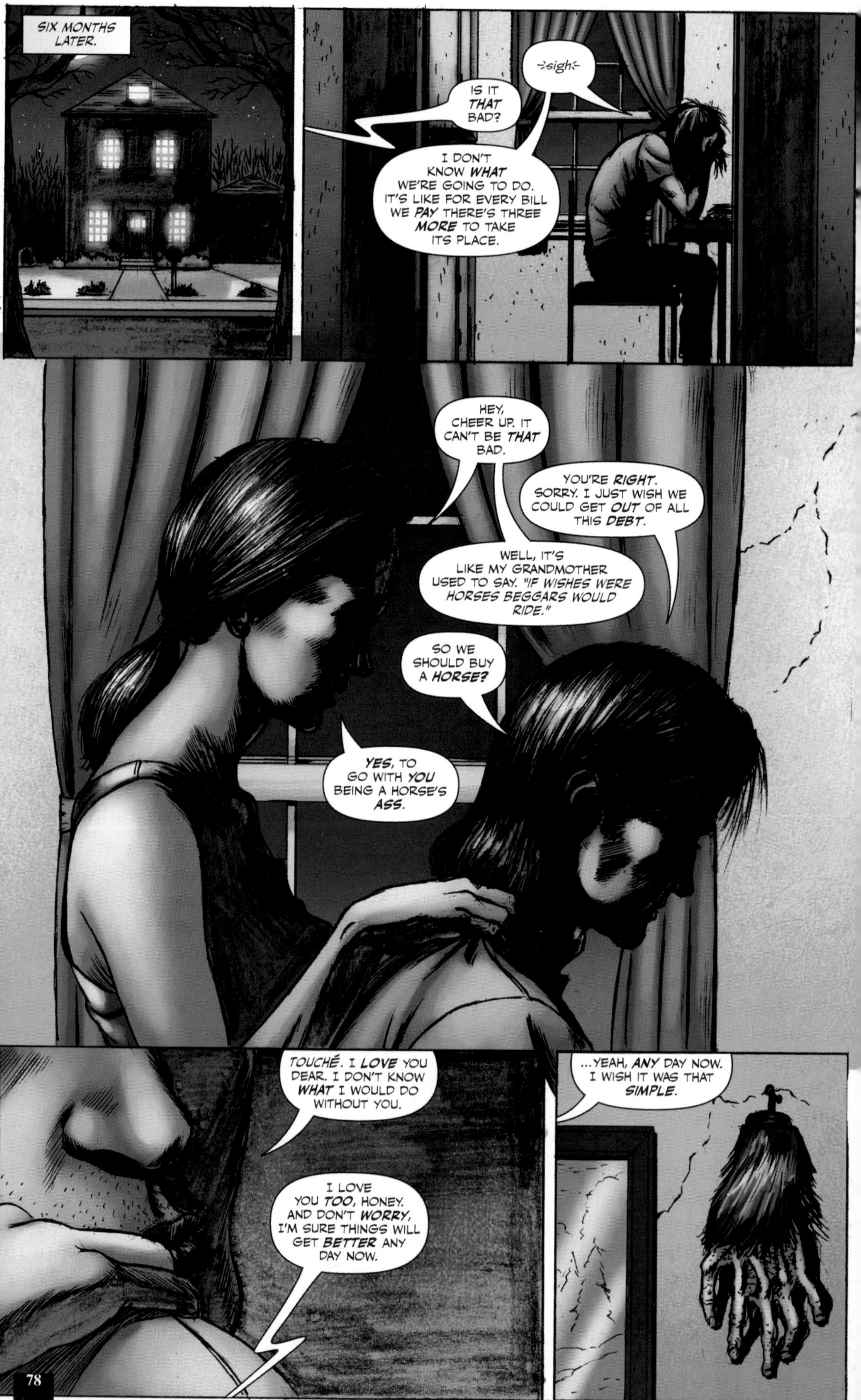
SIX MONTHS LATER.
IS IT THAT BAD?
-sigh-
I DON'T KNOW WHAT WE'RE GOING TO DO. IT'S LIKE FOR EVERY BILL WE PAY THERE'S THREE MORE TO TAKE ITS PLACE.
HEY, CHEER UP. IT CAN'T BE THAT BAD.
YOU'RE RIGHT. SORRY. I JUST WISH WE COULD GET OUT OF ALL THIS DEBT.
WELL, IT'S LIKE MY GRANDMOTHER USED TO SAY. "IF WISHES WERE HORSES BEGGARS WOULD RIDE."
SO WE SHOULD BUY A HORSE?
YES, TO GO WITH YOU BEING A HORSE'S ASS.
TOUCHÉ. I LOVE YOU DEAR. I DON'T KNOW WHAT I WOULD DO WITHOUT YOU.
I LOVE YOU TOO, HONEY. AND DON'T WORRY, I'M SURE THINGS WILL GET BETTER ANY DAY NOW.
...YEAH, ANY DAY NOW. I WISH IT WAS THAT SIMPLE.

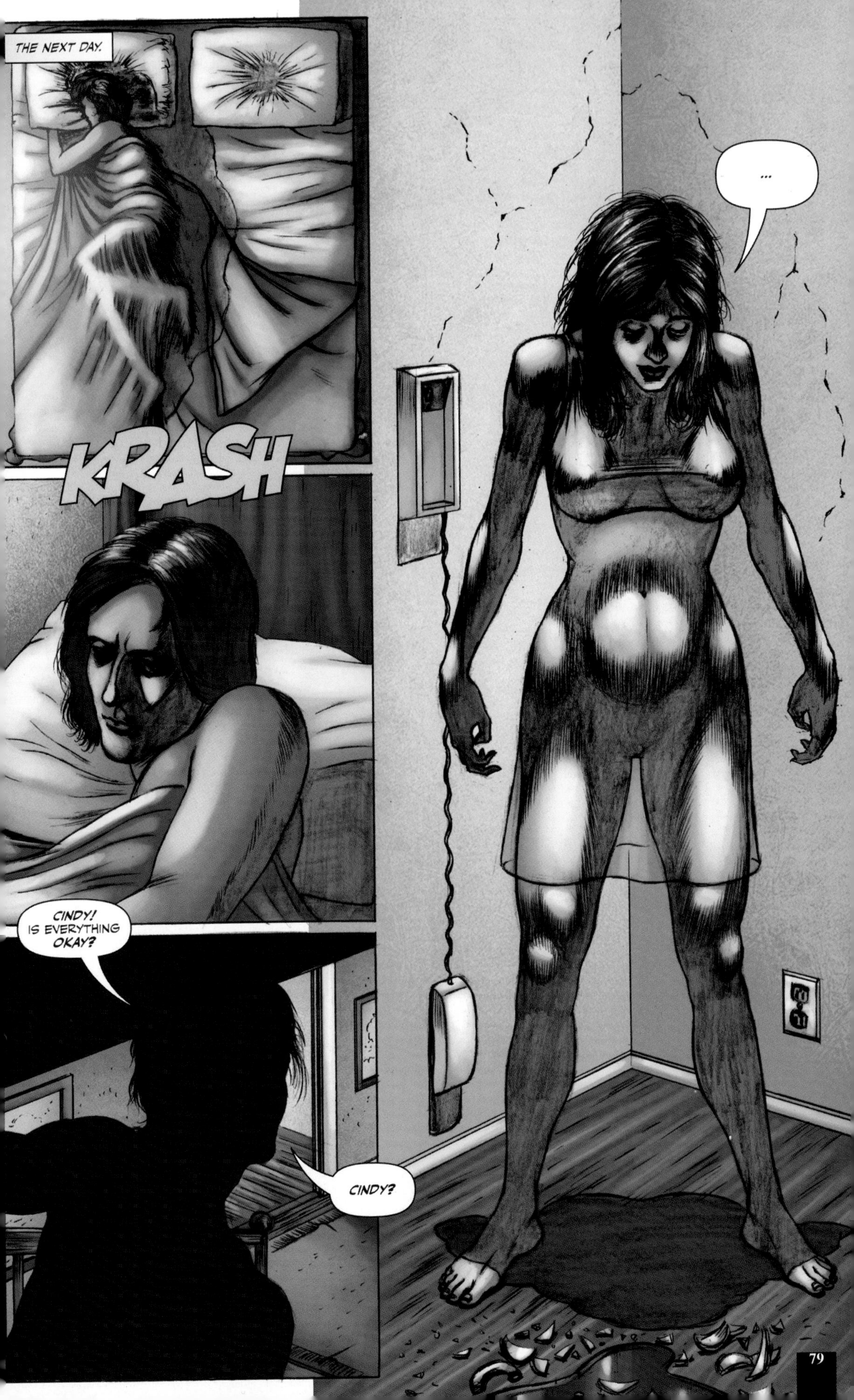
THE NEXT DAY.
KRASH
CINDY! IS EVERYTHING OKAY?
CINDY?
...

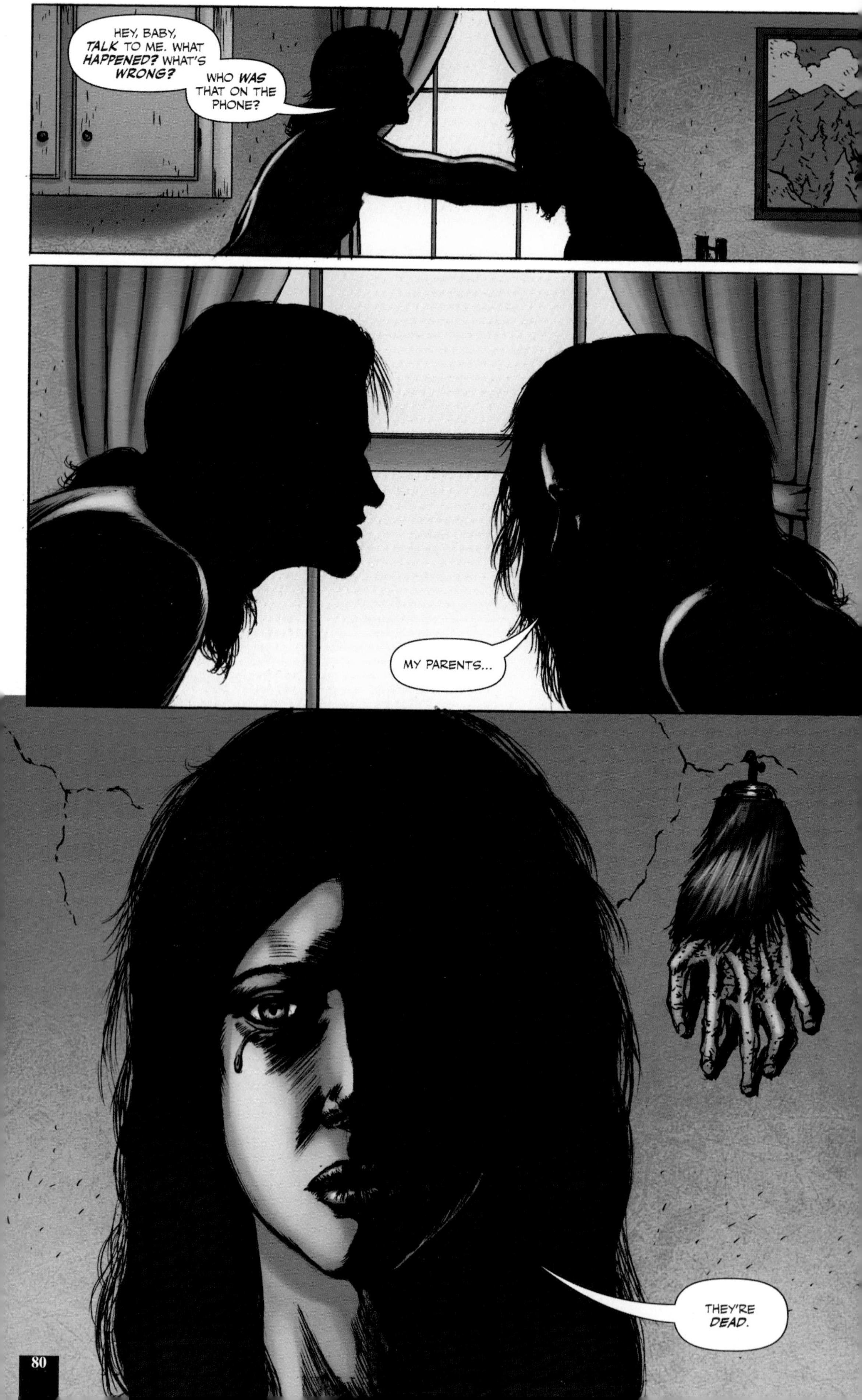
HEY, BABY, TALK TO ME. WHAT HAPPENED? WHAT'S WRONG?
WHO WAS THAT ON THE PHONE?
MY PARENTS...
THEY'RE DEAD.

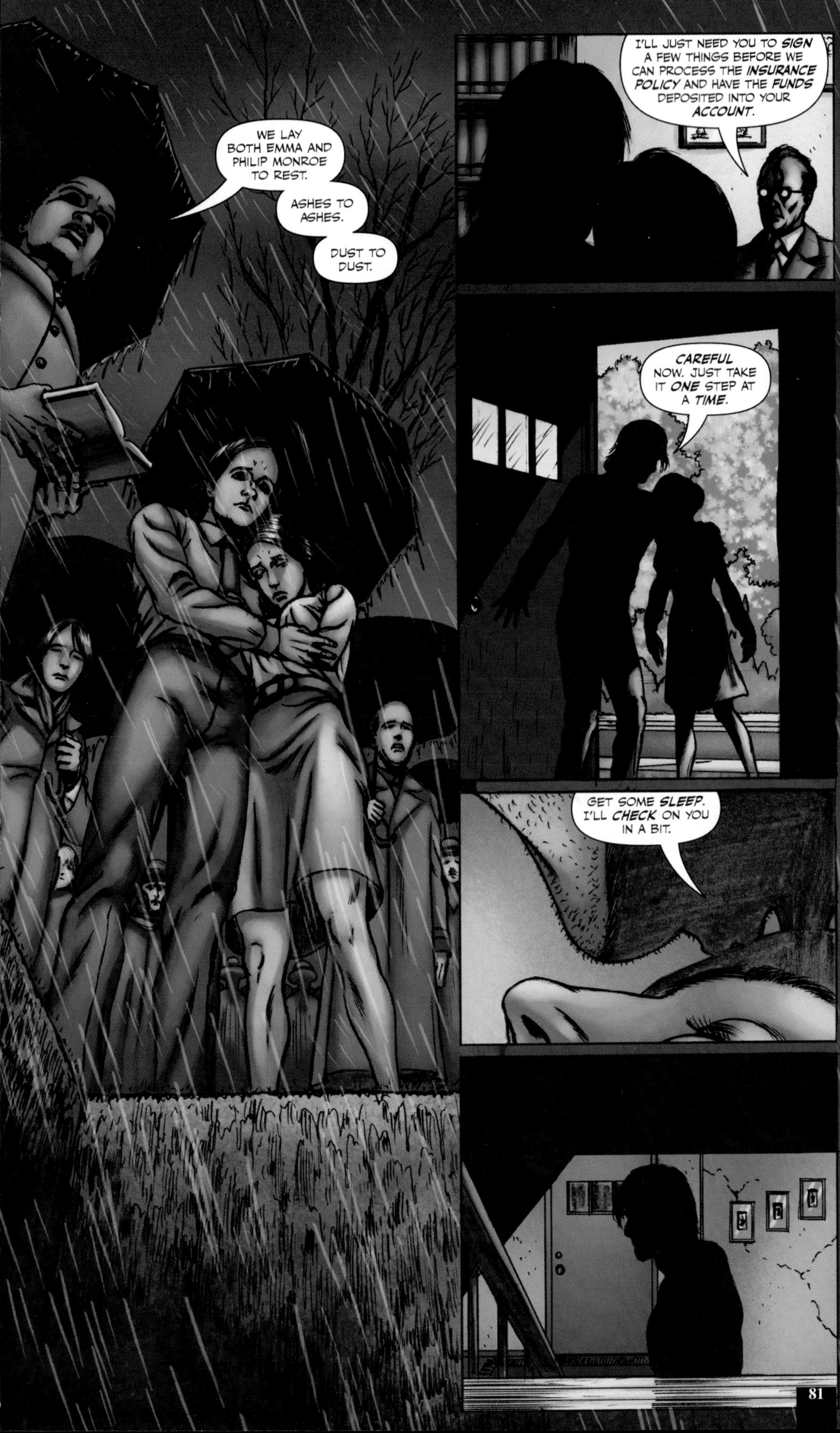
WE LAY BOTH EMMA AND PHILIP MONROE TO REST.
ASHES TO ASHES.
DUST TO DUST.
I'LL JUST NEED YOU TO SIGN A FEW THINGS BEFORE WE CAN PROCESS THE INSURANCE POLICY AND HAVE THE FUNDS DEPOSITED INTO YOUR ACCOUNT.
CAREFUL NOW. JUST TAKE IT ONE STEP AT A TIME.
GET SOME SLEEP. I'LL CHECK ON YOU IN A BIT.

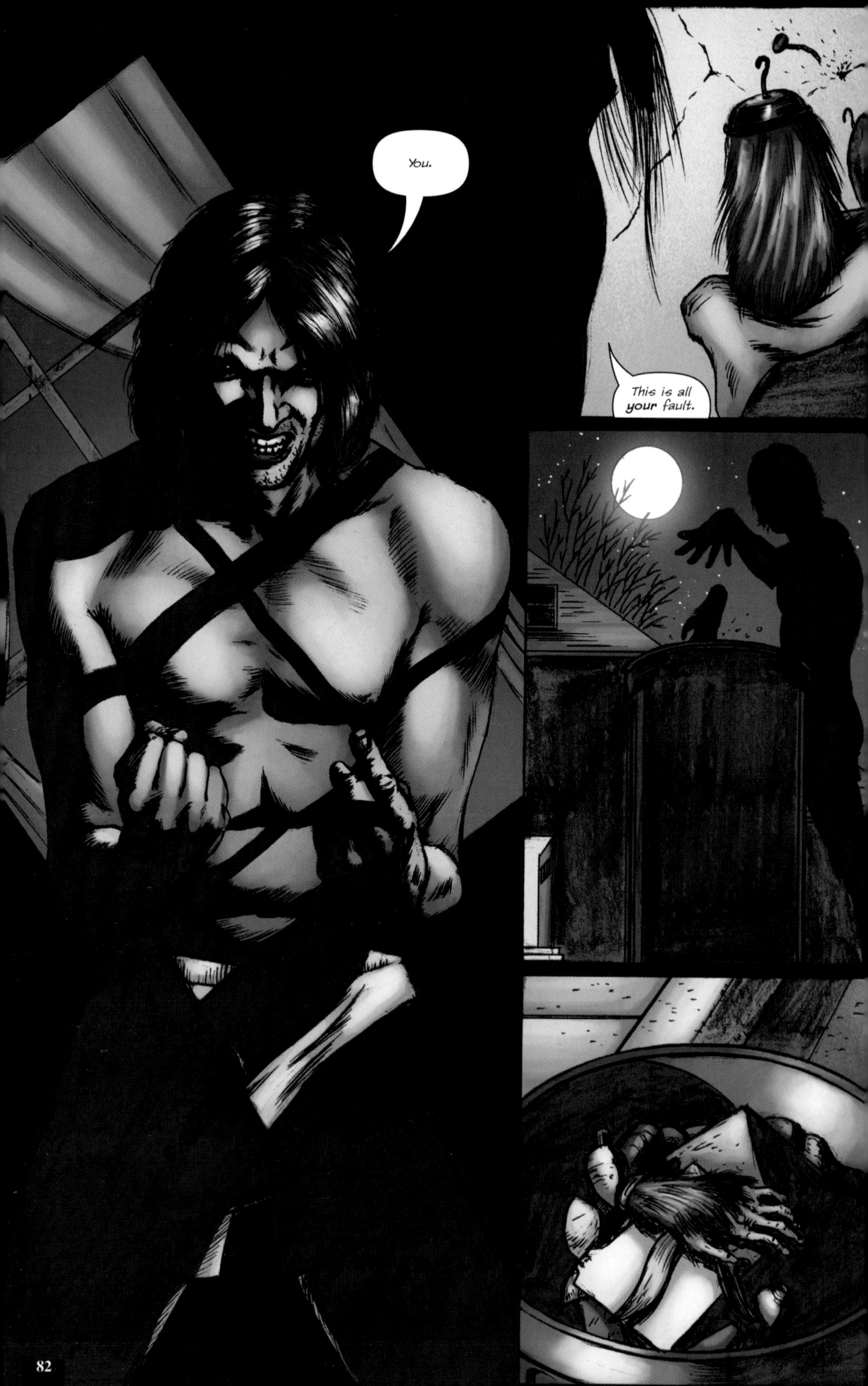

You.
This is all your fault.

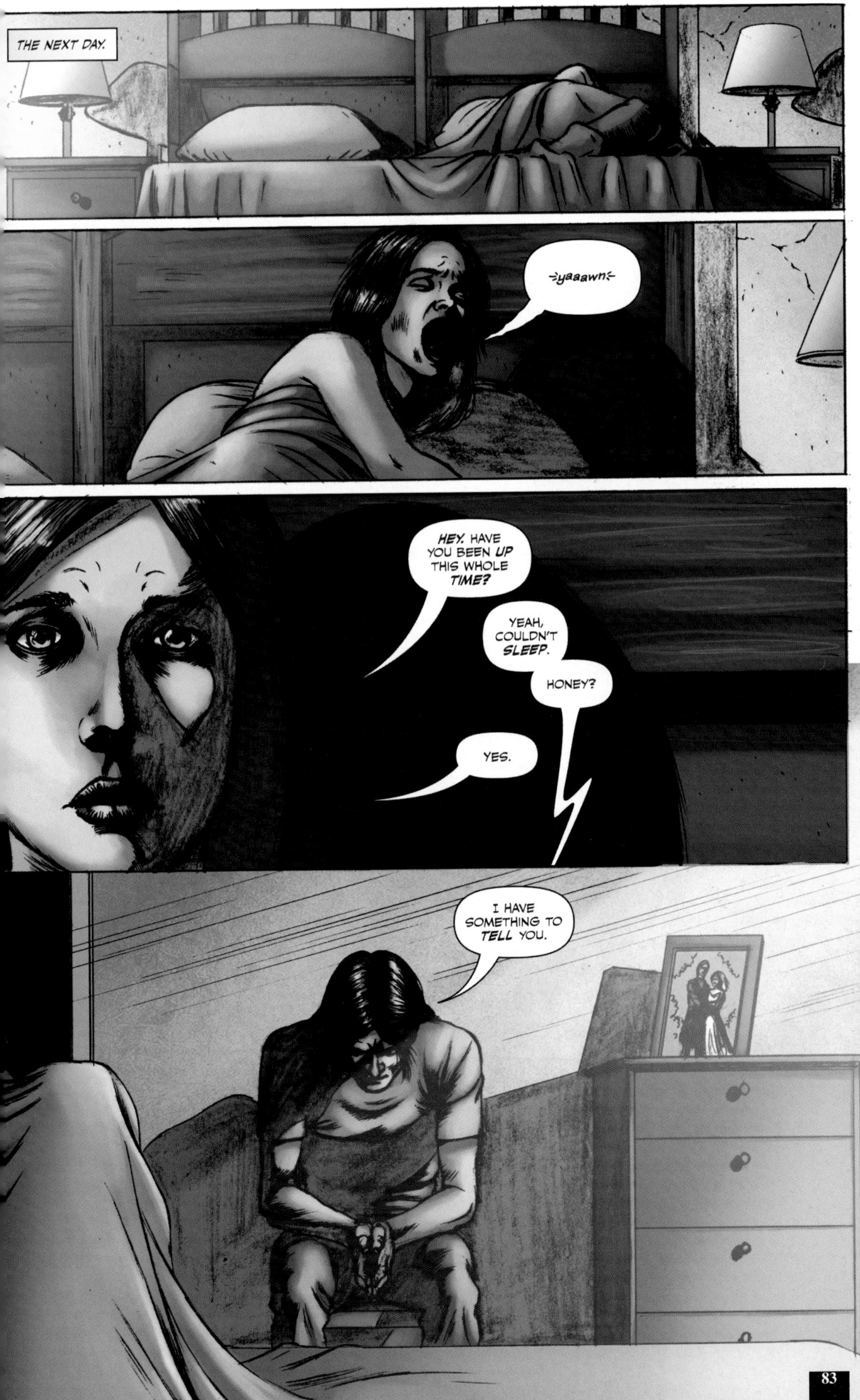

THE NEXT DAY.
~yaaawn~
HEY. HAVE YOU BEEN UP THIS WHOLE TIME?
YEAH, COULDN'T SLEEP.
HONEY?
YES.
I HAVE SOMETHING TO TELL YOU.

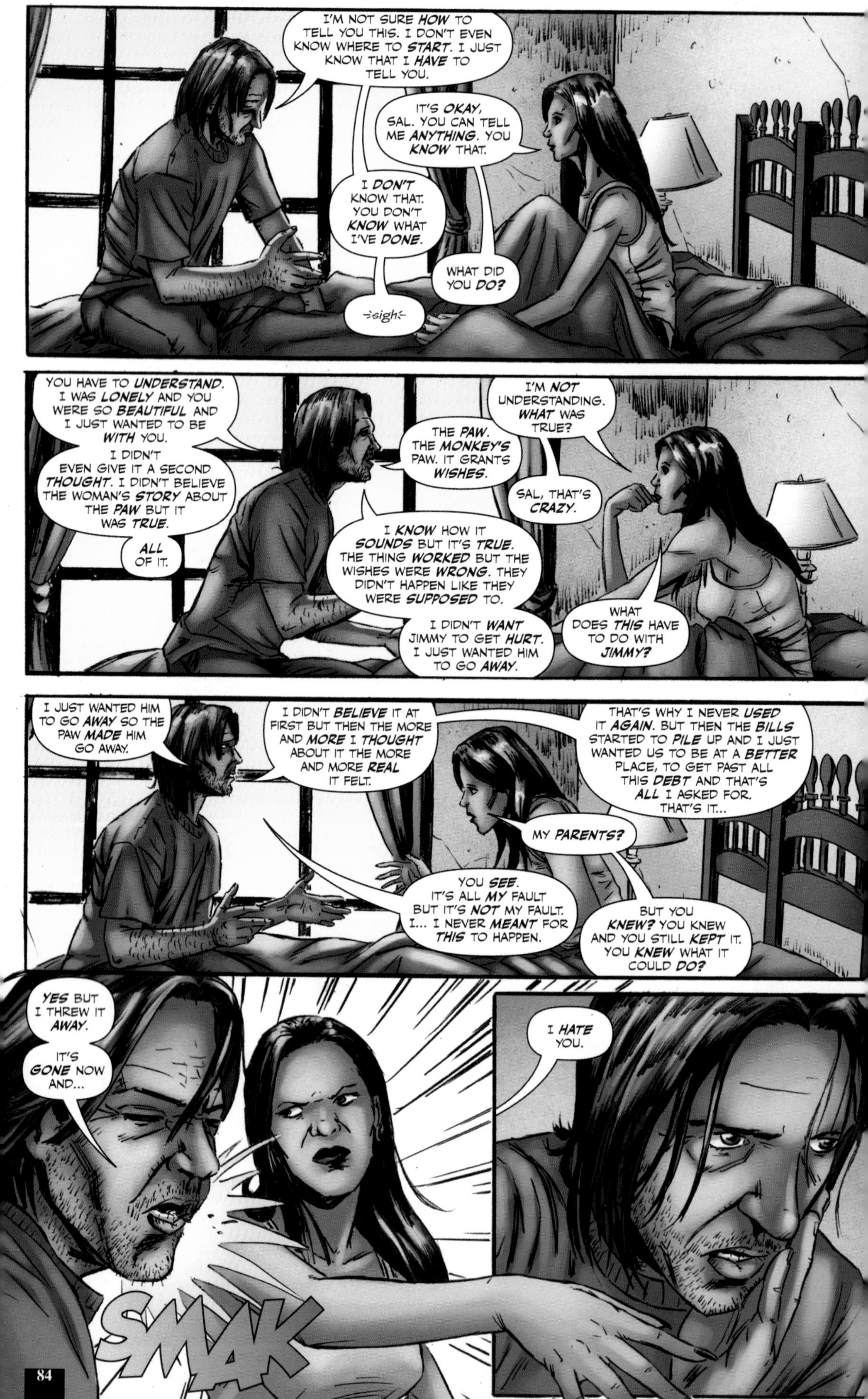
I'M NOT SURE HOW TO TELL YOU THIS. I DON'T EVEN KNOW WHERE TO START. I JUST KNOW THAT I HAVE TO TELL YOU.
IT'S OKAY, SAL. YOU CAN TELL ME ANYTHING. YOU KNOW THAT.
I DON'T KNOW THAT. YOU DON'T KNOW WHAT I'VE DONE.
WHAT DID YOU DO?
sigh
YOU HAVE TO UNDERSTAND. I WAS LONELY AND YOU WERE SO BEAUTIFUL AND I JUST WANTED TO BE WITH YOU.
I DIDN'T EVEN GIVE IT A SECOND THOUGHT. I DIDN'T BELIEVE THE WOMAN'S STORY ABOUT THE PAW BUT IT WAS TRUE.
ALL OF IT.
I'M NOT UNDERSTANDING. WHAT WAS TRUE?
THE PAW. THE MONKEY'S PAW. IT GRANTS WISHES.
SAL, THAT'S CRAZY.
I KNOW HOW IT SOUNDS BUT IT'S TRUE. THE THING WORKED BUT THE WISHES WERE WRONG. THEY DIDN'T HAPPEN LIKE THEY WERE SUPPOSED TO.
I DIDN'T WANT JIMMY TO GET HURT. I JUST WANTED HIM TO GO AWAY.
WHAT DOES THIS HAVE TO DO WITH JIMMY?
I JUST WANTED HIM TO GO AWAY SO THE PAW MADE HIM GO AWAY.
I DIDN'T BELIEVE IT AT FIRST BUT THEN THE MORE AND MORE I THOUGHT ABOUT IT THE MORE AND MORE REAL IT FELT.
THAT'S WHY I NEVER USED IT AGAIN. BUT THEN THE BILLS STARTED TO PILE UP AND I JUST WANTED US TO BE AT A BETTER PLACE, TO GET PAST ALL THIS DEBT AND THAT'S ALL I ASKED FOR. THAT'S IT...
MY PARENTS?
YOU SEE. IT'S ALL MY FAULT BUT IT'S NOT MY FAULT. I... I NEVER MEANT FOR THIS TO HAPPEN.
BUT YOU KNEW? YOU KNEW AND YOU STILL KEPT IT. YOU KNEW WHAT IT COULD DO?
YES BUT I THREW IT AWAY.
IT'S GONE NOW AND...
SMAK
I HATE YOU.

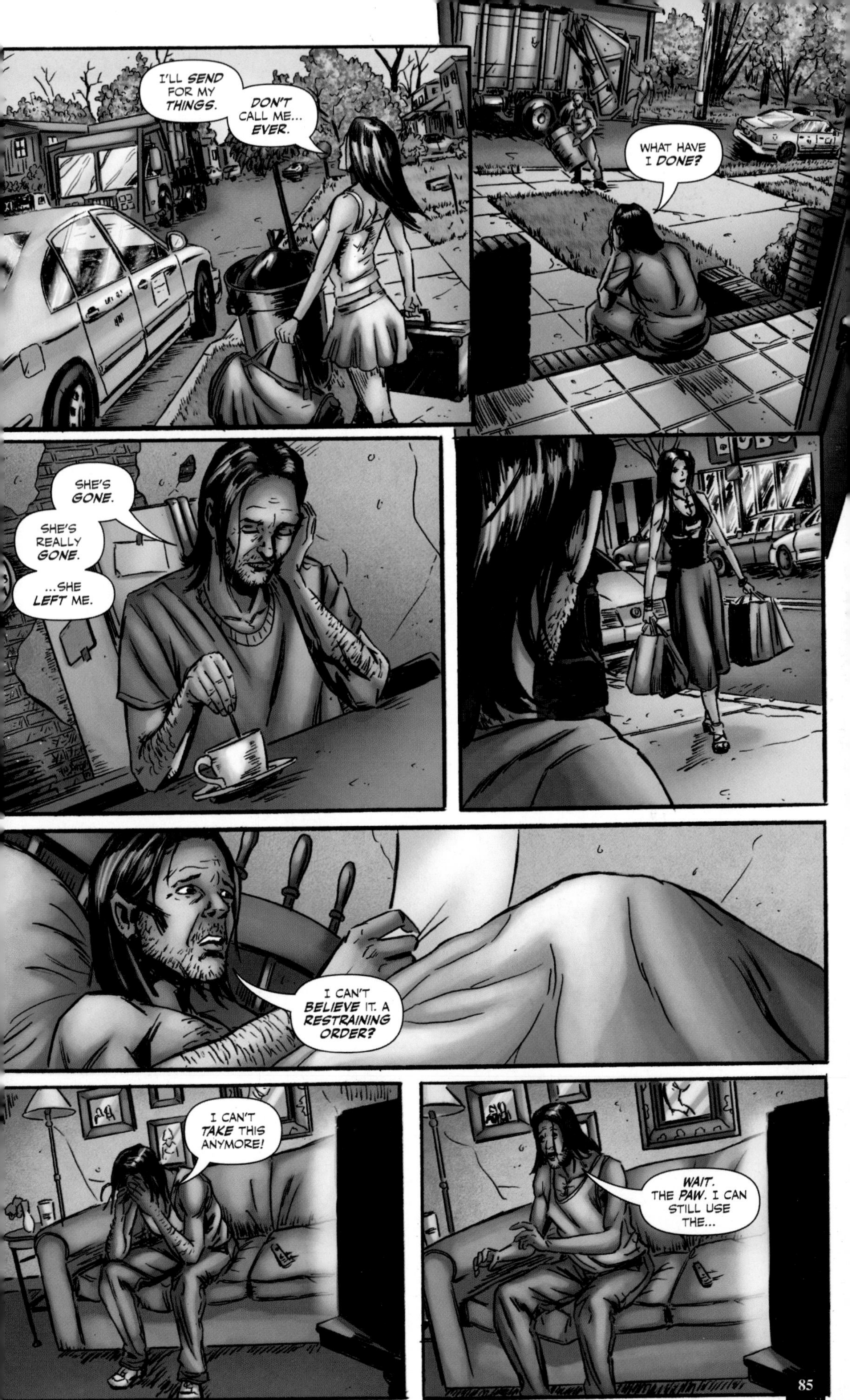

I'LL SEND FOR MY THINGS.
DON'T CALL ME... EVER.
WHAT HAVE I DONE?
SHE'S GONE.
SHE'S REALLY GONE.
...SHE LEFT ME.
I CAN'T BELIEVE IT. A RESTRAINING ORDER?
I CAN'T TAKE THIS ANYMORE!
WAIT. THE PAW. I CAN STILL USE THE...

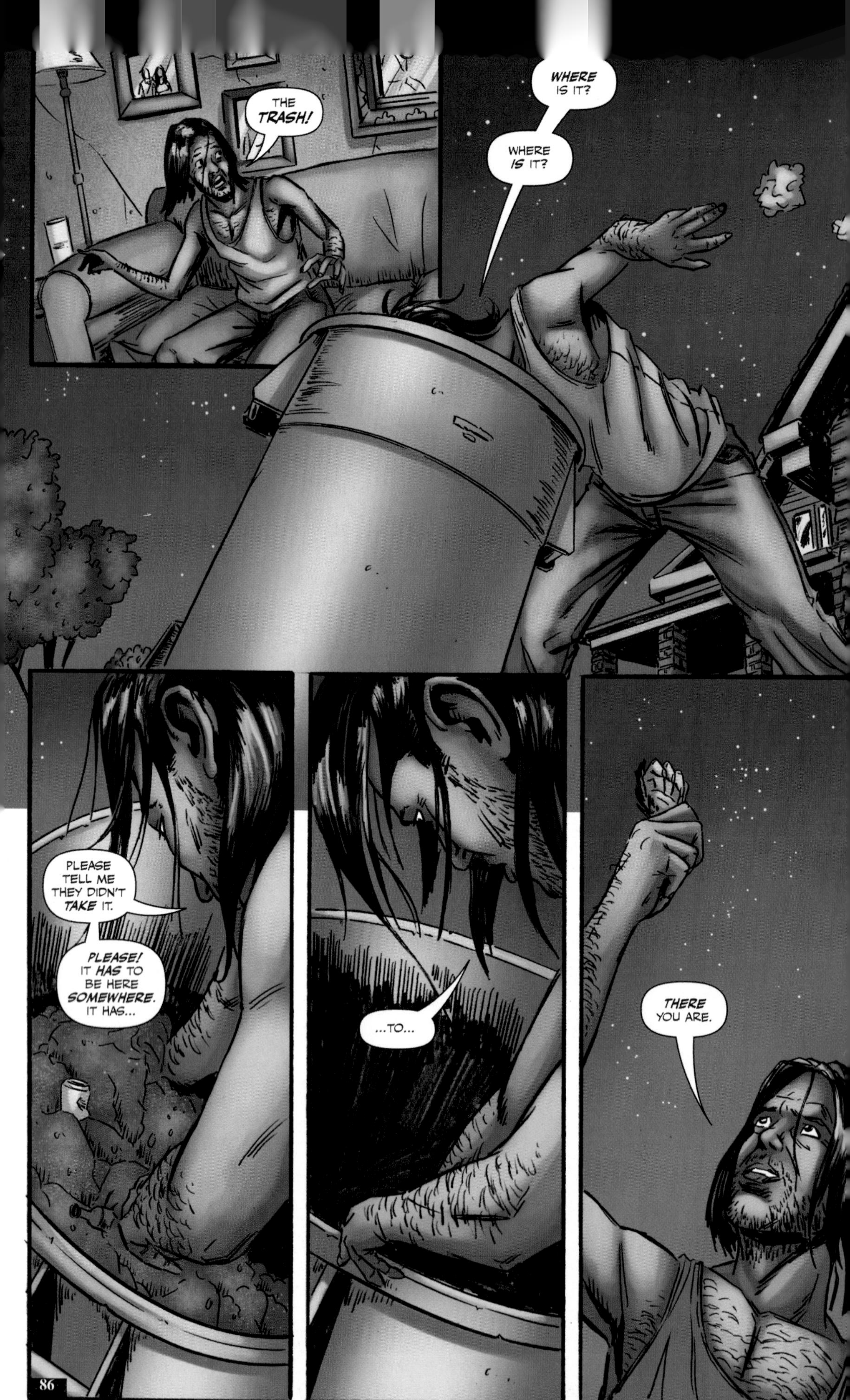
THE TRASH!
WHERE IS IT?
WHERE IS IT?
PLEASE TELL ME THEY DIDN'T TAKE IT.
PLEASE! IT HAS TO BE HERE SOMEWHERE. IT HAS...
...TO...
THERE YOU ARE.

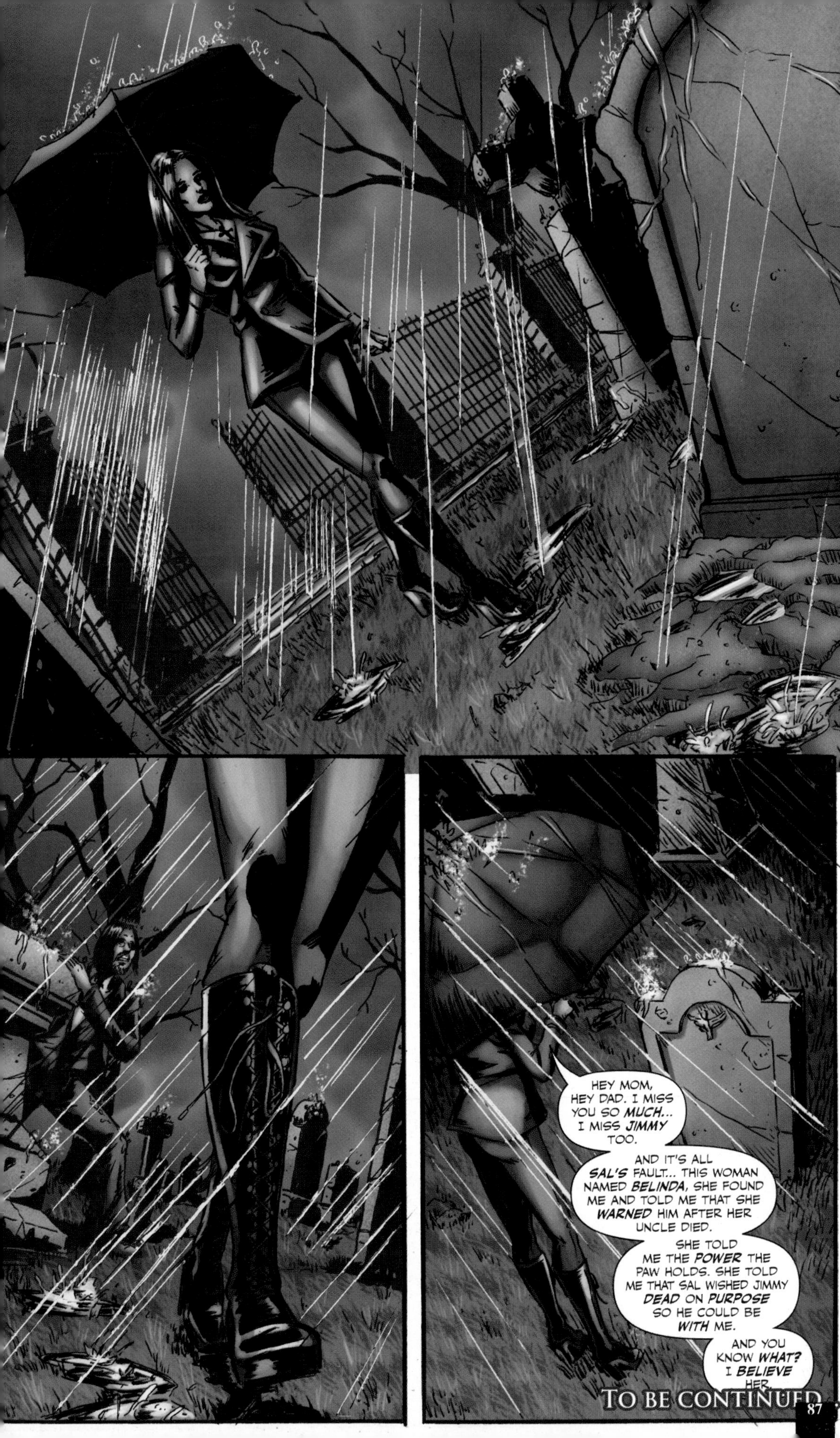
HEY MOM, HEY DAD. I MISS YOU SO MUCH... I MISS JIMMY TOO.
AND IT'S ALL SAL'S FAULT... THIS WOMAN NAMED BELINDA, SHE FOUND ME AND TOLD ME THAT SHE WARNED HIM AFTER HER UNCLE DIED.
SHE TOLD ME THE POWER THE PAW HOLDS. SHE TOLD ME THAT SAL WISHED JIMMY DEAD ON PURPOSE SO HE COULD BE WITH ME.
AND YOU KNOW WHAT? I BELIEVE HER.
TO BE CONTINUED

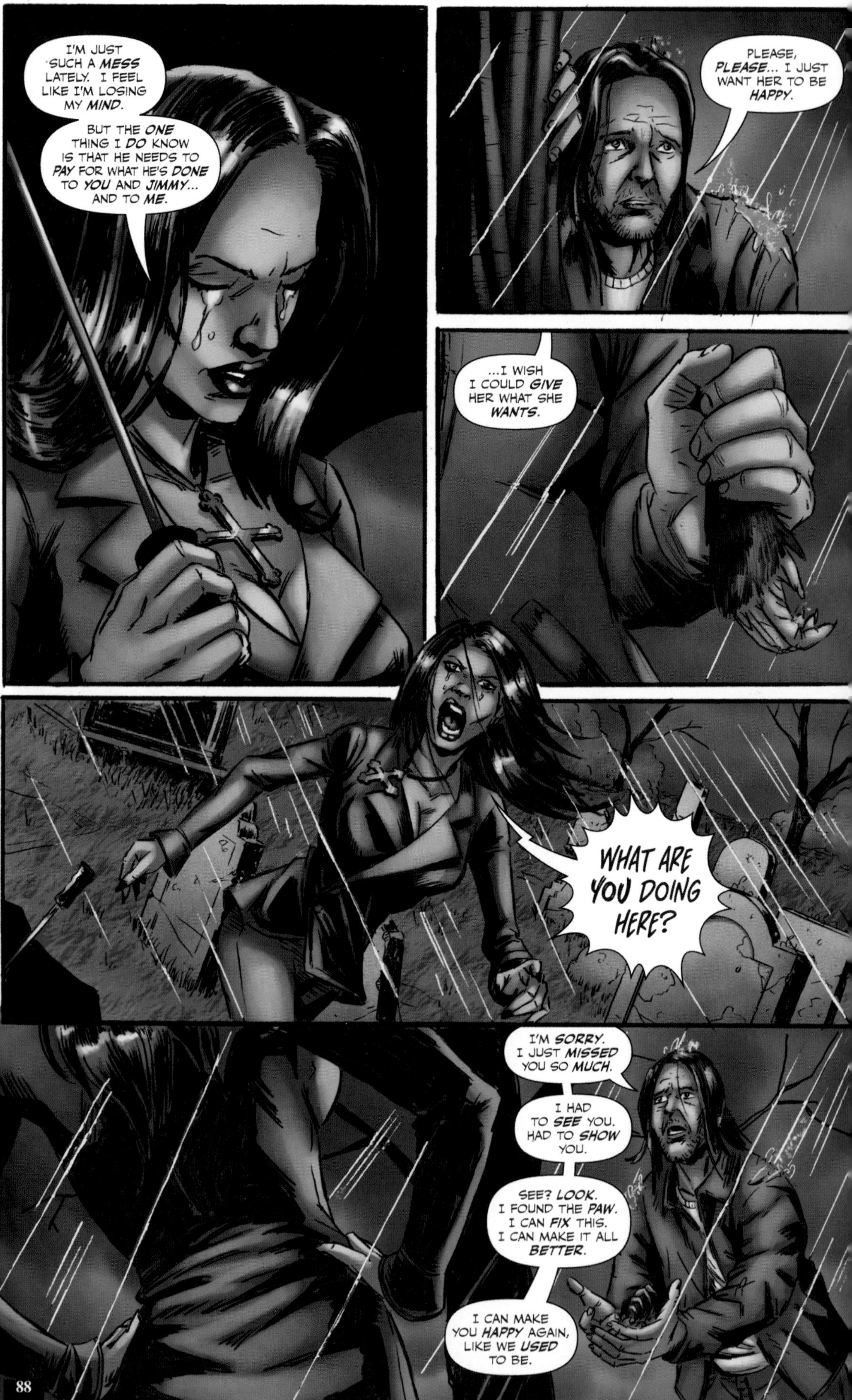
I'M JUST SUCH A MESS LATELY. I FEEL LIKE I'M LOSING MY MIND.
BUT THE ONE THING I DO KNOW IS THAT HE NEEDS TO PAY FOR WHAT HE'S DONE TO YOU AND JIMMY... AND TO ME.
PLEASE, PLEASE... I JUST WANT HER TO BE HAPPY.
...I WISH I COULD GIVE HER WHAT SHE WANTS.
WHAT ARE YOU DOING HERE?
I'M SORRY. I JUST MISSED YOU SO MUCH.
I HAD TO SEE YOU. HAD TO SHOW YOU.
SEE? LOOK. I FOUND THE PAW. I CAN FIX THIS. I CAN MAKE IT ALL BETTER.
I CAN MAKE YOU HAPPY AGAIN, LIKE WE USED TO BE.

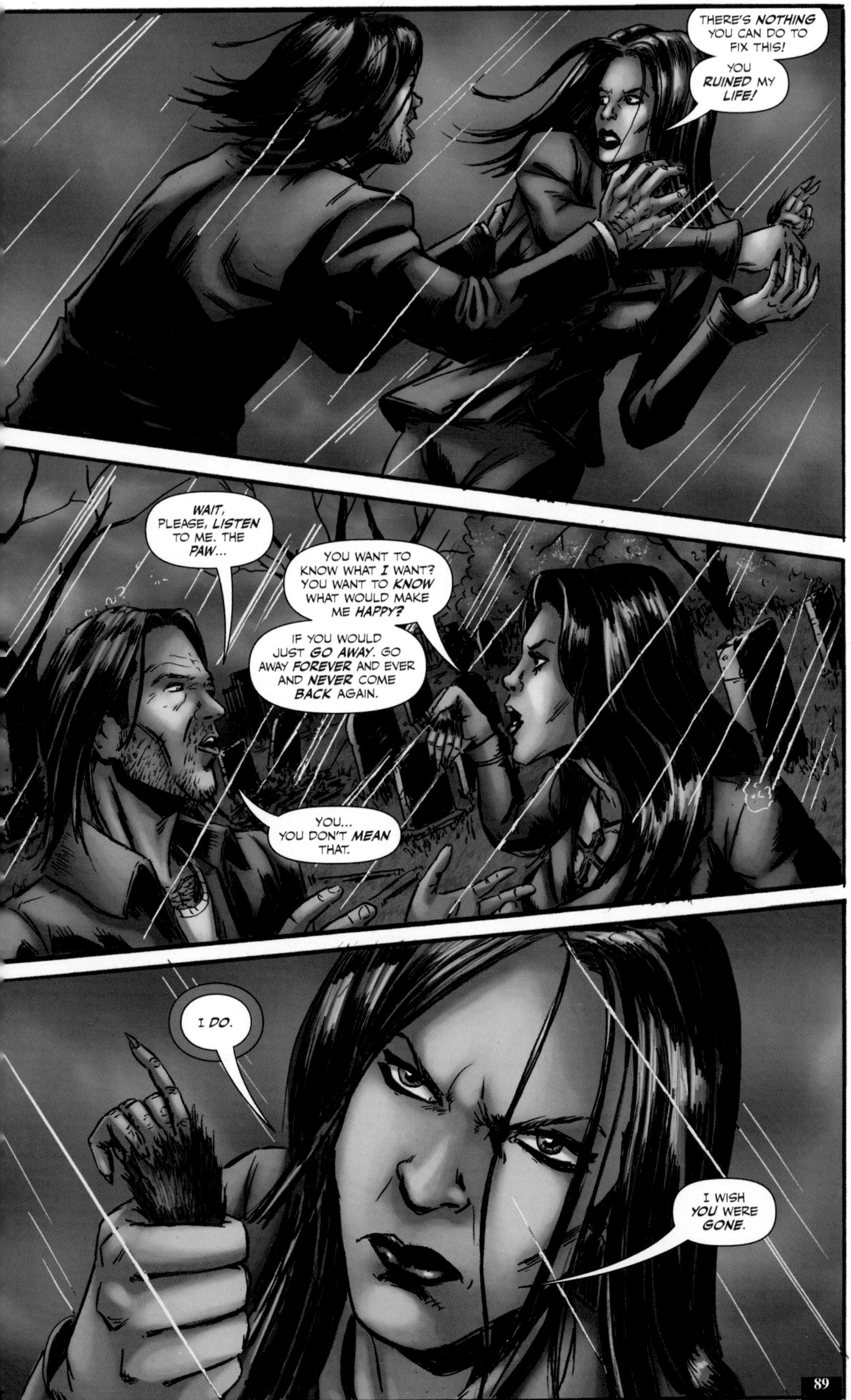
THERE'S NOTHING YOU CAN DO TO FIX THIS!
YOU RUINED MY LIFE!
WAIT, PLEASE, LISTEN TO ME. THE PAW...
YOU WANT TO KNOW WHAT I WANT? YOU WANT TO KNOW WHAT WOULD MAKE ME HAPPY?
IF YOU WOULD JUST GO AWAY. GO AWAY FOREVER AND EVER AND NEVER COME BACK AGAIN.
YOU... YOU DON'T MEAN THAT.
I DO.
I WISH YOU WERE GONE.

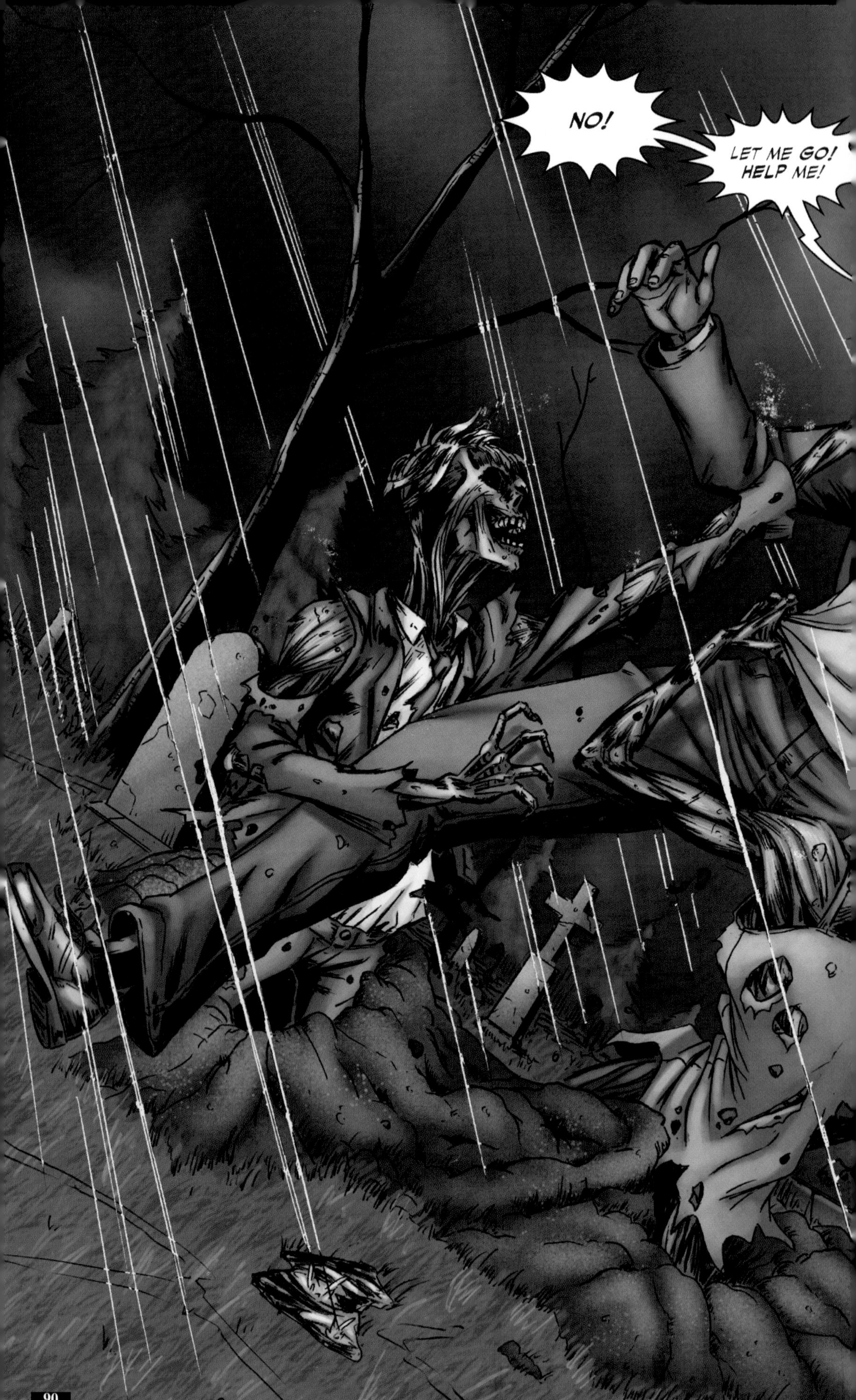
NO!
LET ME GO! HELP ME!

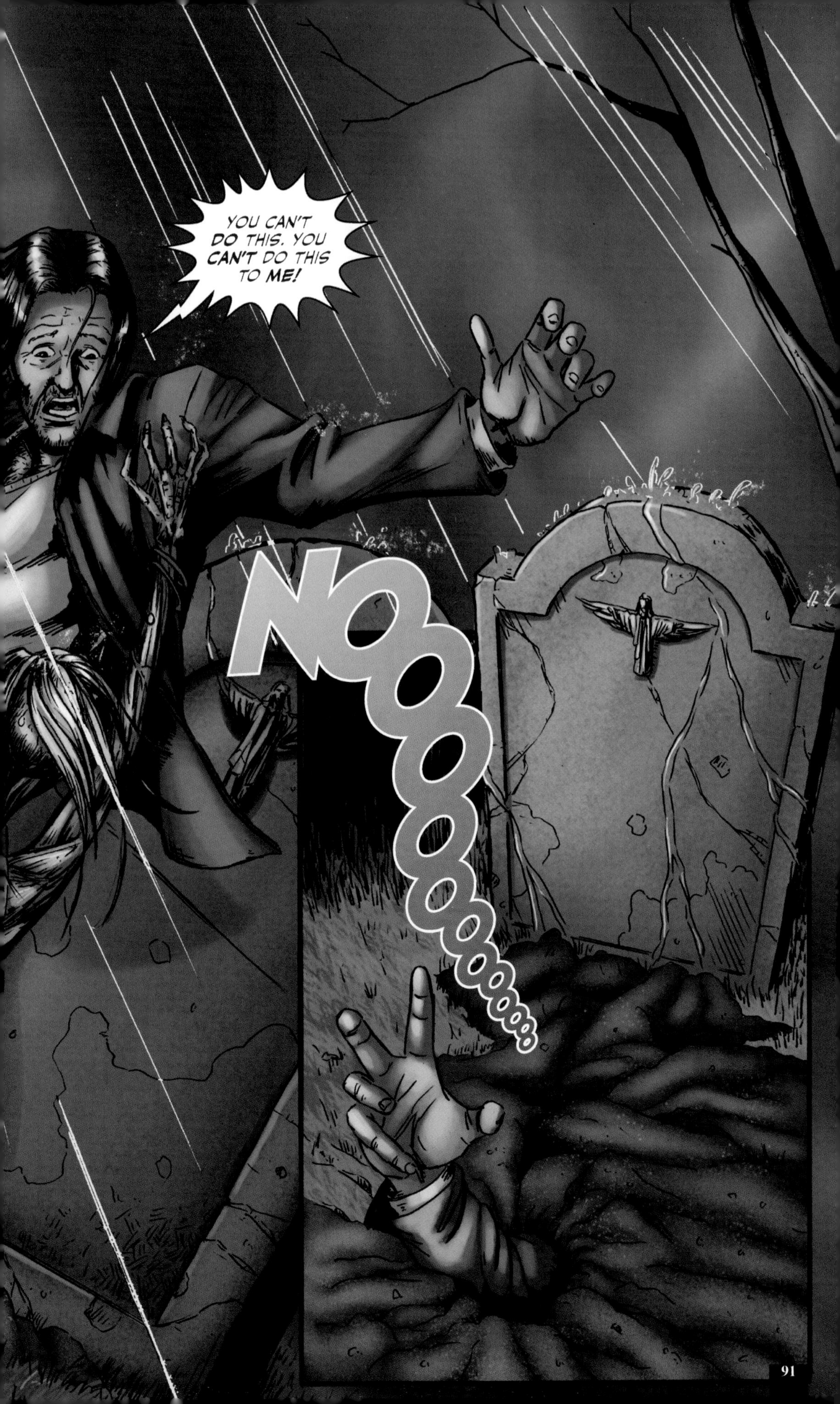
YOU CAN'T DO THIS. YOU CAN'T DO THIS TO ME!
NOOOOOOOOOOO

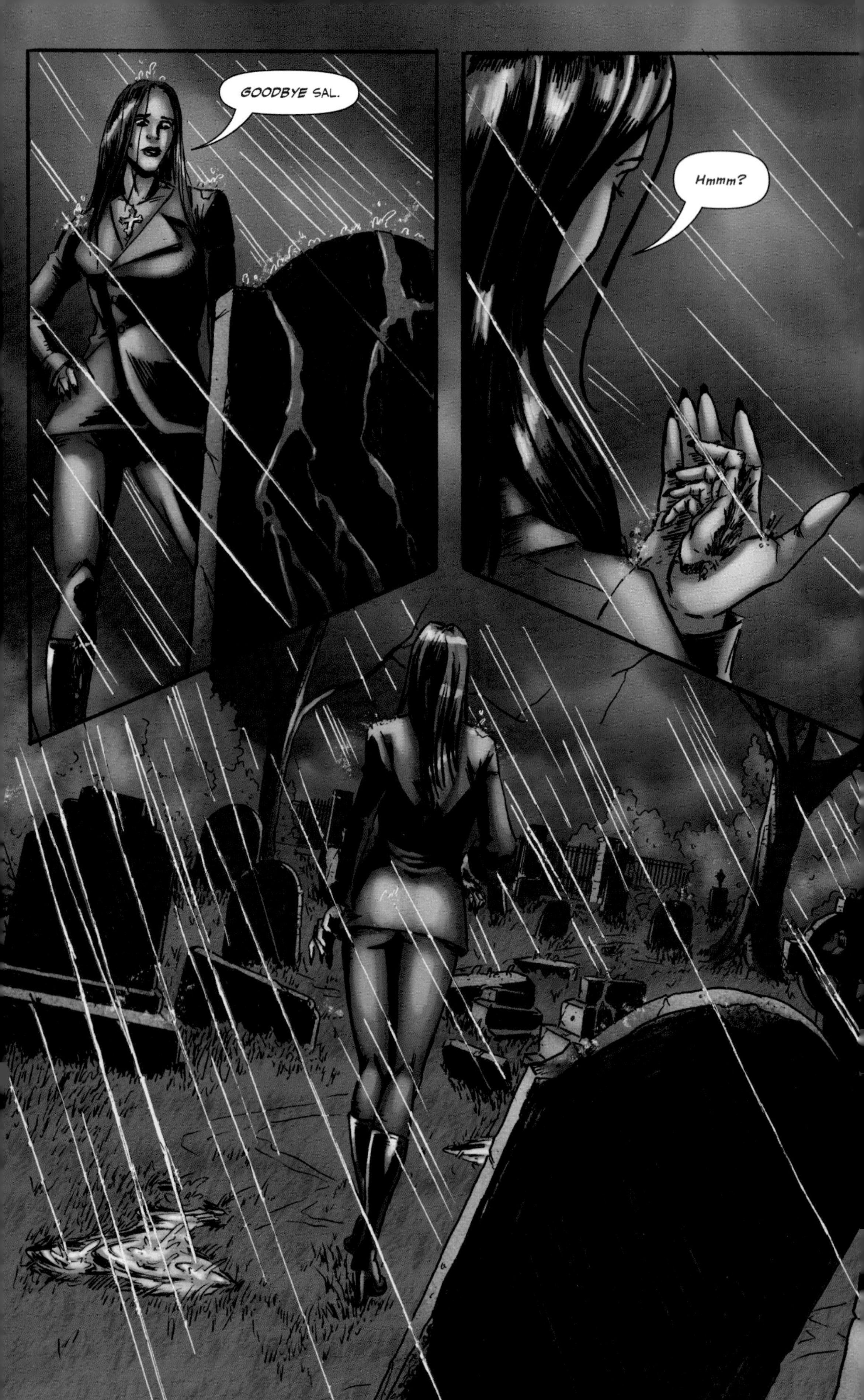
GOODBYE SAL.
Hmmm?

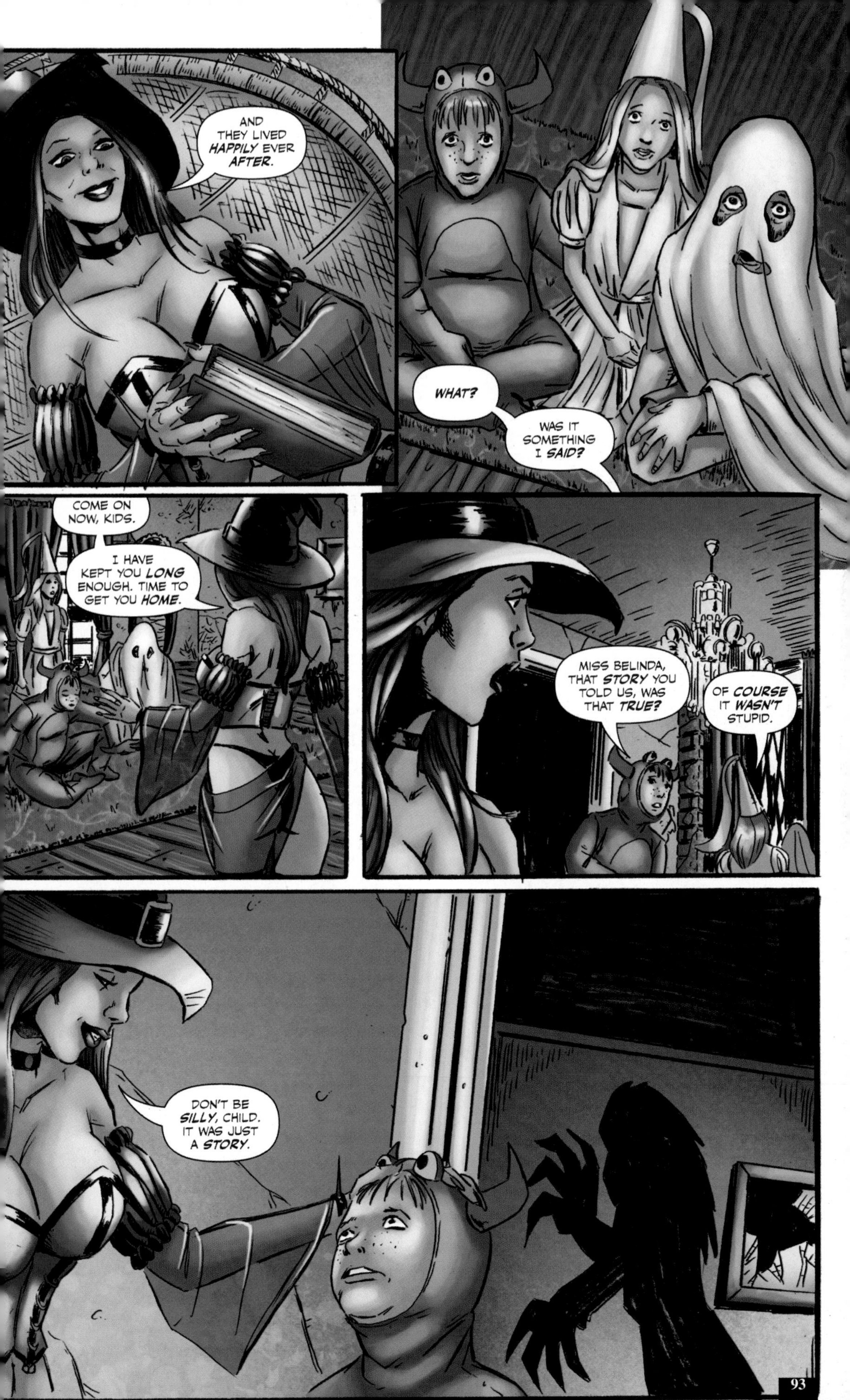
AND THEY LIVED HAPPILY EVER AFTER.
WHAT?
WAS IT SOMETHING I SAID?
COME ON NOW, KIDS.
I HAVE KEPT YOU LONG ENOUGH. TIME TO GET YOU HOME.
MISS BELINDA, THAT STORY YOU TOLD US, WAS THAT TRUE?
OF COURSE IT WASN'T STUPID.
DON'T BE SILLY, CHILD. IT WAS JUST A STORY.

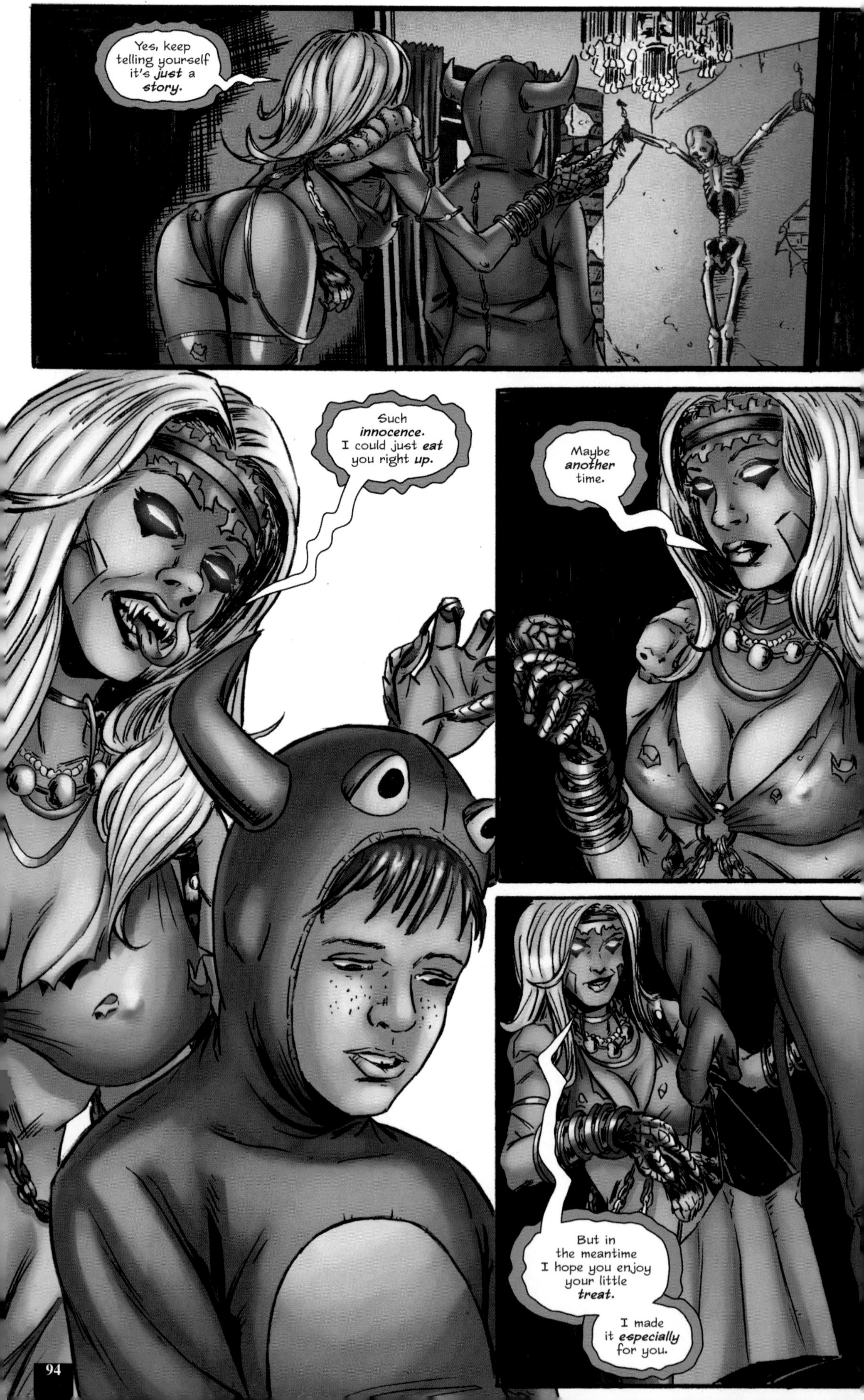

Yes, keep telling yourself it's *just* a *story.*
Such *innocence.* I could just *eat* you right *up.*
Maybe *another* time.
But in the meantime I hope you enjoy your little *treat.*
I made it *especially* for you.

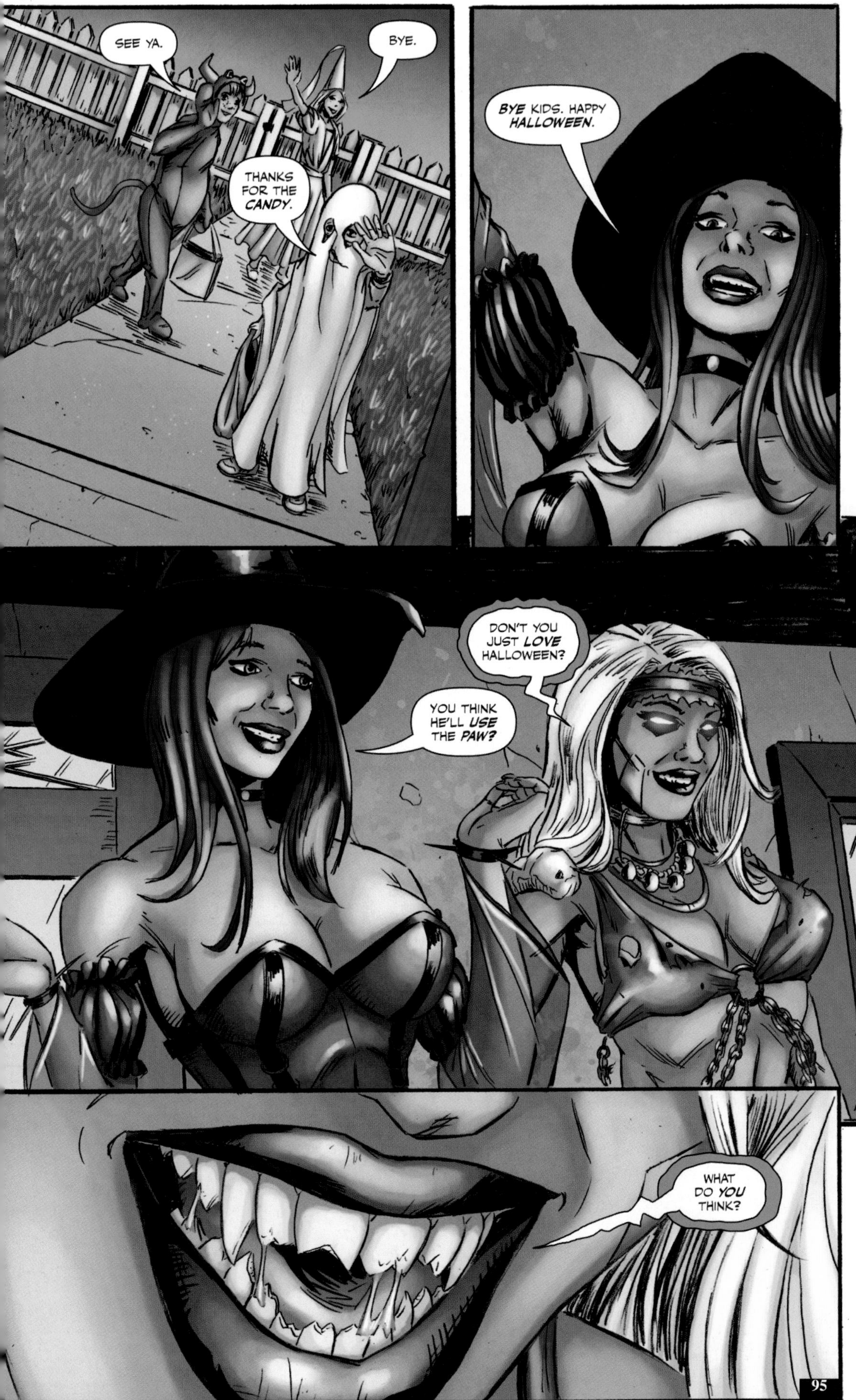
SEE YA.
BYE.
THANKS FOR THE CANDY.
BYE KIDS. HAPPY HALLOWEEN.
DON'T YOU JUST LOVE HALLOWEEN?
YOU THINK HE'LL USE THE PAW?
WHAT DO YOU THINK?

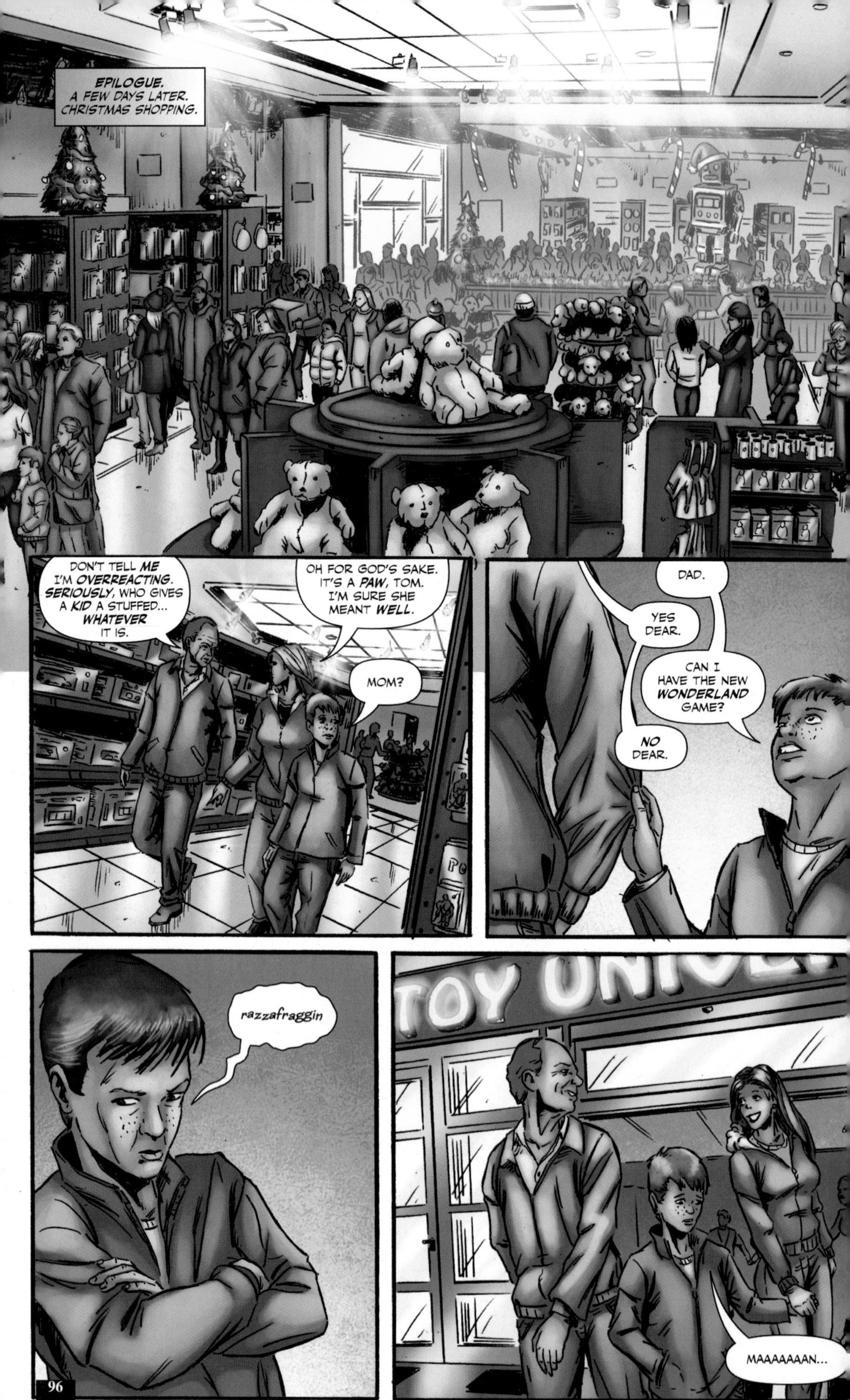
EPILOGUE.
A FEW DAYS LATER.
CHRISTMAS SHOPPING.
DON'T TELL ME I'M OVERREACTING. SERIOUSLY, WHO GIVES A KID A STUFFED... WHATEVER IT IS.
OH FOR GOD'S SAKE. IT'S A PAW, TOM. I'M SURE SHE MEANT WELL.
MOM?
DAD.
YES DEAR.
CAN I HAVE THE NEW WONDERLAND GAME?
NO DEAR.
razzafraggin
TOY UNI
MAAAAAAAN...

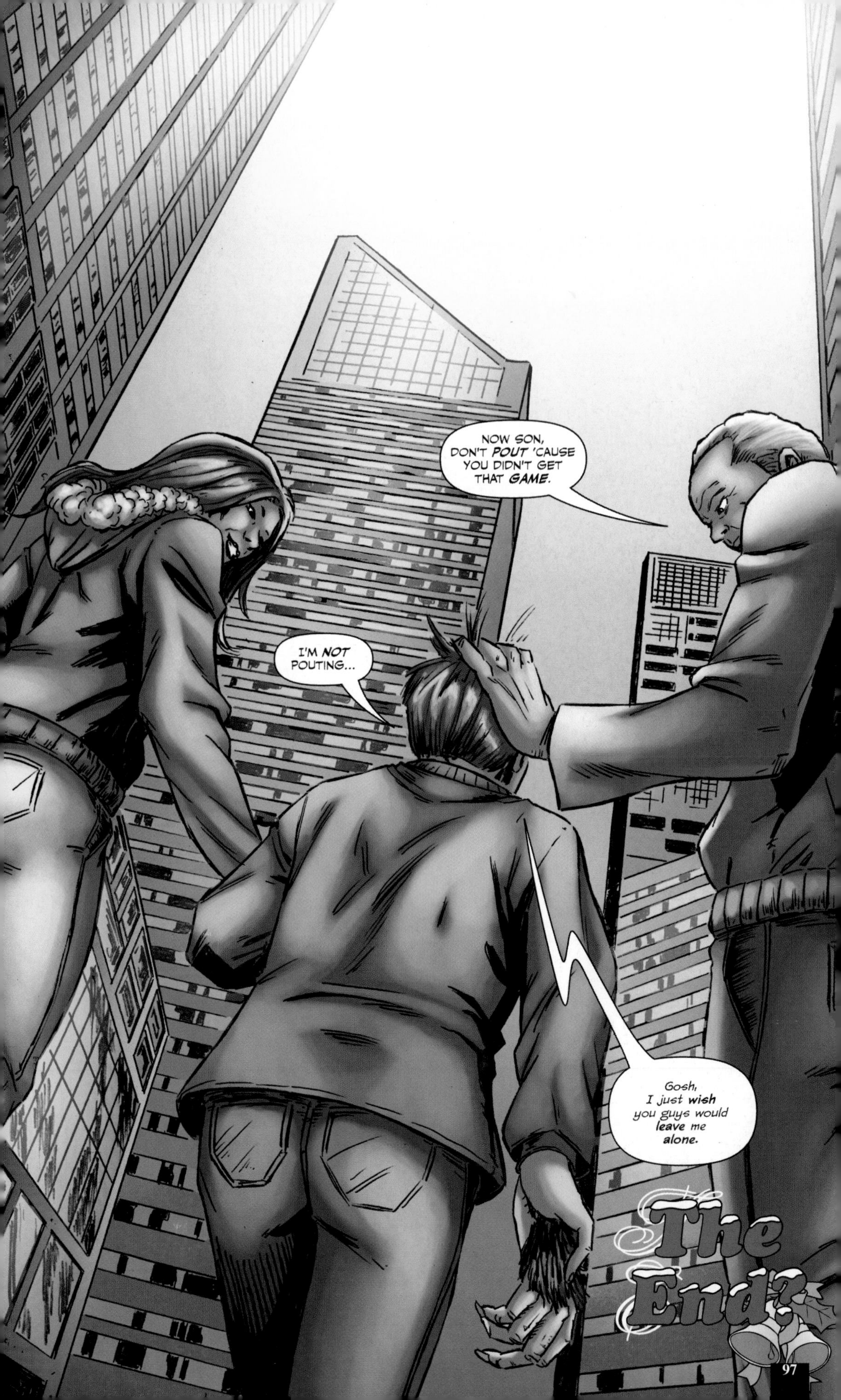
NOW SON, DON'T POUT 'CAUSE YOU DIDN'T GET THAT GAME.
I'M NOT POUTING...
Gosh, I just wish you guys would leave me alone.
The End?

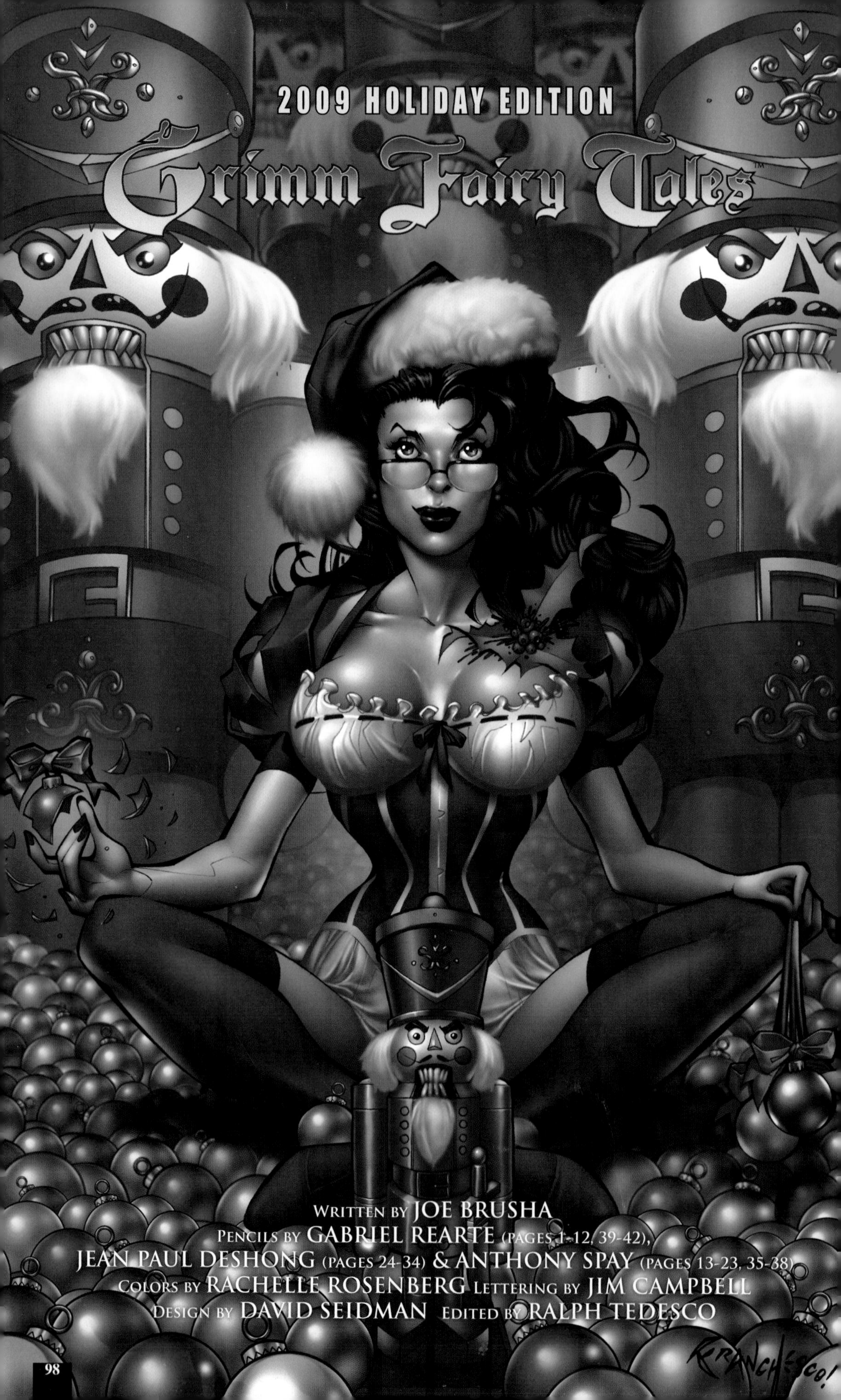
2009 HOLIDAY EDITION
Grimm Fairy Tales™
Written by JOE BRUSHA
Pencils by GABRIEL REARTE (pages 1-12, 39-42),
JEAN PAUL DESHONG (pages 24-34) & ANTHONY SPAY (pages 13-23, 35-38)
Colors by RACHELLE ROSENBERG Lettering by JIM CAMPBELL
Design by DAVID SEIDMAN Edited by RALPH TEDESCO

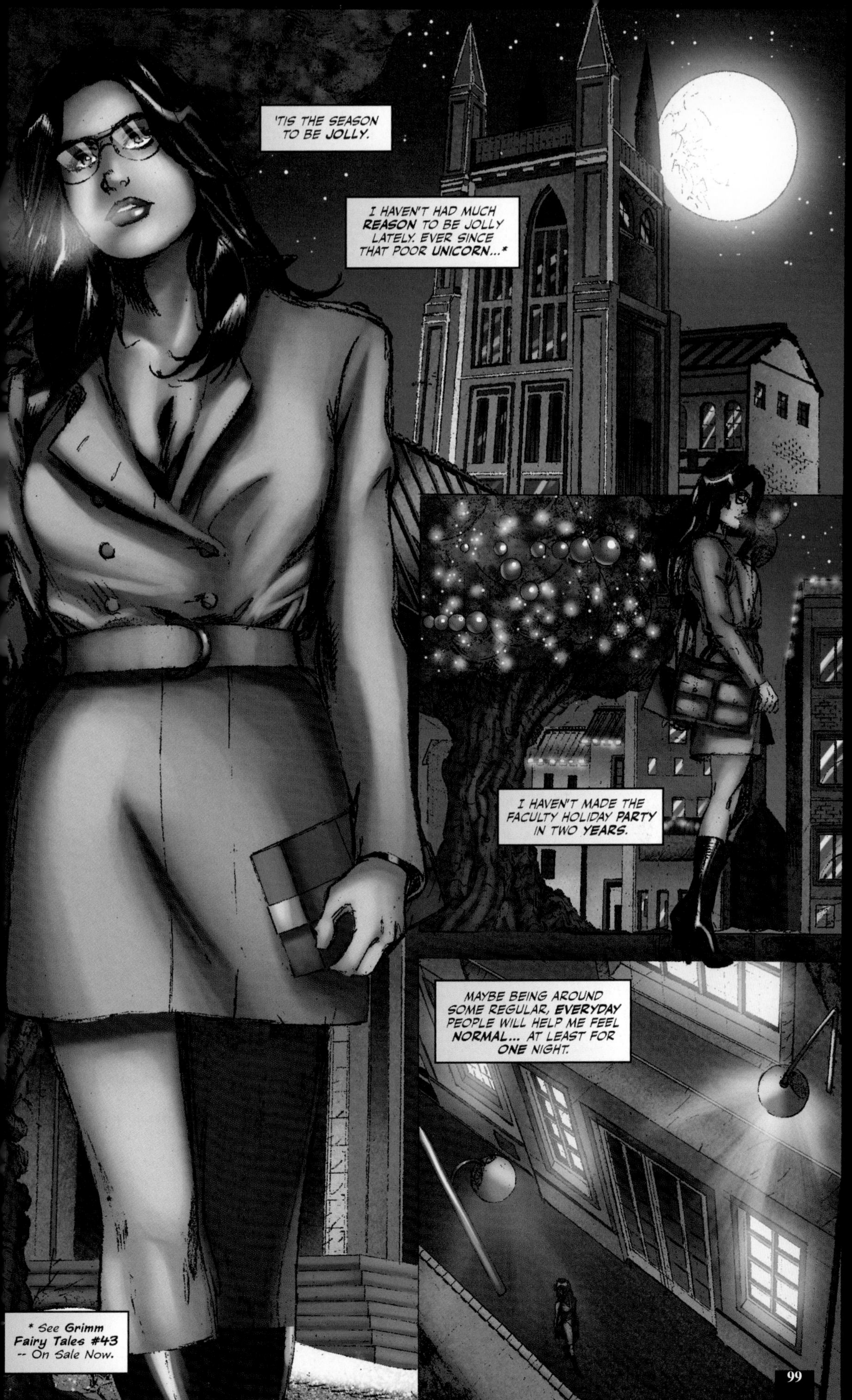
'TIS THE SEASON TO BE JOLLY.
I HAVEN'T HAD MUCH REASON TO BE JOLLY LATELY. EVER SINCE THAT POOR UNICORN...*
I HAVEN'T MADE THE FACULTY HOLIDAY PARTY IN TWO YEARS.
MAYBE BEING AROUND SOME REGULAR, EVERYDAY PEOPLE WILL HELP ME FEEL NORMAL... AT LEAST FOR ONE NIGHT.
* See Grimm Fairy Tales #43 -- On Sale Now.

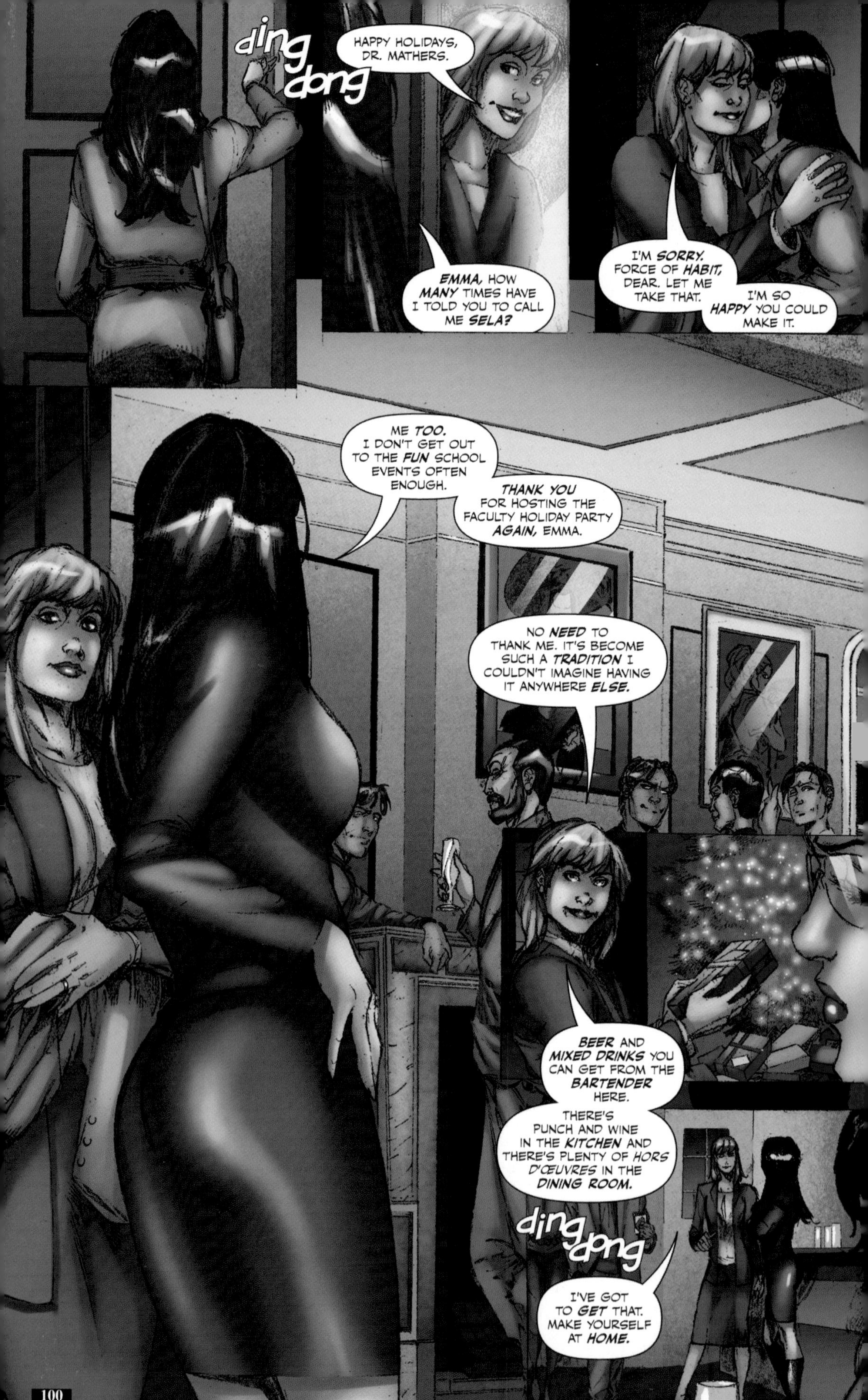
ding dong
HAPPY HOLIDAYS, DR. MATHERS.
EMMA, HOW MANY TIMES HAVE I TOLD YOU TO CALL ME SELA?
I'M SORRY. FORCE OF HABIT, DEAR. LET ME TAKE THAT.
I'M SO HAPPY YOU COULD MAKE IT.
ME TOO. I DON'T GET OUT TO THE FUN SCHOOL EVENTS OFTEN ENOUGH.
THANK YOU FOR HOSTING THE FACULTY HOLIDAY PARTY AGAIN, EMMA.
NO NEED TO THANK ME. IT'S BECOME SUCH A TRADITION I COULDN'T IMAGINE HAVING IT ANYWHERE ELSE.
BEER AND MIXED DRINKS YOU CAN GET FROM THE BARTENDER HERE.
THERE'S PUNCH AND WINE IN THE KITCHEN AND THERE'S PLENTY OF HORS D'ŒUVRES IN THE DINING ROOM.
ding dong
I'VE GOT TO GET THAT. MAKE YOURSELF AT HOME.

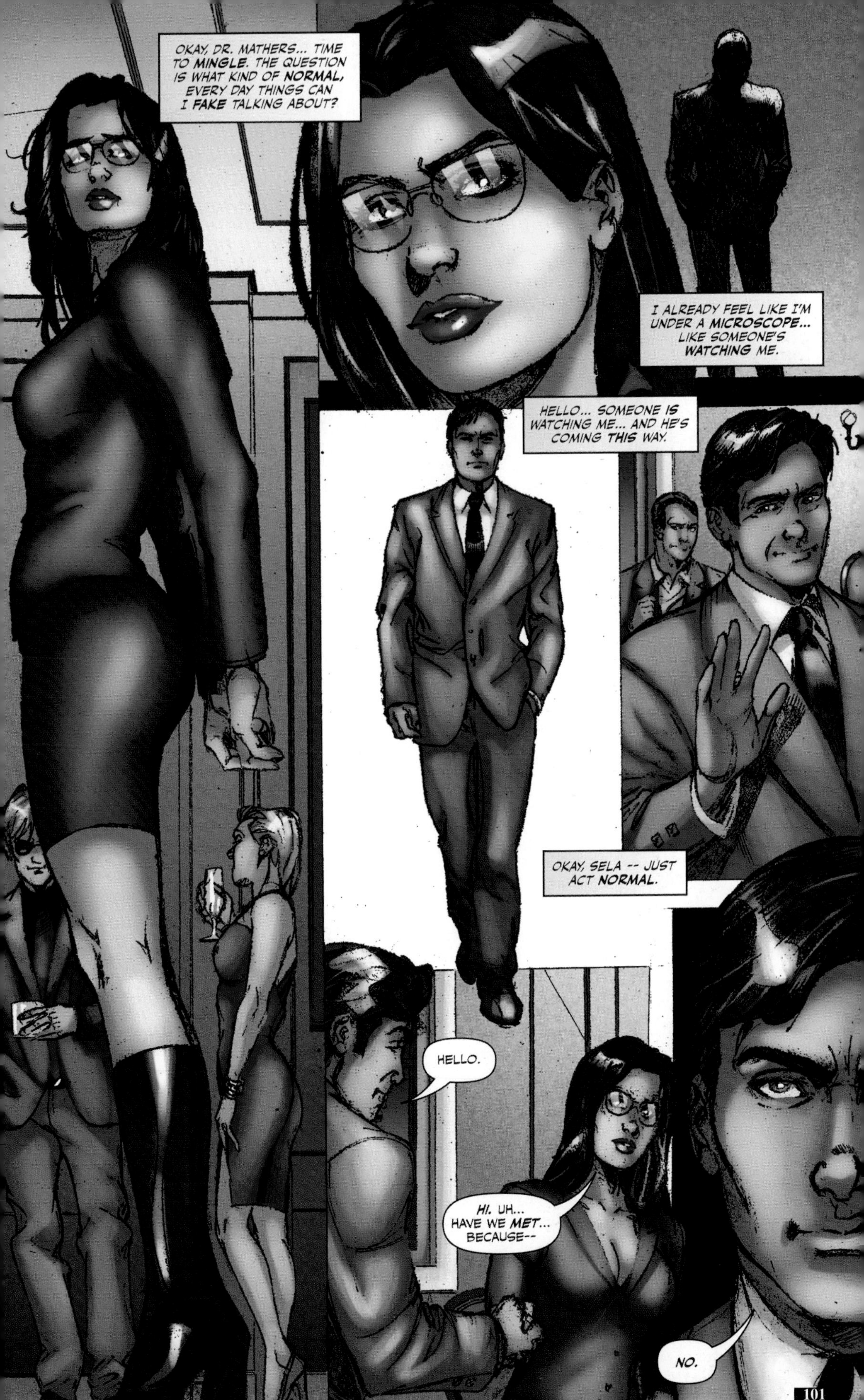
OKAY, DR. MATHERS... TIME TO MINGLE. THE QUESTION IS WHAT KIND OF NORMAL, EVERY DAY THINGS CAN I FAKE TALKING ABOUT?
I ALREADY FEEL LIKE I'M UNDER A MICROSCOPE... LIKE SOMEONE'S WATCHING ME.
HELLO... SOMEONE IS WATCHING ME... AND HE'S COMING THIS WAY.
OKAY, SELA -- JUST ACT NORMAL.
HELLO.
HI. UH... HAVE WE MET... BECAUSE--
NO.

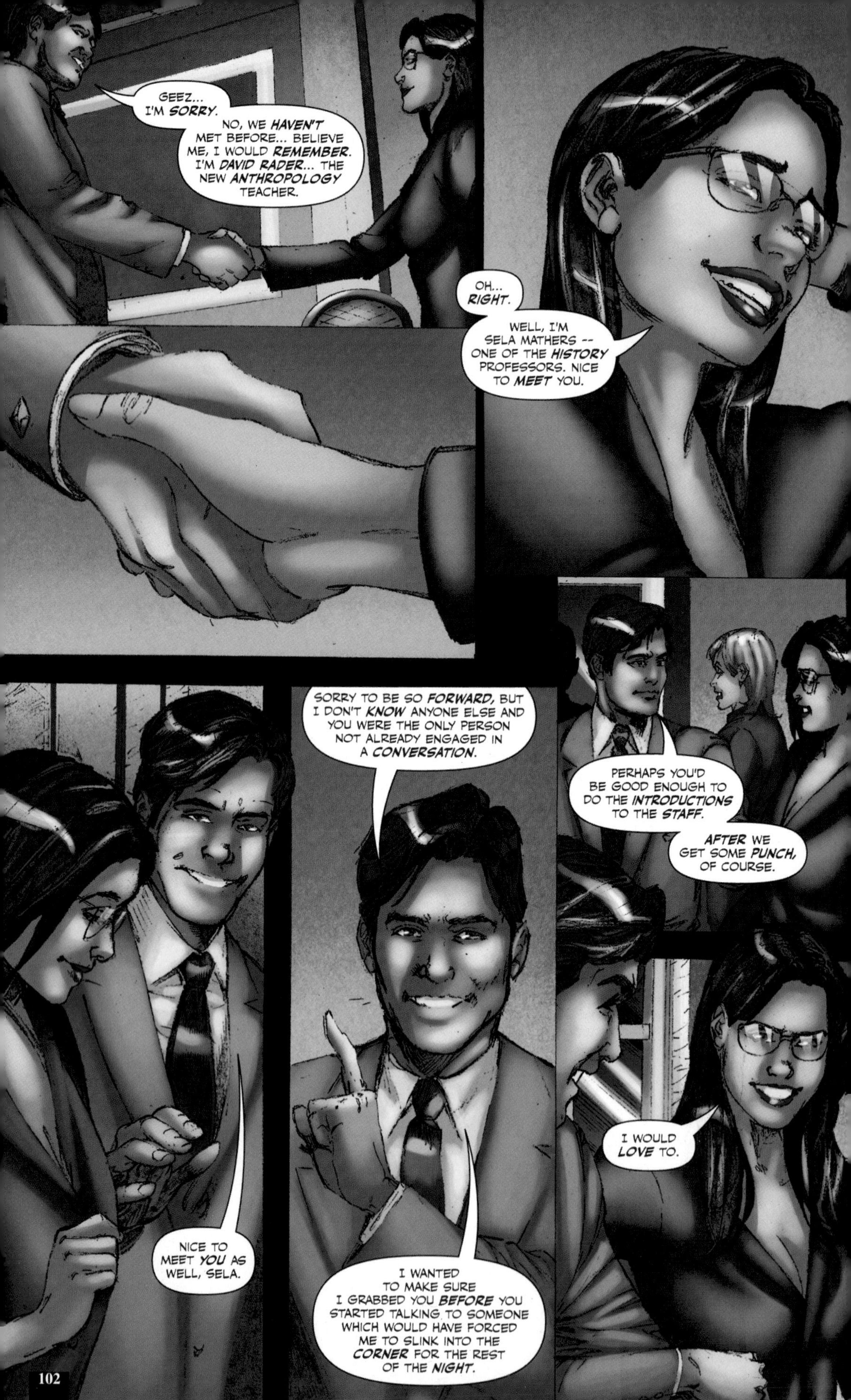
GEEZ... I'M SORRY.
NO, WE HAVEN'T MET BEFORE... BELIEVE ME, I WOULD REMEMBER. I'M DAVID RADER... THE NEW ANTHROPOLOGY TEACHER.
OH... RIGHT.
WELL, I'M SELA MATHERS -- ONE OF THE HISTORY PROFESSORS. NICE TO MEET YOU.
NICE TO MEET YOU AS WELL, SELA.
SORRY TO BE SO FORWARD, BUT I DON'T KNOW ANYONE ELSE AND YOU WERE THE ONLY PERSON NOT ALREADY ENGAGED IN A CONVERSATION.
I WANTED TO MAKE SURE I GRABBED YOU BEFORE YOU STARTED TALKING TO SOMEONE WHICH WOULD HAVE FORCED ME TO SLINK INTO THE CORNER FOR THE REST OF THE NIGHT.
PERHAPS YOU'D BE GOOD ENOUGH TO DO THE INTRODUCTIONS TO THE STAFF.
AFTER WE GET SOME PUNCH, OF COURSE.
I WOULD LOVE TO.

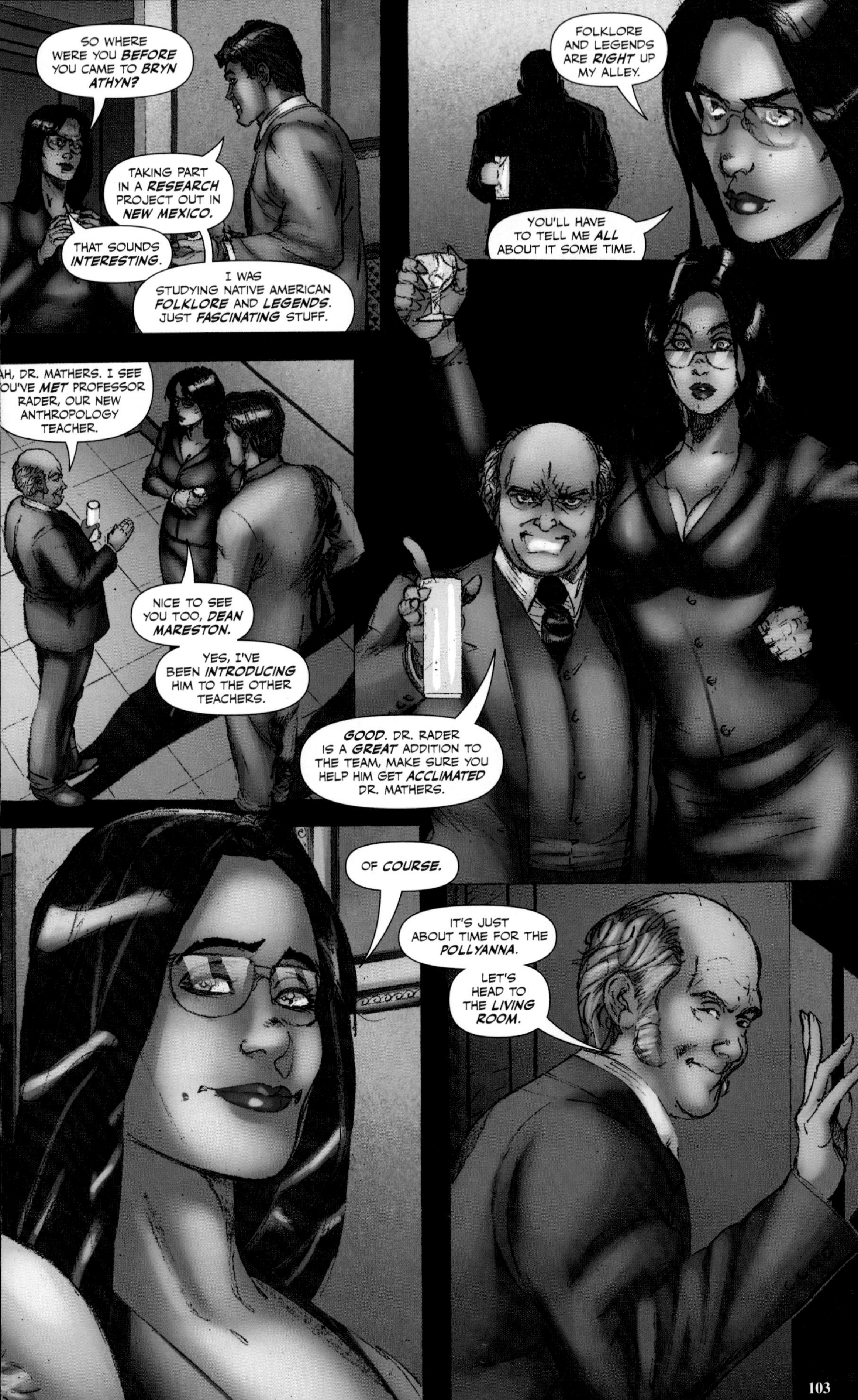
SO WHERE WERE YOU BEFORE YOU CAME TO BRYN ATHYN?
TAKING PART IN A RESEARCH PROJECT OUT IN NEW MEXICO.
THAT SOUNDS INTERESTING.
I WAS STUDYING NATIVE AMERICAN FOLKLORE AND LEGENDS. JUST FASCINATING STUFF.
FOLKLORE AND LEGENDS ARE RIGHT UP MY ALLEY.
YOU'LL HAVE TO TELL ME ALL ABOUT IT SOME TIME.
AH, DR. MATHERS. I SEE YOU'VE MET PROFESSOR RADER, OUR NEW ANTHROPOLOGY TEACHER.
NICE TO SEE YOU TOO, DEAN MARESTON.
YES, I'VE BEEN INTRODUCING HIM TO THE OTHER TEACHERS.
GOOD. DR. RADER IS A GREAT ADDITION TO THE TEAM, MAKE SURE YOU HELP HIM GET ACCLIMATED DR. MATHERS.
OF COURSE.
IT'S JUST ABOUT TIME FOR THE POLLYANNA.
LET'S HEAD TO THE LIVING ROOM.

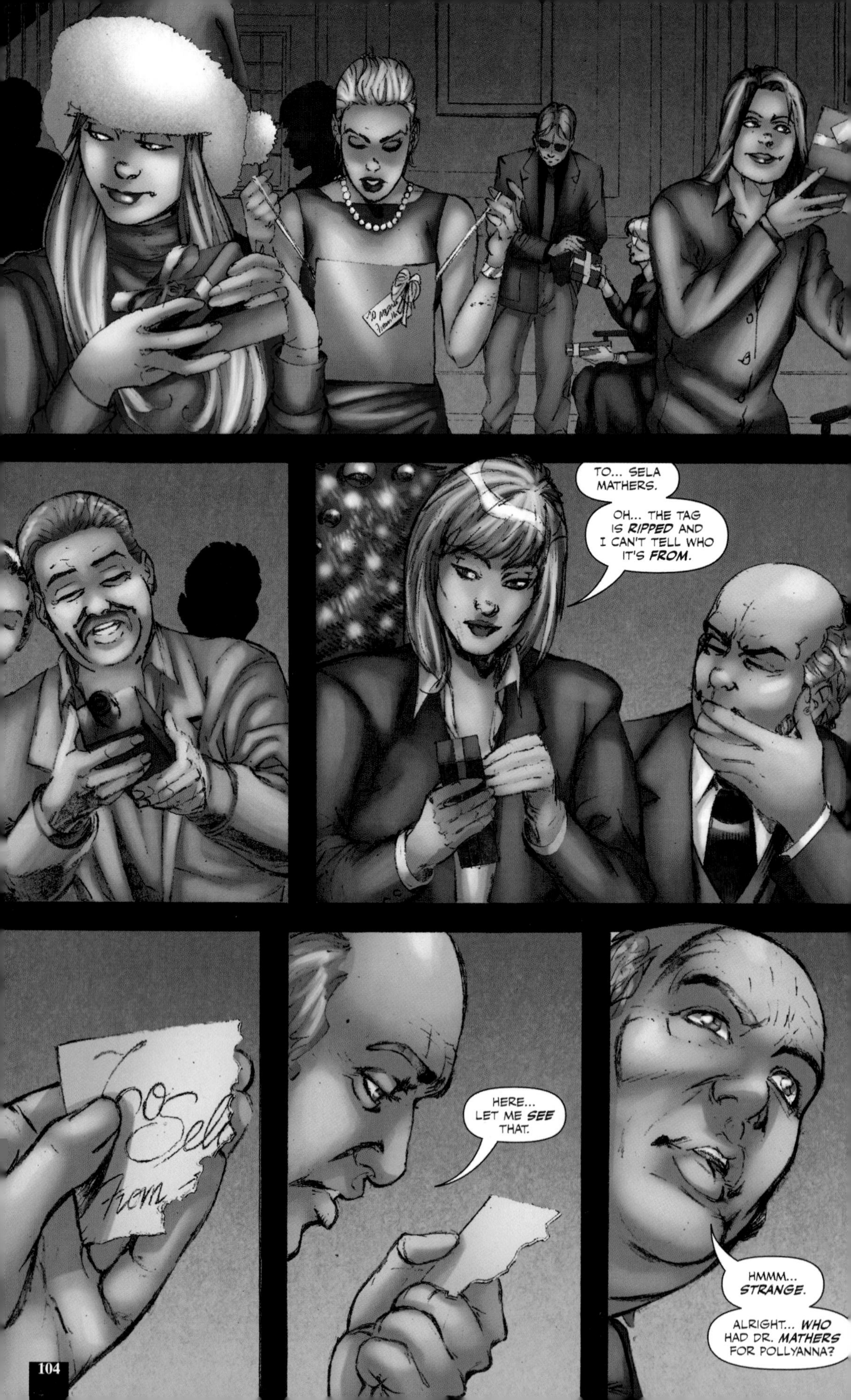
TO... SELA MATHERS.
OH... THE TAG IS RIPPED AND I CAN'T TELL WHO IT'S FROM.
HERE... LET ME SEE THAT.
HMMM... STRANGE.
ALRIGHT... WHO HAD DR. MATHERS FOR POLLYANNA?

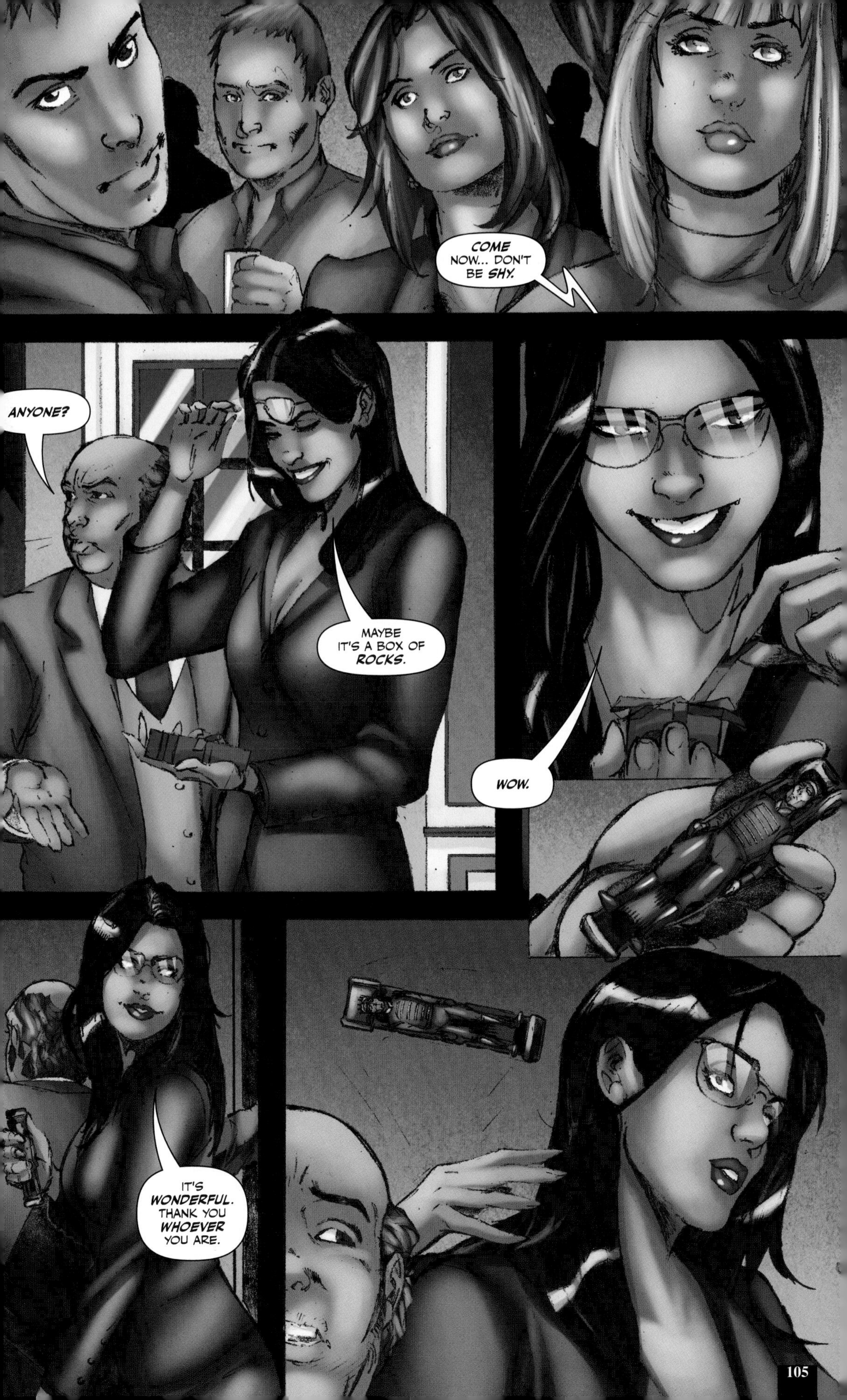
COME NOW... DON'T BE SHY.
ANYONE?
MAYBE IT'S A BOX OF ROCKS.
WOW.
IT'S WONDERFUL. THANK YOU WHOEVER YOU ARE.

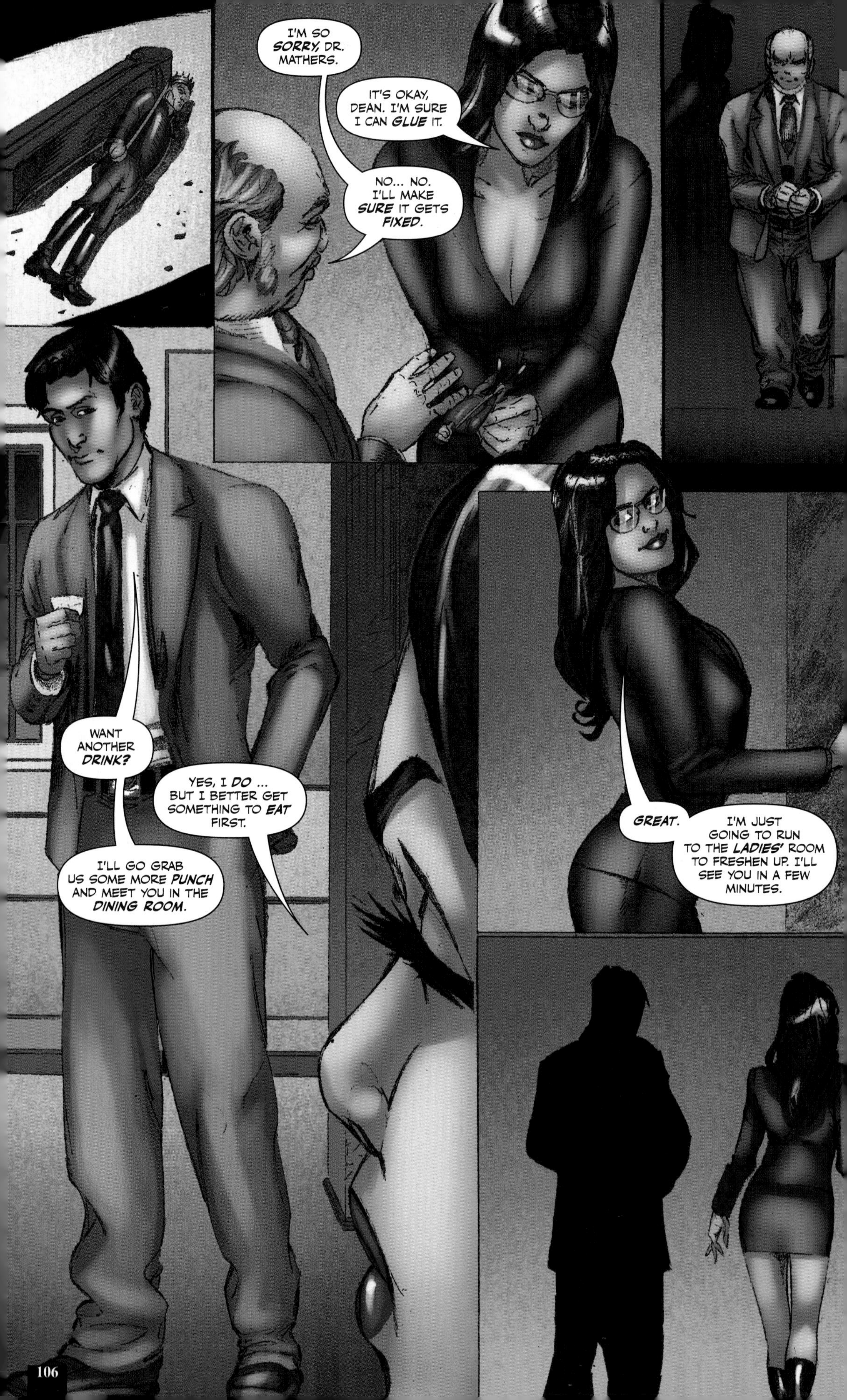
I'M SO SORRY, DR. MATHERS.
IT'S OKAY, DEAN. I'M SURE I CAN GLUE IT.
NO... NO. I'LL MAKE SURE IT GETS FIXED.
WANT ANOTHER DRINK?
YES, I DO ... BUT I BETTER GET SOMETHING TO EAT FIRST.
I'LL GO GRAB US SOME MORE PUNCH AND MEET YOU IN THE DINING ROOM.
GREAT.
I'M JUST GOING TO RUN TO THE LADIES' ROOM TO FRESHEN UP. I'LL SEE YOU IN A FEW MINUTES.

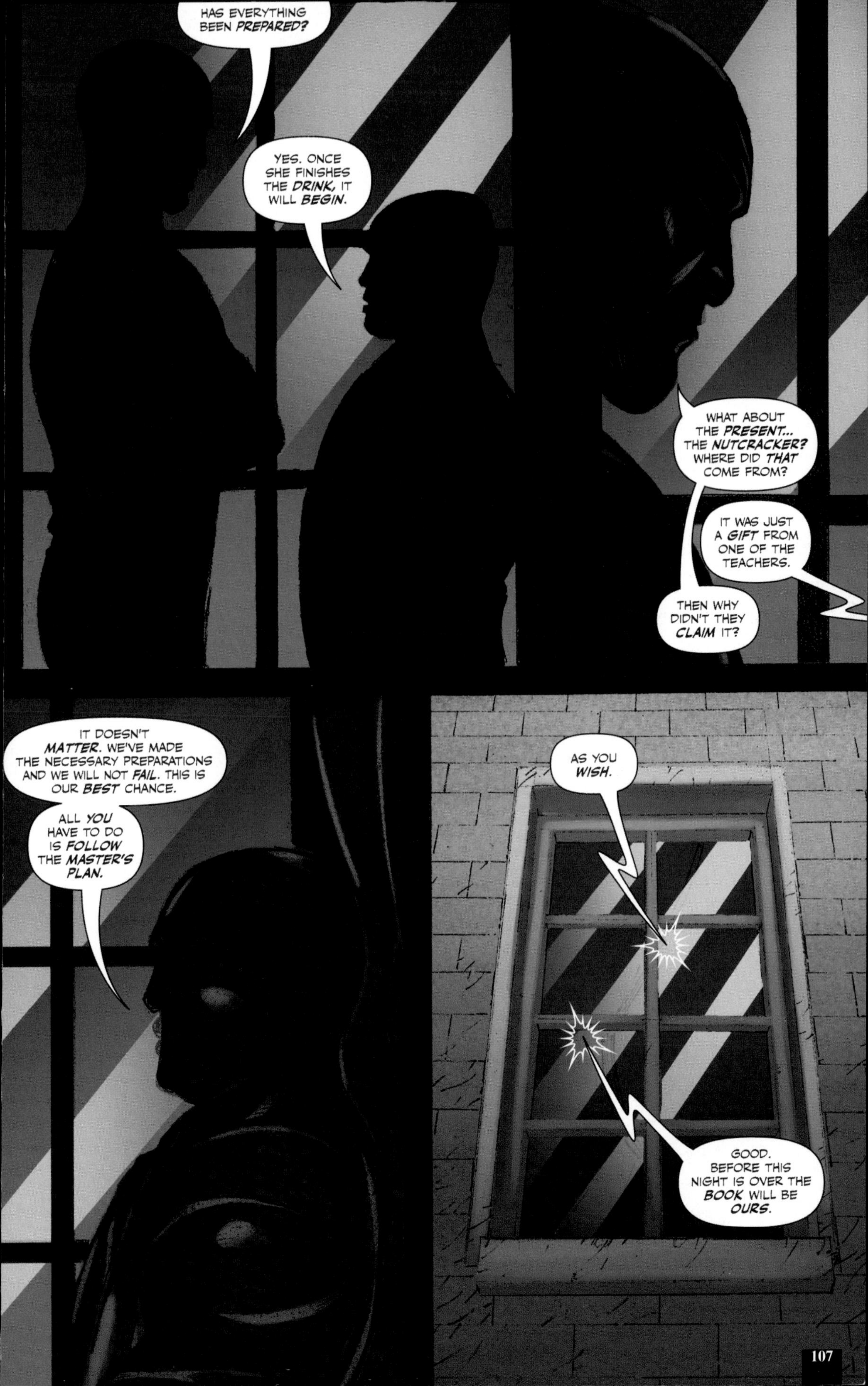
HAS EVERYTHING BEEN PREPARED?
YES. ONCE SHE FINISHES THE DRINK, IT WILL BEGIN.
WHAT ABOUT THE PRESENT... THE NUTCRACKER? WHERE DID THAT COME FROM?
IT WAS JUST A GIFT FROM ONE OF THE TEACHERS.
THEN WHY DIDN'T THEY CLAIM IT?
IT DOESN'T MATTER. WE'VE MADE THE NECESSARY PREPARATIONS AND WE WILL NOT FAIL. THIS IS OUR BEST CHANCE.
ALL YOU HAVE TO DO IS FOLLOW THE MASTER'S PLAN.
AS YOU WISH.
GOOD. BEFORE THIS NIGHT IS OVER THE BOOK WILL BE OURS.

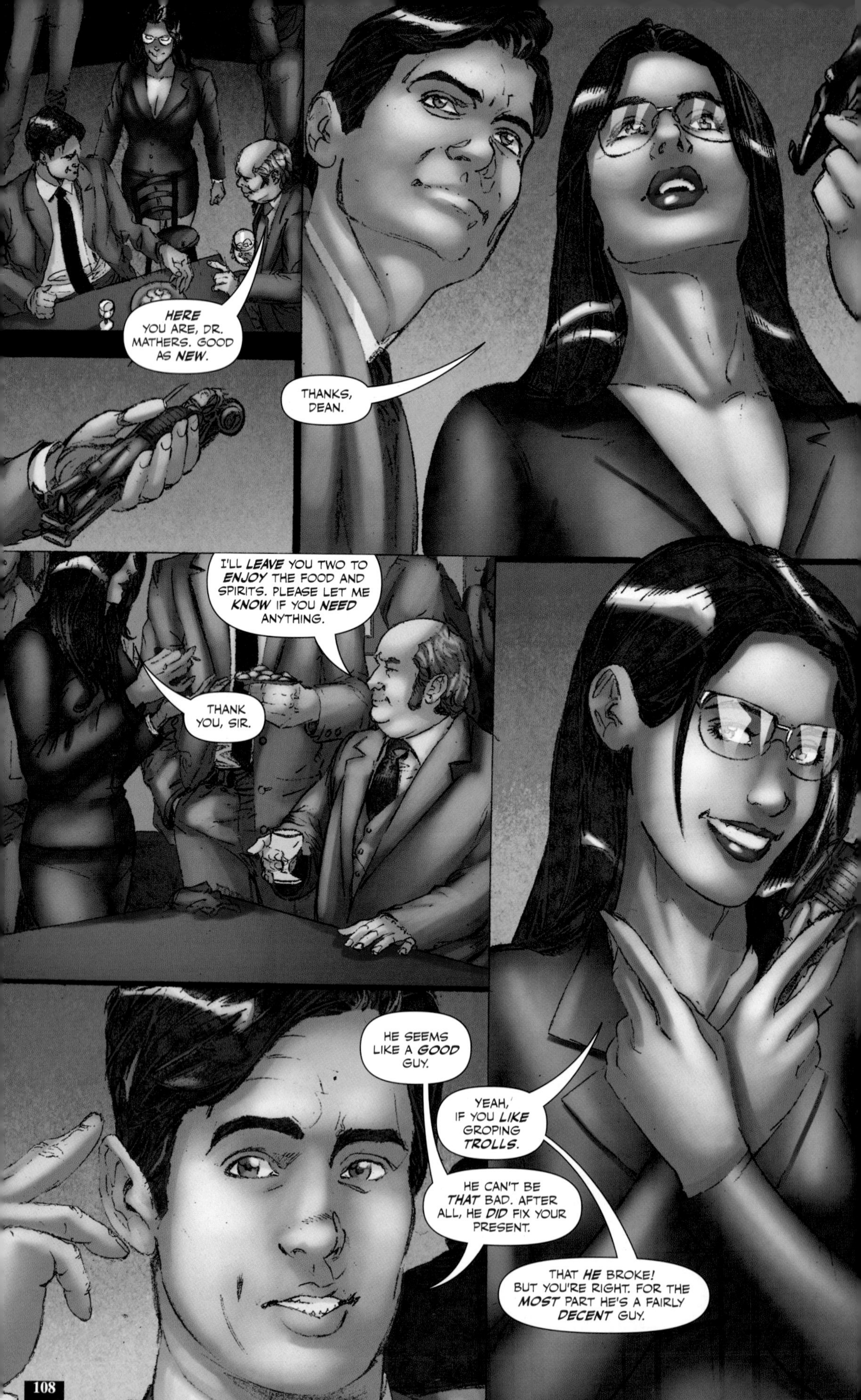
HERE YOU ARE, DR. MATHERS. GOOD AS NEW.
THANKS, DEAN.
I'LL LEAVE YOU TWO TO ENJOY THE FOOD AND SPIRITS. PLEASE LET ME KNOW IF YOU NEED ANYTHING.
THANK YOU, SIR.
HE SEEMS LIKE A GOOD GUY.
YEAH, IF YOU LIKE GROPING TROLLS.
HE CAN'T BE THAT BAD. AFTER ALL, HE DID FIX YOUR PRESENT.
THAT HE BROKE! BUT YOU'RE RIGHT. FOR THE MOST PART HE'S A FAIRLY DECENT GUY.

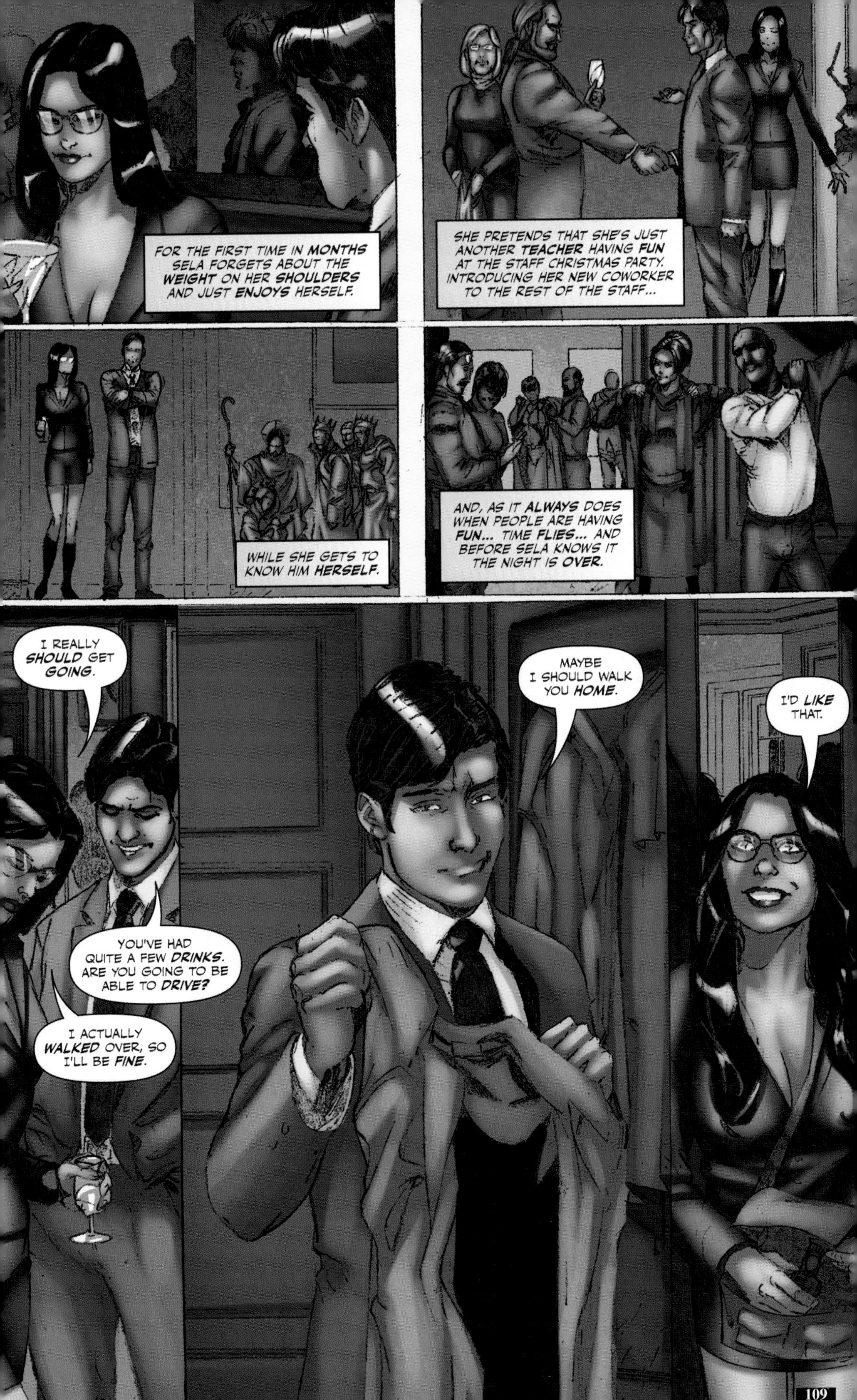
FOR THE FIRST TIME IN MONTHS SELA FORGETS ABOUT THE WEIGHT ON HER SHOULDERS AND JUST ENJOYS HERSELF.
SHE PRETENDS THAT SHE'S JUST ANOTHER TEACHER HAVING FUN AT THE STAFF CHRISTMAS PARTY. INTRODUCING HER NEW COWORKER TO THE REST OF THE STAFF...
WHILE SHE GETS TO KNOW HIM HERSELF.
AND, AS IT ALWAYS DOES WHEN PEOPLE ARE HAVING FUN... TIME FLIES... AND BEFORE SELA KNOWS IT THE NIGHT IS OVER.
I REALLY SHOULD GET GOING.
YOU'VE HAD QUITE A FEW DRINKS. ARE YOU GOING TO BE ABLE TO DRIVE?
I ACTUALLY WALKED OVER, SO I'LL BE FINE.
MAYBE I SHOULD WALK YOU HOME.
I'D LIKE THAT.

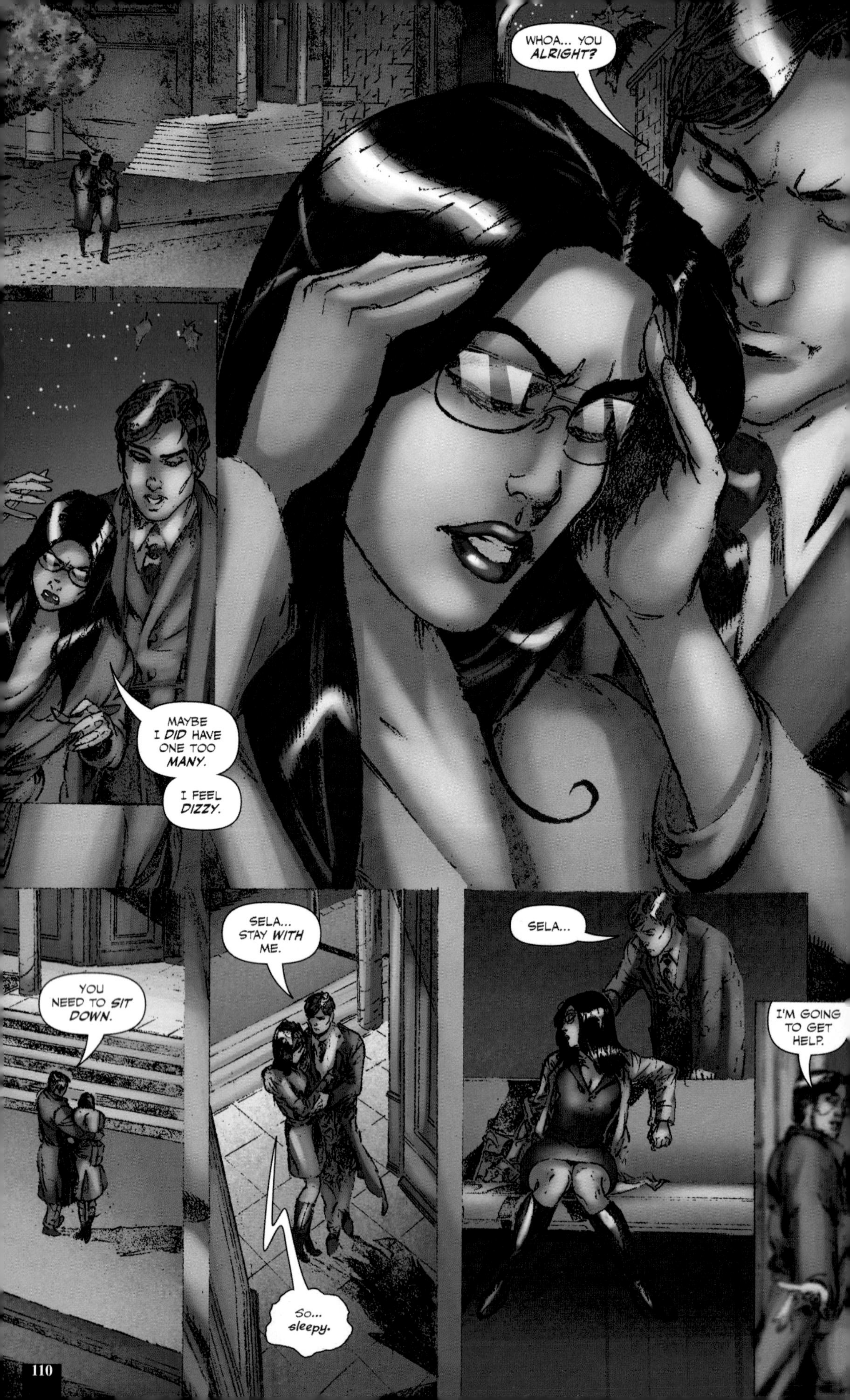
WHOA... YOU ALRIGHT?
MAYBE I DID HAVE ONE TOO MANY.
I FEEL DIZZY.
YOU NEED TO SIT DOWN.
SELA... STAY WITH ME.
So... sleepy.
SELA...
I'M GOING TO GET HELP.

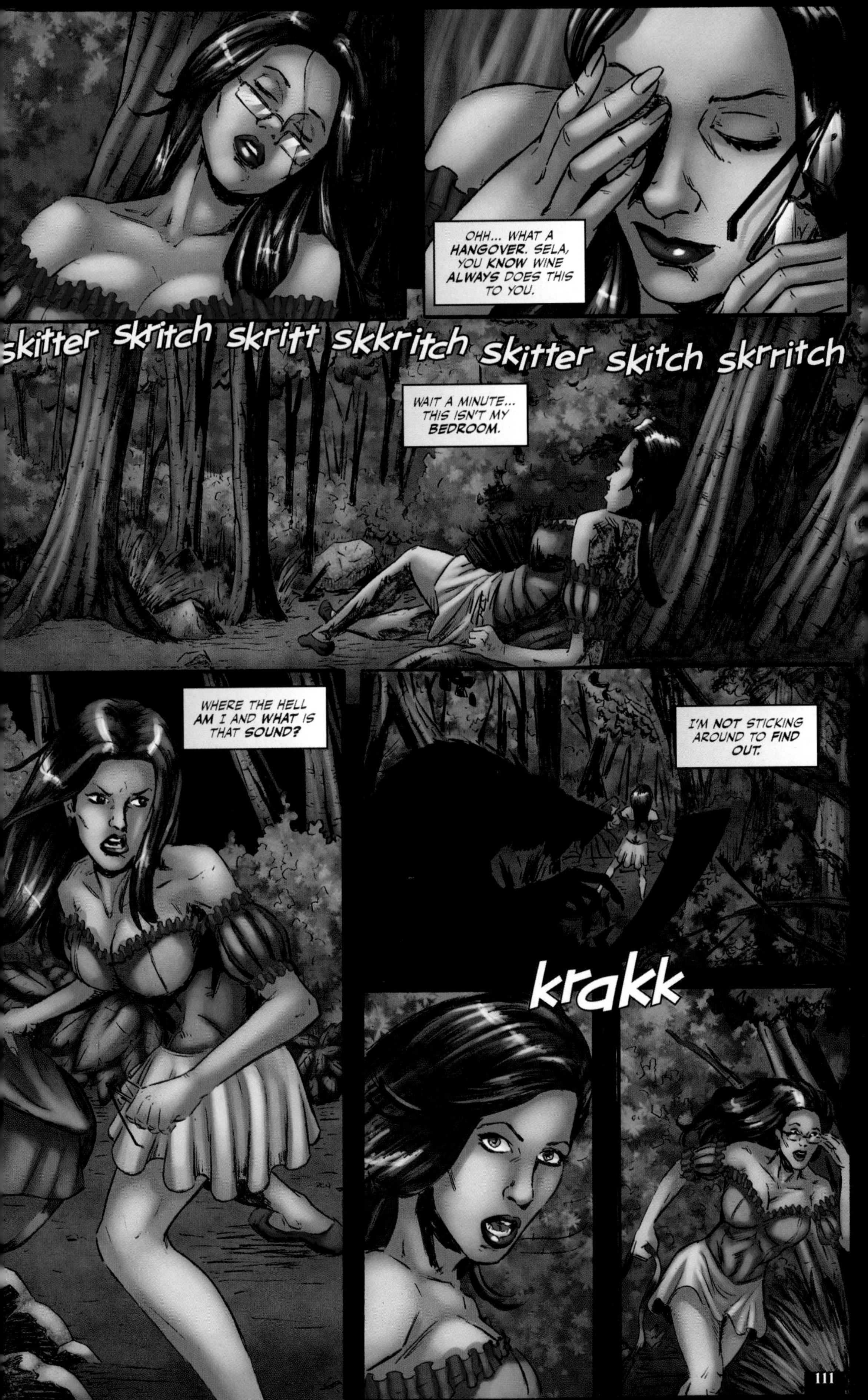
OHH... WHAT A HANGOVER. SELA, YOU KNOW WINE ALWAYS DOES THIS TO YOU.
skitter skritch skritt skkritch skitter skitch skrritch
WAIT A MINUTE... THIS ISN'T MY BEDROOM.
WHERE THE HELL AM I AND WHAT IS THAT SOUND?
I'M NOT STICKING AROUND TO FIND OUT.
krakk

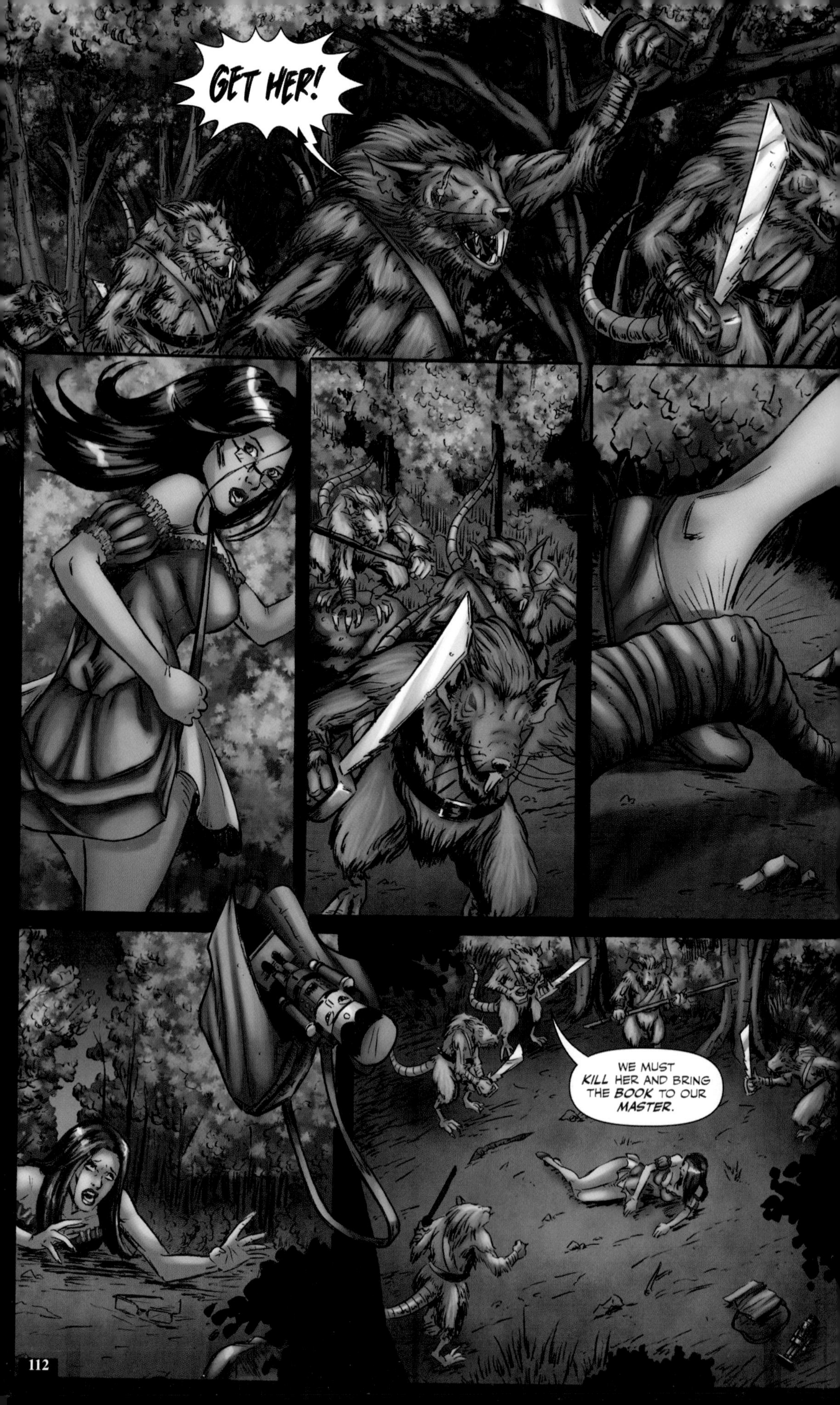
GET HER!
WE MUST KILL HER AND BRING THE BOOK TO OUR MASTER.

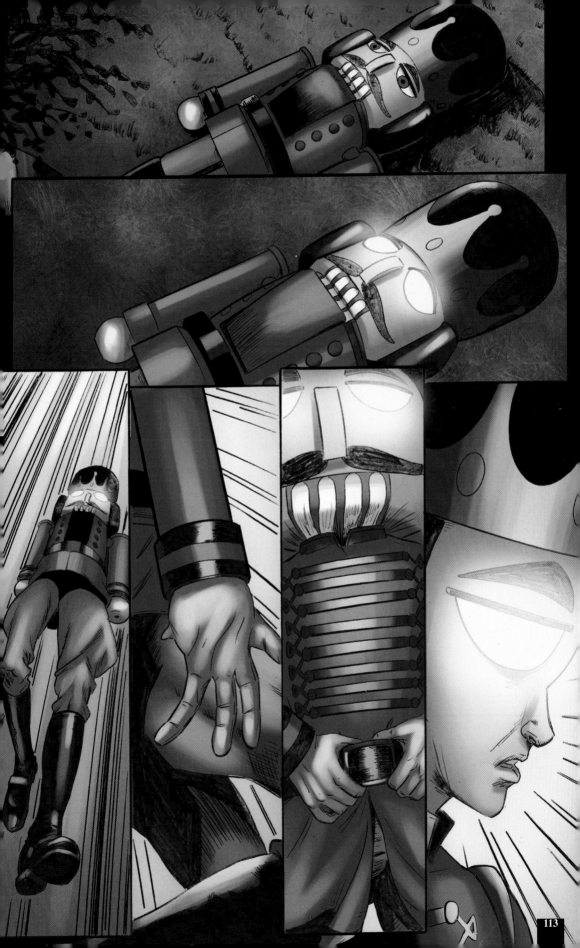

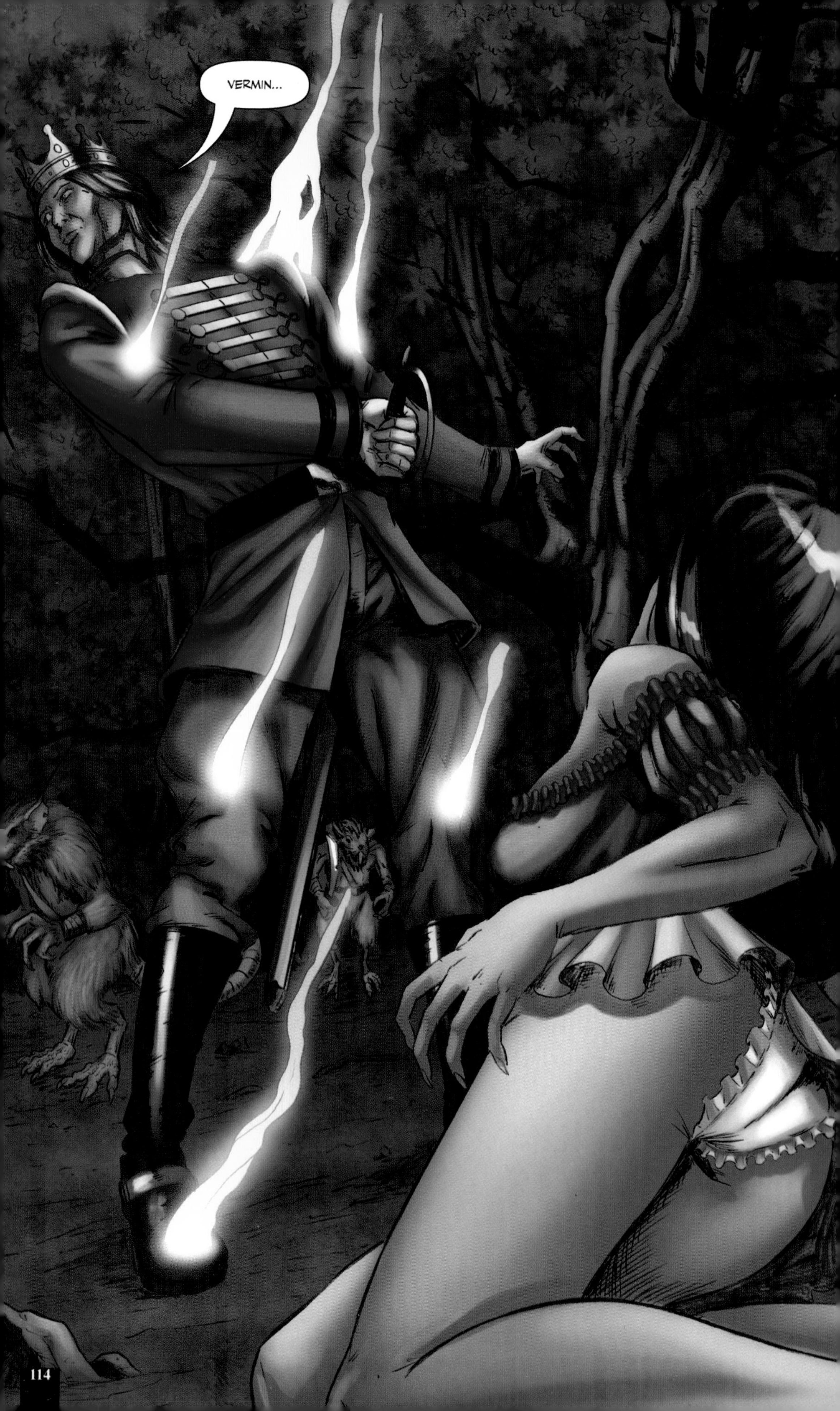
VERMIN...

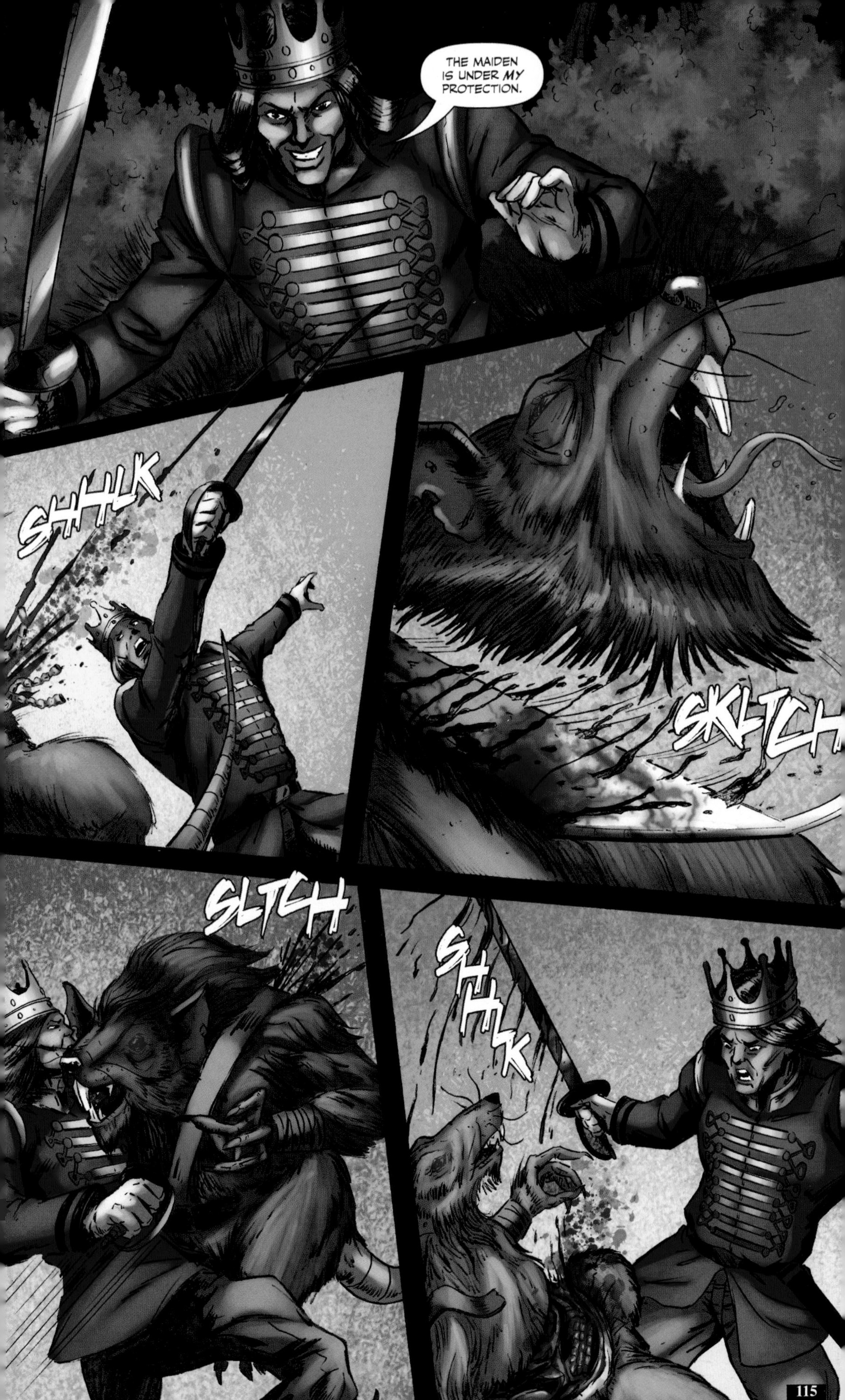
THE MAIDEN IS UNDER MY PROTECTION.
SHHLK
SKLTCH
SLTCH
SHHLK

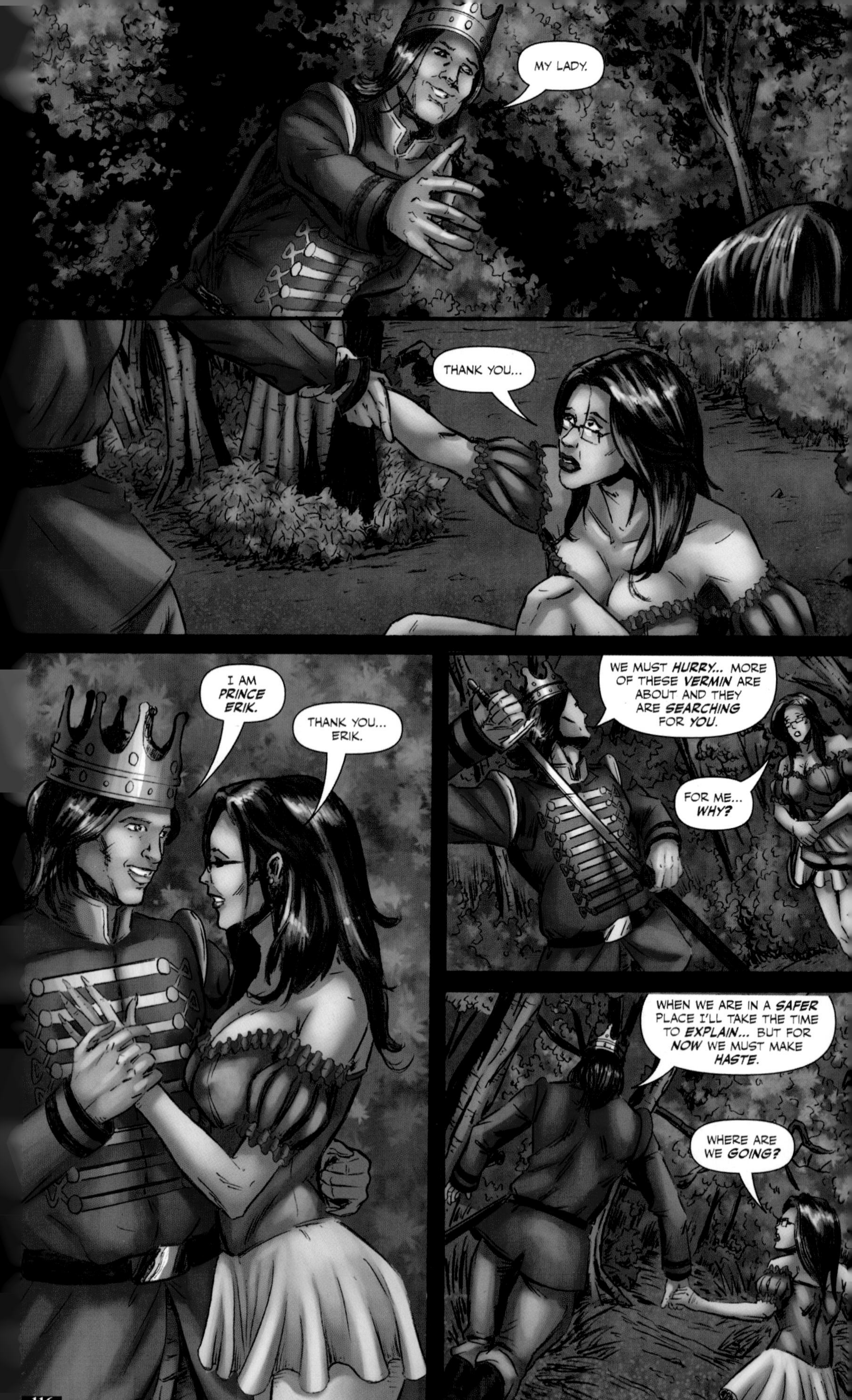
MY LADY.
THANK YOU...
I AM PRINCE ERIK.
THANK YOU... ERIK.
WE MUST HURRY... MORE OF THESE VERMIN ARE ABOUT AND THEY ARE SEARCHING FOR YOU.
FOR ME... WHY?
WHEN WE ARE IN A SAFER PLACE I'LL TAKE THE TIME TO EXPLAIN... BUT FOR NOW WE MUST MAKE HASTE.
WHERE ARE WE GOING?

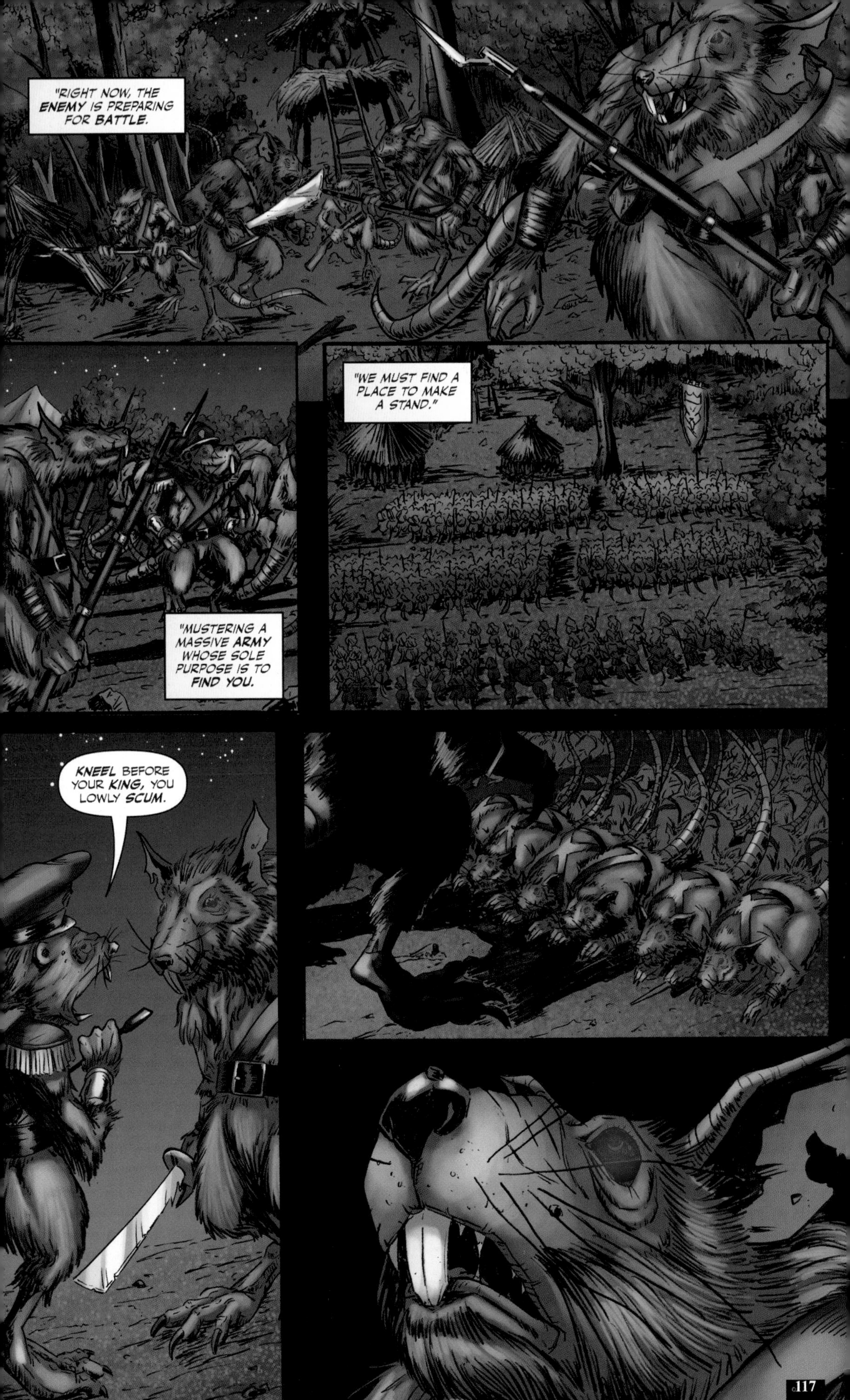
"RIGHT NOW, THE ENEMY IS PREPARING FOR BATTLE.
"MUSTERING A MASSIVE ARMY WHOSE SOLE PURPOSE IS TO FIND YOU.
"WE MUST FIND A PLACE TO MAKE A STAND."
KNEEL BEFORE YOUR KING, YOU LOWLY SCUM.

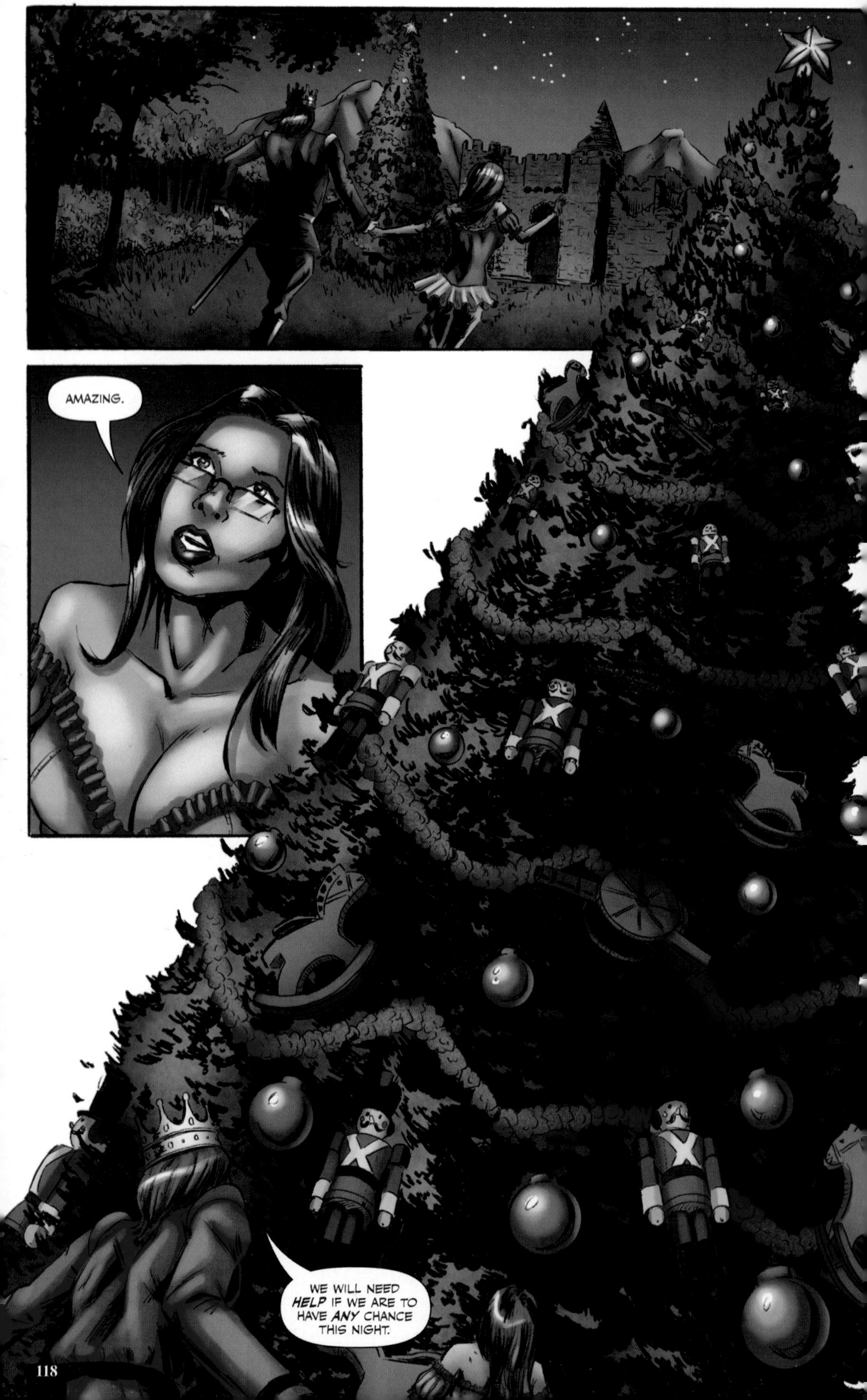
AMAZING.
WE WILL NEED HELP IF WE ARE TO HAVE ANY CHANCE THIS NIGHT.

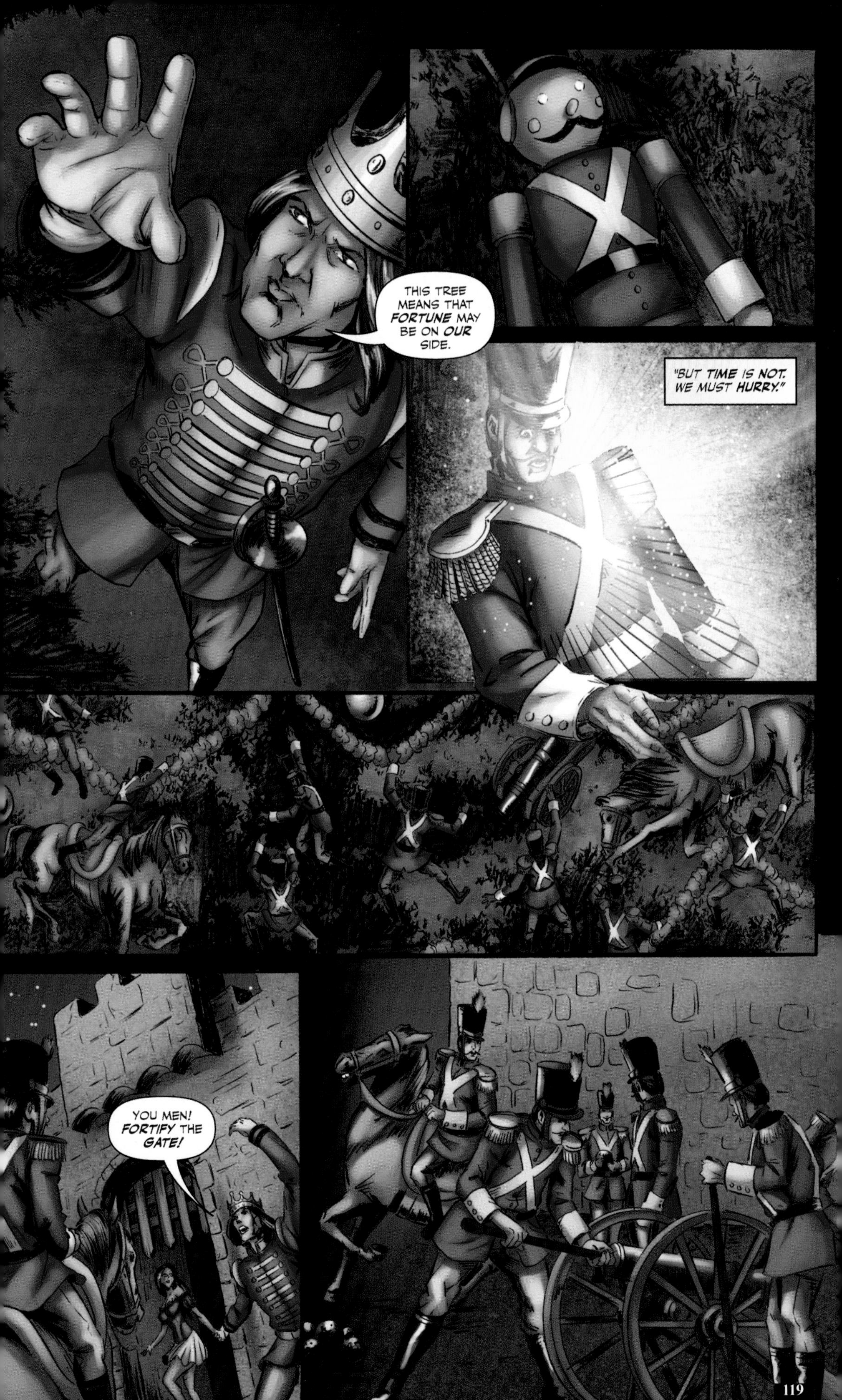
THIS TREE MEANS THAT FORTUNE MAY BE ON OUR SIDE.
"BUT TIME IS NOT. WE MUST HURRY."
YOU MEN! FORTIFY THE GATE!

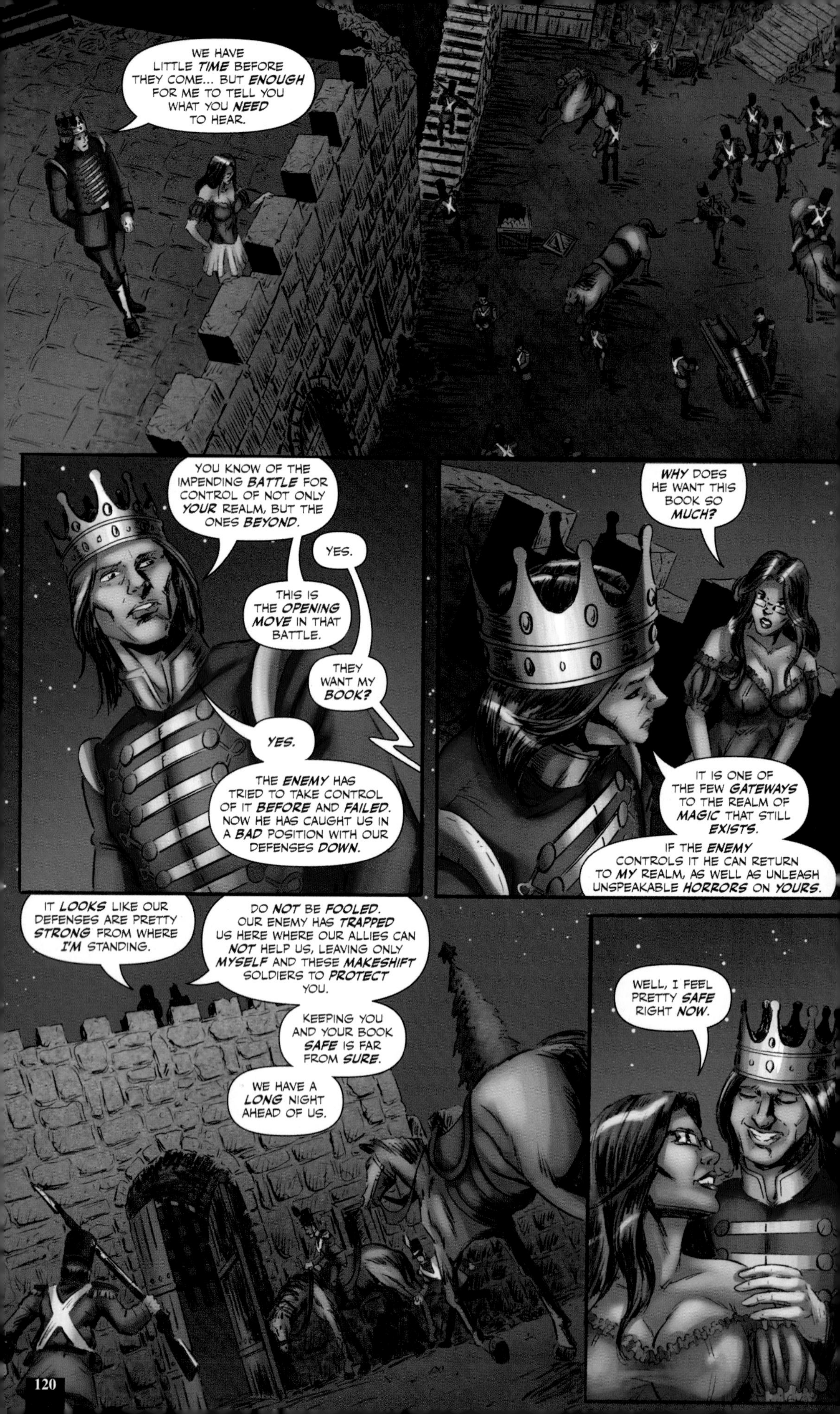
WE HAVE LITTLE TIME BEFORE THEY COME... BUT ENOUGH FOR ME TO TELL YOU WHAT YOU NEED TO HEAR.
YOU KNOW OF THE IMPENDING BATTLE FOR CONTROL OF NOT ONLY YOUR REALM, BUT THE ONES BEYOND.
YES.
THIS IS THE OPENING MOVE IN THAT BATTLE.
THEY WANT MY BOOK?
YES.
THE ENEMY HAS TRIED TO TAKE CONTROL OF IT BEFORE AND FAILED. NOW HE HAS CAUGHT US IN A BAD POSITION WITH OUR DEFENSES DOWN.
WHY DOES HE WANT THIS BOOK SO MUCH?
IT IS ONE OF THE FEW GATEWAYS TO THE REALM OF MAGIC THAT STILL EXISTS.
IF THE ENEMY CONTROLS IT HE CAN RETURN TO MY REALM, AS WELL AS UNLEASH UNSPEAKABLE HORRORS ON YOURS.
IT LOOKS LIKE OUR DEFENSES ARE PRETTY STRONG FROM WHERE I'M STANDING.
DO NOT BE FOOLED. OUR ENEMY HAS TRAPPED US HERE WHERE OUR ALLIES CAN NOT HELP US, LEAVING ONLY MYSELF AND THESE MAKESHIFT SOLDIERS TO PROTECT YOU.
KEEPING YOU AND YOUR BOOK SAFE IS FAR FROM SURE.
WE HAVE A LONG NIGHT AHEAD OF US.
WELL, I FEEL PRETTY SAFE RIGHT NOW.

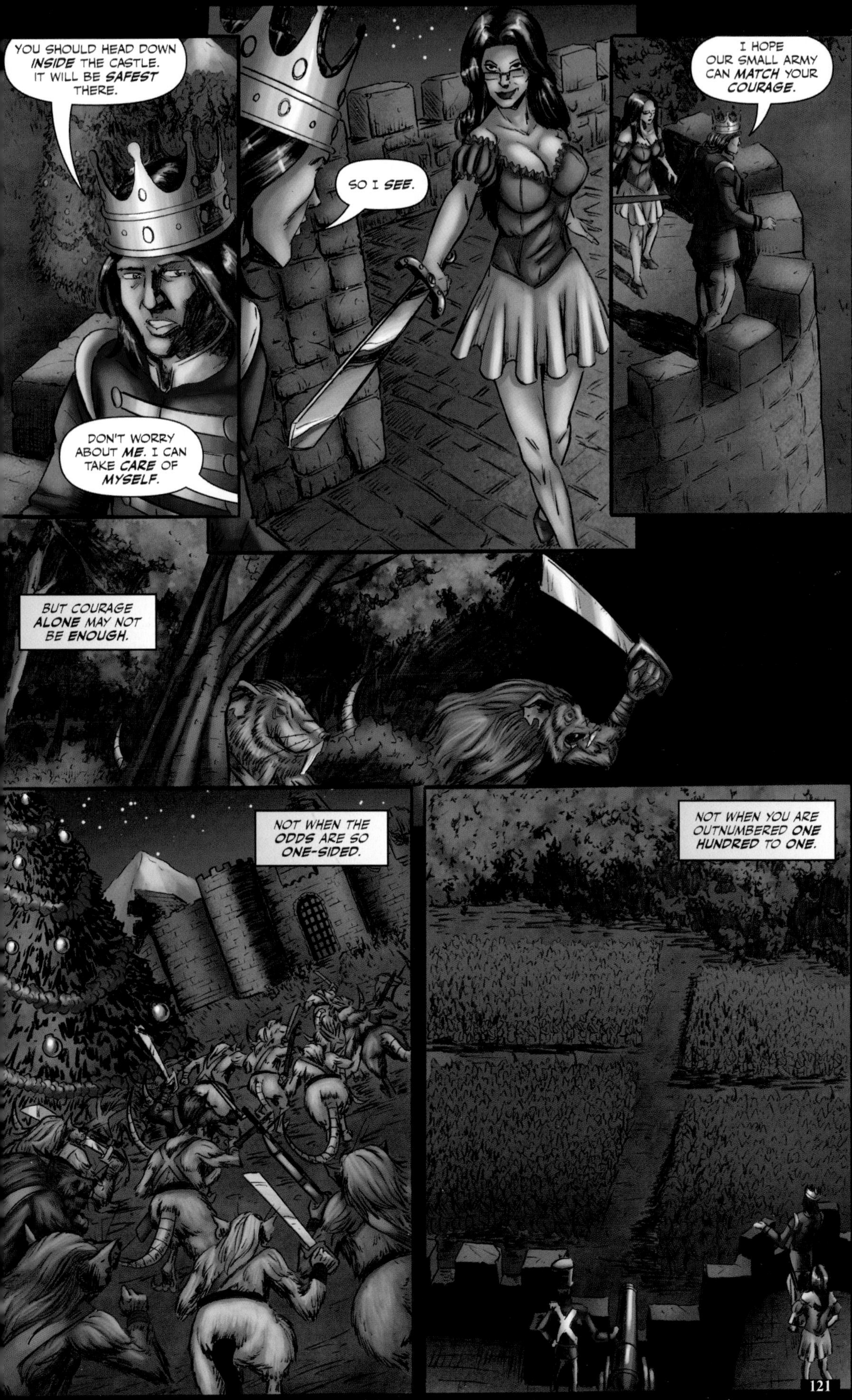
YOU SHOULD HEAD DOWN INSIDE THE CASTLE. IT WILL BE SAFEST THERE.
DON'T WORRY ABOUT ME. I CAN TAKE CARE OF MYSELF.
SO I SEE.
I HOPE OUR SMALL ARMY CAN MATCH YOUR COURAGE.
BUT COURAGE ALONE MAY NOT BE ENOUGH.
NOT WHEN THE ODDS ARE SO ONE-SIDED.
NOT WHEN YOU ARE OUTNUMBERED ONE HUNDRED TO ONE.

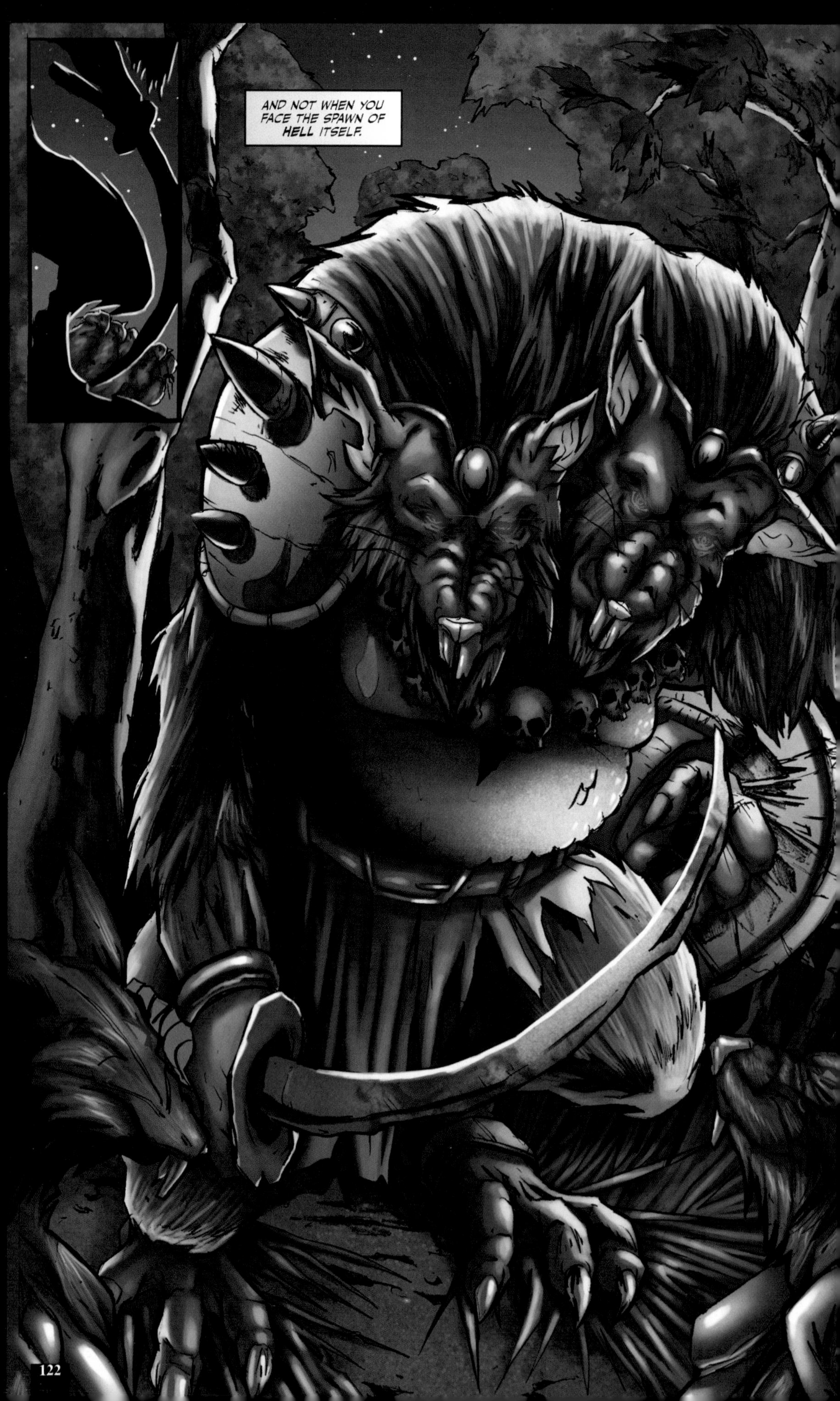
AND NOT WHEN YOU FACE THE SPAWN OF HELL ITSELF.

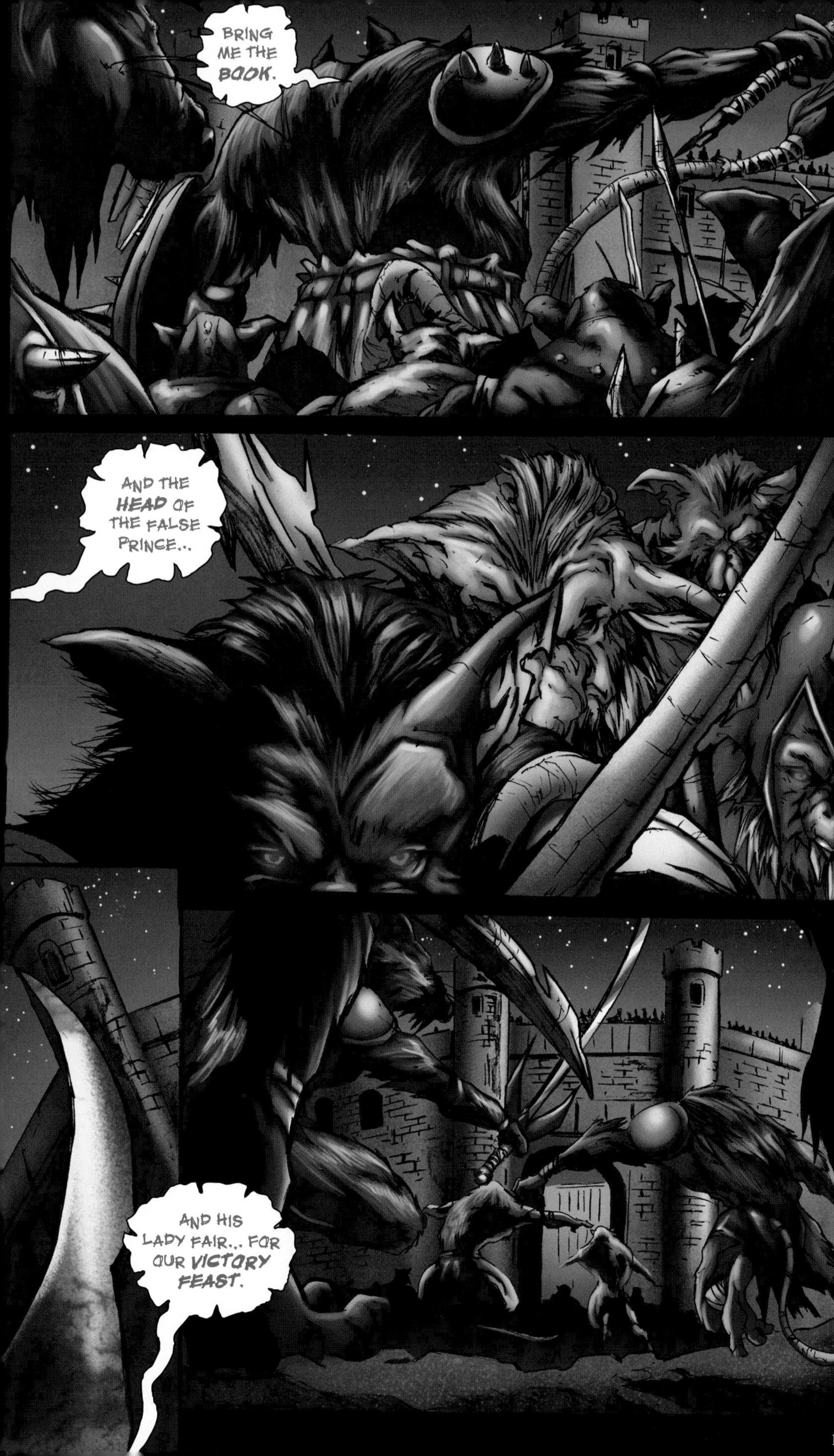
BRING ME THE BOOK.
AND THE HEAD OF THE FALSE PRINCE...
AND HIS LADY FAIR... FOR OUR VICTORY FEAST.

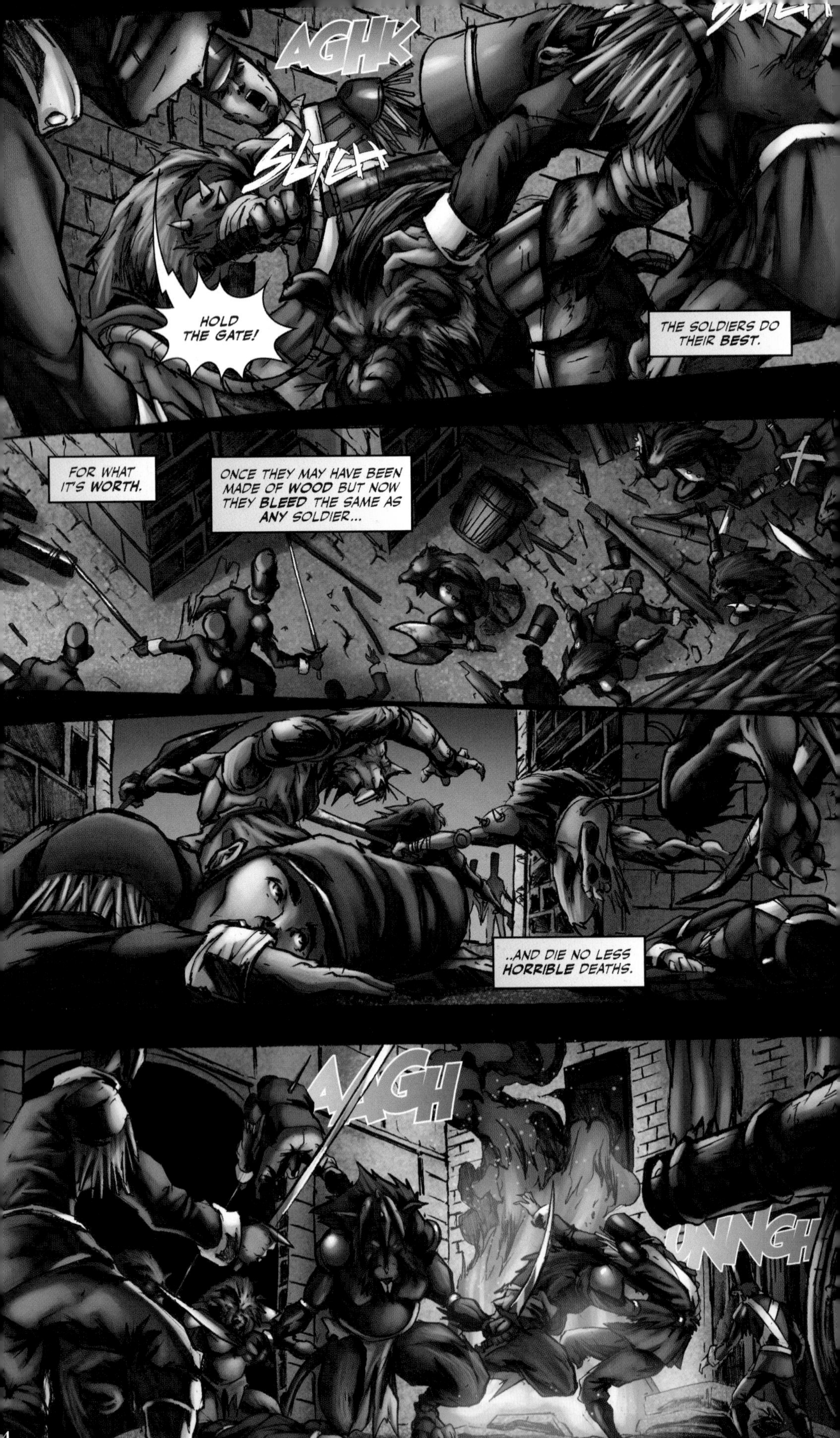
AGHK
SLTCH
HOLD THE GATE!
THE SOLDIERS DO THEIR BEST.
FOR WHAT IT'S WORTH.
ONCE THEY MAY HAVE BEEN MADE OF WOOD BUT NOW THEY BLEED THE SAME AS ANY SOLDIER...
..AND DIE NO LESS HORRIBLE DEATHS.
AAGH
UNNGH

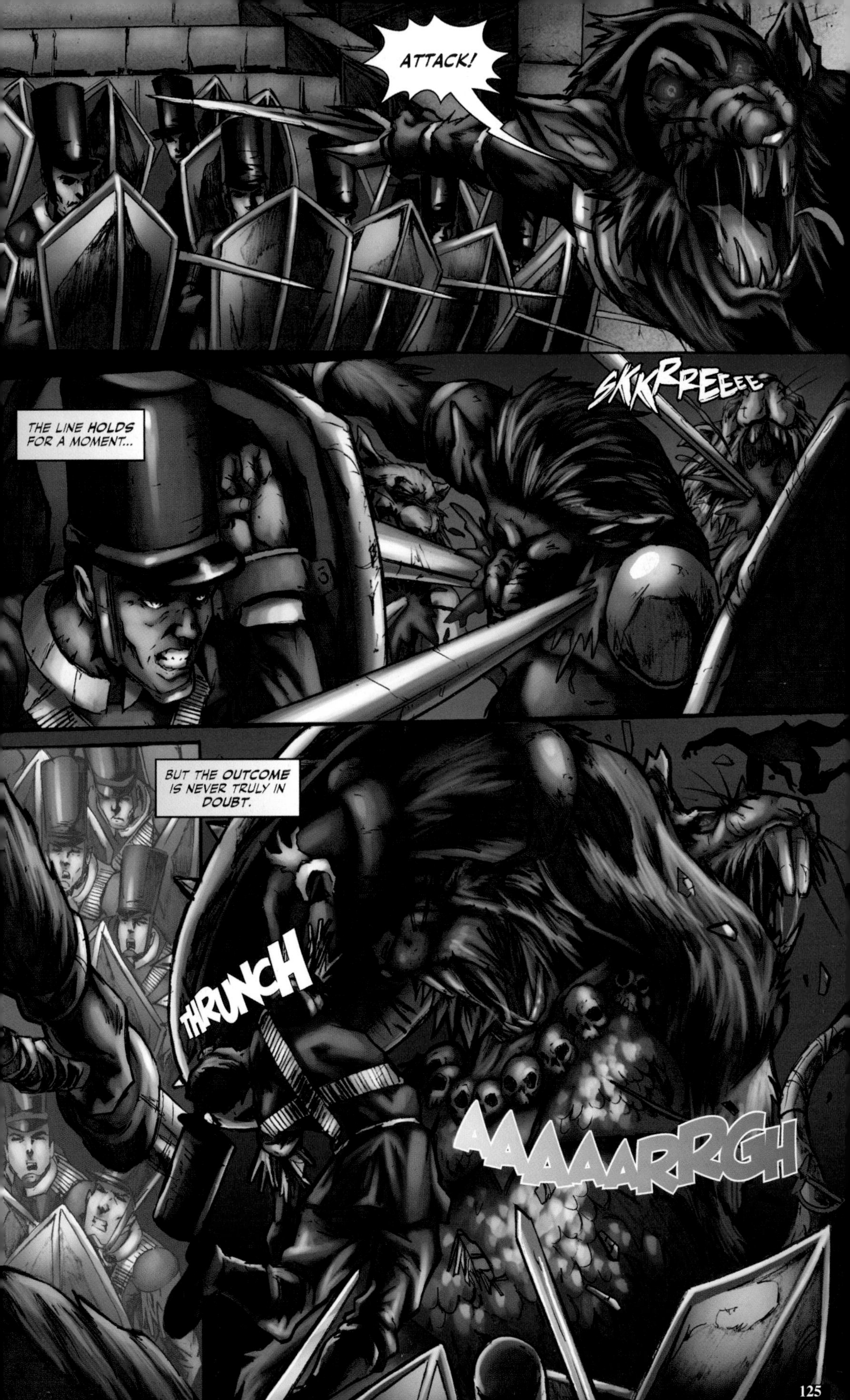
ATTACK!
SKKRREEEEE
THE LINE HOLDS FOR A MOMENT...
BUT THE OUTCOME IS NEVER TRULY IN DOUBT.
THRUNCH
AAAAAARRGH

THINGS DO NOT GO MUCH BETTER ON THE SECOND LEVEL.

BUT EVEN AS HOPE FADES...

SKLTCH

COURAGE REMAINS.

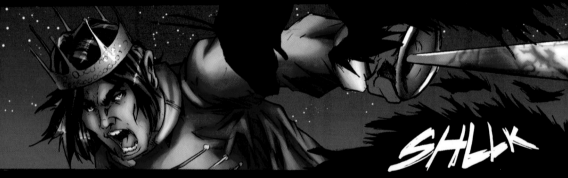

SHLLK

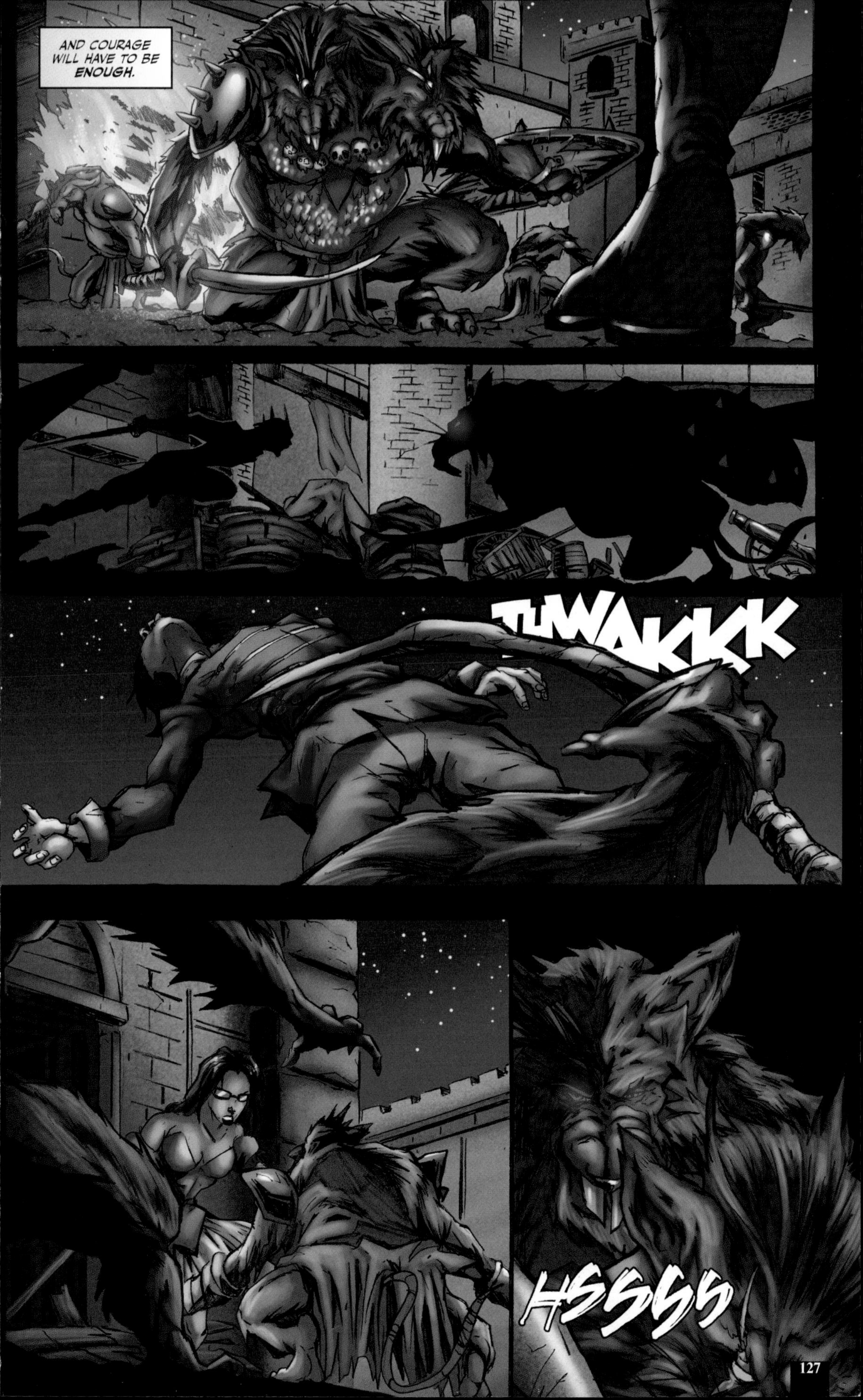
AND COURAGE WILL HAVE TO BE ENOUGH.
TWAKKK
HSSSS

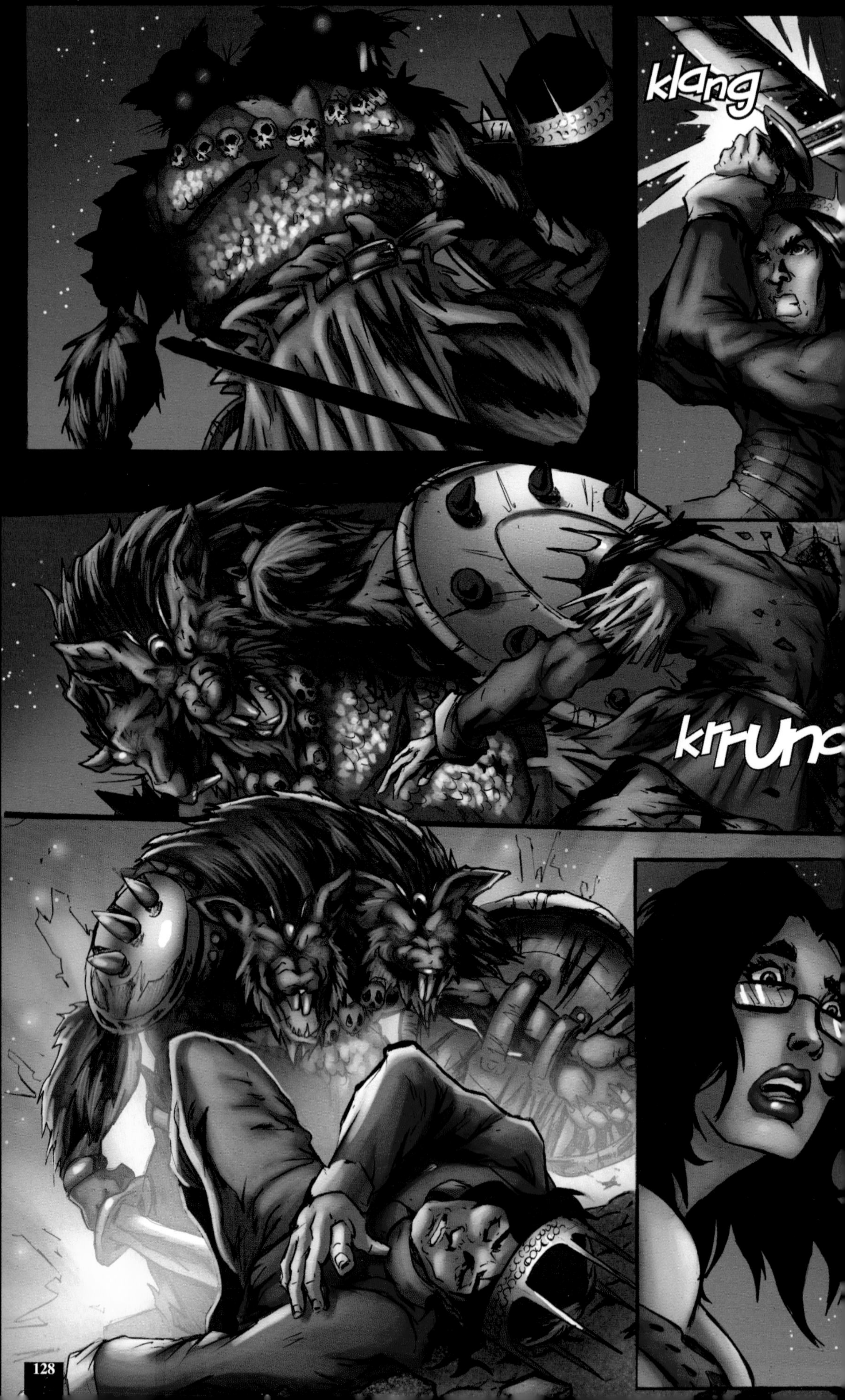
klang
krrunc

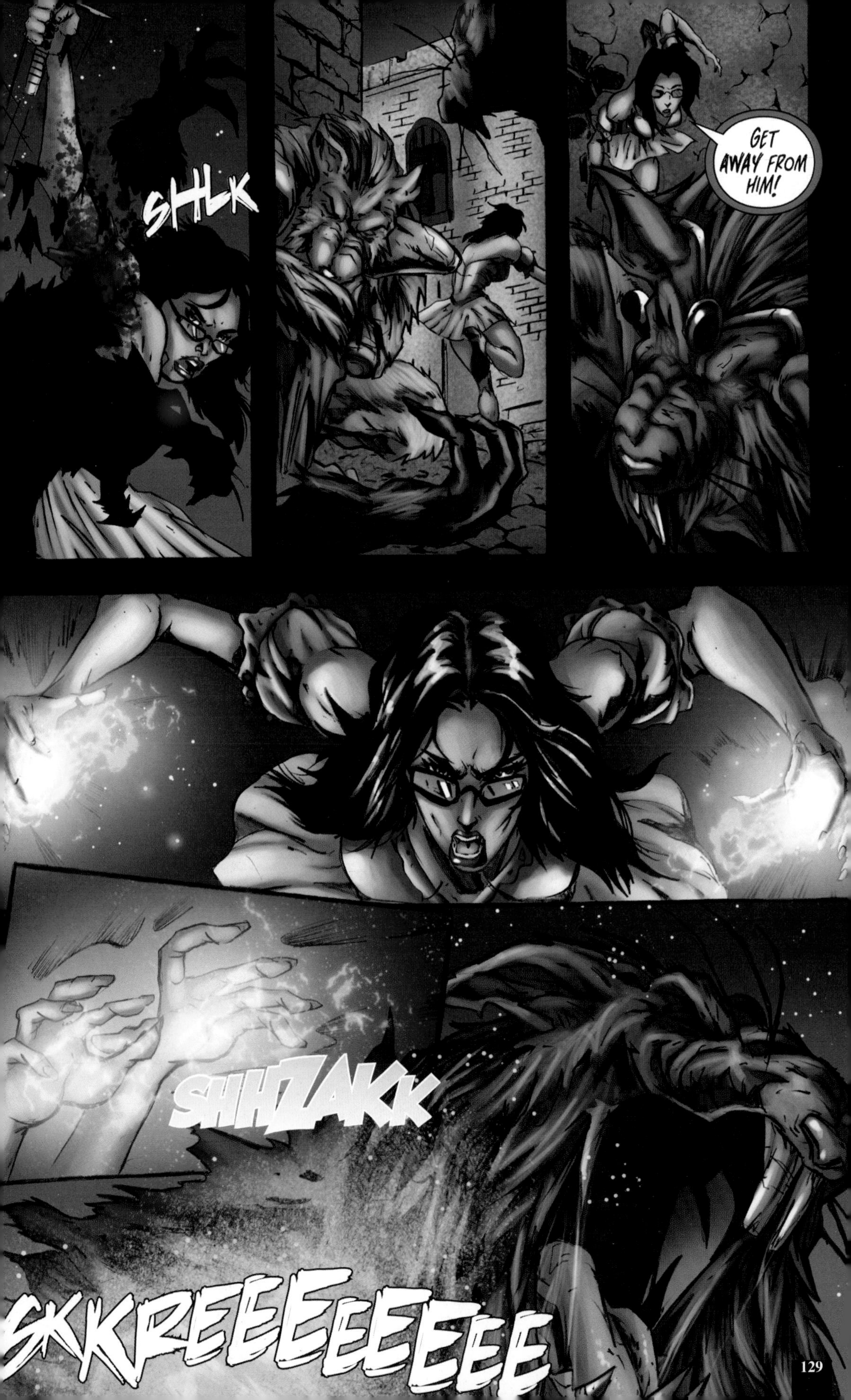
SHLK
GET AWAY FROM HIM!
SHHZAKK
SKREEEEEEEEE

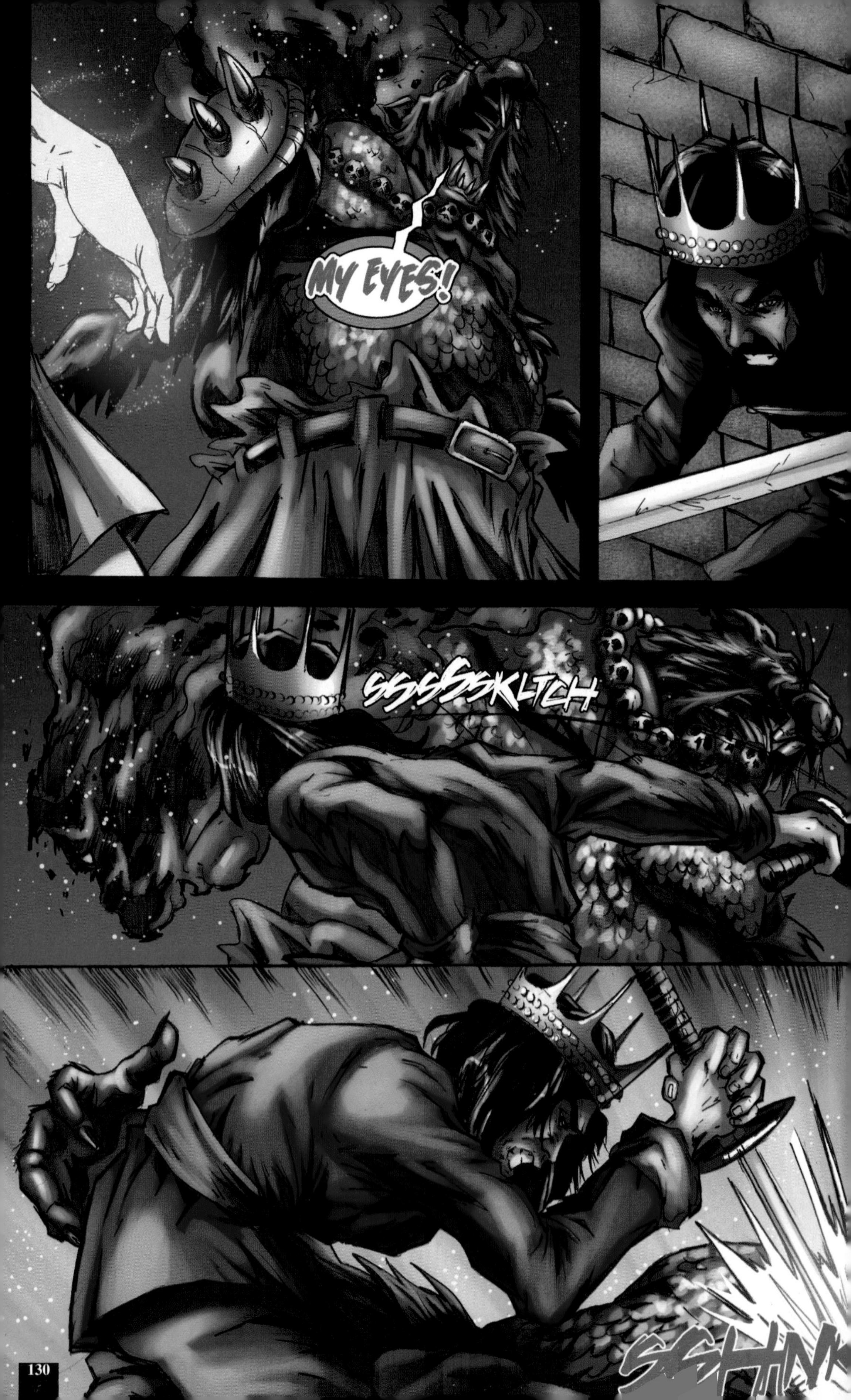
MY EYES!
SSSSSSKLTCH
SCHNK

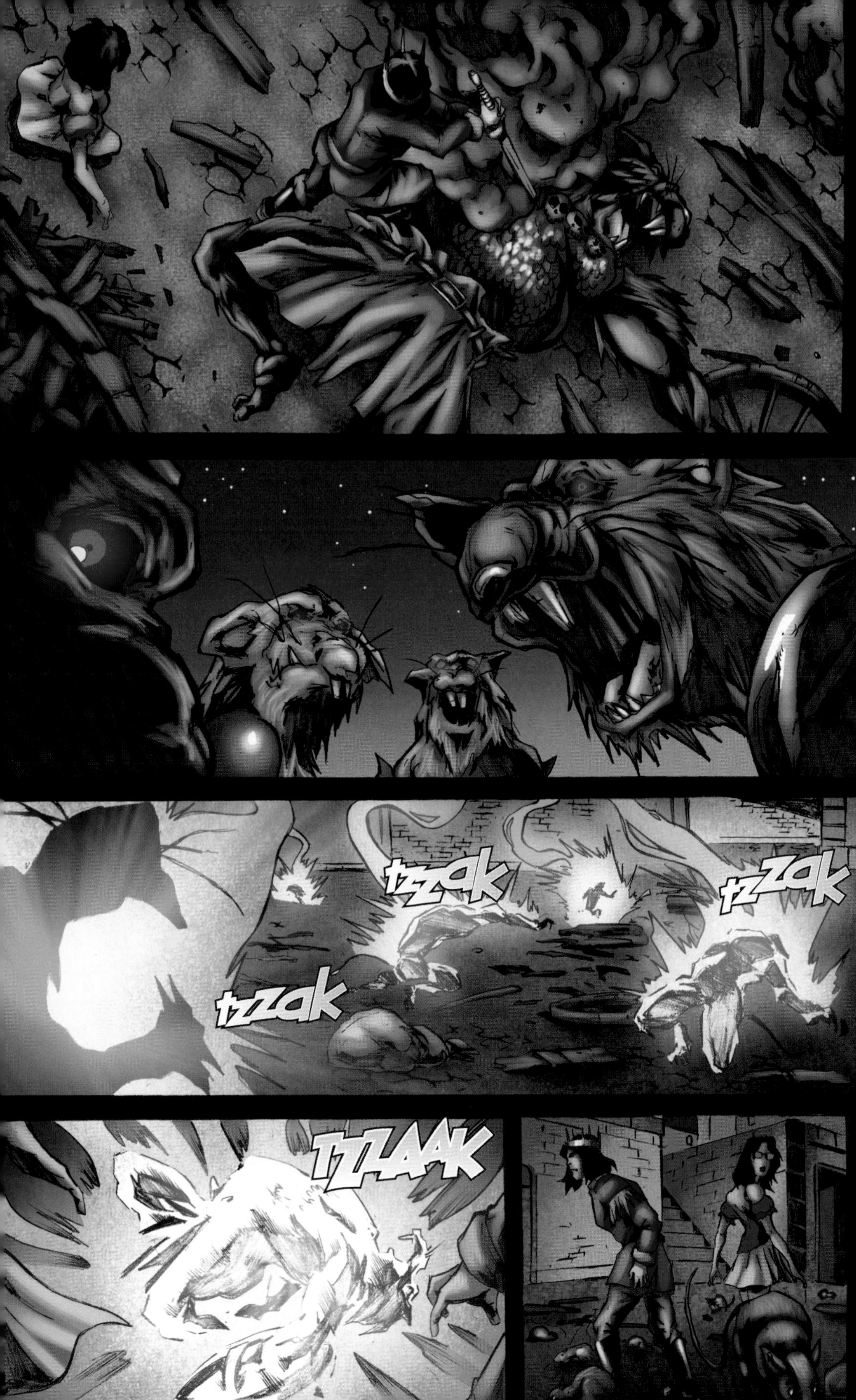
tzzak
tzzak
tzzak
TZZAAK

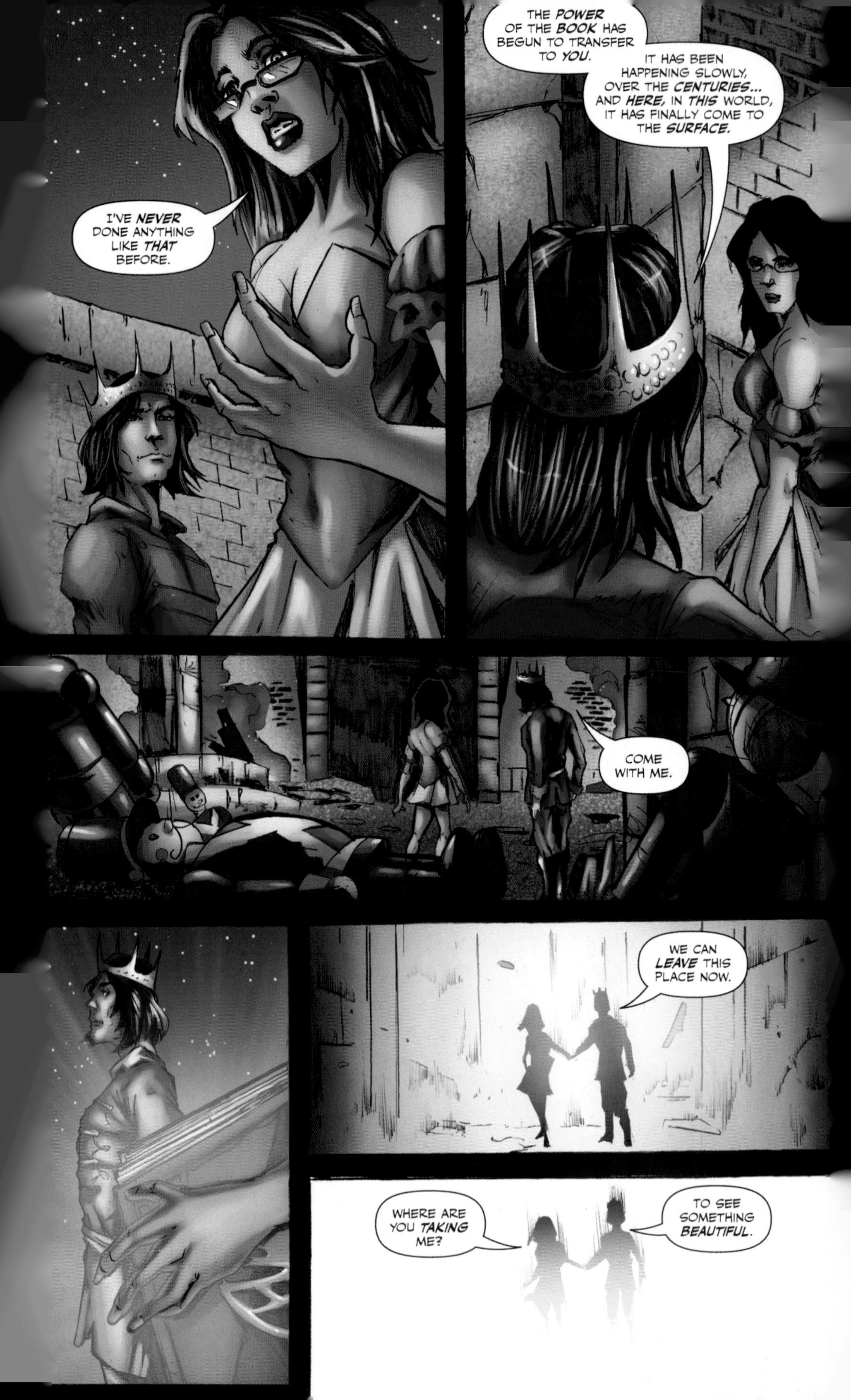
I'VE NEVER DONE ANYTHING LIKE THAT BEFORE.
THE POWER OF THE BOOK HAS BEGUN TO TRANSFER TO YOU.
IT HAS BEEN HAPPENING SLOWLY, OVER THE CENTURIES... AND HERE, IN THIS WORLD, IT HAS FINALLY COME TO THE SURFACE.
COME WITH ME.
WE CAN LEAVE THIS PLACE NOW.
WHERE ARE YOU TAKING ME?
TO SEE SOMETHING BEAUTIFUL.

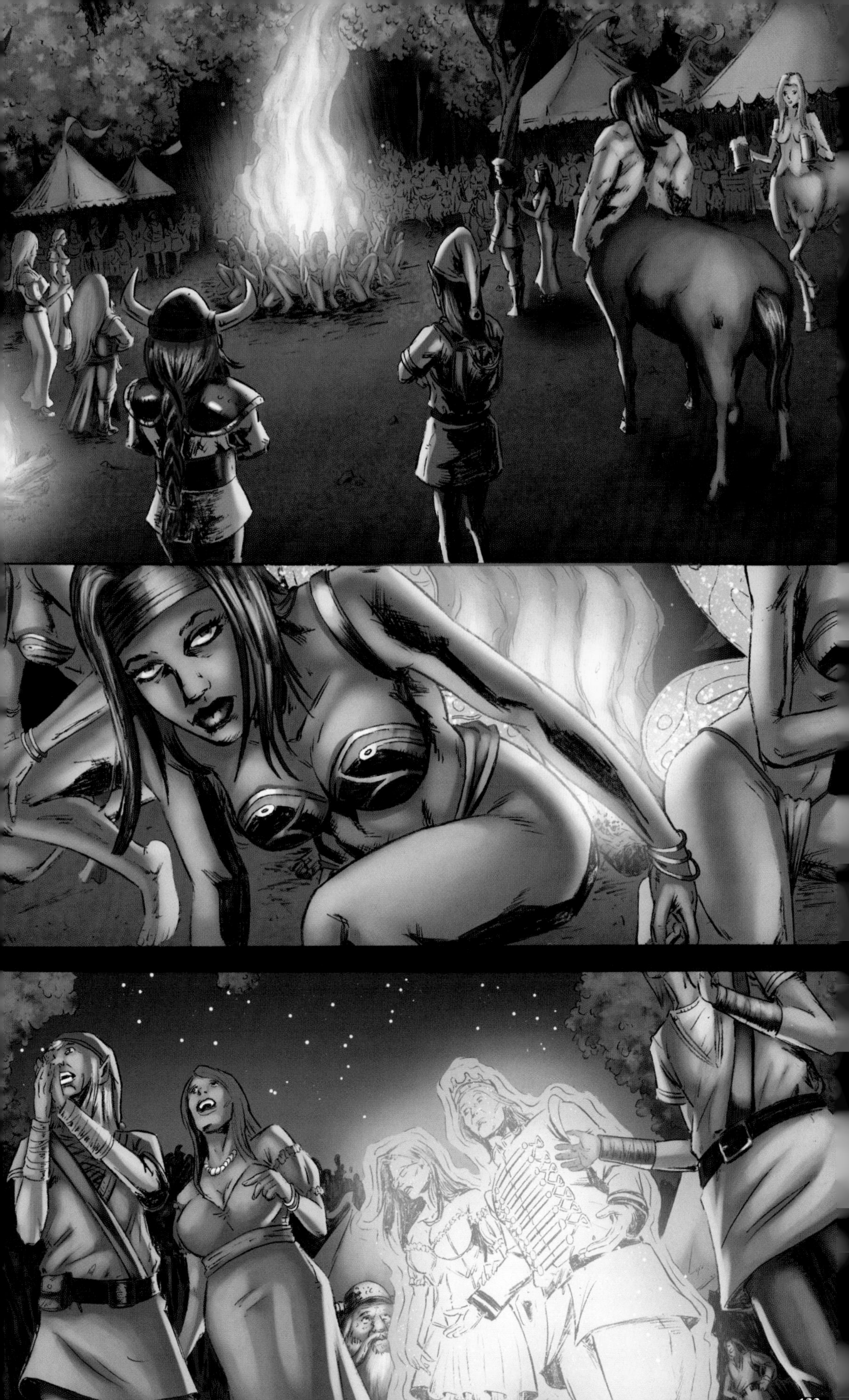

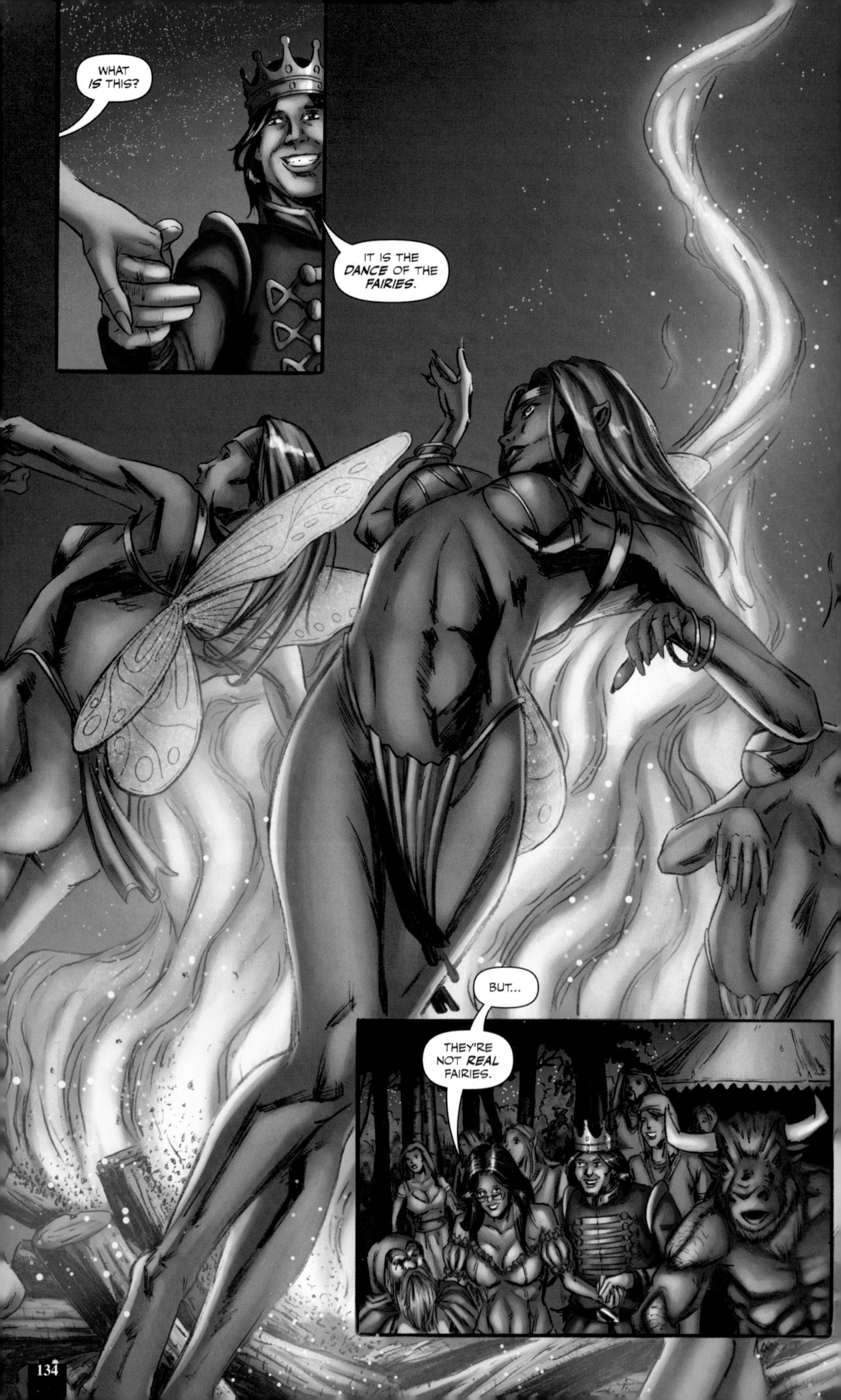
WHAT *IS* THIS?
IT IS THE *DANCE* OF THE *FAIRIES*.
BUT...
THEY'RE NOT *REAL* FAIRIES.

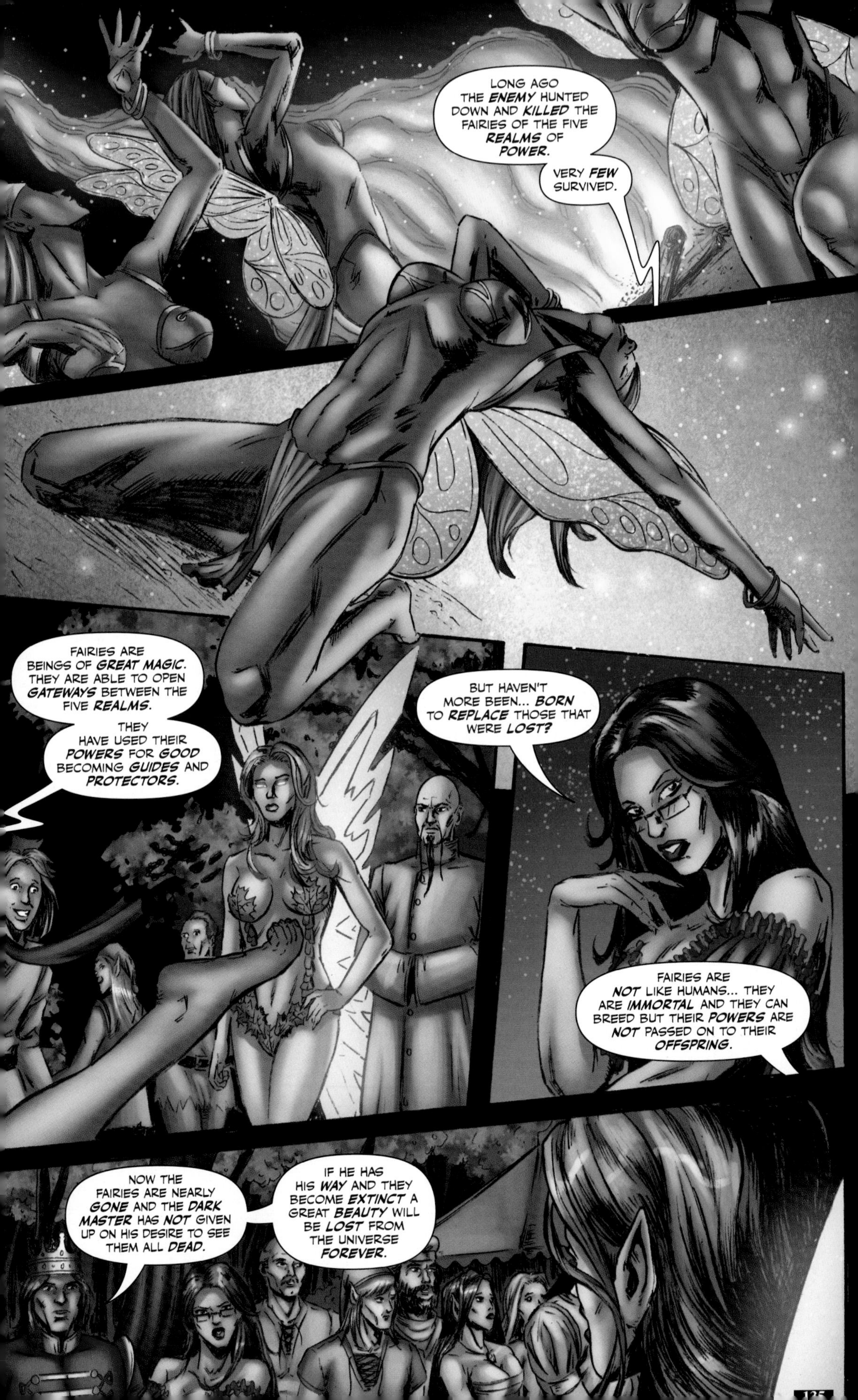
LONG AGO THE ENEMY HUNTED DOWN AND KILLED THE FAIRIES OF THE FIVE REALMS OF POWER.
VERY FEW SURVIVED.
FAIRIES ARE BEINGS OF GREAT MAGIC. THEY ARE ABLE TO OPEN GATEWAYS BETWEEN THE FIVE REALMS.
THEY HAVE USED THEIR POWERS FOR GOOD BECOMING GUIDES AND PROTECTORS.
BUT HAVEN'T MORE BEEN... BORN TO REPLACE THOSE THAT WERE LOST?
FAIRIES ARE NOT LIKE HUMANS... THEY ARE IMMORTAL AND THEY CAN BREED BUT THEIR POWERS ARE NOT PASSED ON TO THEIR OFFSPRING.
NOW THE FAIRIES ARE NEARLY GONE AND THE DARK MASTER HAS NOT GIVEN UP ON HIS DESIRE TO SEE THEM ALL DEAD.
IF HE HAS HIS WAY AND THEY BECOME EXTINCT A GREAT BEAUTY WILL BE LOST FROM THE UNIVERSE FOREVER.

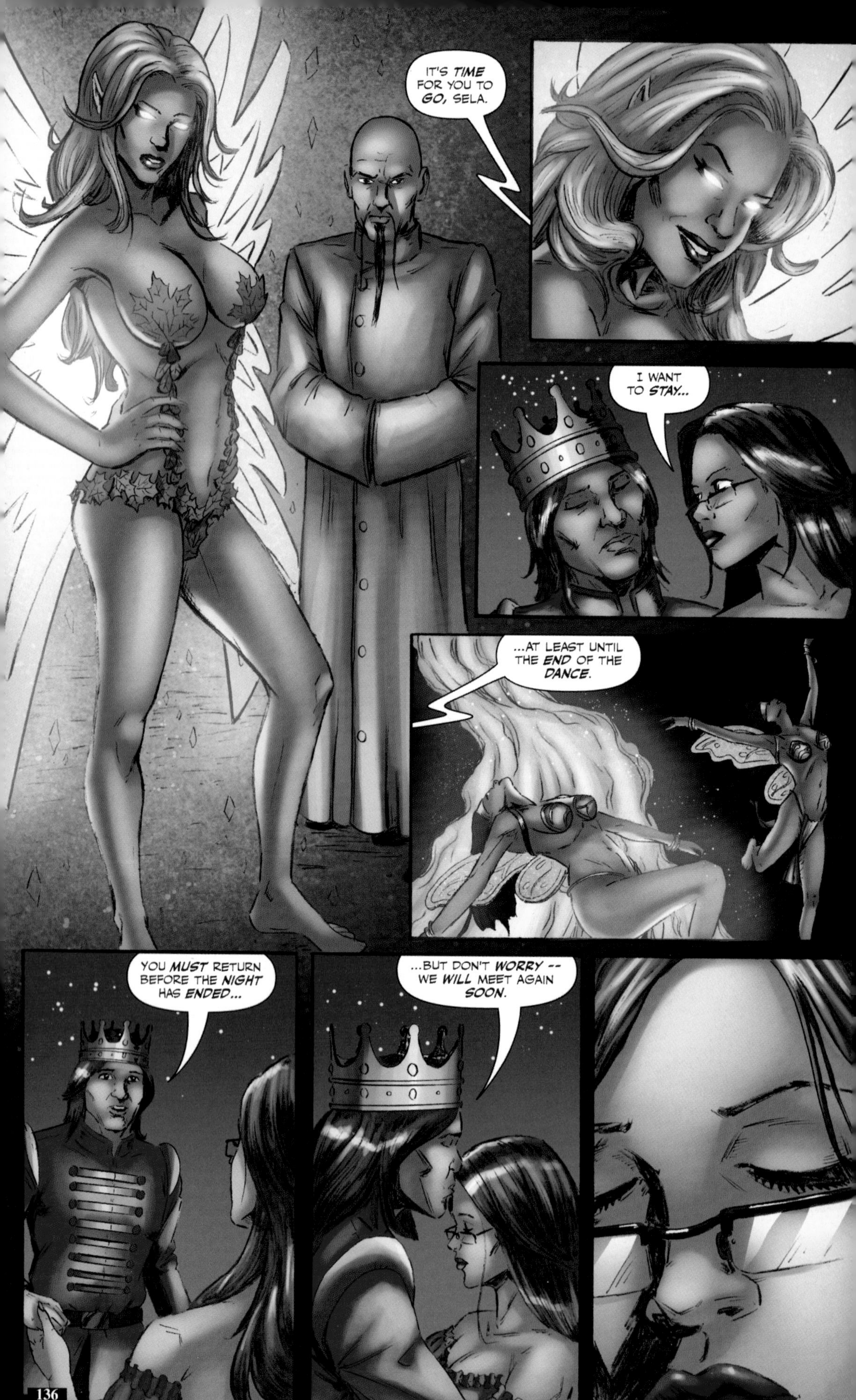
IT'S TIME FOR YOU TO GO, SELA.
I WANT TO STAY...
...AT LEAST UNTIL THE END OF THE DANCE.
YOU MUST RETURN BEFORE THE NIGHT HAS ENDED...
...BUT DON'T WORRY -- WE WILL MEET AGAIN SOON.

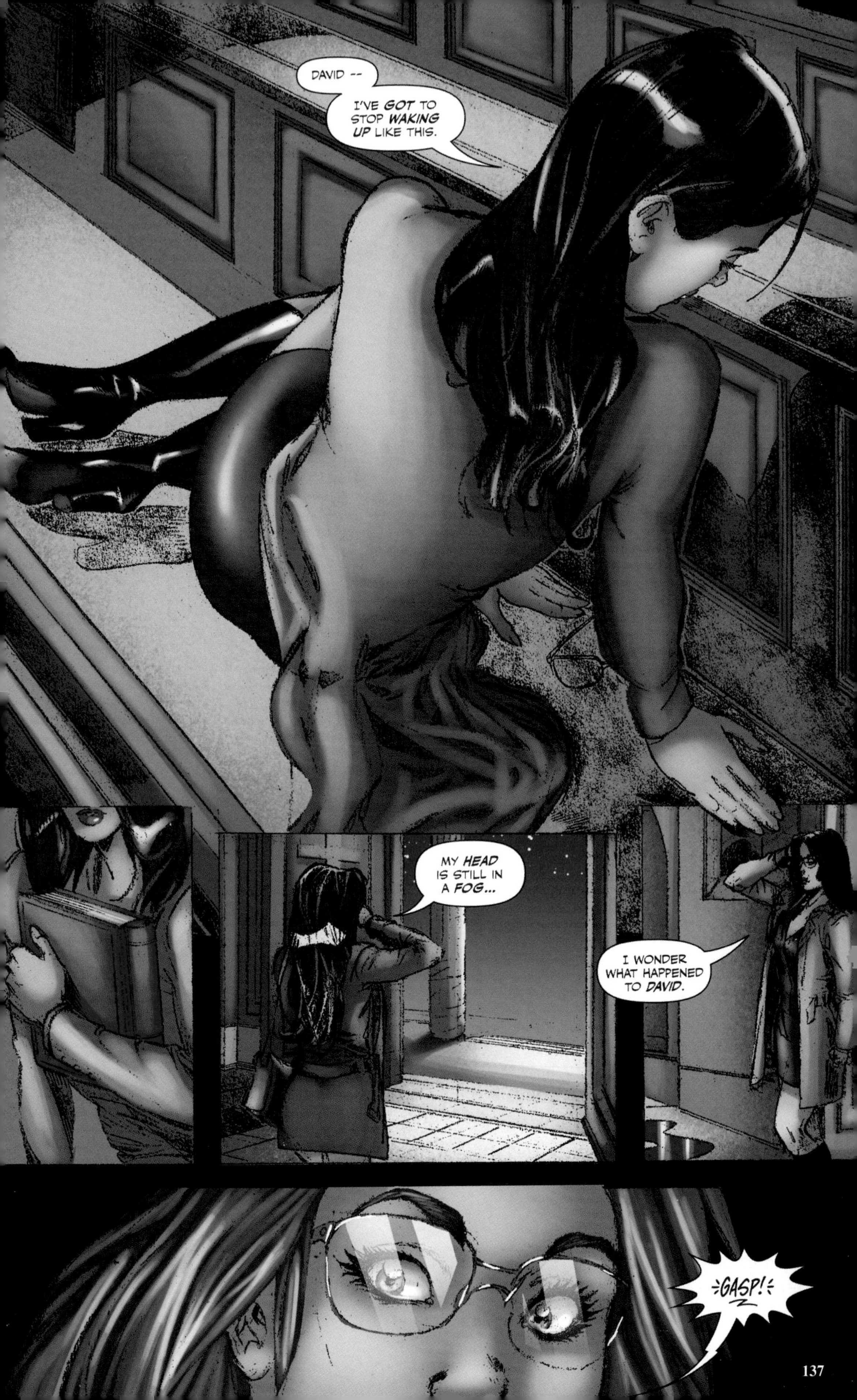
DAVID --
I'VE GOT TO STOP WAKING UP LIKE THIS.
MY HEAD IS STILL IN A FOG...
I WONDER WHAT HAPPENED TO DAVID.
GASP!

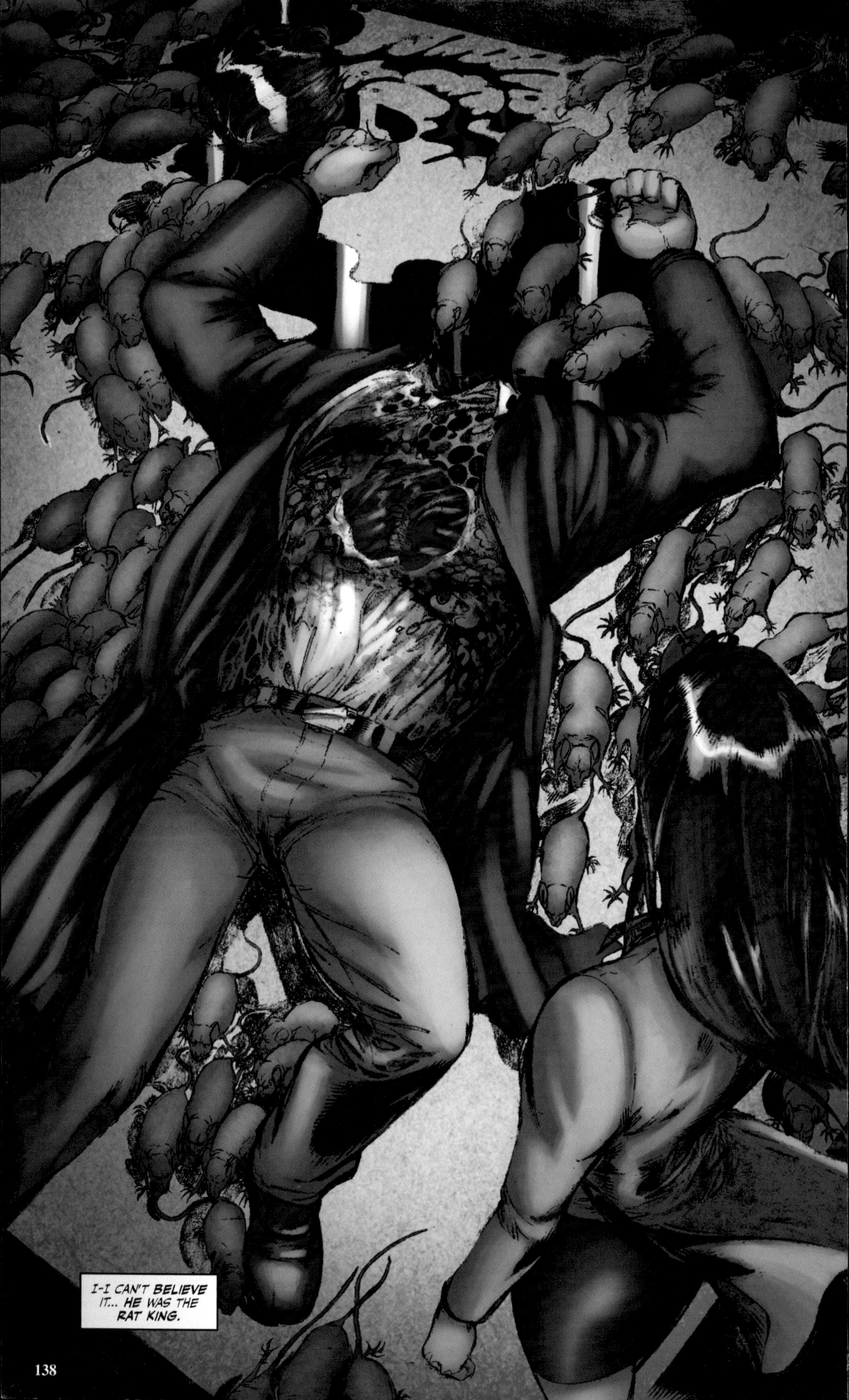
I-I CAN'T BELIEVE IT... HE WAS THE RAT KING.

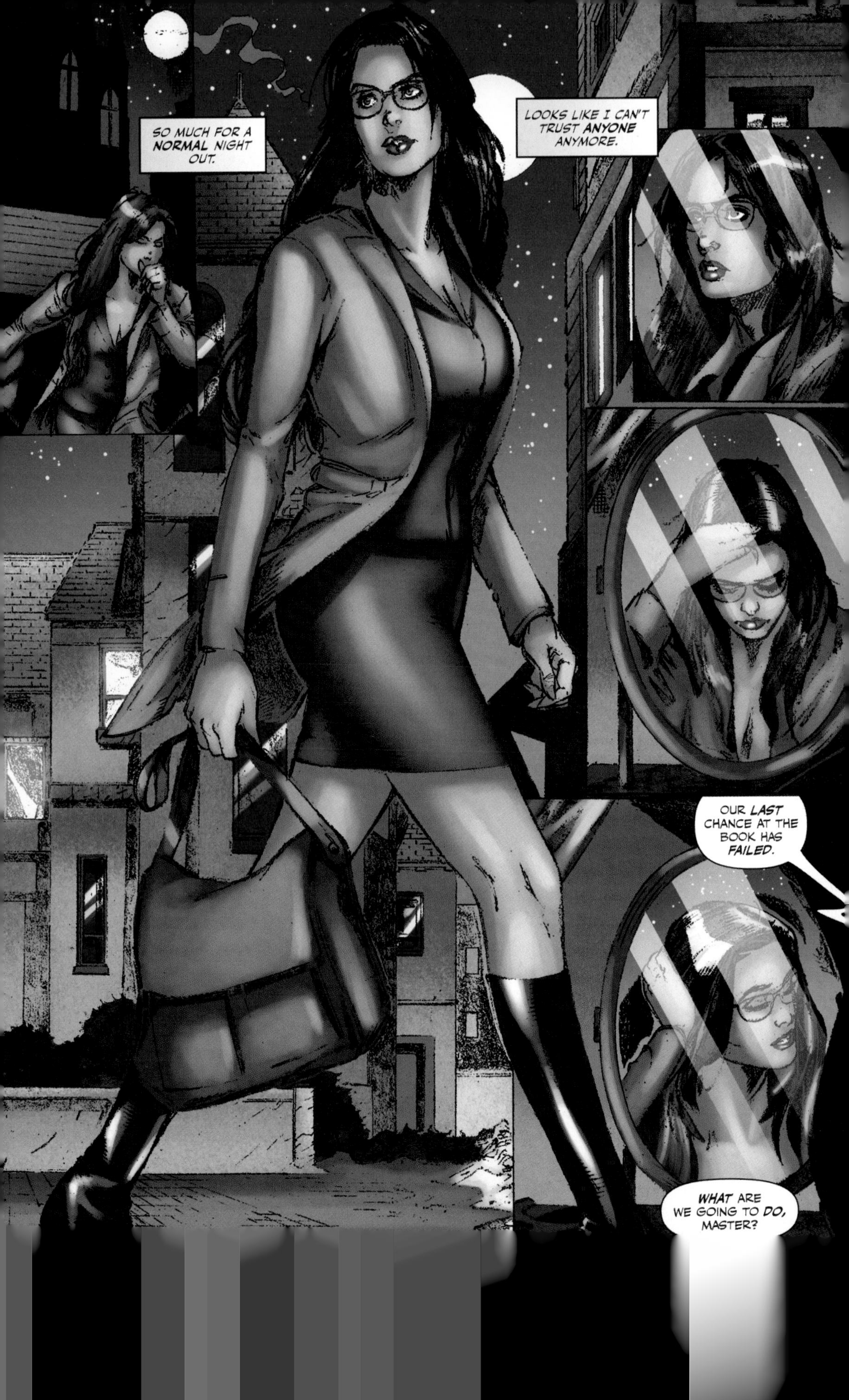
SO MUCH FOR A NORMAL NIGHT OUT.
LOOKS LIKE I CAN'T TRUST ANYONE ANYMORE.
OUR LAST CHANCE AT THE BOOK HAS FAILED.
WHAT ARE WE GOING TO DO, MASTER?

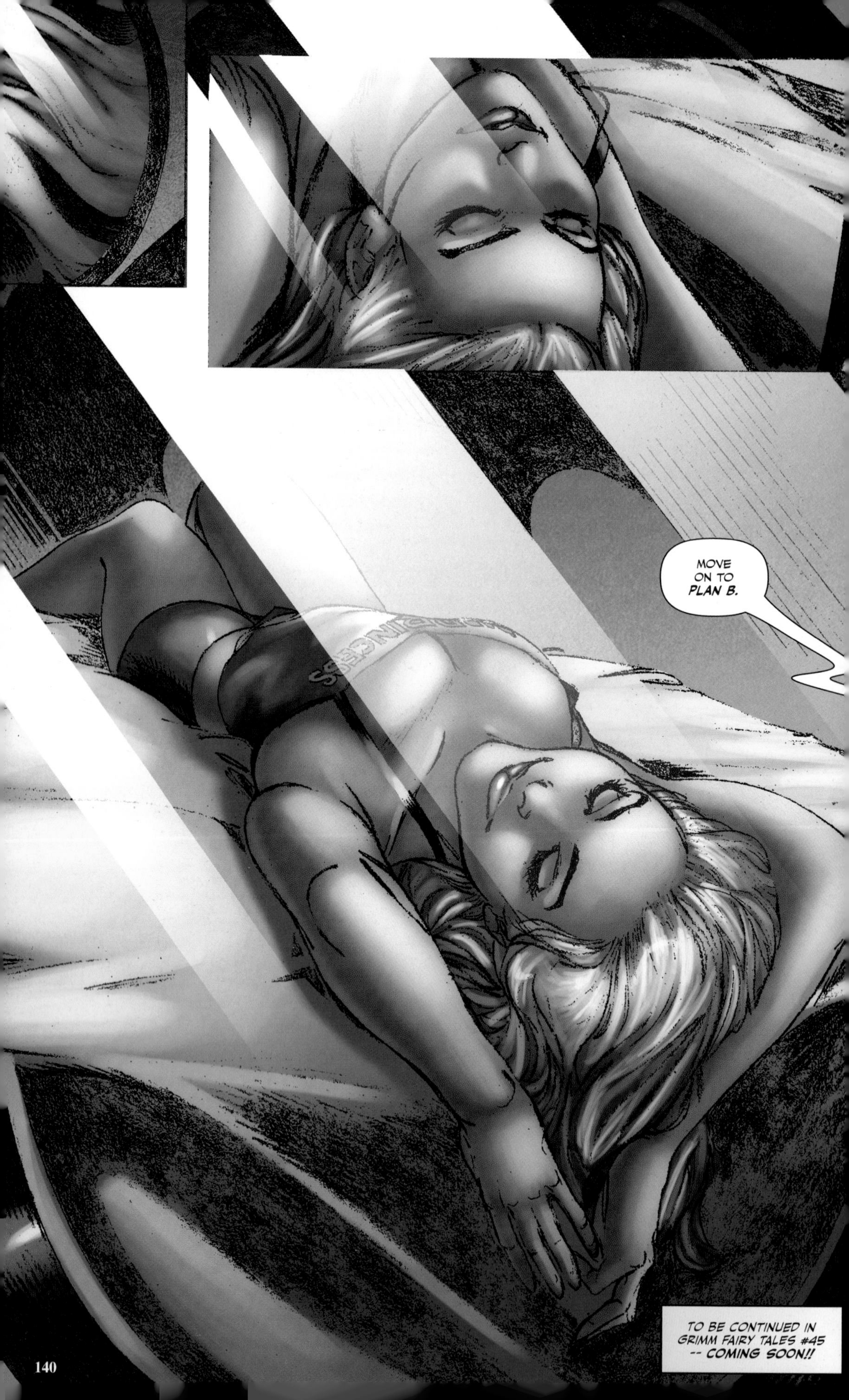
MOVE ON TO PLAN B.
TO BE CONTINUED IN GRIMM FAIRY TALES #45 -- COMING SOON!!

Grimm Fairy Tales

Different Seasons

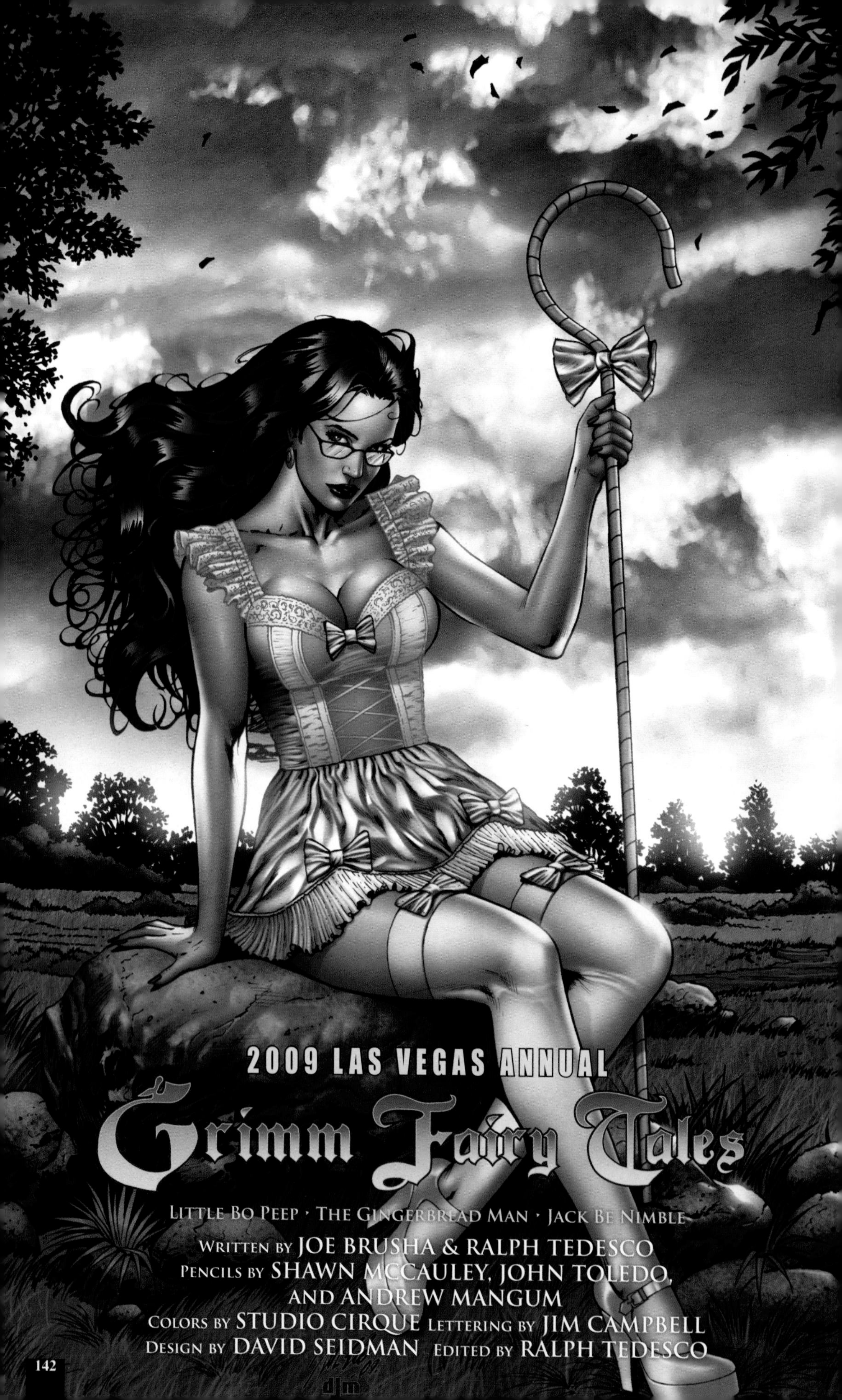
2009 LAS VEGAS ANNUAL
Grimm Fairy Tales
Little Bo Peep · The Gingerbread Man · Jack Be Nimble
Written by JOE BRUSHA & RALPH TEDESCO
Pencils by SHAWN MCCAULEY, JOHN TOLEDO, AND ANDREW MANGUM
Colors by STUDIO CIRQUE Lettering by JIM CAMPBELL
Design by DAVID SEIDMAN Edited by RALPH TEDESCO

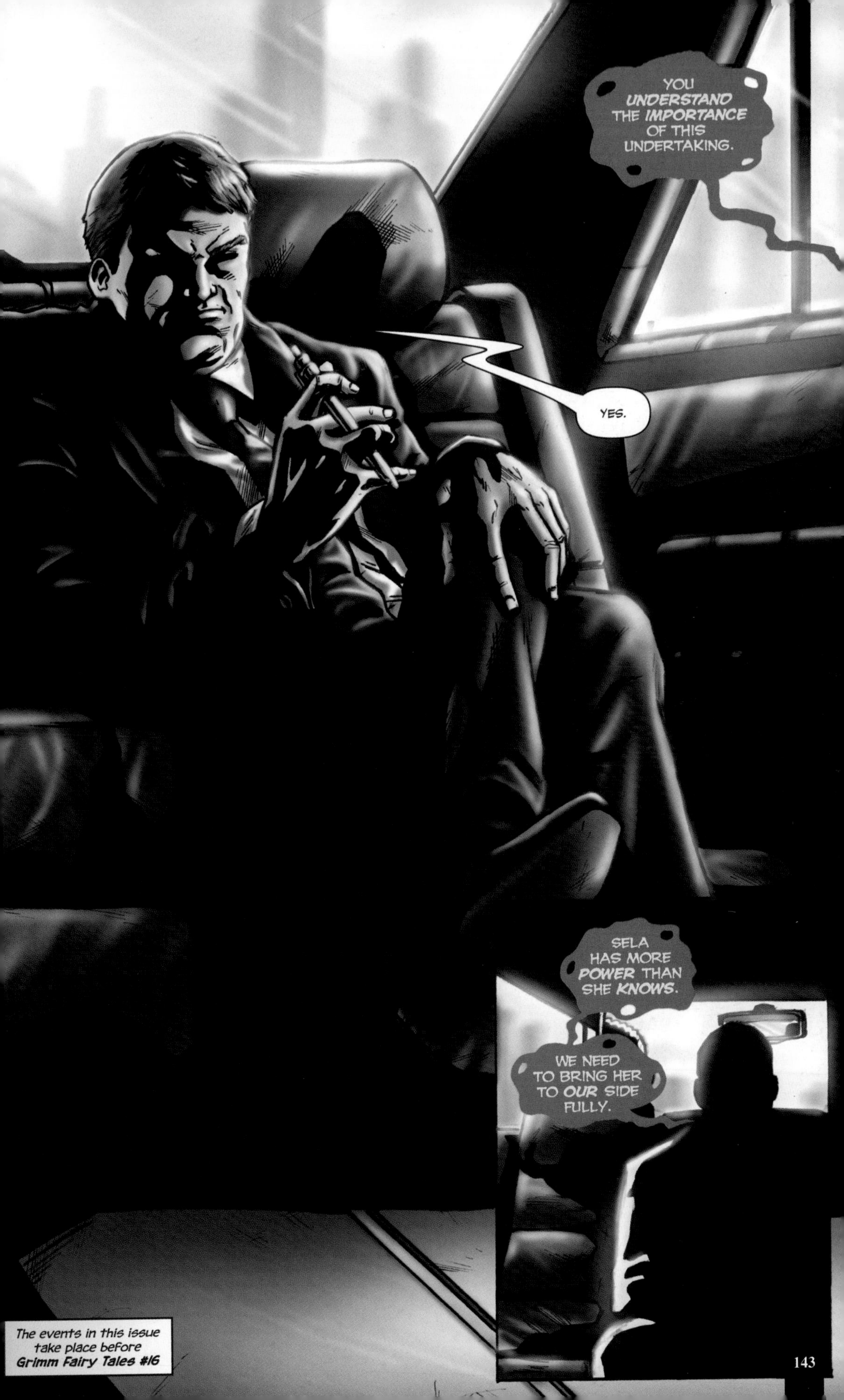

YOU UNDERSTAND THE IMPORTANCE OF THIS UNDERTAKING.
YES.
SELA HAS MORE POWER THAN SHE KNOWS.
WE NEED TO BRING HER TO OUR SIDE FULLY.
The events in this issue take place before Grimm Fairy Tales #16

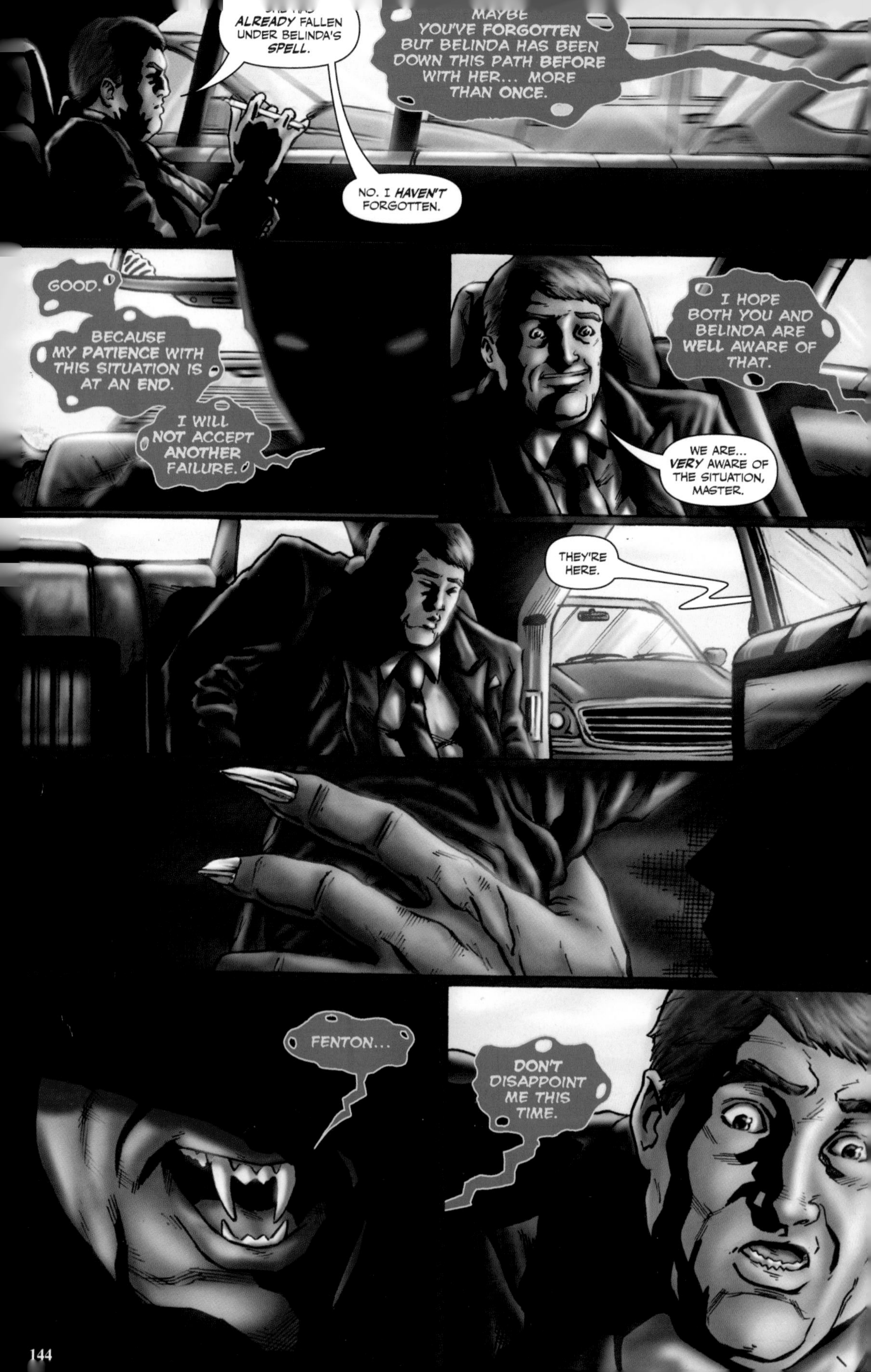
ALREADY FALLEN UNDER BELINDA'S SPELL.
MAYBE YOU'VE FORGOTTEN BUT BELINDA HAS BEEN DOWN THIS PATH BEFORE WITH HER... MORE THAN ONCE.
NO. I HAVEN'T FORGOTTEN.
GOOD.
BECAUSE MY PATIENCE WITH THIS SITUATION IS AT AN END.
I WILL NOT ACCEPT ANOTHER FAILURE.
I HOPE BOTH YOU AND BELINDA ARE WELL AWARE OF THAT.
WE ARE... VERY AWARE OF THE SITUATION, MASTER.
THEY'RE HERE.
FENTON...
DON'T DISAPPOINT ME THIS TIME.

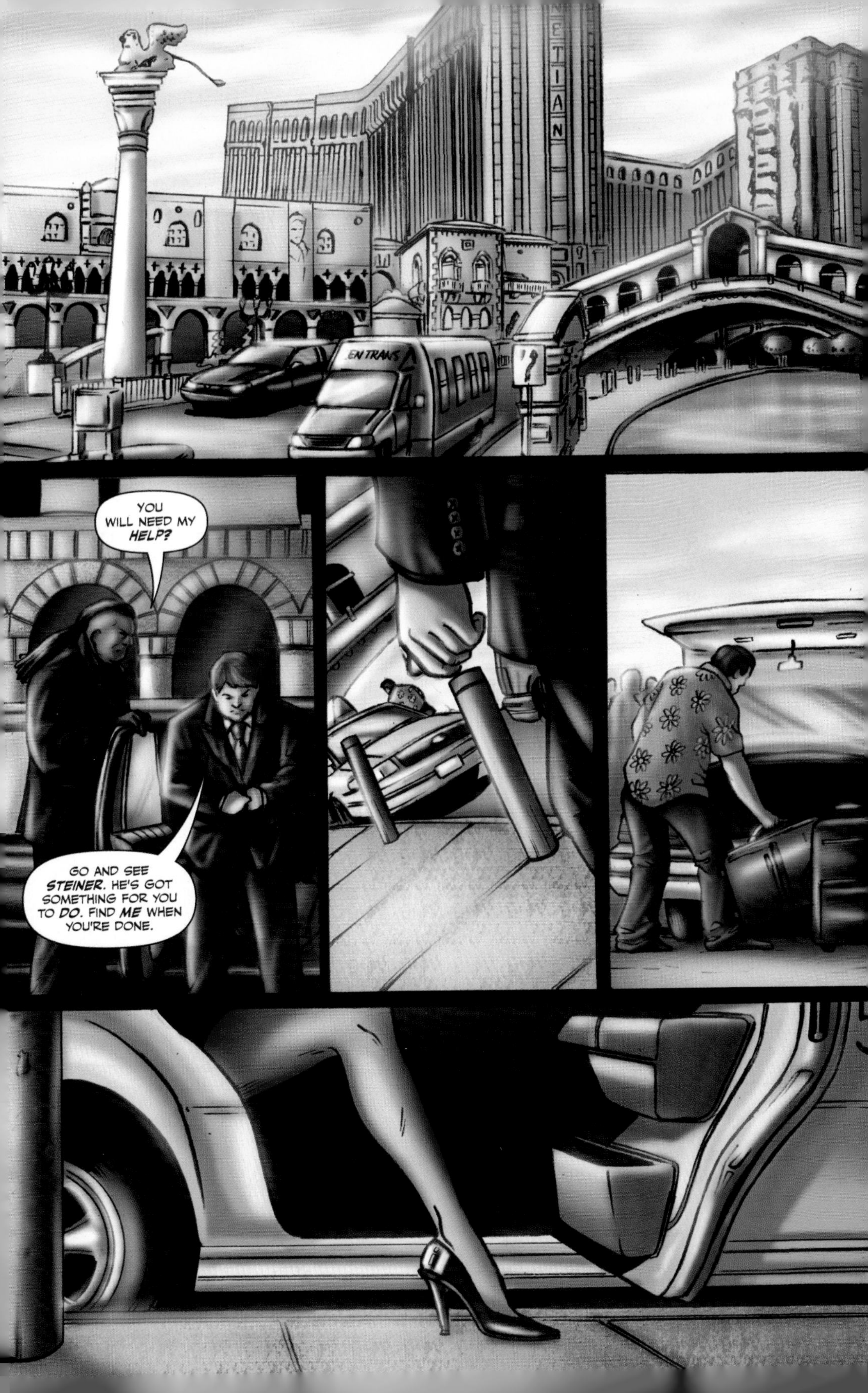

NETIAN
EN TRANS
YOU WILL NEED MY HELP?
GO AND SEE STEINER. HE'S GOT SOMETHING FOR YOU TO DO. FIND ME WHEN YOU'RE DONE.

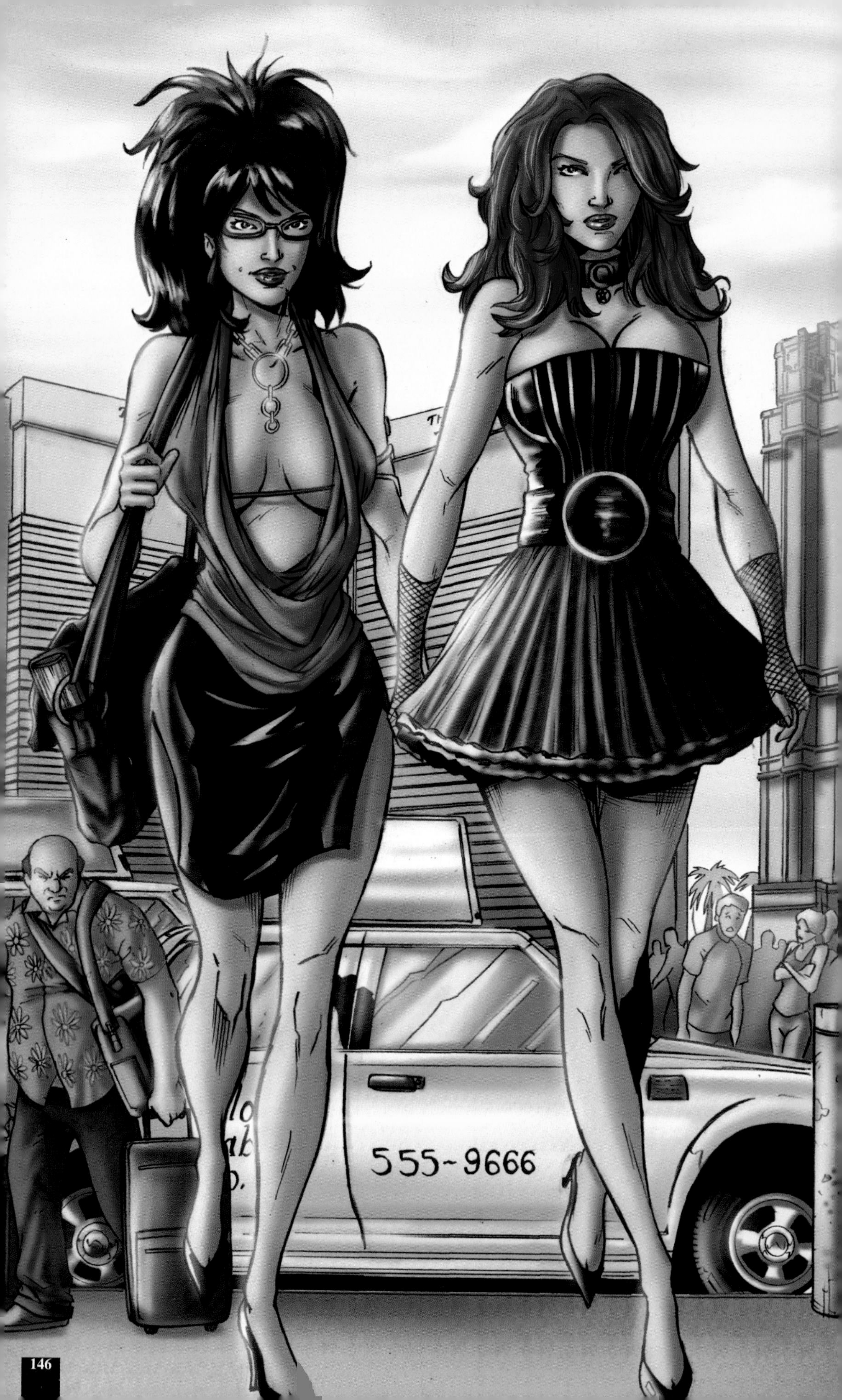
555-9666

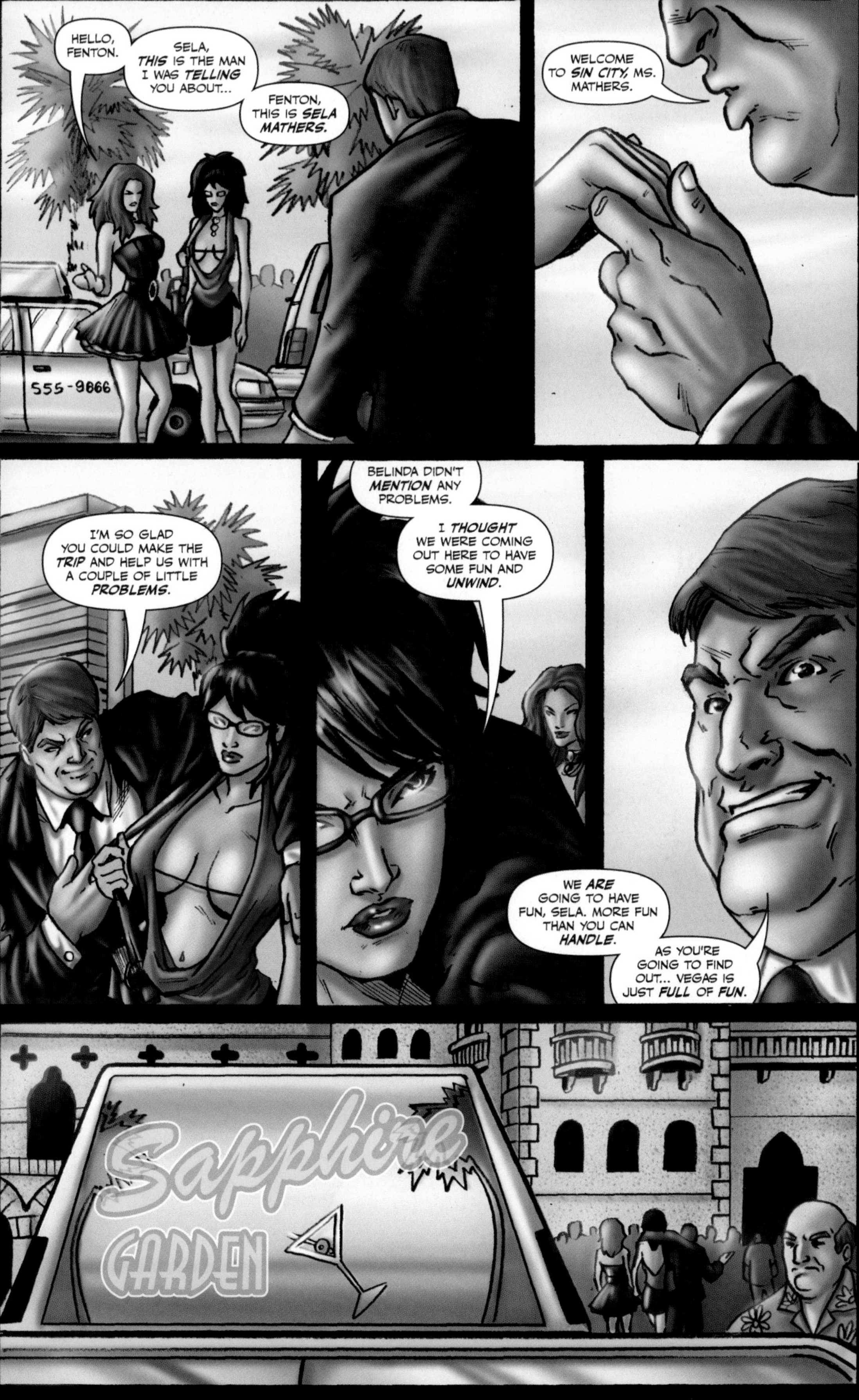
HELLO, FENTON.
SELA, *THIS* IS THE MAN I WAS *TELLING* YOU ABOUT...
FENTON, THIS IS *SELA MATHERS.*
555-9866
WELCOME TO *SIN CITY,* MS. MATHERS.
I'M SO GLAD YOU COULD MAKE THE *TRIP* AND HELP US WITH A COUPLE OF LITTLE *PROBLEMS*.
BELINDA DIDN'T *MENTION* ANY PROBLEMS.
I *THOUGHT* WE WERE COMING OUT HERE TO HAVE SOME FUN AND *UNWIND*.
WE *ARE* GOING TO HAVE FUN, SELA. MORE FUN THAN YOU CAN *HANDLE*.
AS YOU'RE GOING TO FIND OUT... VEGAS IS JUST *FULL* OF *FUN*.
Sapphire
GARDEN

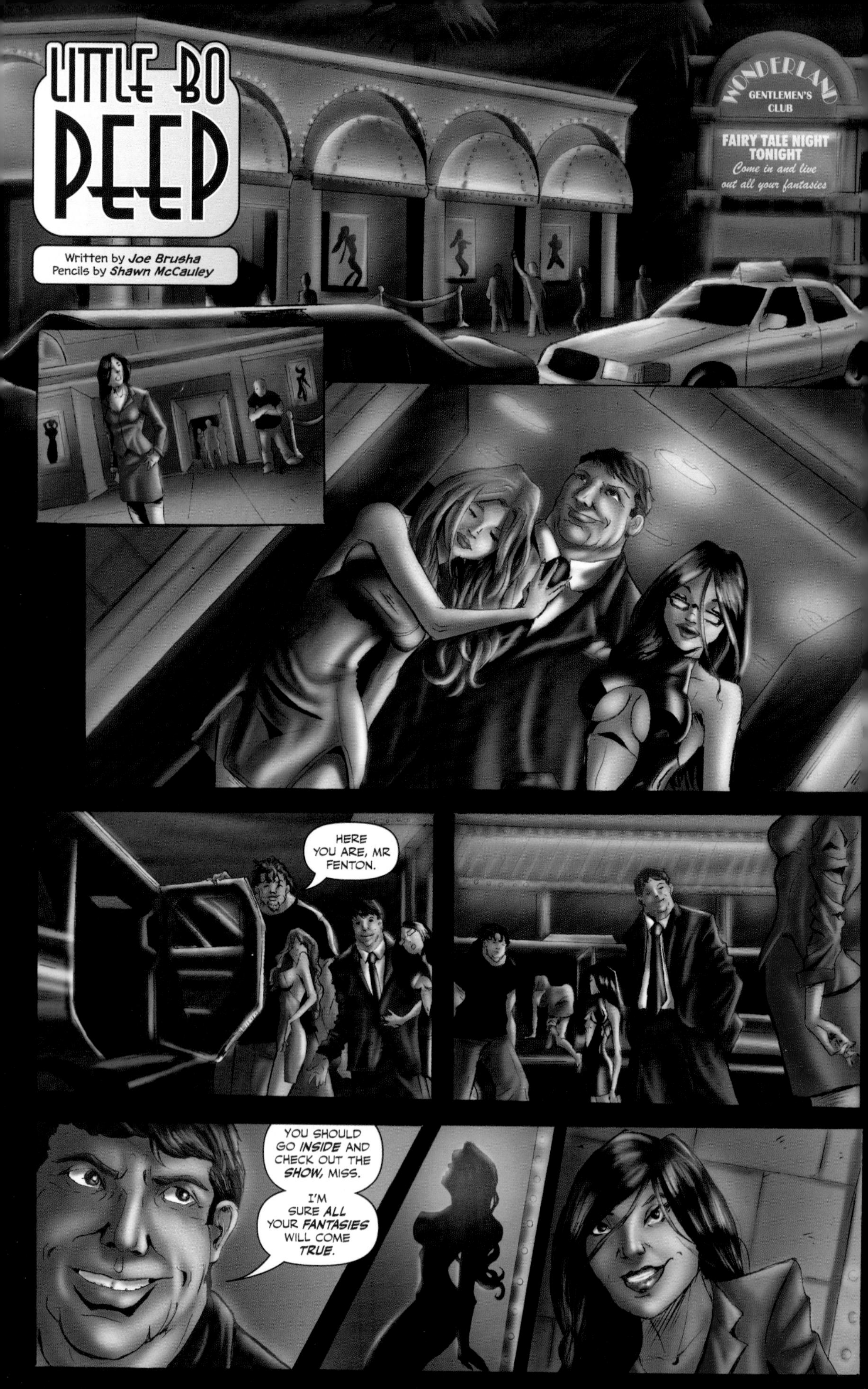

LITTLE BO PEEP
Written by Joe Brusha
Pencils by Shawn McCauley
WONDERLAND GENTLEMEN'S CLUB
FAIRY TALE NIGHT TONIGHT
Come in and live out all your fantasies
HERE YOU ARE, MR FENTON.
YOU SHOULD GO INSIDE AND CHECK OUT THE SHOW, MISS.
I'M SURE ALL YOUR FANTASIES WILL COME TRUE.

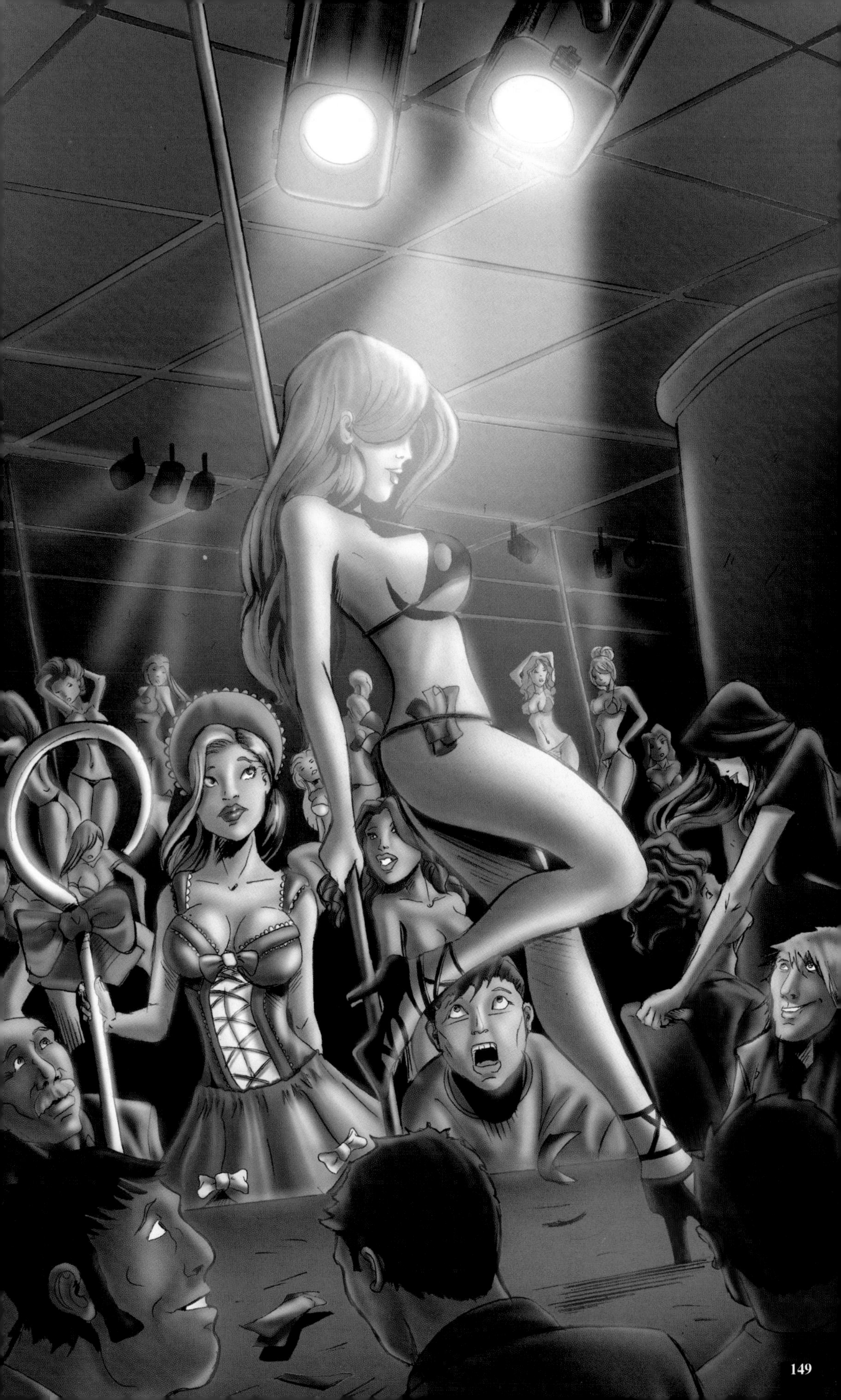

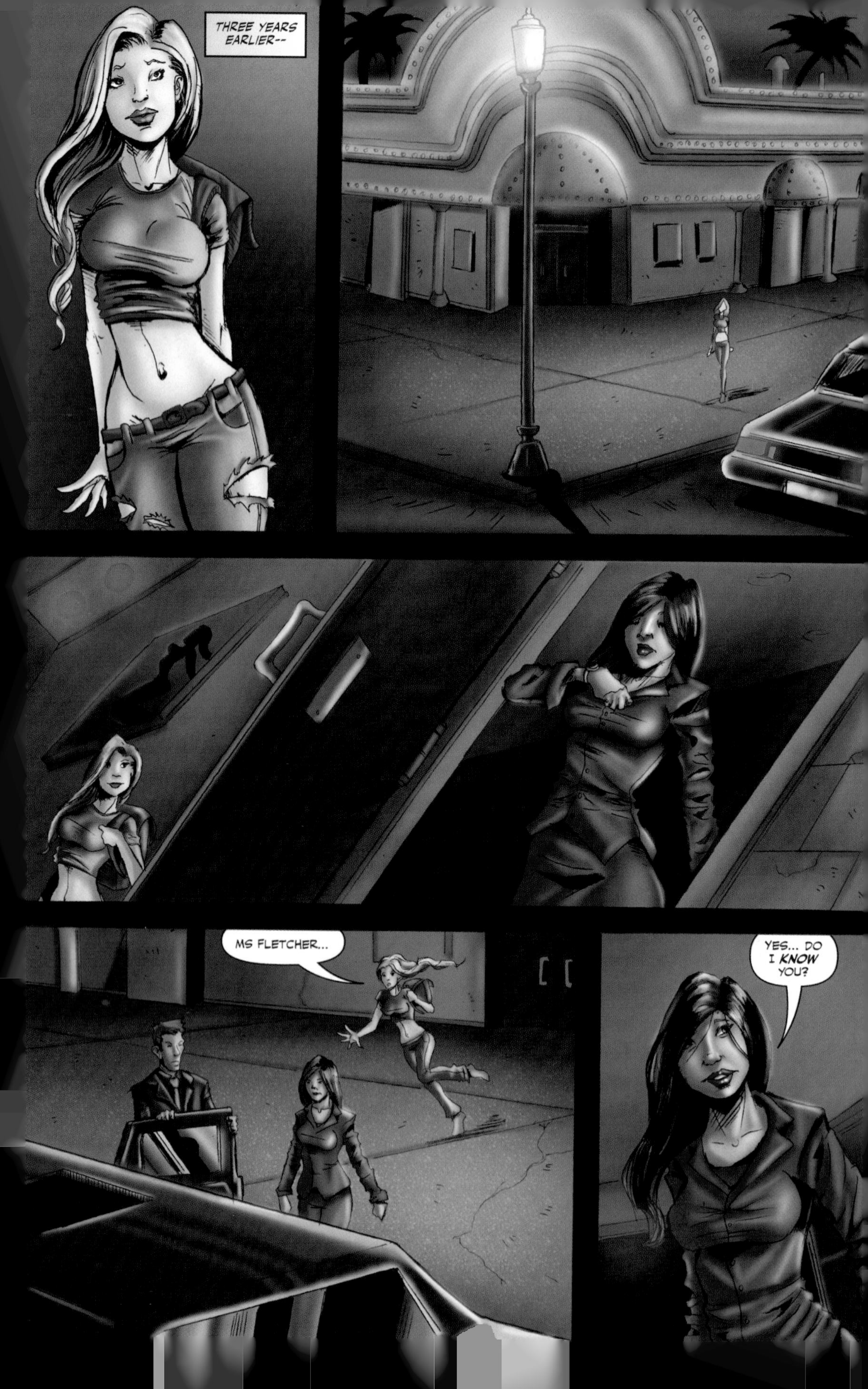
THREE YEARS EARLIER--
MS FLETCHER...
YES... DO I KNOW YOU?

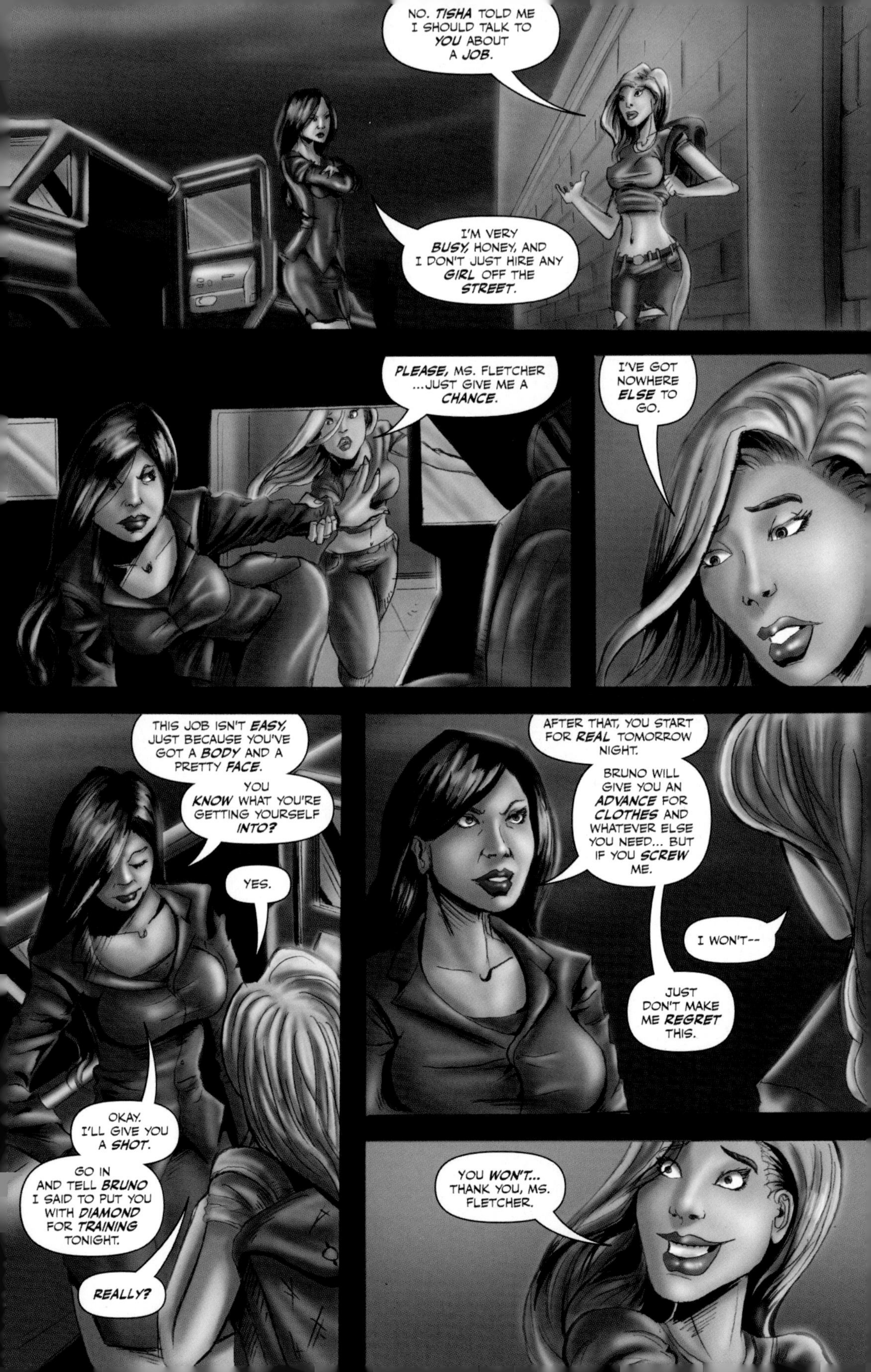
NO. TISHA TOLD ME I SHOULD TALK TO YOU ABOUT A JOB.
I'M VERY BUSY, HONEY, AND I DON'T JUST HIRE ANY GIRL OFF THE STREET.
PLEASE, MS. FLETCHER ...JUST GIVE ME A CHANCE.
I'VE GOT NOWHERE ELSE TO GO.
THIS JOB ISN'T EASY, JUST BECAUSE YOU'VE GOT A BODY AND A PRETTY FACE.
YOU KNOW WHAT YOU'RE GETTING YOURSELF INTO?
YES.
OKAY. I'LL GIVE YOU A SHOT.
GO IN AND TELL BRUNO I SAID TO PUT YOU WITH DIAMOND FOR TRAINING TONIGHT.
REALLY?
AFTER THAT, YOU START FOR REAL TOMORROW NIGHT.
BRUNO WILL GIVE YOU AN ADVANCE FOR CLOTHES AND WHATEVER ELSE YOU NEED... BUT IF YOU SCREW ME.
I WON'T--
JUST DON'T MAKE ME REGRET THIS.
YOU WON'T... THANK YOU, MS. FLETCHER.

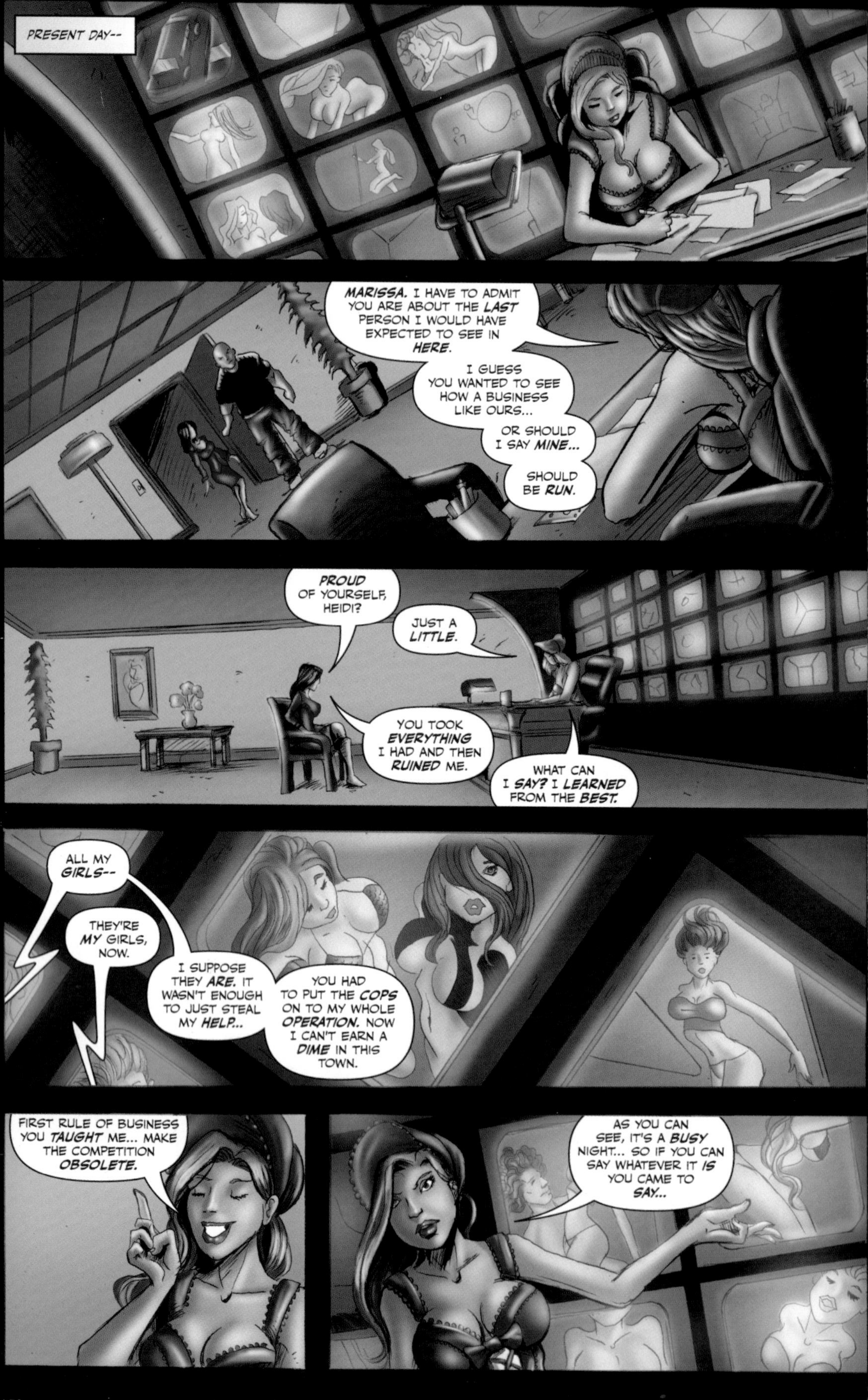
PRESENT DAY--
MARISSA. I HAVE TO ADMIT YOU ARE ABOUT THE LAST PERSON I WOULD HAVE EXPECTED TO SEE IN HERE.
I GUESS YOU WANTED TO SEE HOW A BUSINESS LIKE OURS...
OR SHOULD I SAY MINE...
SHOULD BE RUN.
PROUD OF YOURSELF, HEIDI?
JUST A LITTLE.
YOU TOOK EVERYTHING I HAD AND THEN RUINED ME.
WHAT CAN I SAY? I LEARNED FROM THE BEST.
ALL MY GIRLS--
THEY'RE MY GIRLS, NOW.
I SUPPOSE THEY ARE. IT WASN'T ENOUGH TO JUST STEAL MY HELP...
YOU HAD TO PUT THE COPS ON TO MY WHOLE OPERATION. NOW I CAN'T EARN A DIME IN THIS TOWN.
FIRST RULE OF BUSINESS YOU TAUGHT ME... MAKE THE COMPETITION OBSOLETE.
AS YOU CAN SEE, IT'S A BUSY NIGHT... SO IF YOU CAN SAY WHATEVER IT IS YOU CAME TO SAY...

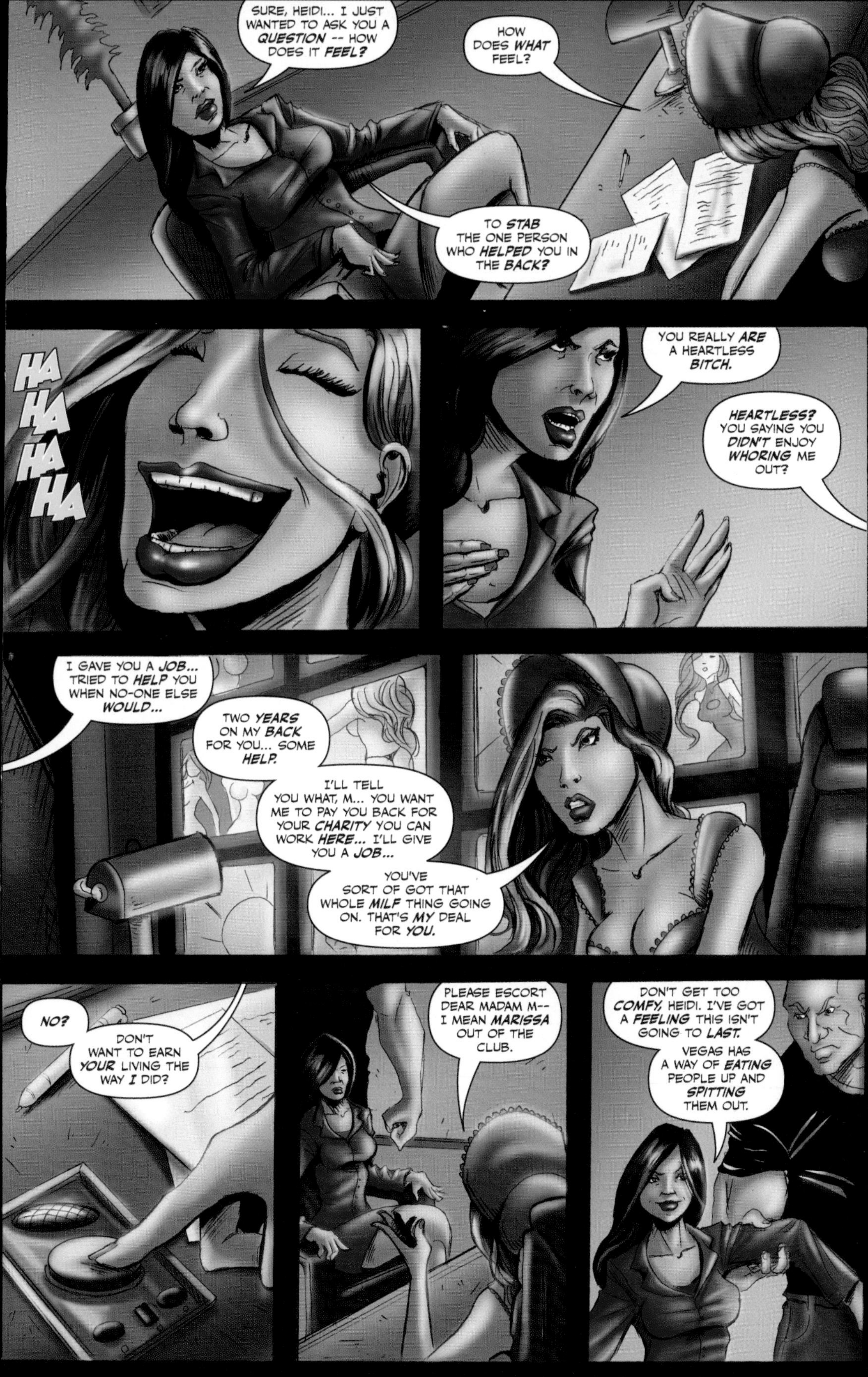
SURE, HEIDI... I JUST WANTED TO ASK YOU A QUESTION -- HOW DOES IT FEEL?
HOW DOES WHAT FEEL?
TO STAB THE ONE PERSON WHO HELPED YOU IN THE BACK?
HA HA HA HA
YOU REALLY ARE A HEARTLESS BITCH.
HEARTLESS? YOU SAYING YOU DIDN'T ENJOY WHORING ME OUT?
I GAVE YOU A JOB... TRIED TO HELP YOU WHEN NO-ONE ELSE WOULD...
TWO YEARS ON MY BACK FOR YOU... SOME HELP.
I'LL TELL YOU WHAT, M... YOU WANT ME TO PAY YOU BACK FOR YOUR CHARITY YOU CAN WORK HERE... I'LL GIVE YOU A JOB...
YOU'VE SORT OF GOT THAT WHOLE MILF THING GOING ON. THAT'S MY DEAL FOR YOU.
NO?
DON'T WANT TO EARN YOUR LIVING THE WAY I DID?
PLEASE ESCORT DEAR MADAM M-- I MEAN MARISSA OUT OF THE CLUB.
DON'T GET TOO COMFY, HEIDI. I'VE GOT A FEELING THIS ISN'T GOING TO LAST.
VEGAS HAS A WAY OF EATING PEOPLE UP AND SPITTING THEM OUT.

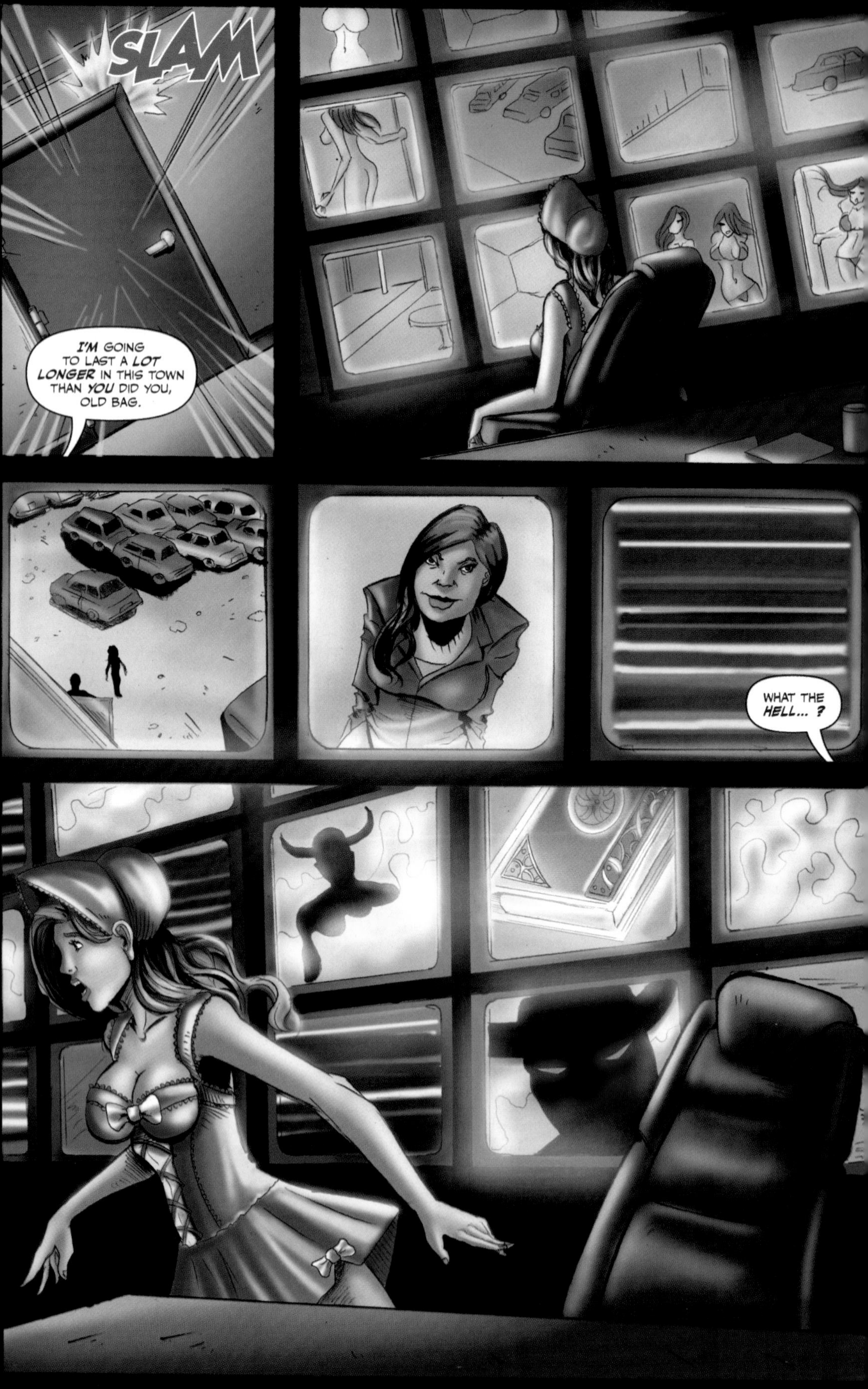

SLAM
I'M GOING TO LAST A LOT LONGER IN THIS TOWN THAN YOU DID YOU, OLD BAG.
WHAT THE HELL... ?

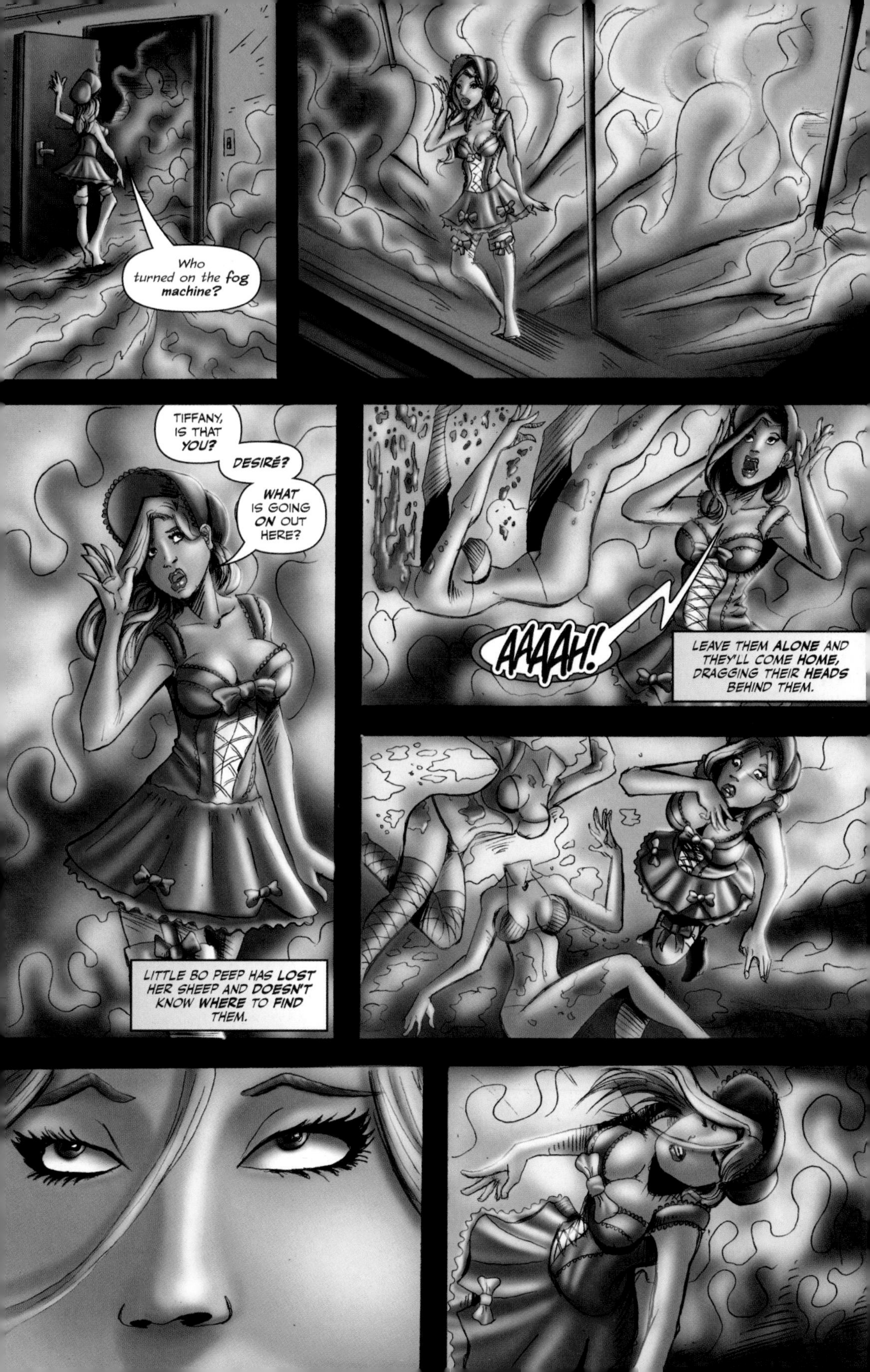
Who turned on the fog machine?
TIFFANY, IS THAT YOU?
DESIRÉ?
WHAT IS GOING ON OUT HERE?
LITTLE BO PEEP HAS LOST HER SHEEP AND DOESN'T KNOW WHERE TO FIND THEM.
AAAAH!
LEAVE THEM ALONE AND THEY'LL COME HOME, DRAGGING THEIR HEADS BEHIND THEM.

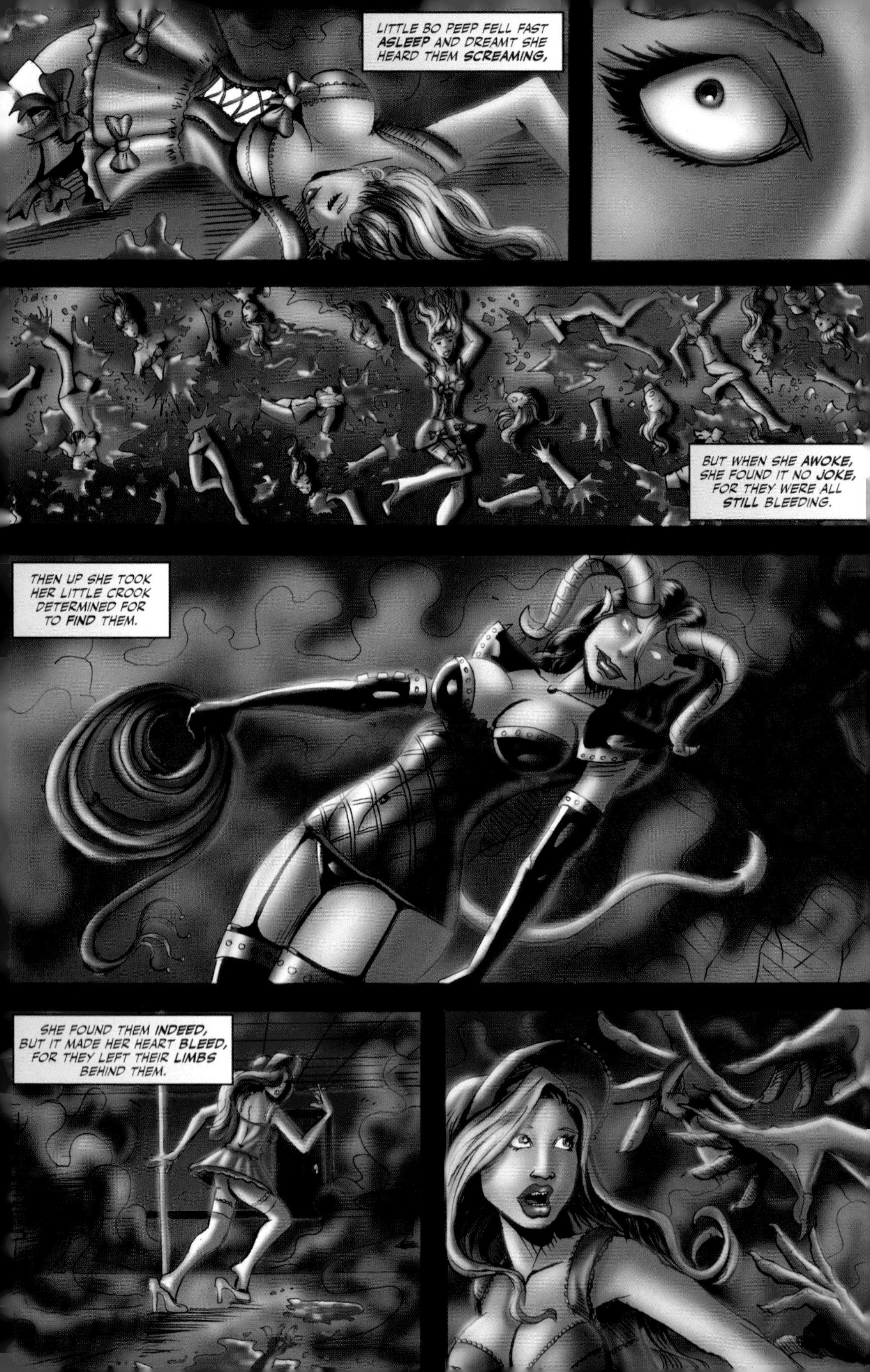
LITTLE BO PEEP FELL FAST ASLEEP AND DREAMT SHE HEARD THEM SCREAMING,
BUT WHEN SHE AWOKE, SHE FOUND IT NO JOKE, FOR THEY WERE ALL STILL BLEEDING.
THEN UP SHE TOOK HER LITTLE CROOK DETERMINED FOR TO FIND THEM.
SHE FOUND THEM INDEED, BUT IT MADE HER HEART BLEED, FOR THEY LEFT THEIR LIMBS BEHIND THEM.

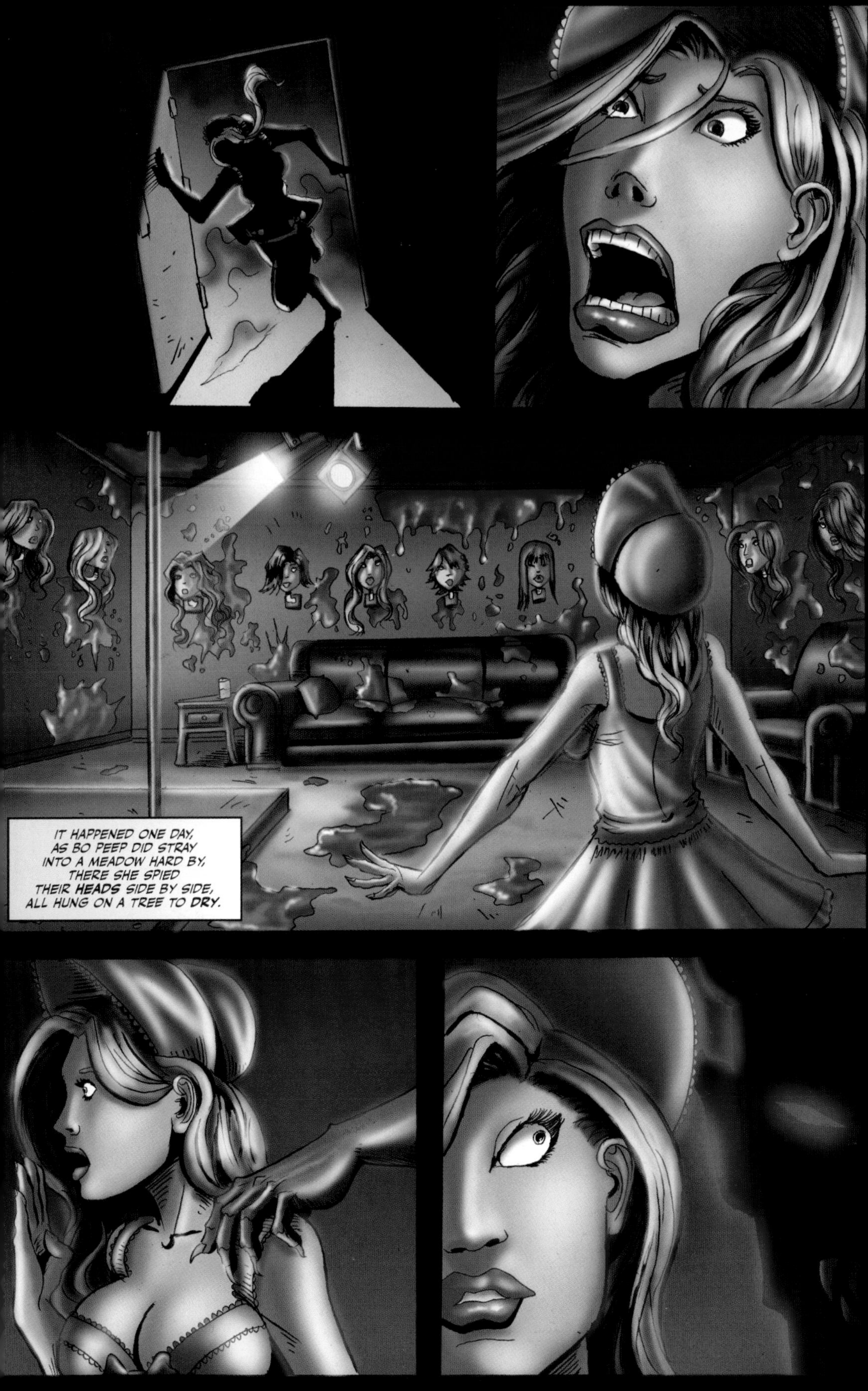
IT HAPPENED ONE DAY,
AS BO PEEP DID STRAY
INTO A MEADOW HARD BY,
THERE SHE SPIED
THEIR **HEADS** SIDE BY SIDE,
ALL HUNG ON A TREE TO **DRY**.

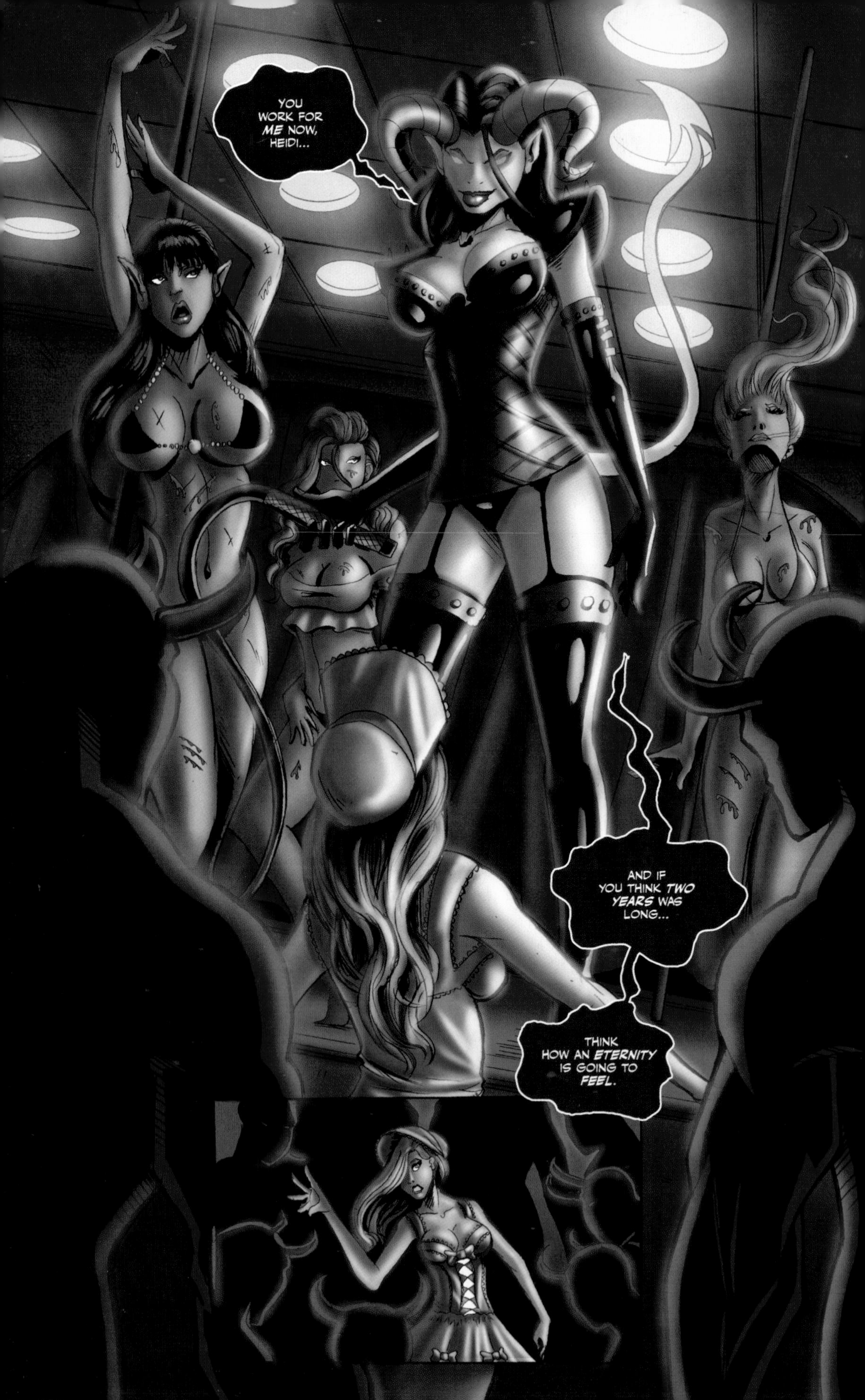
YOU WORK FOR *ME* NOW, HEIDI...
AND IF YOU THINK *TWO YEARS* WAS LONG...
THINK HOW AN *ETERNITY* IS GOING TO *FEEL*.

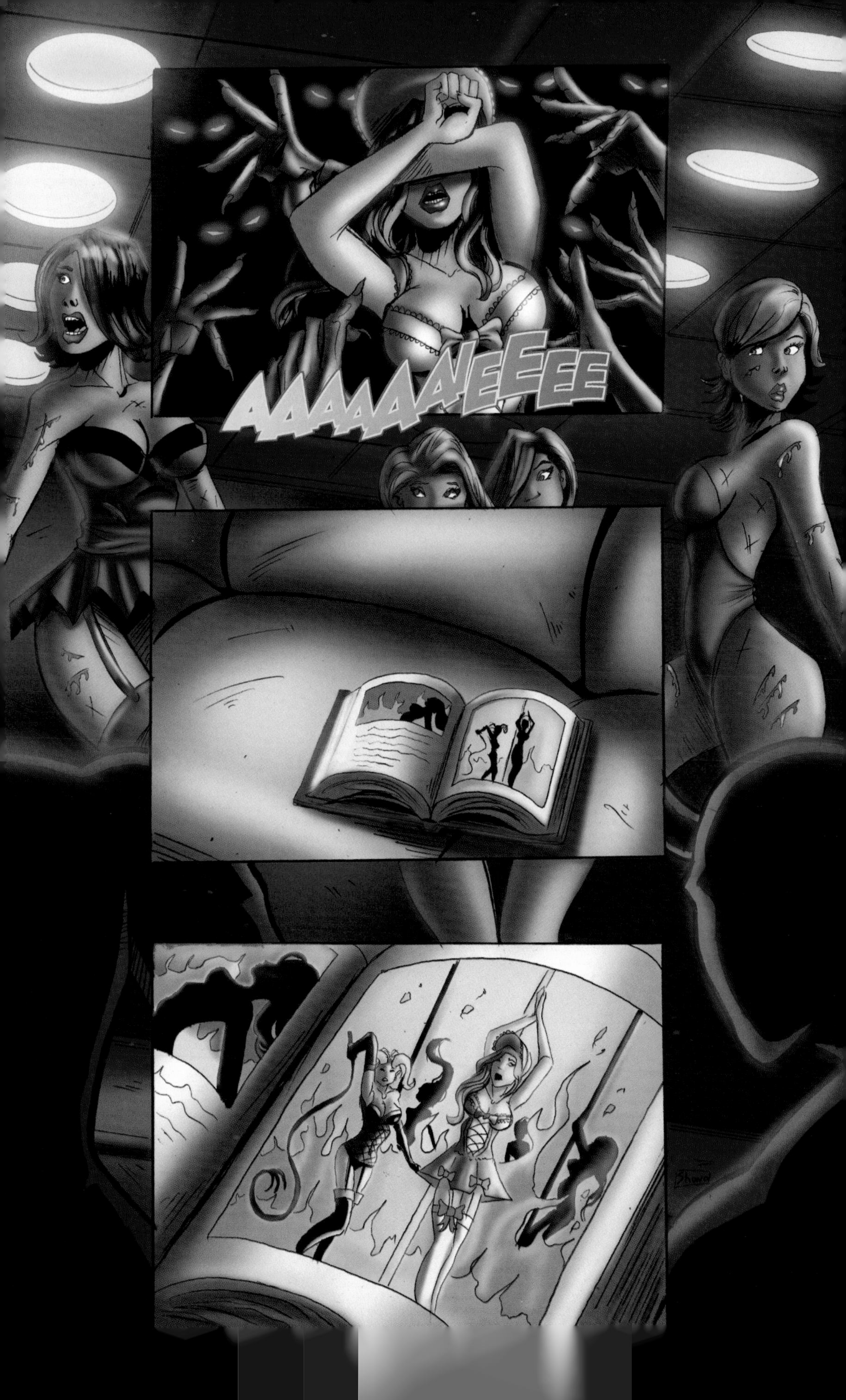
AAAAAAIEEEee

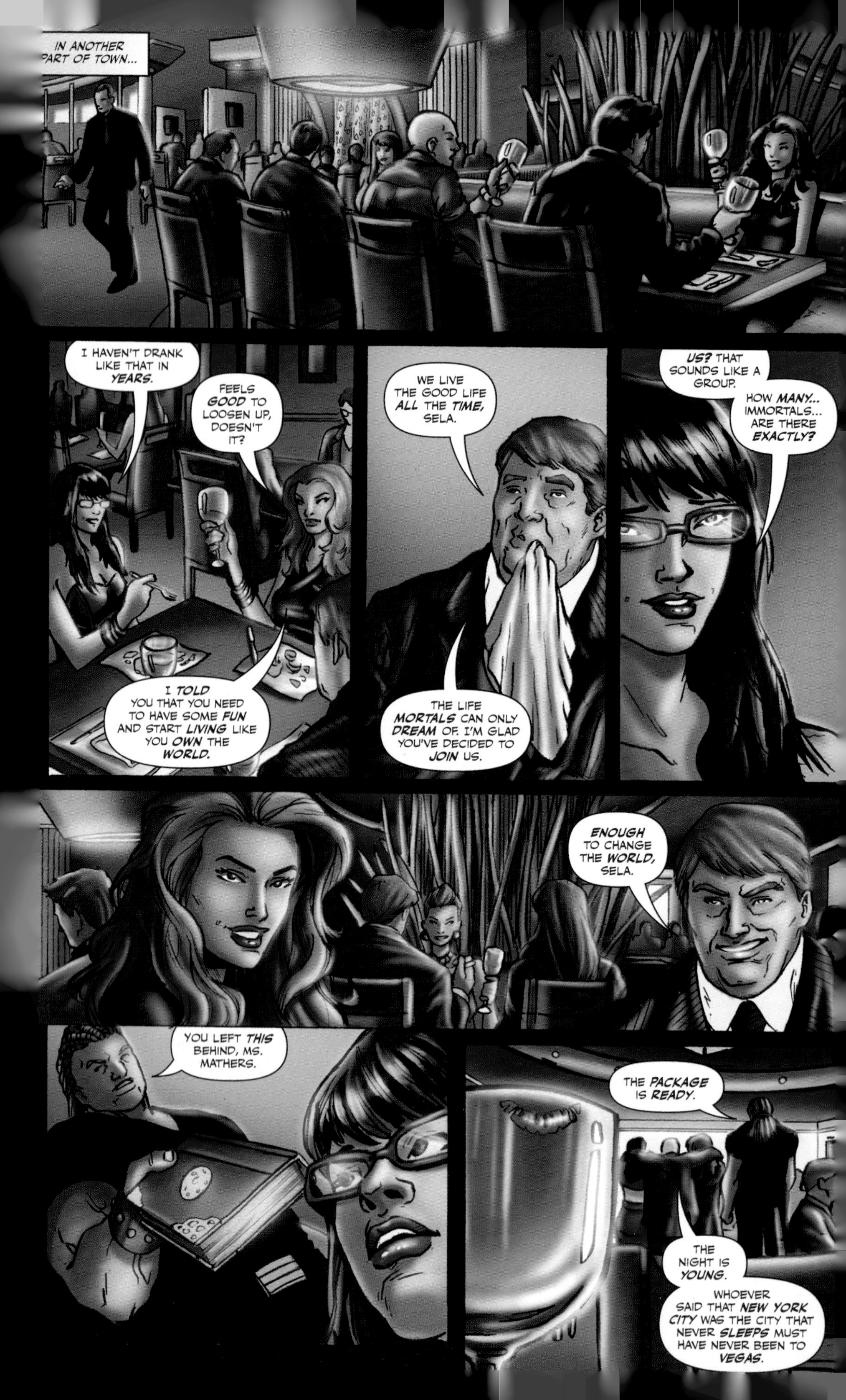
IN ANOTHER PART OF TOWN...
I HAVEN'T DRANK LIKE THAT IN YEARS.
FEELS GOOD TO LOOSEN UP, DOESN'T IT?
I TOLD YOU THAT YOU NEED TO HAVE SOME FUN AND START LIVING LIKE YOU OWN THE WORLD.
WE LIVE THE GOOD LIFE ALL THE TIME, SELA.
THE LIFE MORTALS CAN ONLY DREAM OF. I'M GLAD YOU'VE DECIDED TO JOIN US.
US? THAT SOUNDS LIKE A GROUP.
HOW MANY... IMMORTALS... ARE THERE EXACTLY?
ENOUGH TO CHANGE THE WORLD, SELA.
YOU LEFT THIS BEHIND, MS. MATHERS.
THE PACKAGE IS READY.
THE NIGHT IS YOUNG.
WHOEVER SAID THAT NEW YORK CITY WAS THE CITY THAT NEVER SLEEPS MUST HAVE NEVER BEEN TO VEGAS.

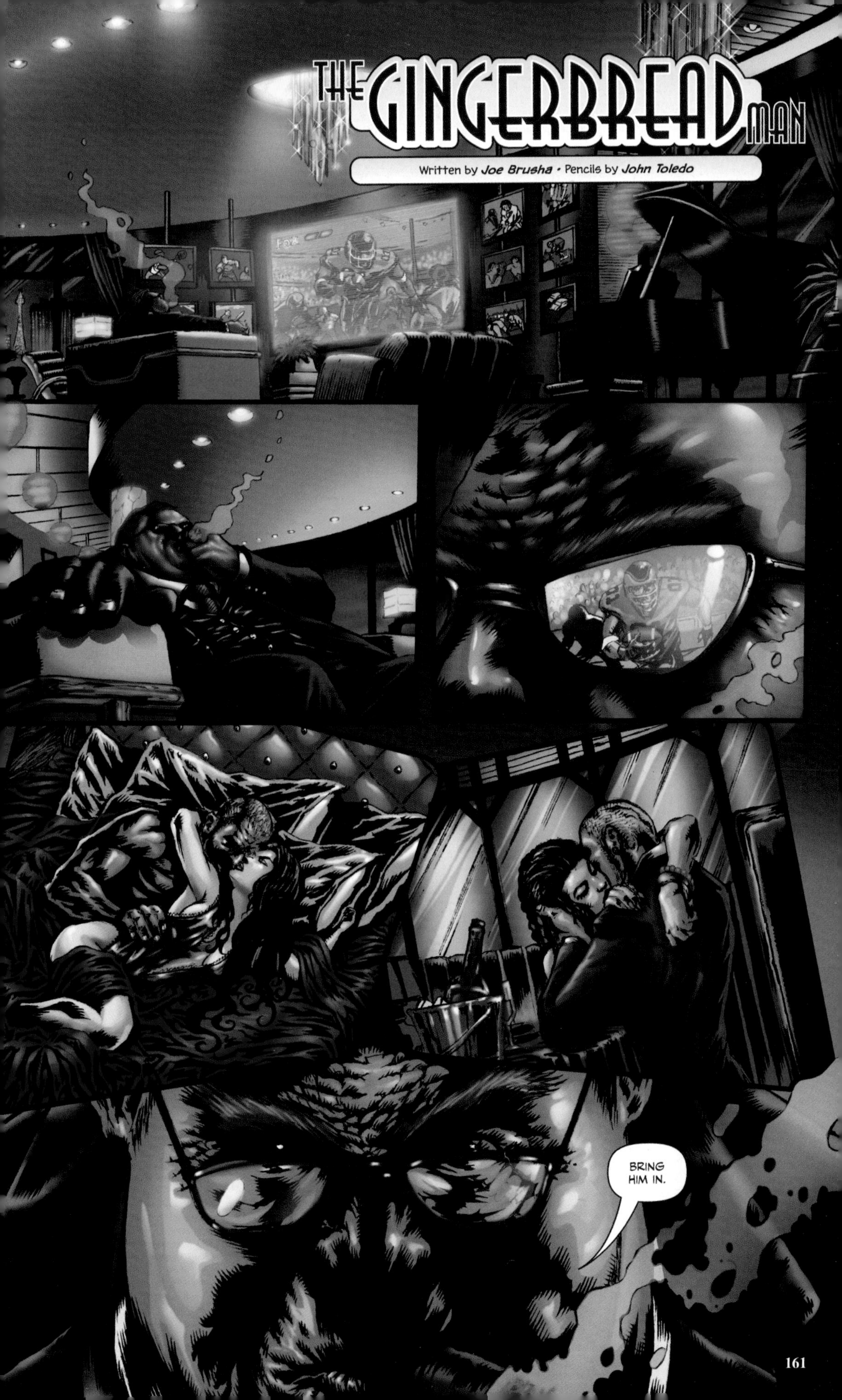
THE GINGERBREAD MAN
Written by Joe Brusha • Pencils by John Toledo
BRING HIM IN.

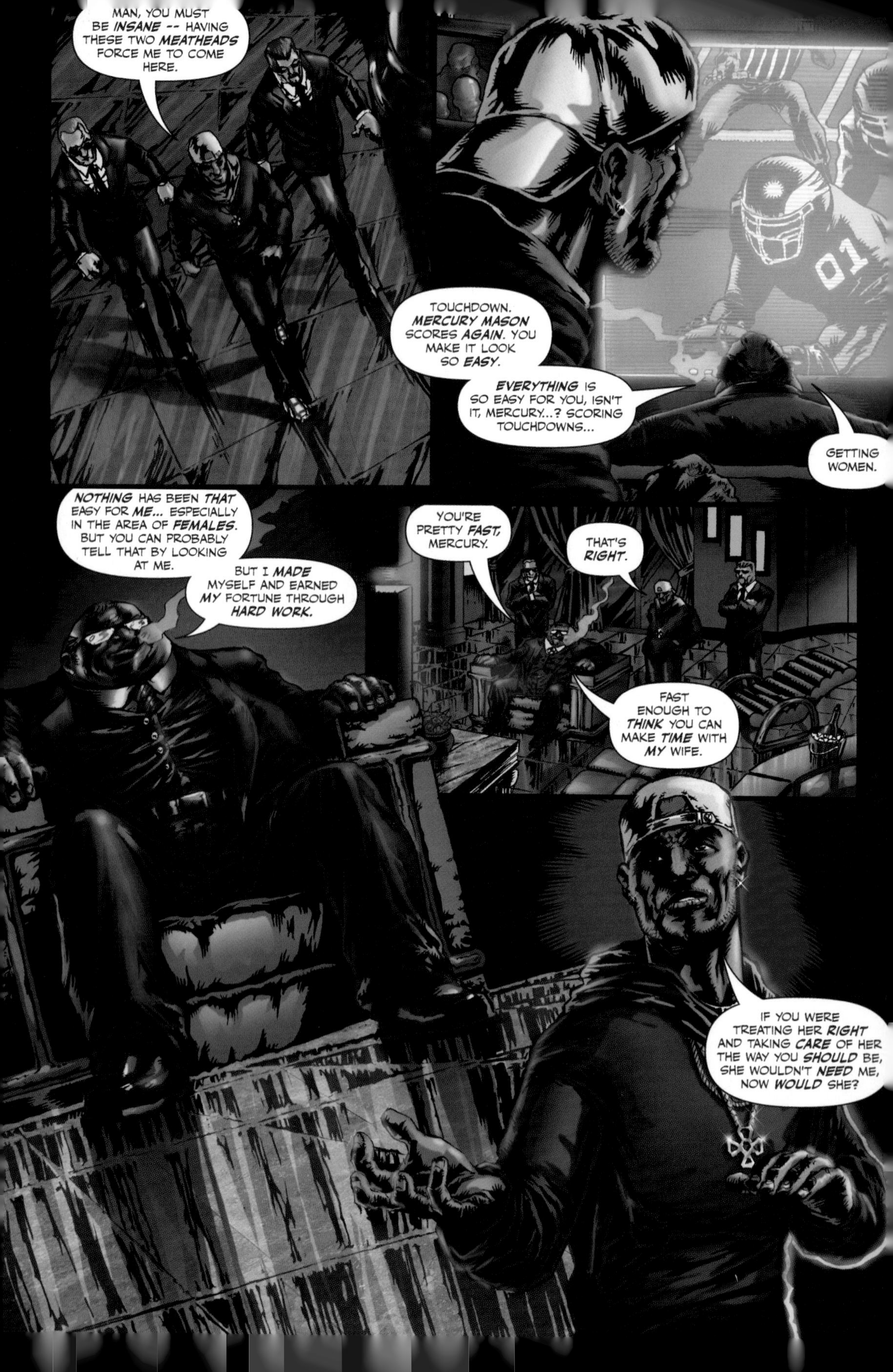

MAN, YOU MUST BE INSANE -- HAVING THESE TWO MEATHEADS FORCE ME TO COME HERE.
TOUCHDOWN. MERCURY MASON SCORES AGAIN. YOU MAKE IT LOOK SO EASY.
EVERYTHING IS SO EASY FOR YOU, ISN'T IT, MERCURY...? SCORING TOUCHDOWNS...
GETTING WOMEN.
NOTHING HAS BEEN THAT EASY FOR ME... ESPECIALLY IN THE AREA OF FEMALES. BUT YOU CAN PROBABLY TELL THAT BY LOOKING AT ME.
BUT I MADE MYSELF AND EARNED MY FORTUNE THROUGH HARD WORK.
YOU'RE PRETTY FAST, MERCURY.
THAT'S RIGHT.
FAST ENOUGH TO THINK YOU CAN MAKE TIME WITH MY WIFE.
IF YOU WERE TREATING HER RIGHT AND TAKING CARE OF HER THE WAY YOU SHOULD BE, SHE WOULDN'T NEED ME, NOW WOULD SHE?

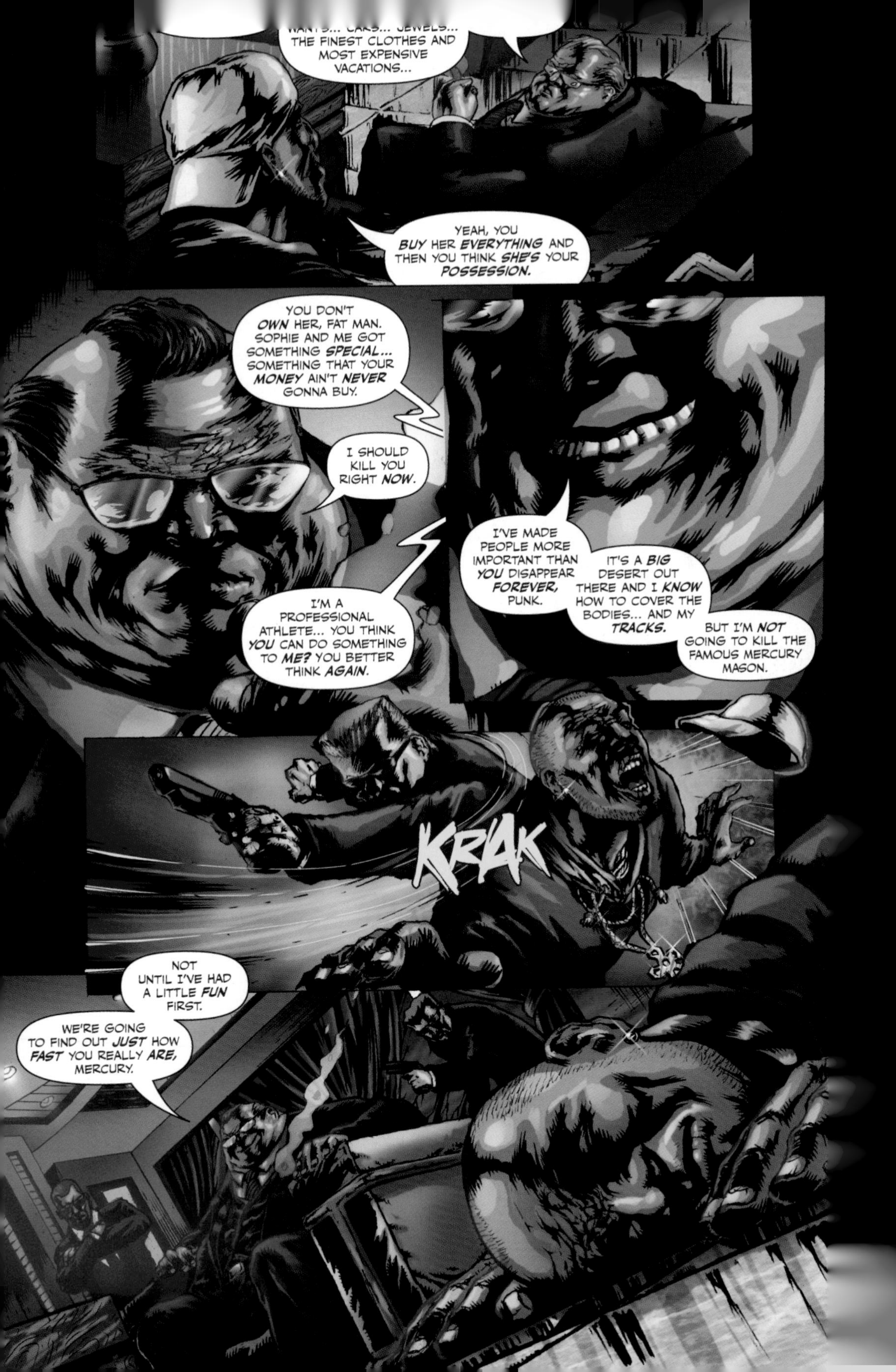
THE FINEST CLOTHES AND MOST EXPENSIVE VACATIONS...
YEAH, YOU BUY HER EVERYTHING AND THEN YOU THINK SHE'S YOUR POSSESSION.
YOU DON'T OWN HER, FAT MAN. SOPHIE AND ME GOT SOMETHING SPECIAL... SOMETHING THAT YOUR MONEY AIN'T NEVER GONNA BUY.
I SHOULD KILL YOU RIGHT NOW.
I'M A PROFESSIONAL ATHLETE... YOU THINK YOU CAN DO SOMETHING TO ME? YOU BETTER THINK AGAIN.
I'VE MADE PEOPLE MORE IMPORTANT THAN YOU DISAPPEAR FOREVER, PUNK.
IT'S A BIG DESERT OUT THERE AND I KNOW HOW TO COVER THE BODIES... AND MY TRACKS.
BUT I'M NOT GOING TO KILL THE FAMOUS MERCURY MASON.
KRAK
NOT UNTIL I'VE HAD A LITTLE FUN FIRST.
WE'RE GOING TO FIND OUT JUST HOW FAST YOU REALLY ARE, MERCURY.

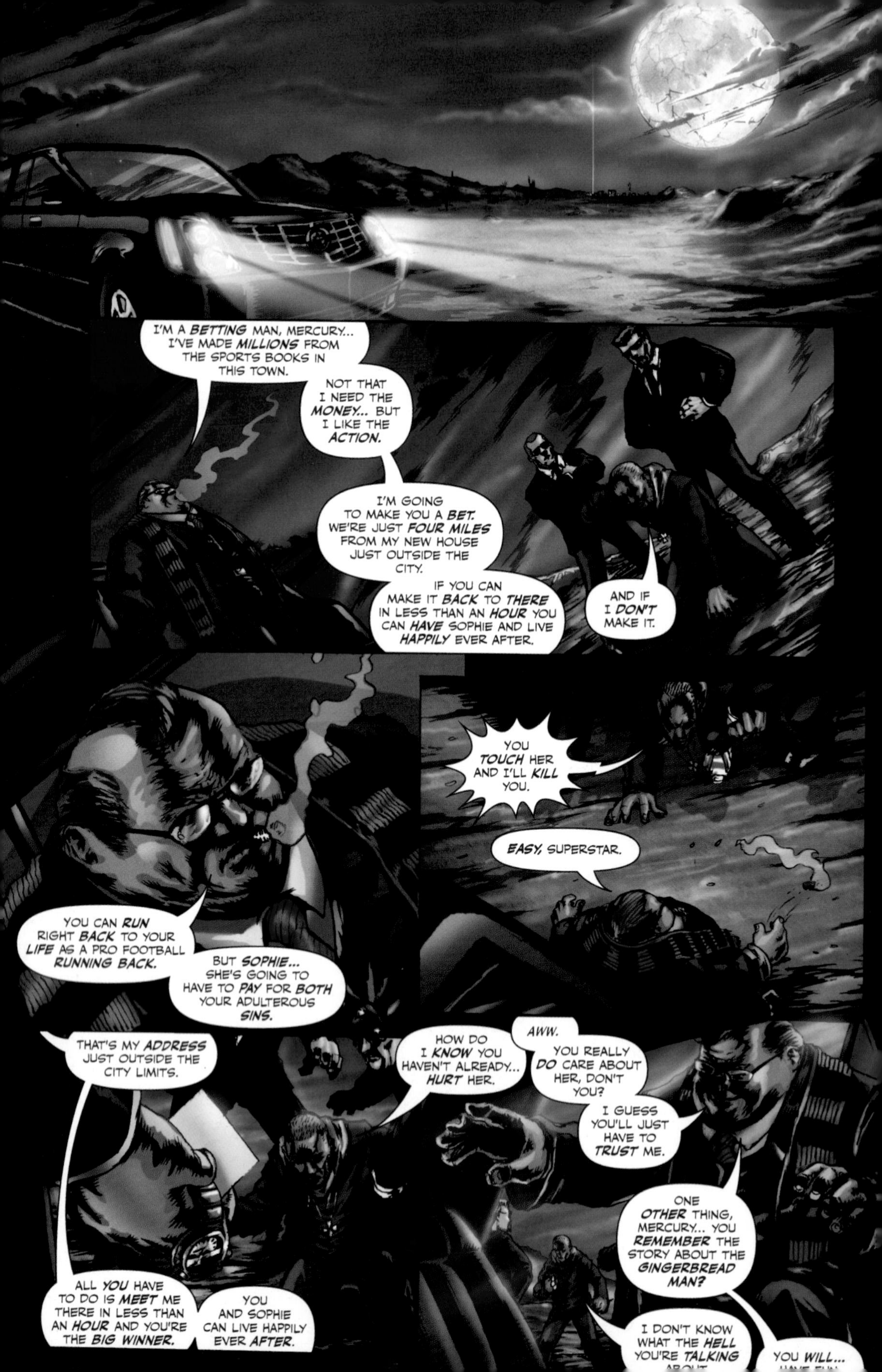
I'M A BETTING MAN, MERCURY... I'VE MADE MILLIONS FROM THE SPORTS BOOKS IN THIS TOWN.
NOT THAT I NEED THE MONEY... BUT I LIKE THE ACTION.
I'M GOING TO MAKE YOU A BET. WE'RE JUST FOUR MILES FROM MY NEW HOUSE JUST OUTSIDE THE CITY.
IF YOU CAN MAKE IT BACK TO THERE IN LESS THAN AN HOUR YOU CAN HAVE SOPHIE AND LIVE HAPPILY EVER AFTER.
AND IF I DON'T MAKE IT.
YOU CAN RUN RIGHT BACK TO YOUR LIFE AS A PRO FOOTBALL RUNNING BACK.
BUT SOPHIE... SHE'S GOING TO HAVE TO PAY FOR BOTH YOUR ADULTEROUS SINS.
YOU TOUCH HER AND I'LL KILL YOU.
EASY, SUPERSTAR.
THAT'S MY ADDRESS JUST OUTSIDE THE CITY LIMITS.
ALL YOU HAVE TO DO IS MEET ME THERE IN LESS THAN AN HOUR AND YOU'RE THE BIG WINNER.
YOU AND SOPHIE CAN LIVE HAPPILY EVER AFTER.
HOW DO I KNOW YOU HAVEN'T ALREADY... HURT HER.
AWW.
YOU REALLY DO CARE ABOUT HER, DON'T YOU?
I GUESS YOU'LL JUST HAVE TO TRUST ME.
ONE OTHER THING, MERCURY... YOU REMEMBER THE STORY ABOUT THE GINGERBREAD MAN?
I DON'T KNOW WHAT THE HELL YOU'RE TALKING
YOU WILL...

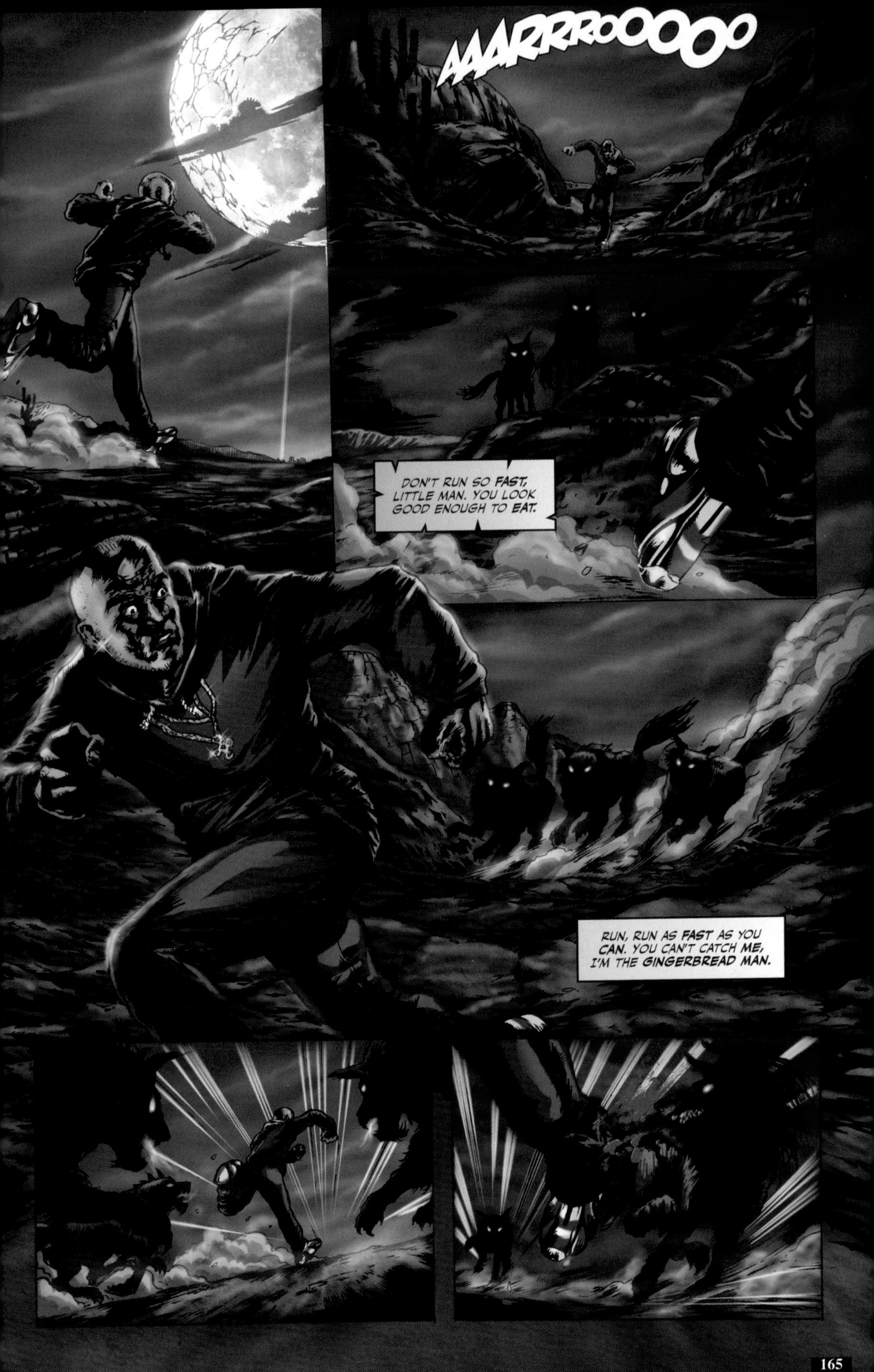
AAARRROOOOO
DON'T RUN SO FAST, LITTLE MAN. YOU LOOK GOOD ENOUGH TO EAT.
RUN, RUN AS FAST AS YOU CAN. YOU CAN'T CATCH ME, I'M THE GINGERBREAD MAN.

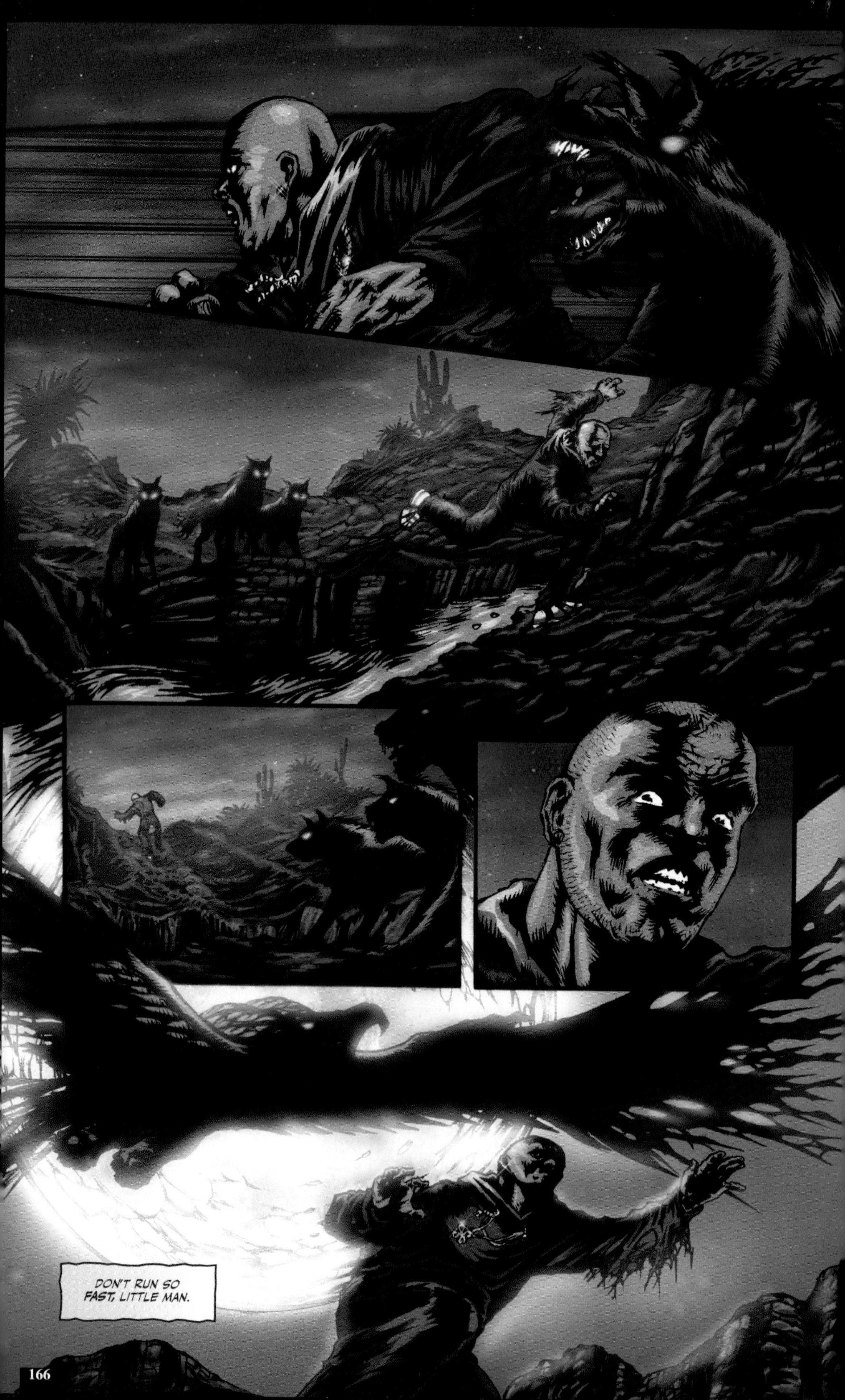
DON'T RUN SO
FAST, LITTLE MAN.

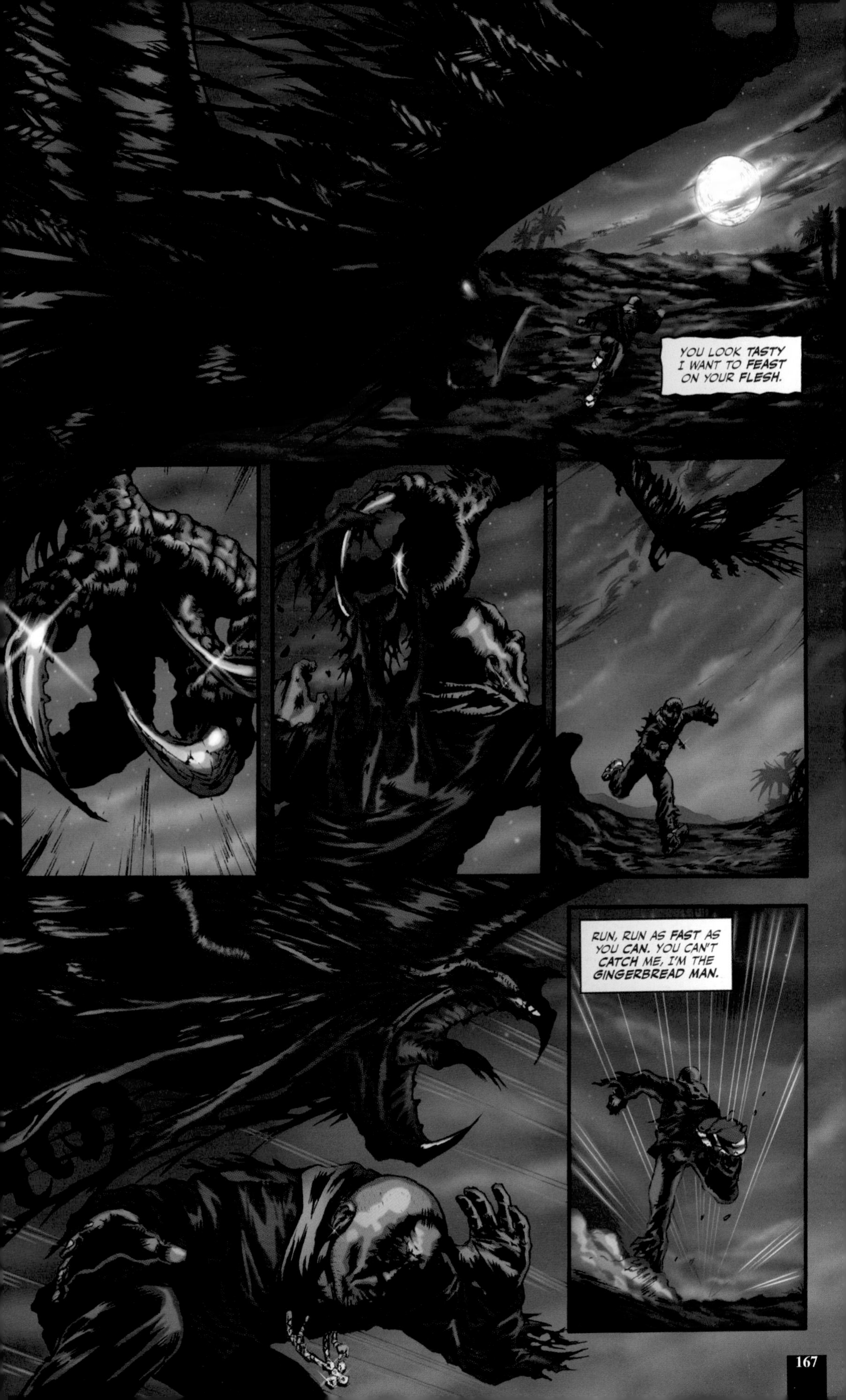
YOU LOOK TASTY I WANT TO FEAST ON YOUR FLESH.
RUN, RUN AS FAST AS YOU CAN. YOU CAN'T CATCH ME, I'M THE GINGERBREAD MAN.

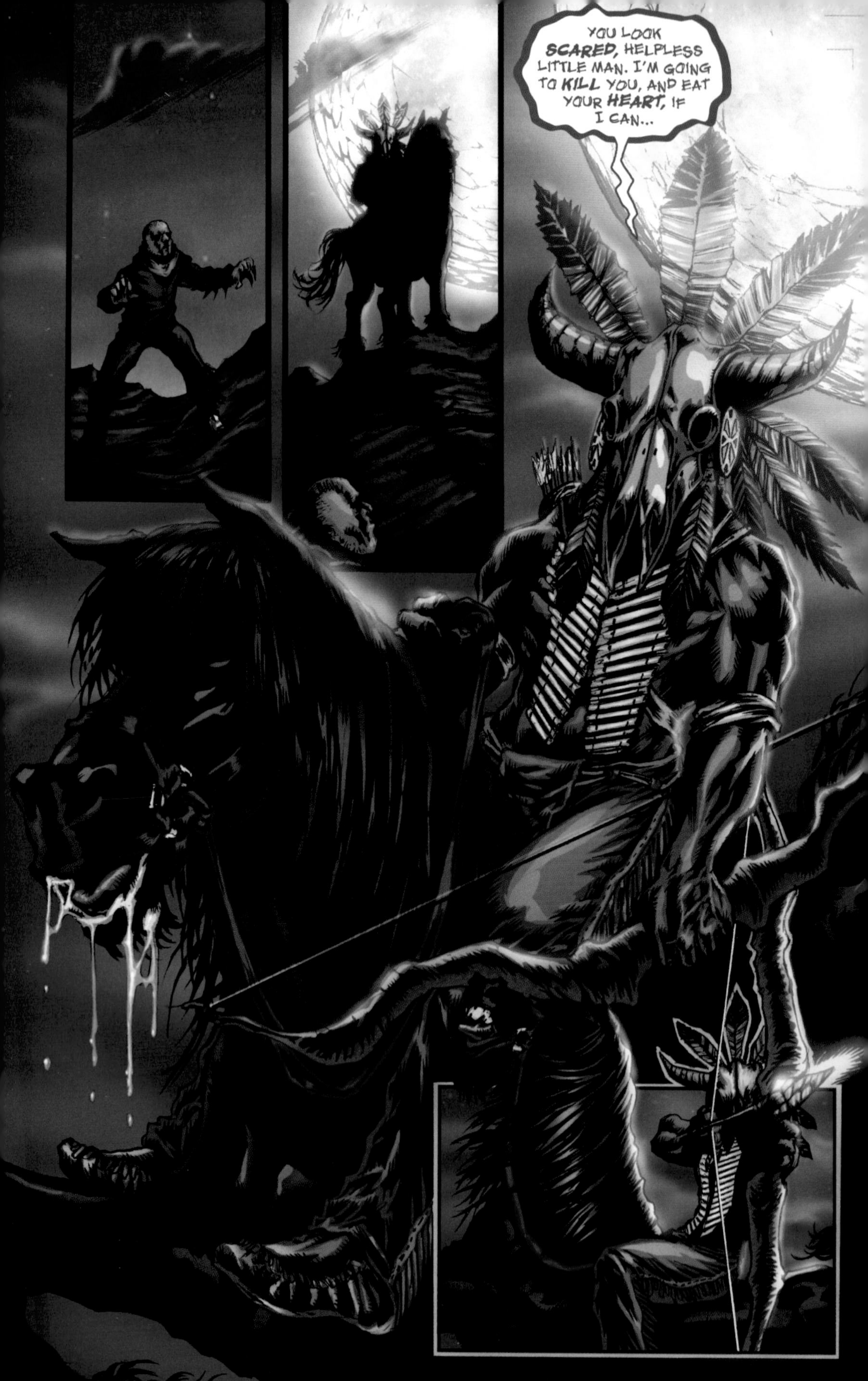
YOU LOOK SCARED, HELPLESS LITTLE MAN. I'M GOING TO KILL YOU, AND EAT YOUR HEART, IF I CAN...

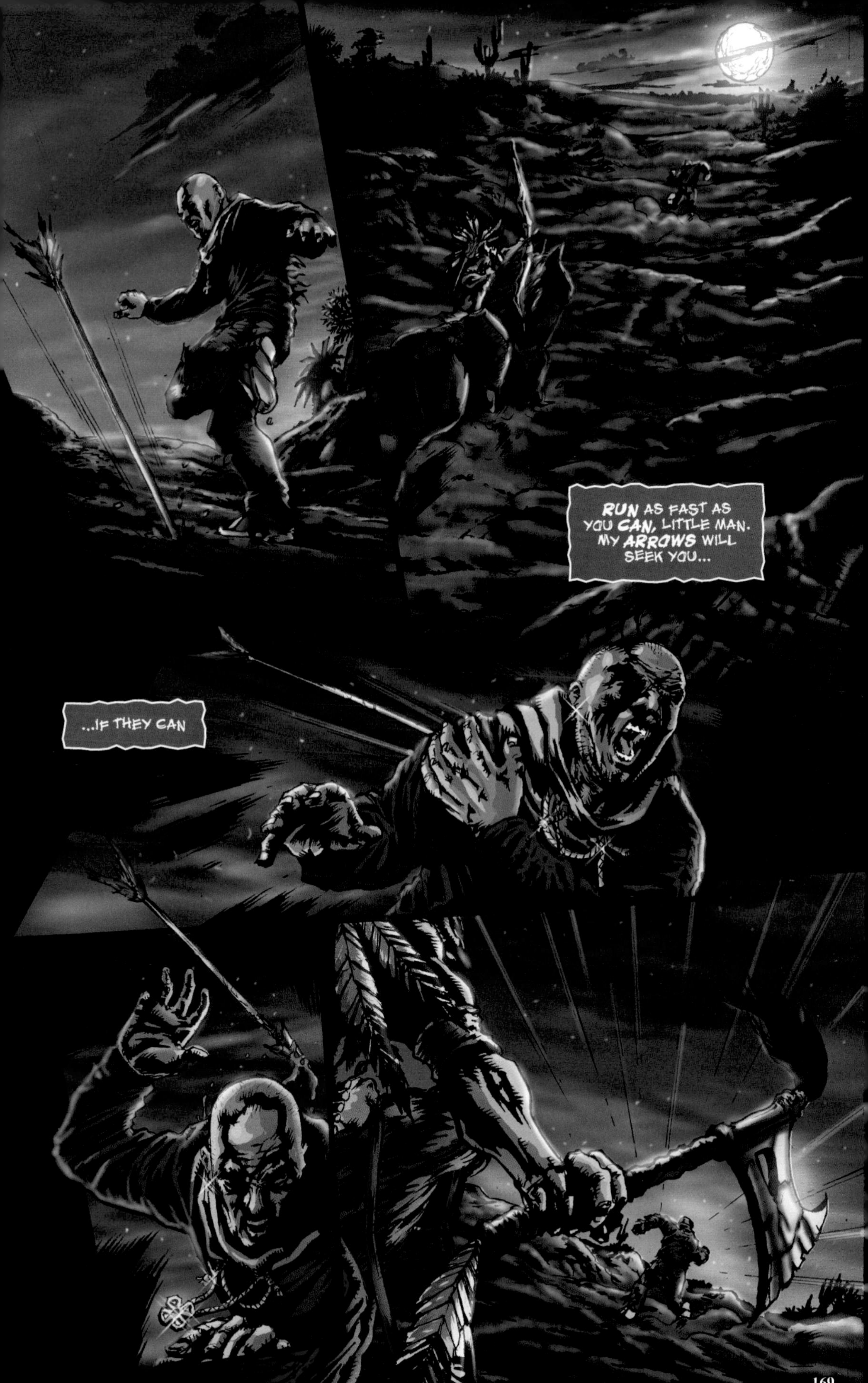
RUN AS FAST AS YOU CAN, LITTLE MAN. MY ARROWS WILL SEEK YOU...
...IF THEY CAN

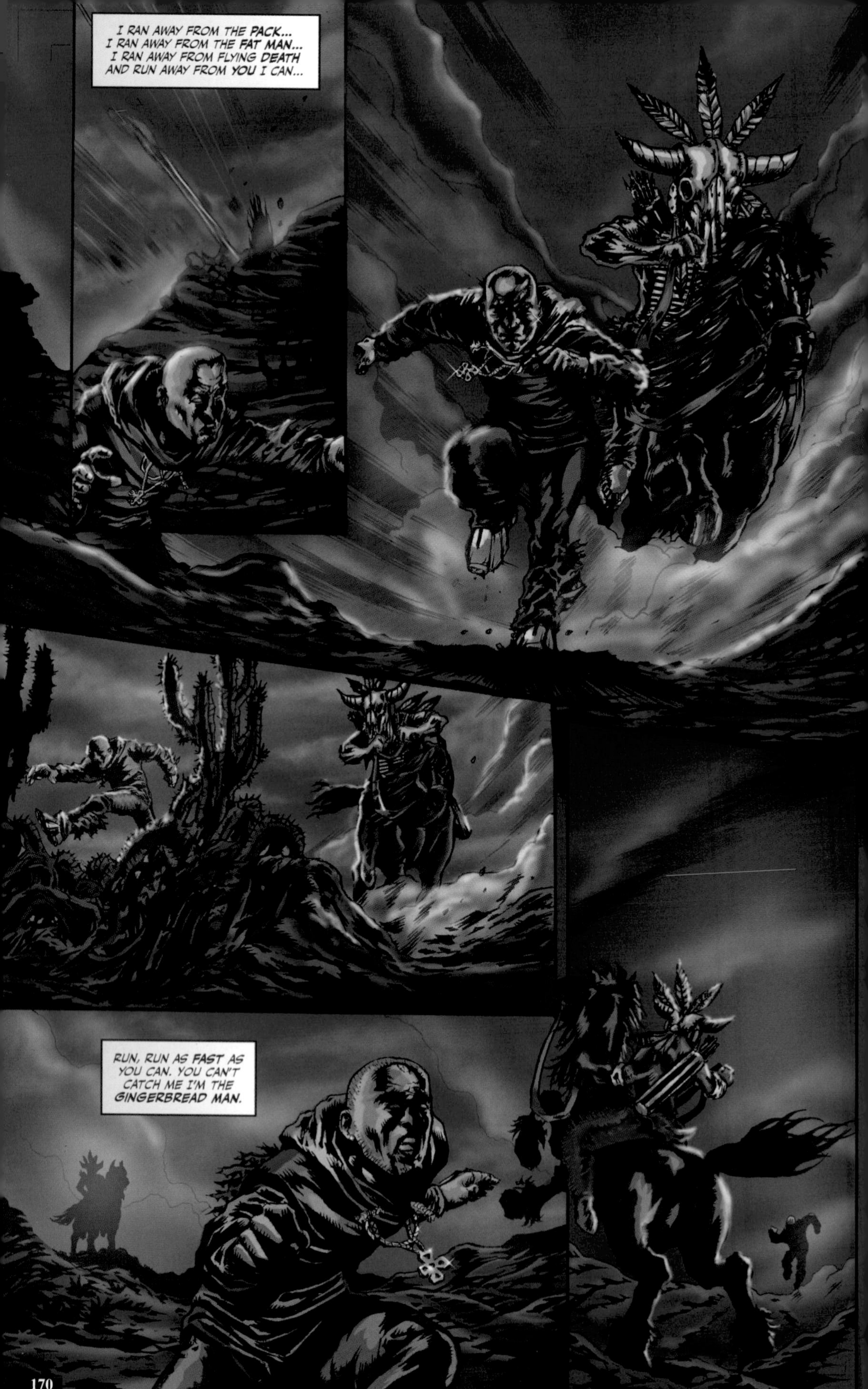
I RAN AWAY FROM THE PACK...
I RAN AWAY FROM THE FAT MAN...
I RAN AWAY FROM FLYING DEATH
AND RUN AWAY FROM YOU I CAN...
RUN, RUN AS FAST AS YOU CAN. YOU CAN'T CATCH ME I'M THE GINGERBREAD MAN.

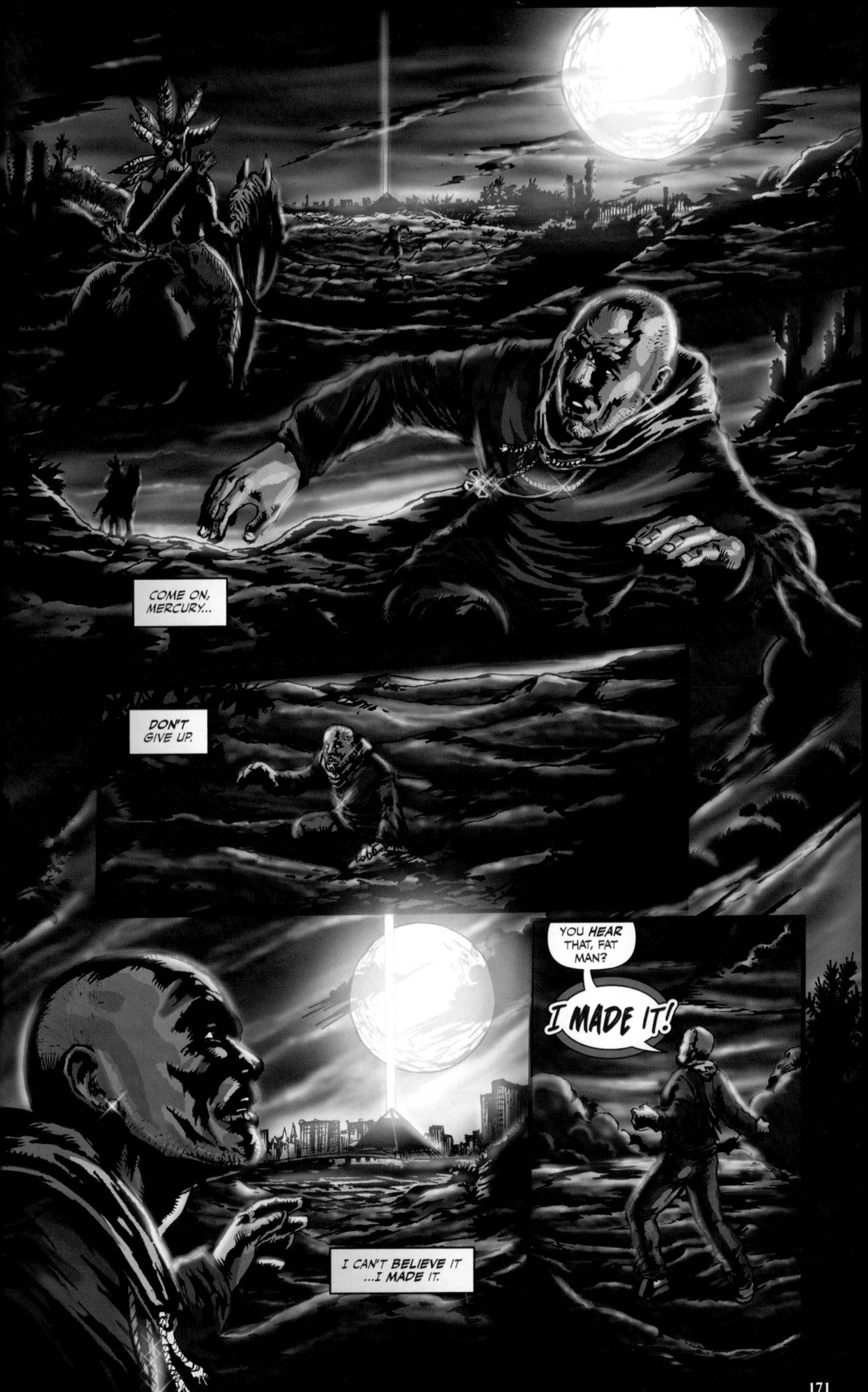
COME ON, MERCURY...
DON'T GIVE UP.
I CAN'T BELIEVE IT ...I MADE IT.
YOU HEAR THAT, FAT MAN?
I MADE IT!

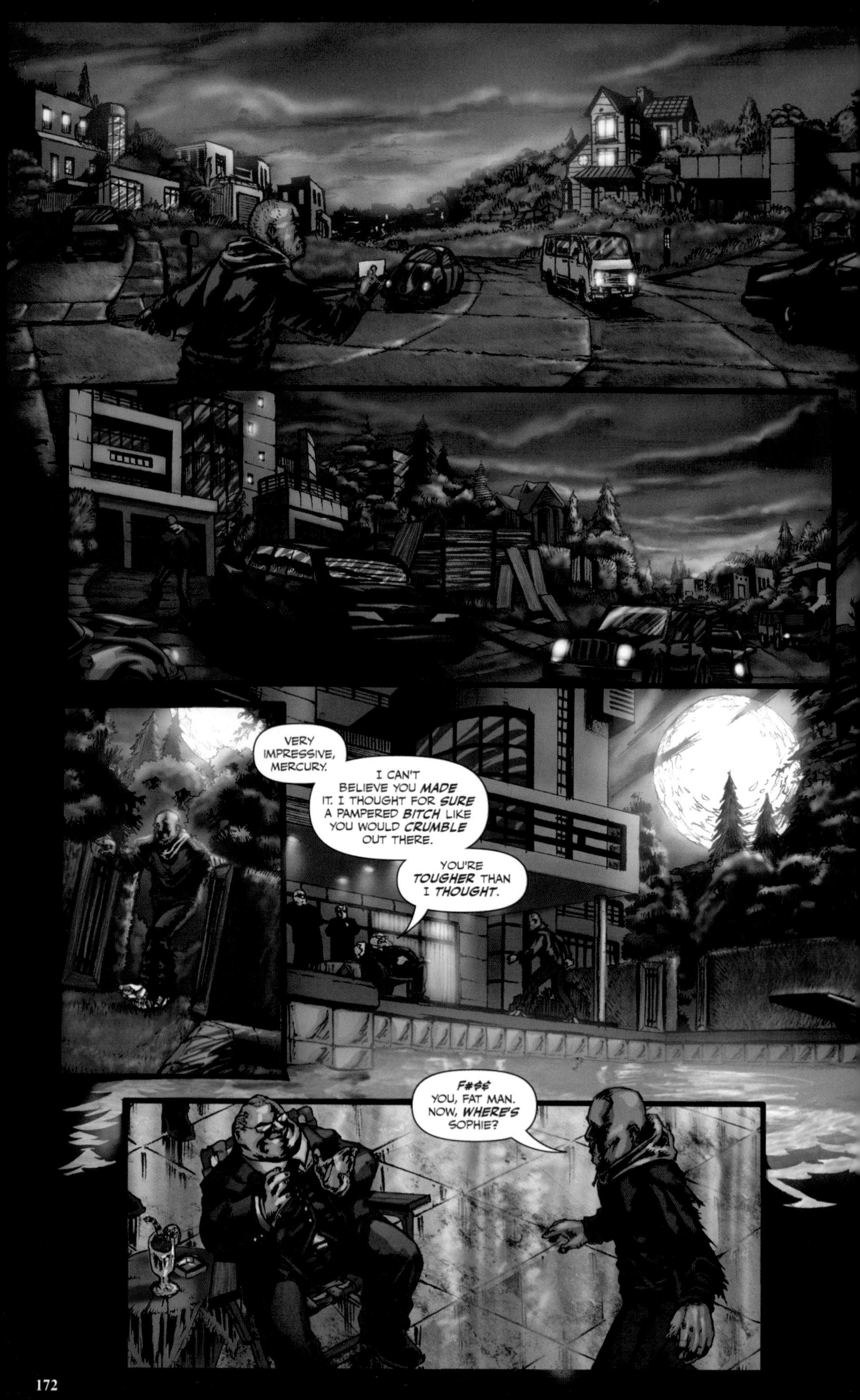
VERY IMPRESSIVE, MERCURY.
I CAN'T BELIEVE YOU MADE IT. I THOUGHT FOR SURE A PAMPERED BITCH LIKE YOU WOULD CRUMBLE OUT THERE.
YOU'RE TOUGHER THAN I THOUGHT.
F#$$ YOU, FAT MAN. NOW, WHERE'S SOPHIE?

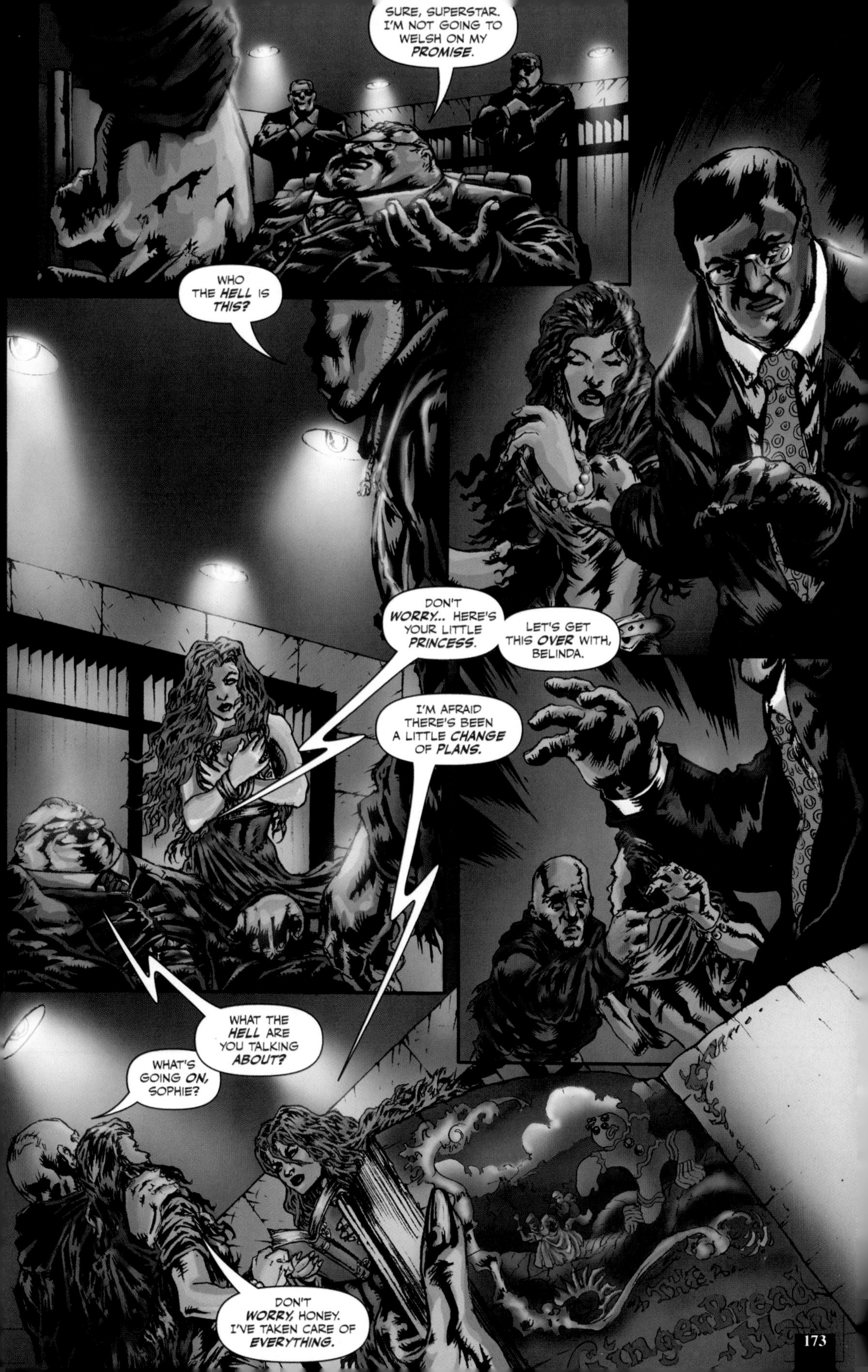
SURE, SUPERSTAR. I'M NOT GOING TO WELSH ON MY PROMISE.
WHO THE HELL IS THIS?
DON'T WORRY... HERE'S YOUR LITTLE PRINCESS.
LET'S GET THIS OVER WITH, BELINDA.
I'M AFRAID THERE'S BEEN A LITTLE CHANGE OF PLANS.
WHAT THE HELL ARE YOU TALKING ABOUT?
WHAT'S GOING ON, SOPHIE?
DON'T WORRY, HONEY. I'VE TAKEN CARE OF EVERYTHING.
The Gingerbread Man

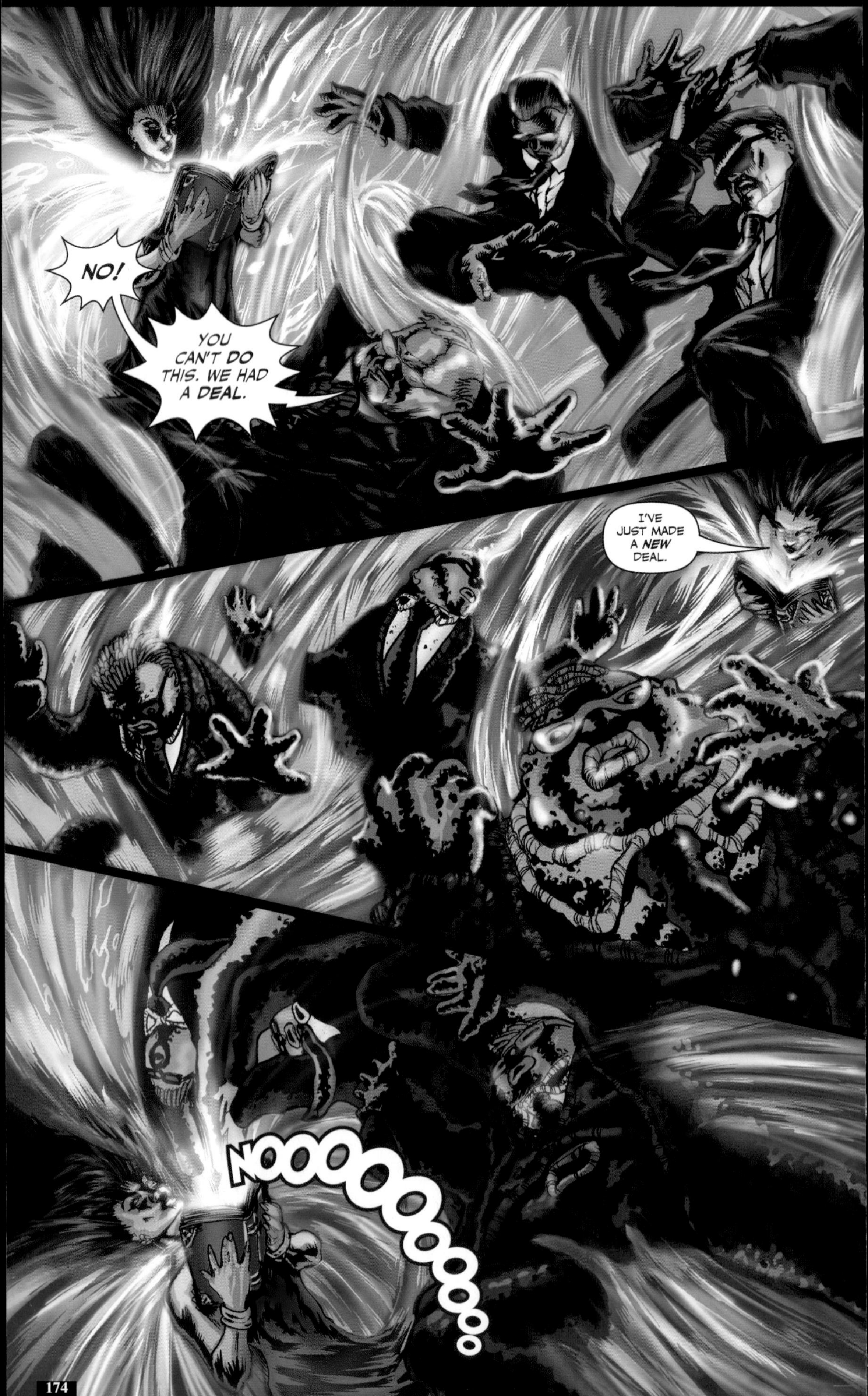
NO!
YOU CAN'T DO THIS. WE HAD A DEAL.
I'VE JUST MADE A NEW DEAL.
NOOOOOOOOOOOOO

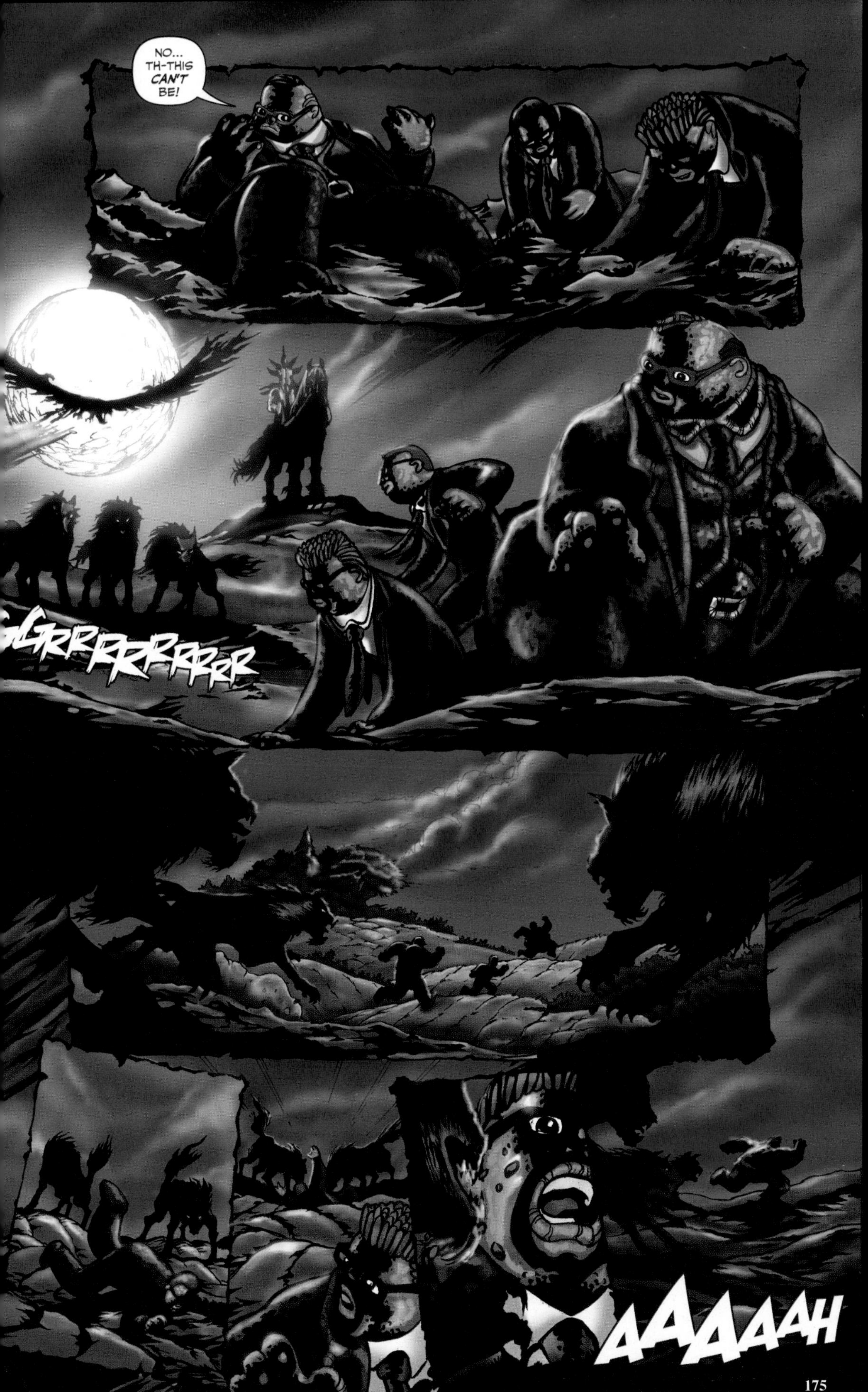
NO... TH-THIS CAN'T BE!
GRRRRRRRRRR
AAAAAH

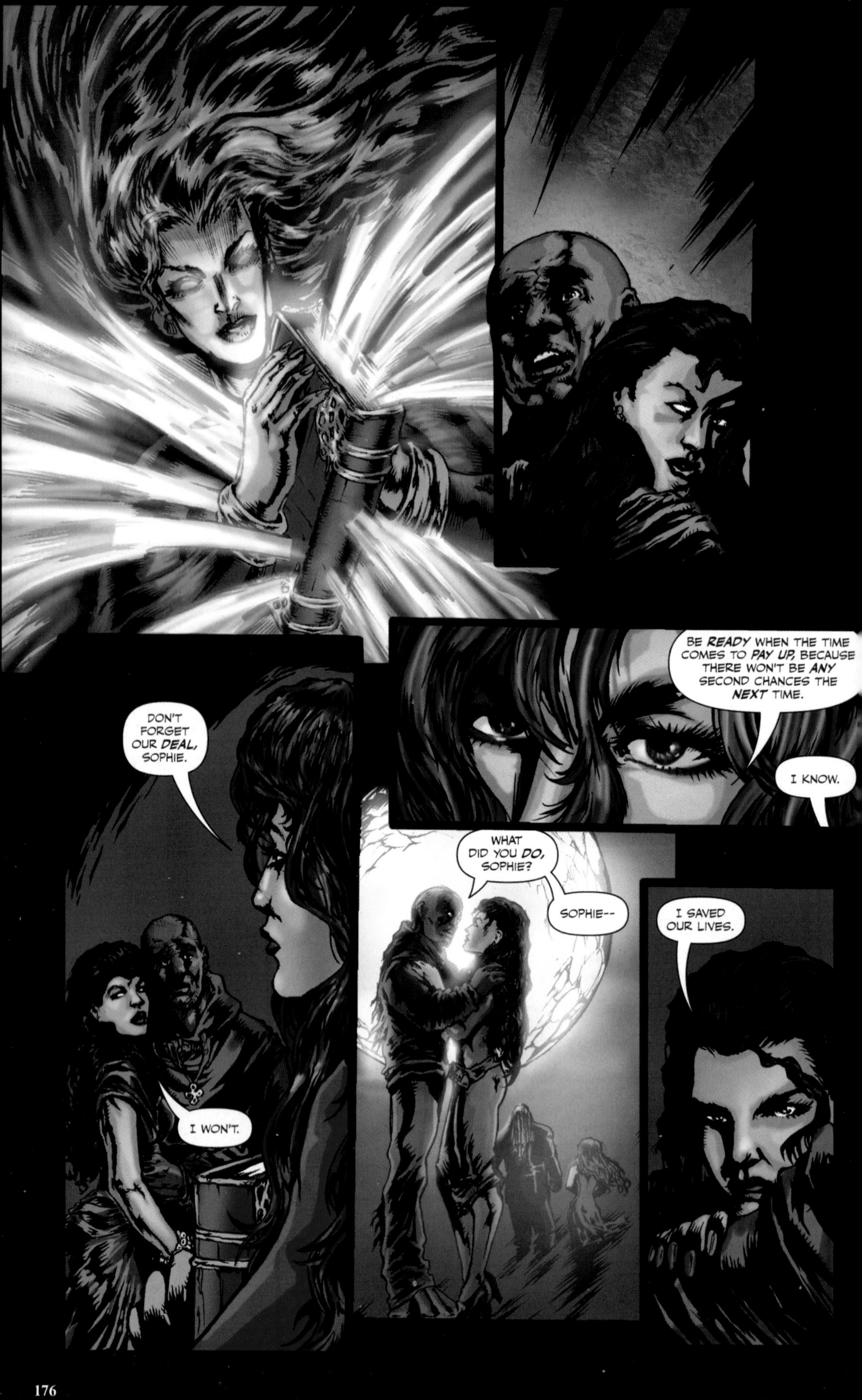
BE READY WHEN THE TIME COMES TO PAY UP, BECAUSE THERE WON'T BE ANY SECOND CHANCES THE NEXT TIME.
I KNOW.
DON'T FORGET OUR DEAL, SOPHIE.
I WON'T.
WHAT DID YOU DO, SOPHIE?
SOPHIE--
I SAVED OUR LIVES.

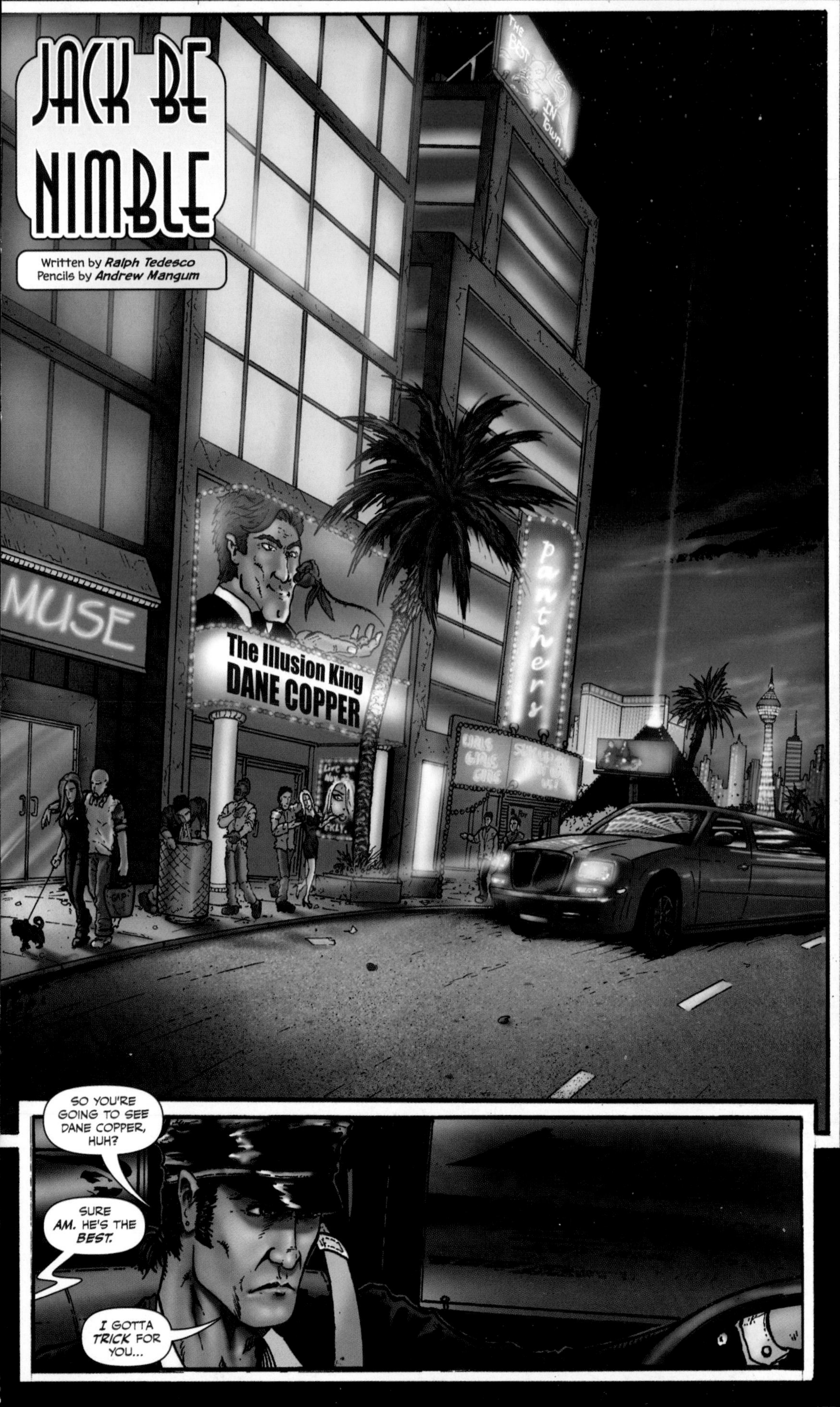
JACK BE NIMBLE
Written by Ralph Tedesco
Pencils by Andrew Mangum
MUSE
The Illusion King
DANE COPPER
Panthers
SO YOU'RE GOING TO SEE DANE COPPER, HUH?
SURE AM. HE'S THE BEST.
I GOTTA TRICK FOR YOU...

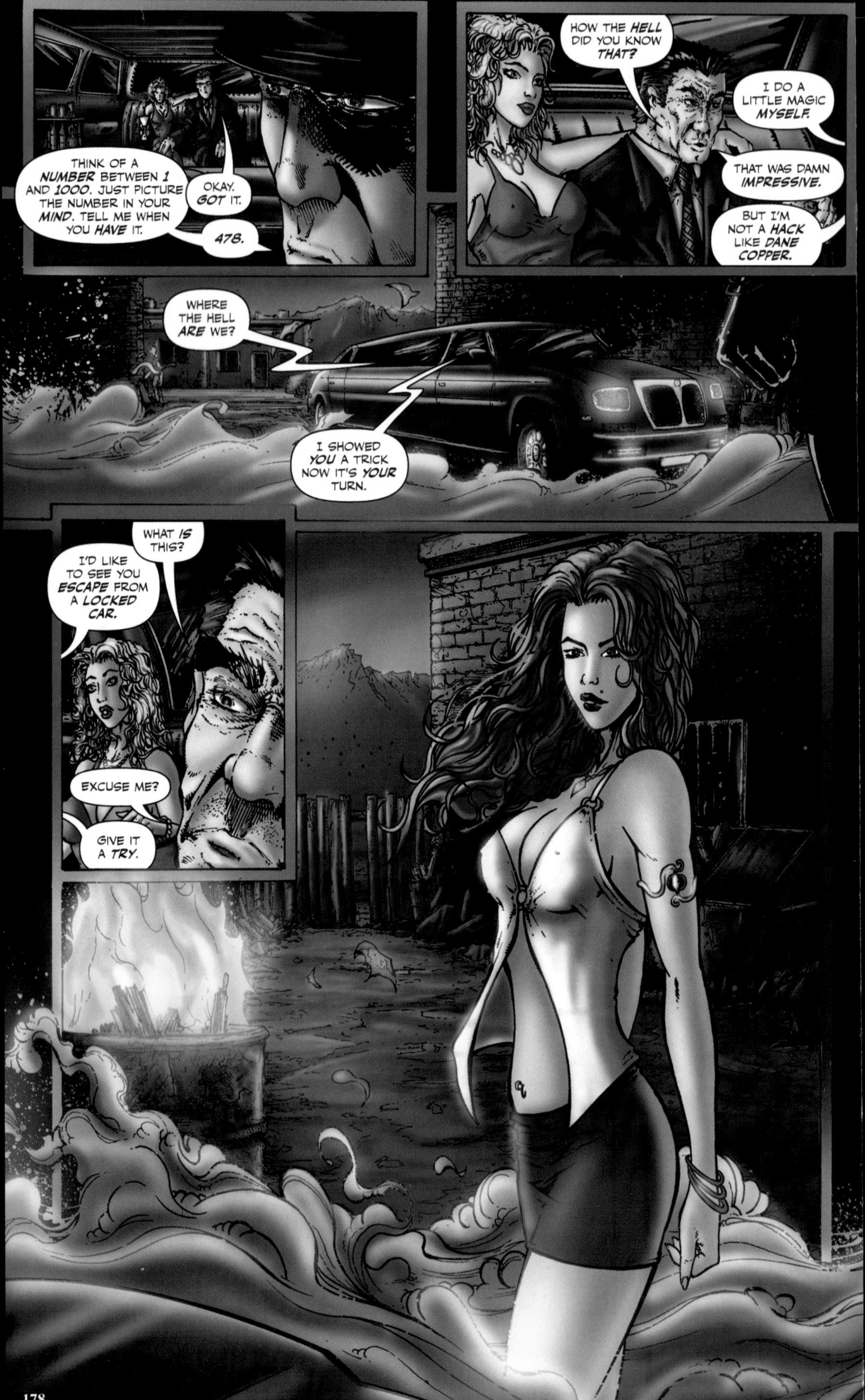
THINK OF A NUMBER BETWEEN 1 AND 1000. JUST PICTURE THE NUMBER IN YOUR MIND. TELL ME WHEN YOU HAVE IT.
OKAY. GOT IT.
478.
HOW THE HELL DID YOU KNOW THAT?
I DO A LITTLE MAGIC MYSELF.
THAT WAS DAMN IMPRESSIVE.
BUT I'M NOT A HACK LIKE DANE COPPER.
WHERE THE HELL ARE WE?
I SHOWED YOU A TRICK NOW IT'S YOUR TURN.
WHAT IS THIS?
I'D LIKE TO SEE YOU ESCAPE FROM A LOCKED CAR.
EXCUSE ME?
GIVE IT A TRY.

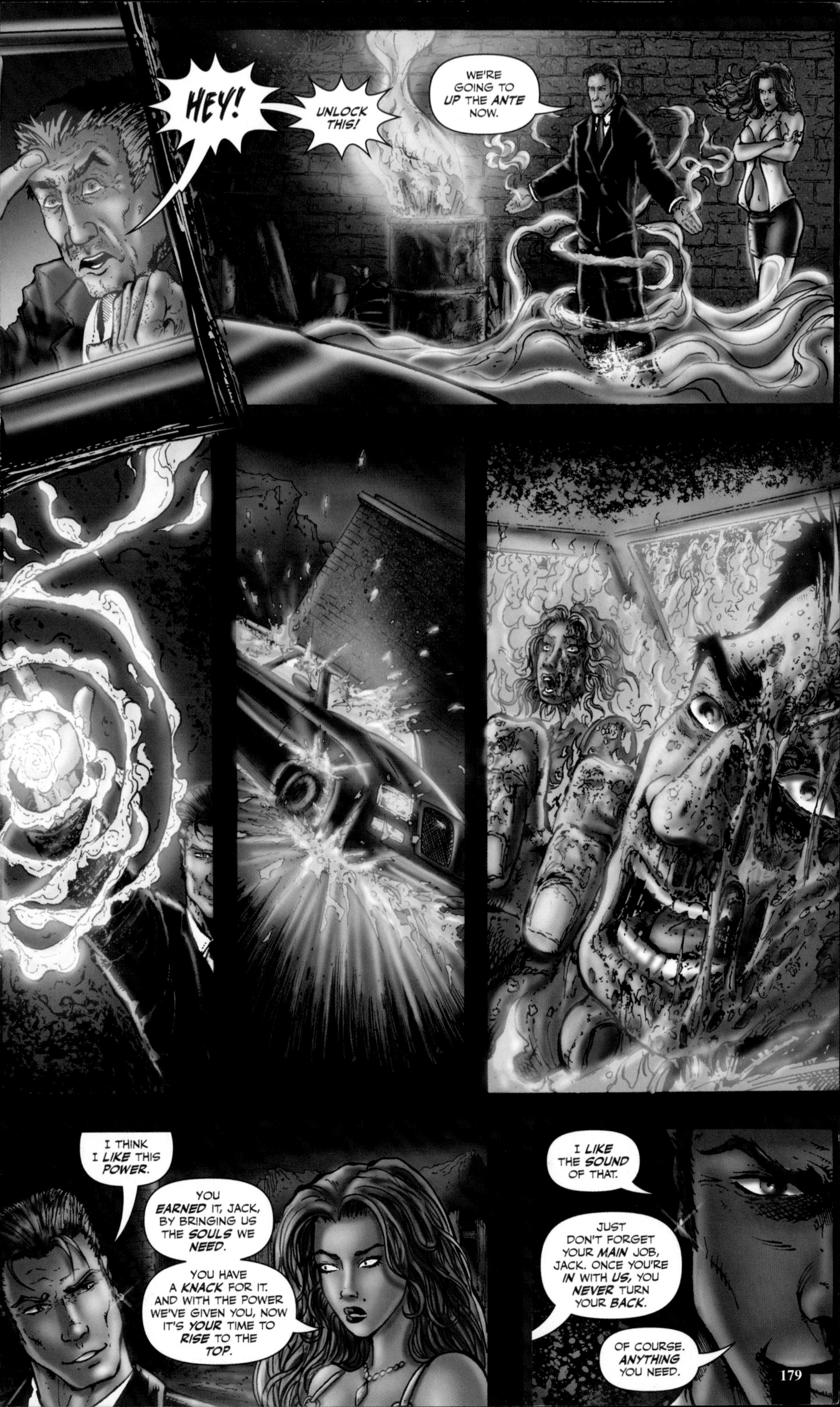
HEY!
UNLOCK THIS!
WE'RE GOING TO UP THE ANTE NOW.
I THINK I LIKE THIS POWER.
YOU EARNED IT, JACK, BY BRINGING US THE SOULS WE NEED.
YOU HAVE A KNACK FOR IT. AND WITH THE POWER WE'VE GIVEN YOU, NOW IT'S YOUR TIME TO RISE TO THE TOP.
I LIKE THE SOUND OF THAT.
JUST DON'T FORGET YOUR MAIN JOB, JACK. ONCE YOU'RE IN WITH US, YOU NEVER TURN YOUR BACK.
OF COURSE. ANYTHING YOU NEED.

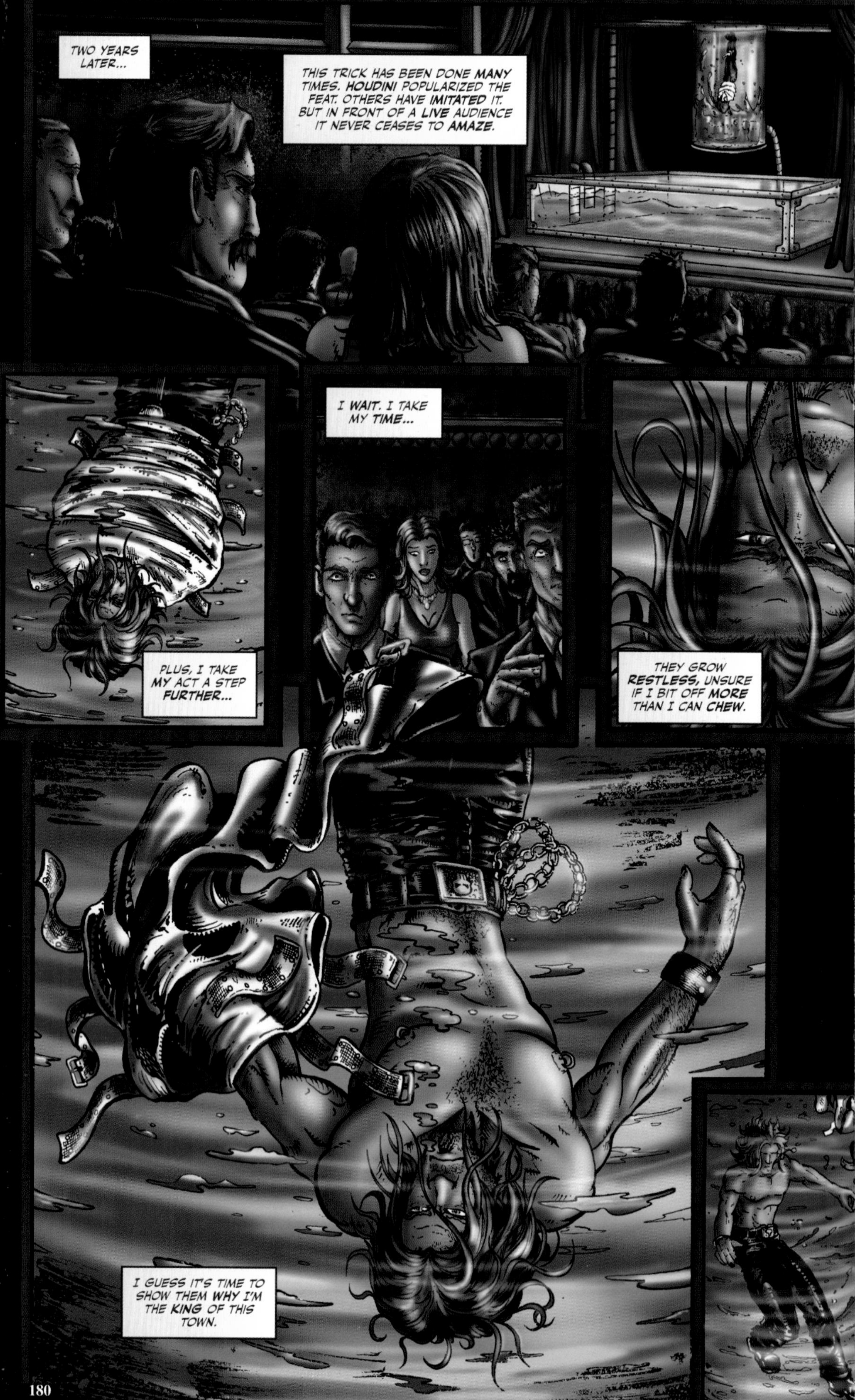
TWO YEARS LATER...
THIS TRICK HAS BEEN DONE MANY TIMES. HOUDINI POPULARIZED THE FEAT. OTHERS HAVE IMITATED IT. BUT IN FRONT OF A LIVE AUDIENCE IT NEVER CEASES TO AMAZE.
PLUS, I TAKE MY ACT A STEP FURTHER...
I WAIT. I TAKE MY TIME...
THEY GROW RESTLESS, UNSURE IF I BIT OFF MORE THAN I CAN CHEW.
I GUESS IT'S TIME TO SHOW THEM WHY I'M THE KING OF THIS TOWN.

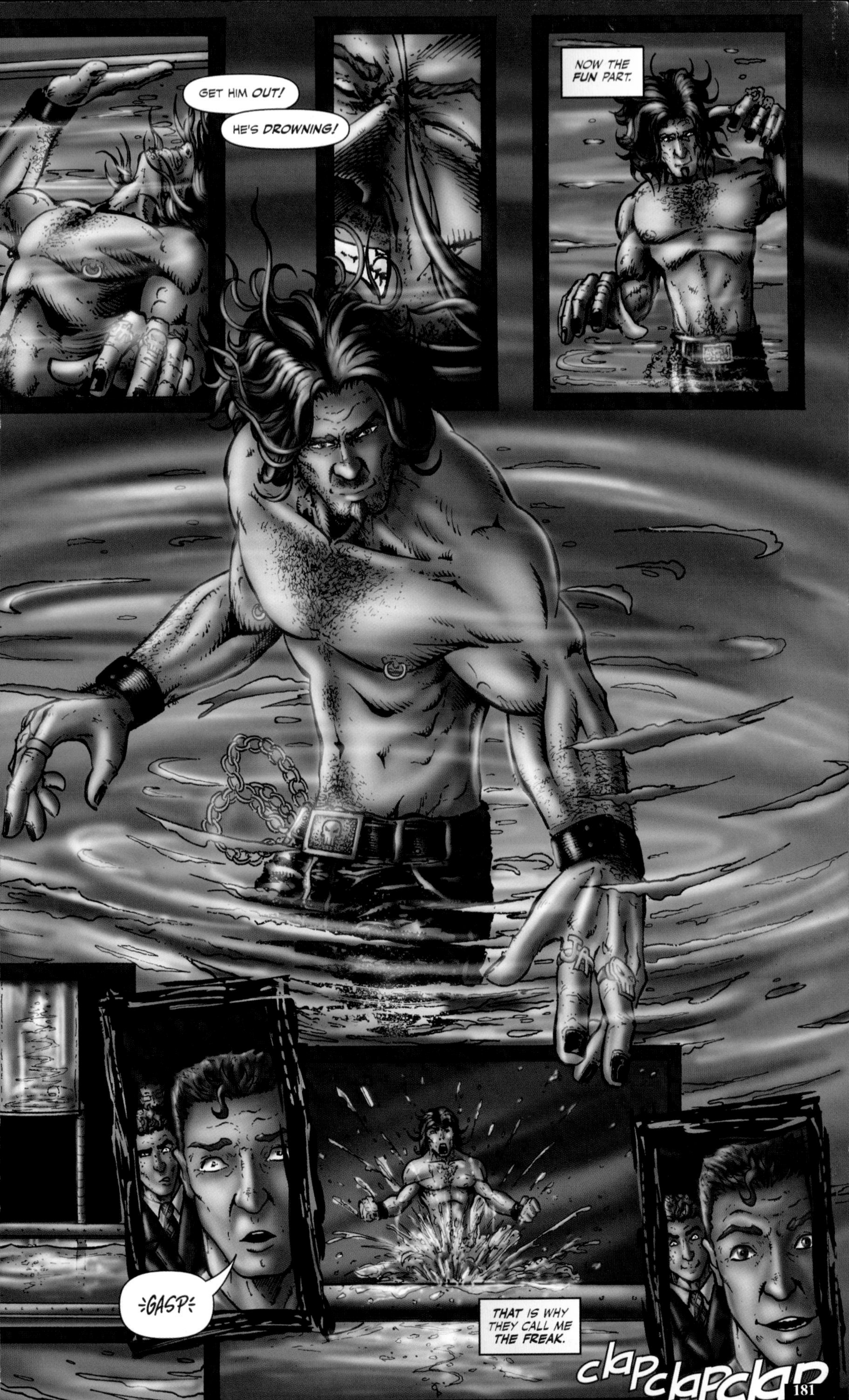
GET HIM OUT!
HE'S DROWNING!
NOW THE FUN PART.
GASP
THAT IS WHY THEY CALL ME THE FREAK.
clapclapclap

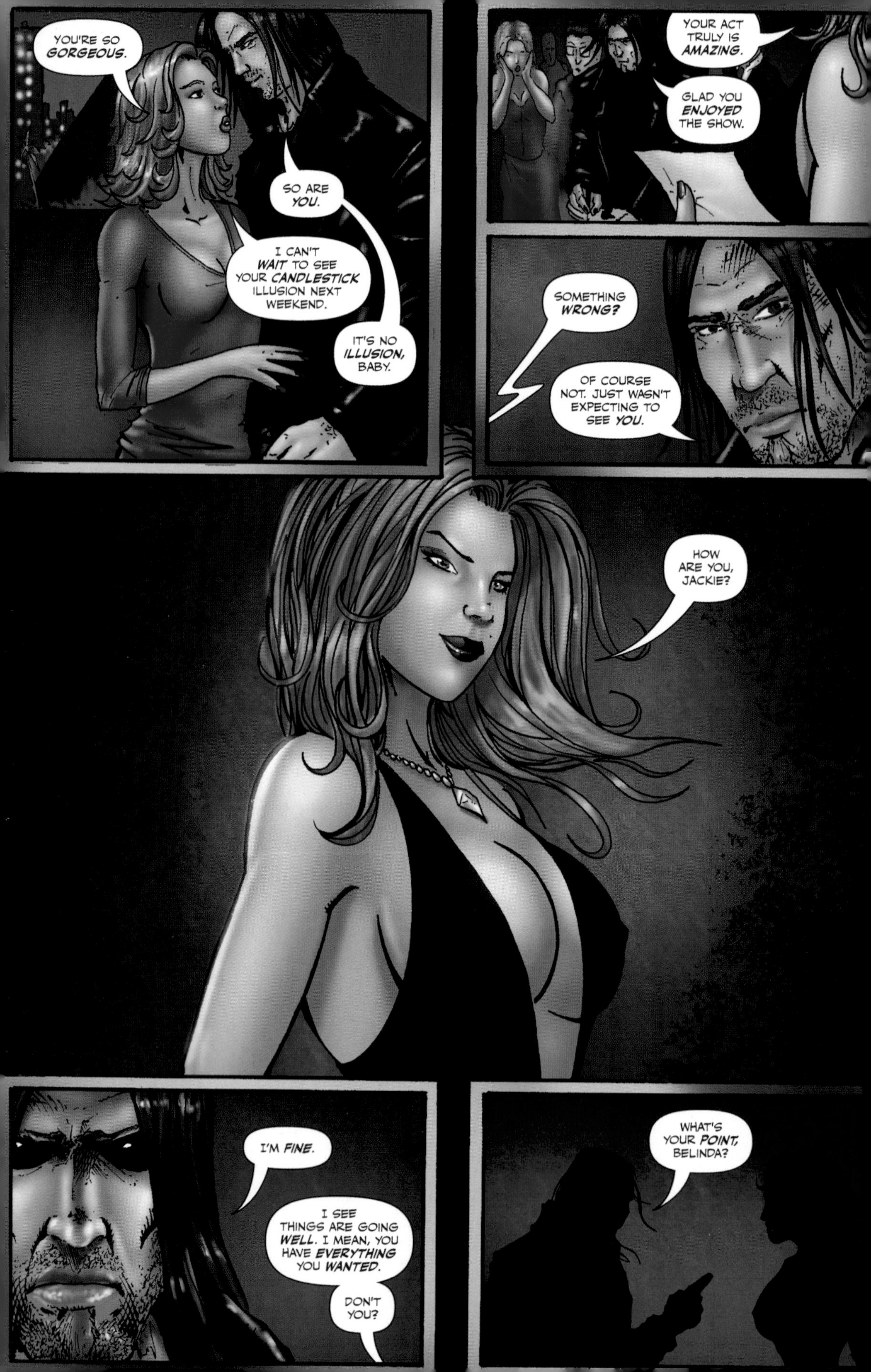
YOU'RE SO *GORGEOUS*.
SO ARE *YOU*.
I CAN'T *WAIT* TO SEE YOUR *CANDLESTICK* ILLUSION NEXT WEEKEND.
IT'S NO *ILLUSION*, BABY.
YOUR ACT TRULY IS *AMAZING*.
GLAD YOU *ENJOYED* THE SHOW.
SOMETHING *WRONG?*
OF COURSE NOT. JUST WASN'T EXPECTING TO SEE *YOU*.
HOW ARE YOU, JACKIE?
I'M *FINE*.
I SEE THINGS ARE GOING *WELL*. I MEAN, YOU HAVE *EVERYTHING* YOU *WANTED*.
DON'T YOU?
WHAT'S YOUR *POINT*, BELINDA?

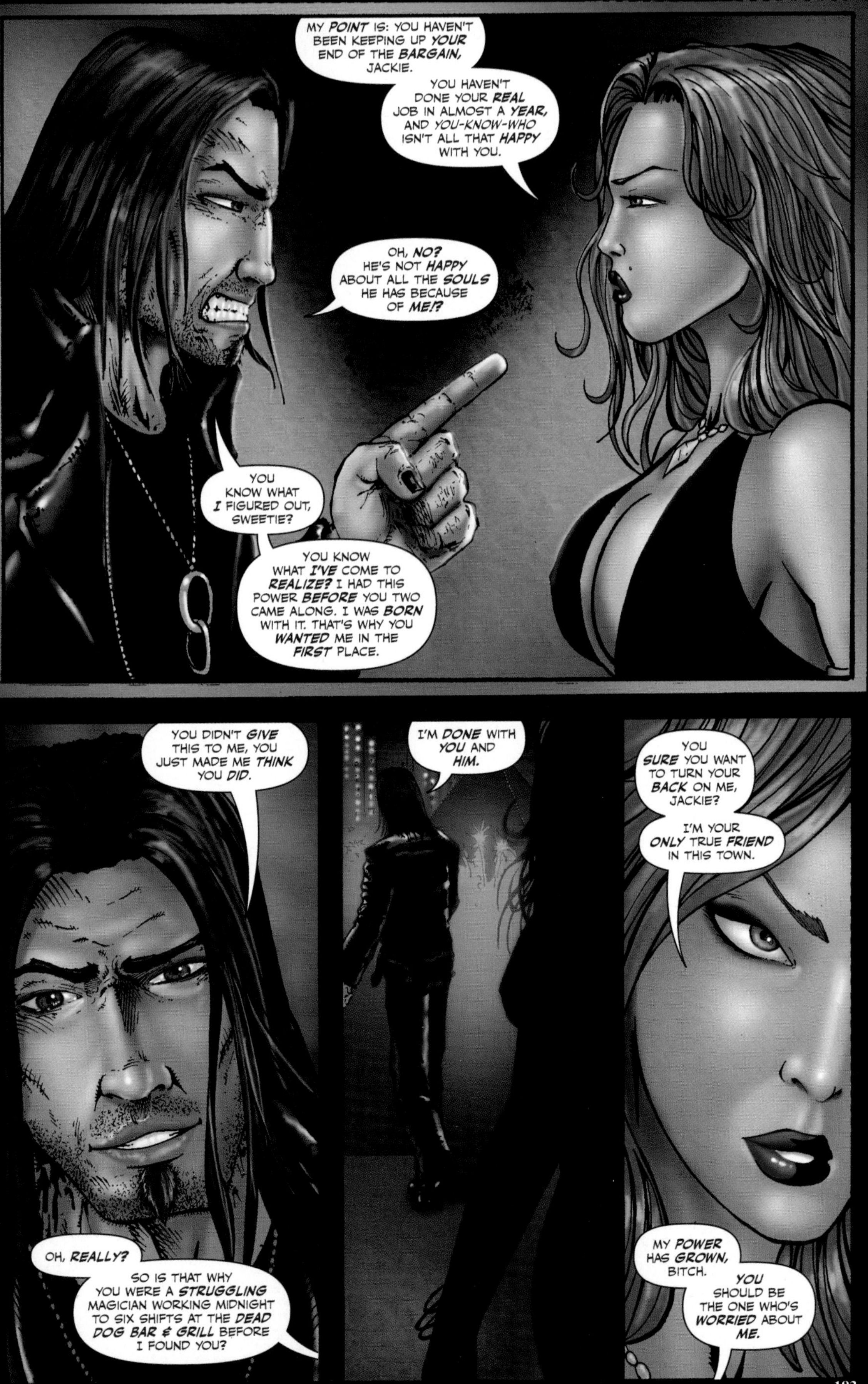
MY POINT IS: YOU HAVEN'T BEEN KEEPING UP YOUR END OF THE BARGAIN, JACKIE.
YOU HAVEN'T DONE YOUR REAL JOB IN ALMOST A YEAR, AND YOU-KNOW-WHO ISN'T ALL THAT HAPPY WITH YOU.
OH, NO? HE'S NOT HAPPY ABOUT ALL THE SOULS HE HAS BECAUSE OF ME!?
YOU KNOW WHAT I FIGURED OUT, SWEETIE?
YOU KNOW WHAT I'VE COME TO REALIZE? I HAD THIS POWER BEFORE YOU TWO CAME ALONG. I WAS BORN WITH IT. THAT'S WHY YOU WANTED ME IN THE FIRST PLACE.
YOU DIDN'T GIVE THIS TO ME, YOU JUST MADE ME THINK YOU DID.
OH, REALLY?
SO IS THAT WHY YOU WERE A STRUGGLING MAGICIAN WORKING MIDNIGHT TO SIX SHIFTS AT THE DEAD DOG BAR & GRILL BEFORE I FOUND YOU?
I'M DONE WITH YOU AND HIM.
YOU SURE YOU WANT TO TURN YOUR BACK ON ME, JACKIE?
I'M YOUR ONLY TRUE FRIEND IN THIS TOWN.
MY POWER HAS GROWN, BITCH.
YOU SHOULD BE THE ONE WHO'S WORRIED ABOUT ME.

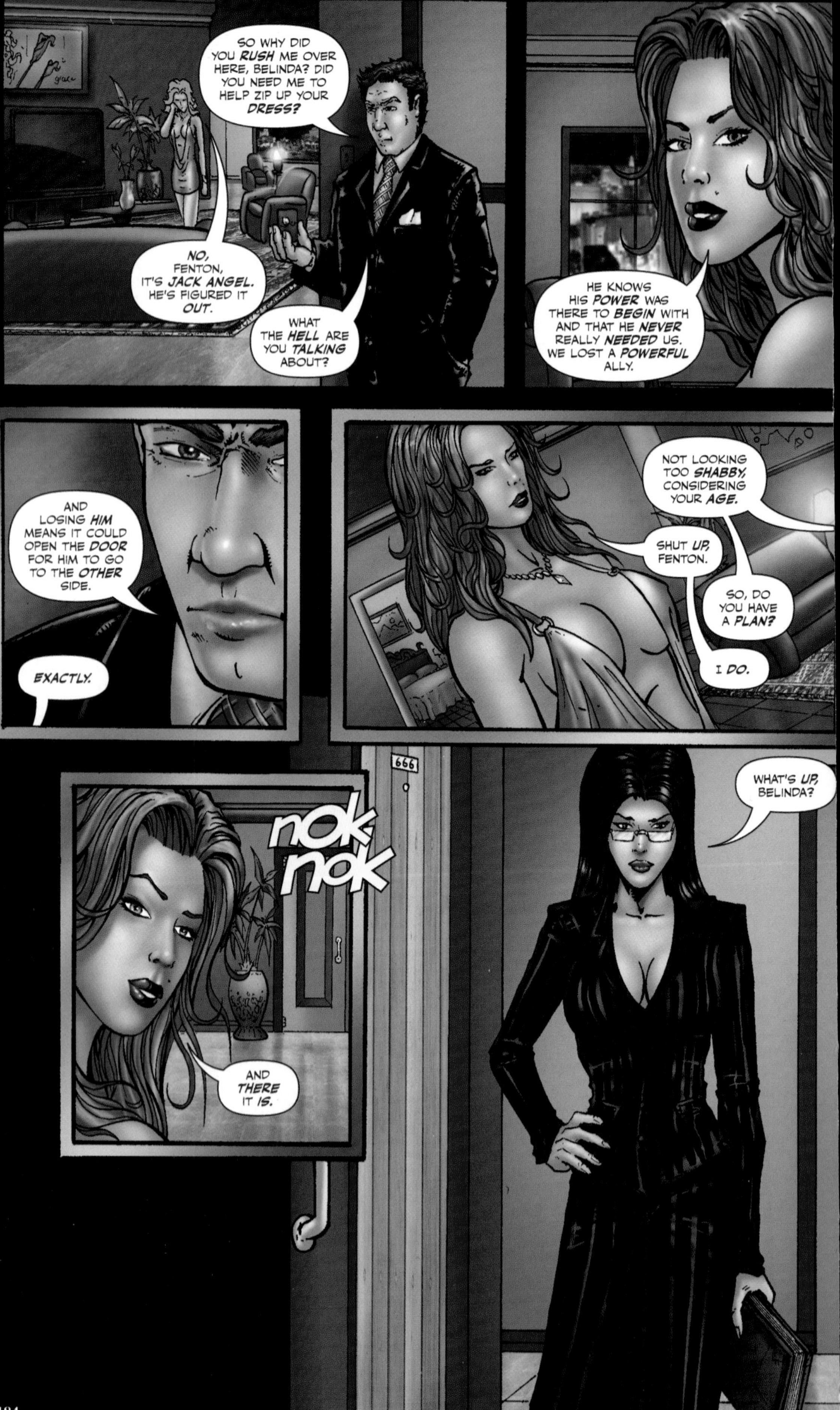

SO WHY DID YOU RUSH ME OVER HERE, BELINDA? DID YOU NEED ME TO HELP ZIP UP YOUR DRESS?
NO, FENTON, IT'S JACK ANGEL. HE'S FIGURED IT OUT.
WHAT THE HELL ARE YOU TALKING ABOUT?
HE KNOWS HIS POWER WAS THERE TO BEGIN WITH AND THAT HE NEVER REALLY NEEDED US. WE LOST A POWERFUL ALLY.
AND LOSING HIM MEANS IT COULD OPEN THE DOOR FOR HIM TO GO TO THE OTHER SIDE.
EXACTLY.
NOT LOOKING TOO SHABBY, CONSIDERING YOUR AGE.
SHUT UP, FENTON.
SO, DO YOU HAVE A PLAN?
I DO.
666
nok nok
AND THERE IT IS.
WHAT'S UP, BELINDA?

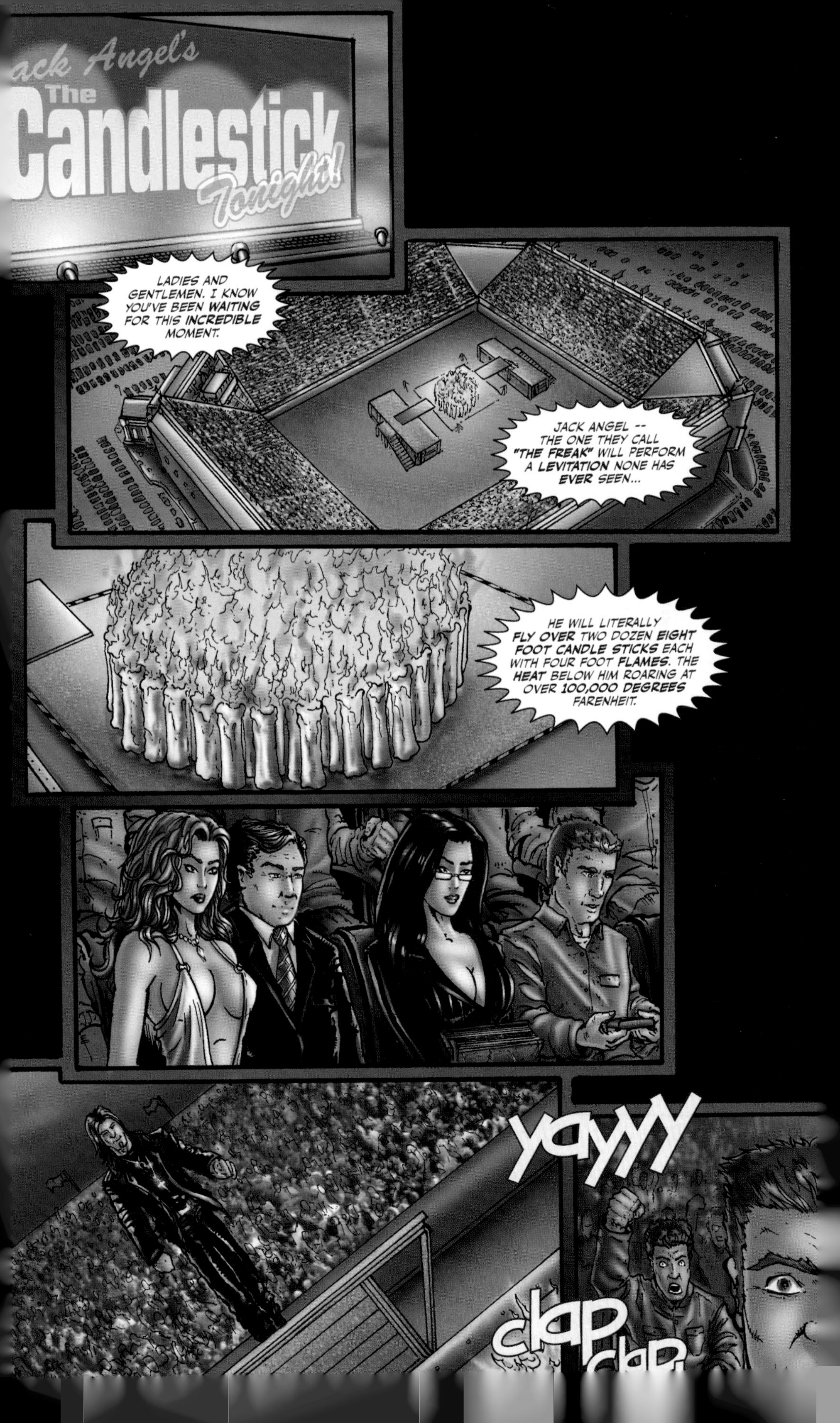
ack Angel's The Candlestick Tonight!
LADIES AND GENTLEMEN. I KNOW YOU'VE BEEN WAITING FOR THIS INCREDIBLE MOMENT.
JACK ANGEL -- THE ONE THEY CALL "THE FREAK" WILL PERFORM A LEVITATION NONE HAS EVER SEEN...
HE WILL LITERALLY FLY OVER TWO DOZEN EIGHT FOOT CANDLE STICKS EACH WITH FOUR FOOT FLAMES. THE HEAT BELOW HIM ROARING AT OVER 100,000 DEGREES FARENHEIT.
yayyy
clap

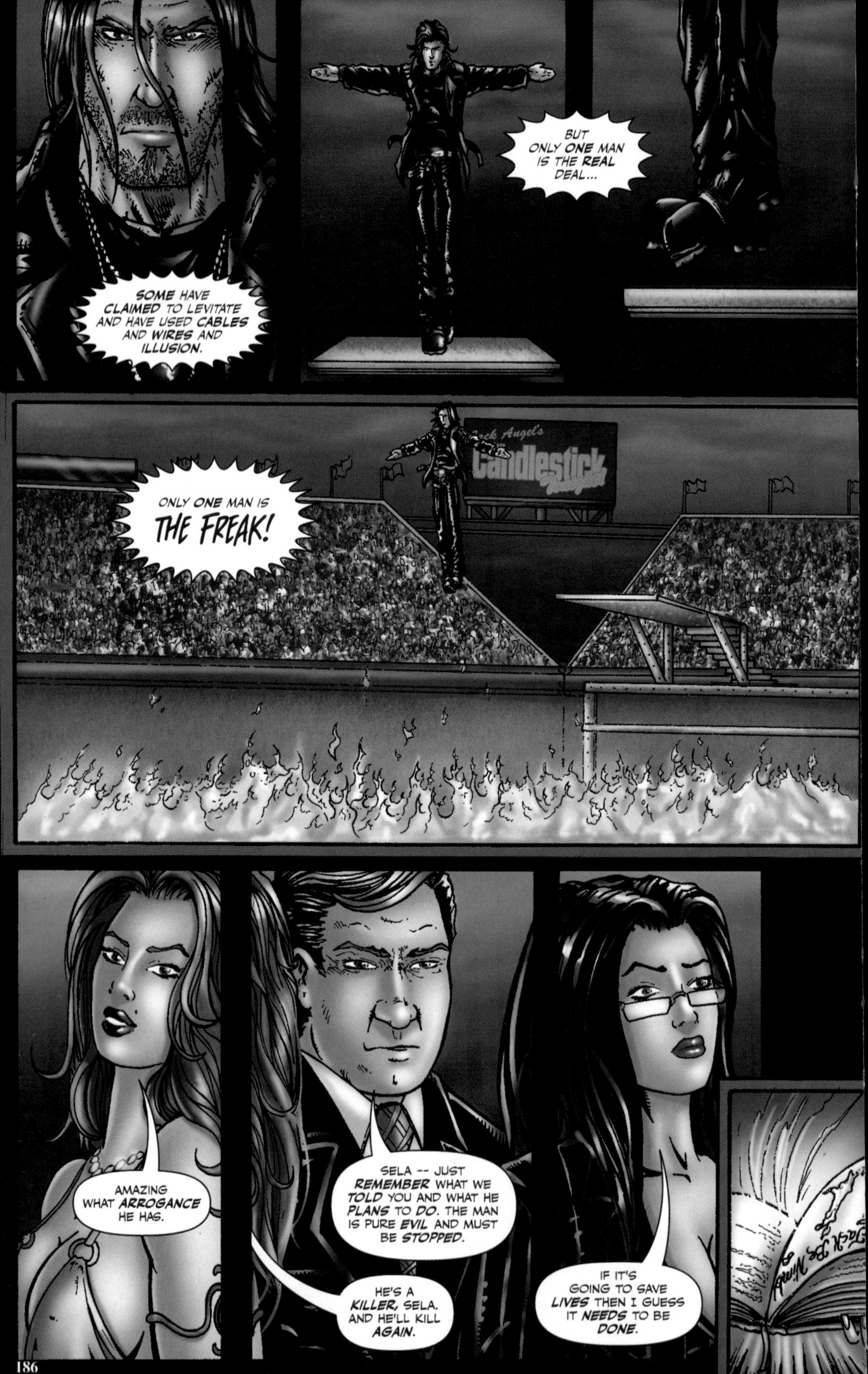
SOME HAVE CLAIMED TO LEVITATE AND HAVE USED CABLES AND WIRES AND ILLUSION.
BUT ONLY ONE MAN IS THE REAL DEAL...
ONLY ONE MAN IS THE FREAK!
Candlestick
AMAZING WHAT ARROGANCE HE HAS.
SELA -- JUST REMEMBER WHAT WE TOLD YOU AND WHAT HE PLANS TO DO. THE MAN IS PURE EVIL AND MUST BE STOPPED.
HE'S A KILLER, SELA. AND HE'LL KILL AGAIN.
IF IT'S GOING TO SAVE LIVES THEN I GUESS IT NEEDS TO BE DONE.

No!
This can't
be...

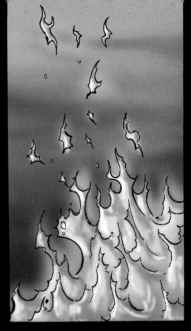

NOOOOOOOOOOOOOO

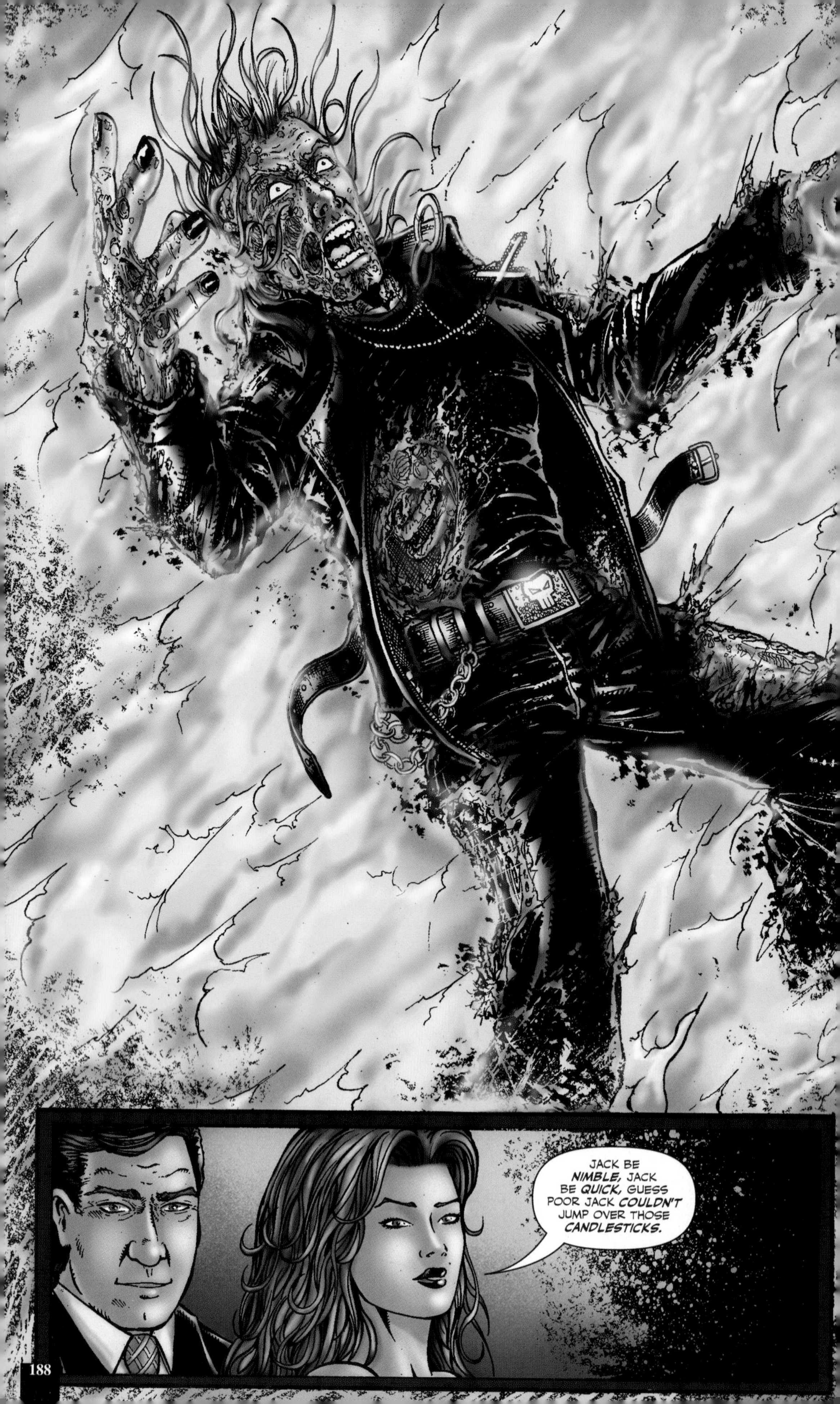
JACK BE NIMBLE, JACK BE QUICK, GUESS POOR JACK COULDN'T JUMP OVER THOSE CANDLESTICKS.

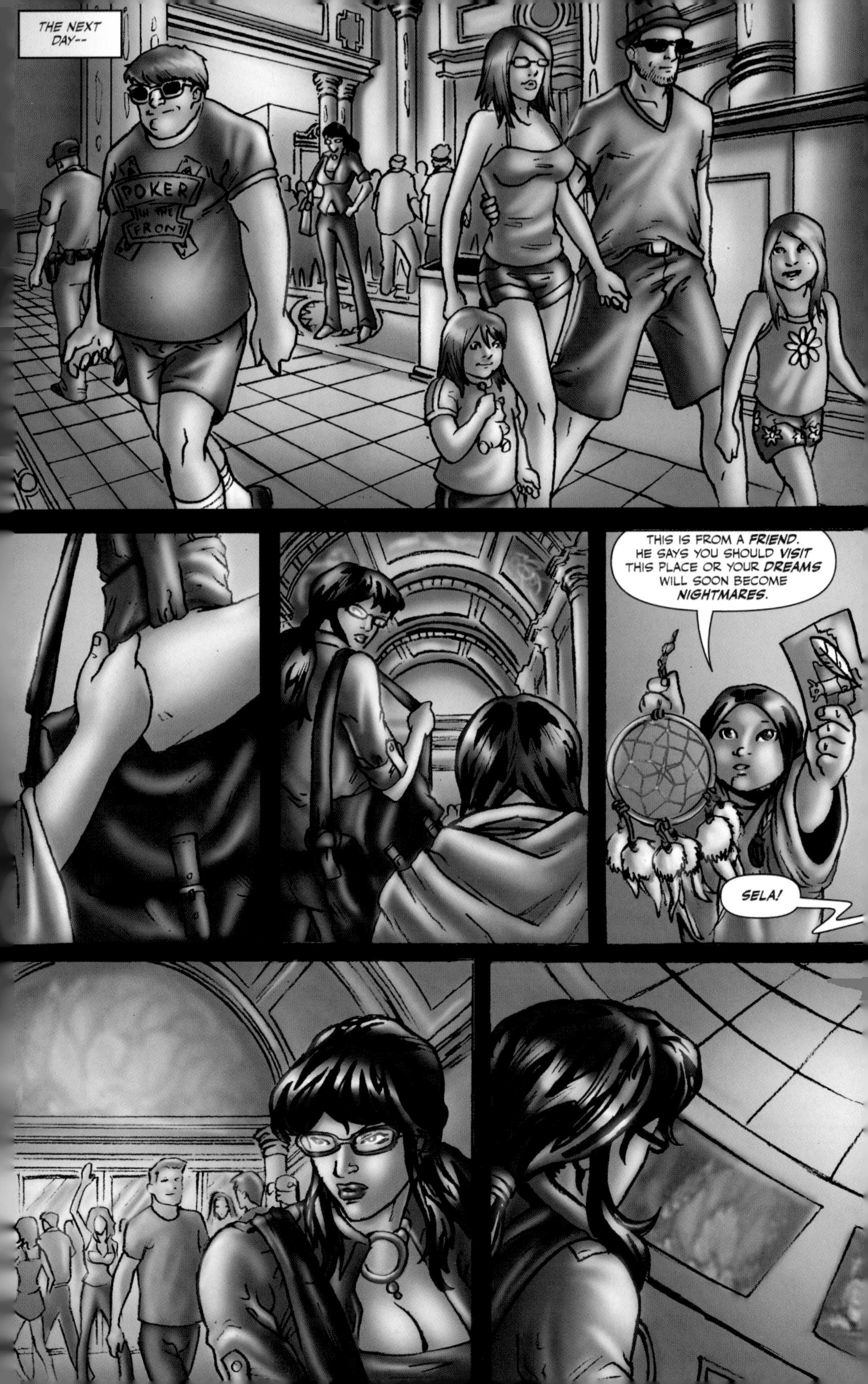
THE NEXT DAY--
POKER IN THE FRONT
THIS IS FROM A FRIEND. HE SAYS YOU SHOULD VISIT THIS PLACE OR YOUR DREAMS WILL SOON BECOME NIGHTMARES.
SELA!

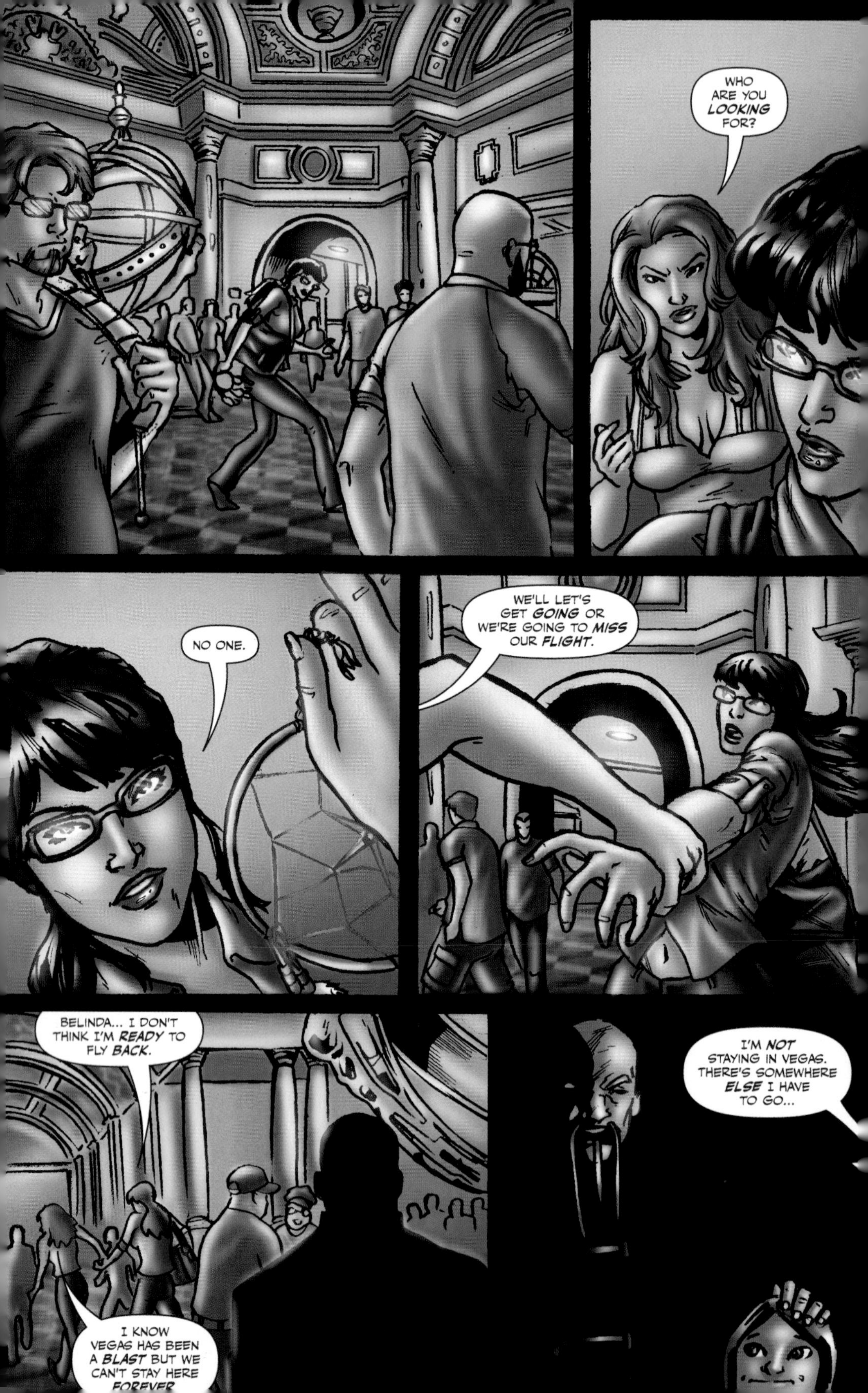
WHO ARE YOU LOOKING FOR?
NO ONE.
WE'LL LET'S GET GOING OR WE'RE GOING TO MISS OUR FLIGHT.
BELINDA... I DON'T THINK I'M READY TO FLY BACK.
I KNOW VEGAS HAS BEEN A BLAST BUT WE CAN'T STAY HERE FOREVER
I'M NOT STAYING IN VEGAS. THERE'S SOMEWHERE ELSE I HAVE TO GO...

Grimm Fairy Tales
Different Seasons

COVER GALLERY

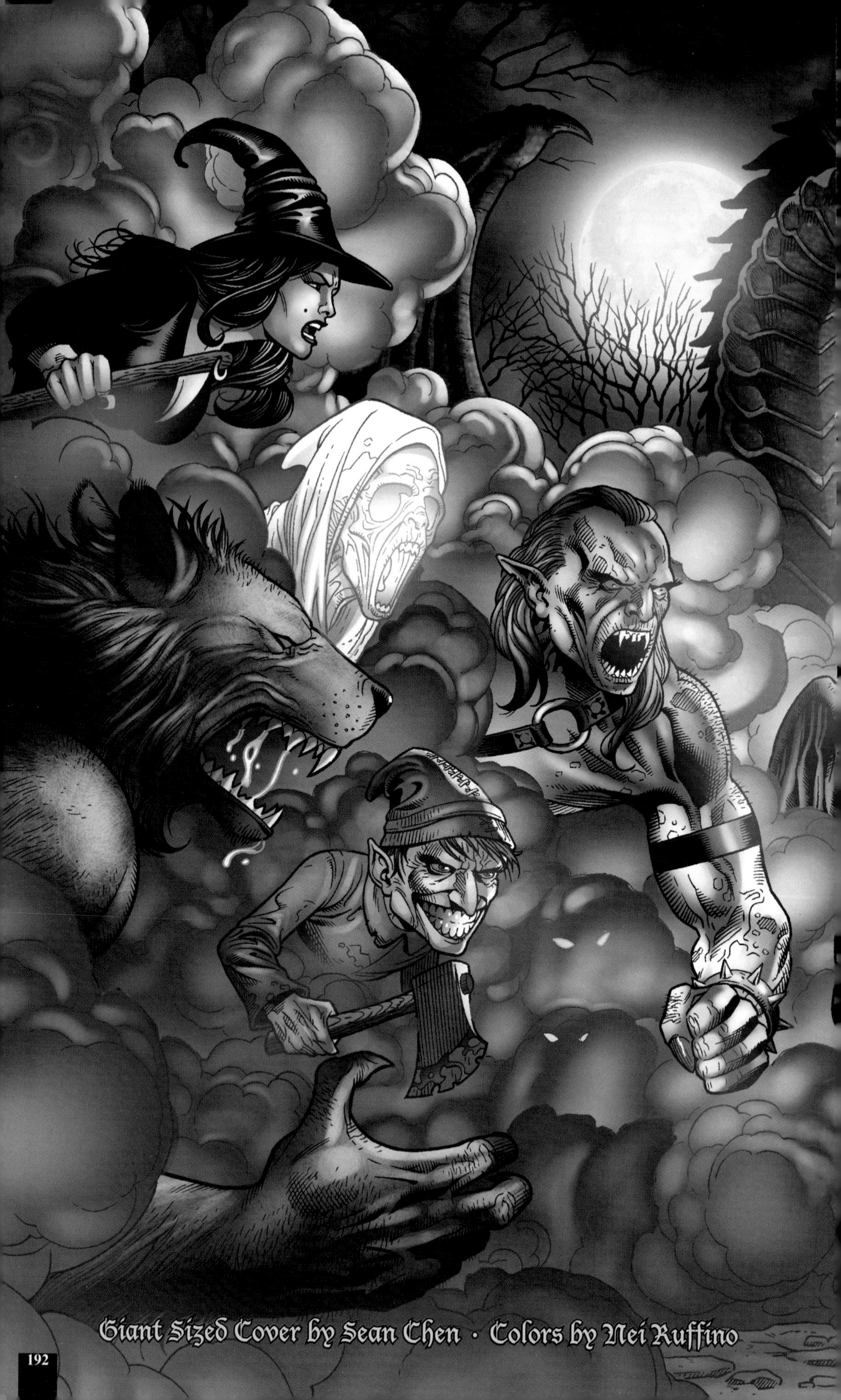

Giant Sized Cover by Sean Chen · Colors by Nei Ruffino

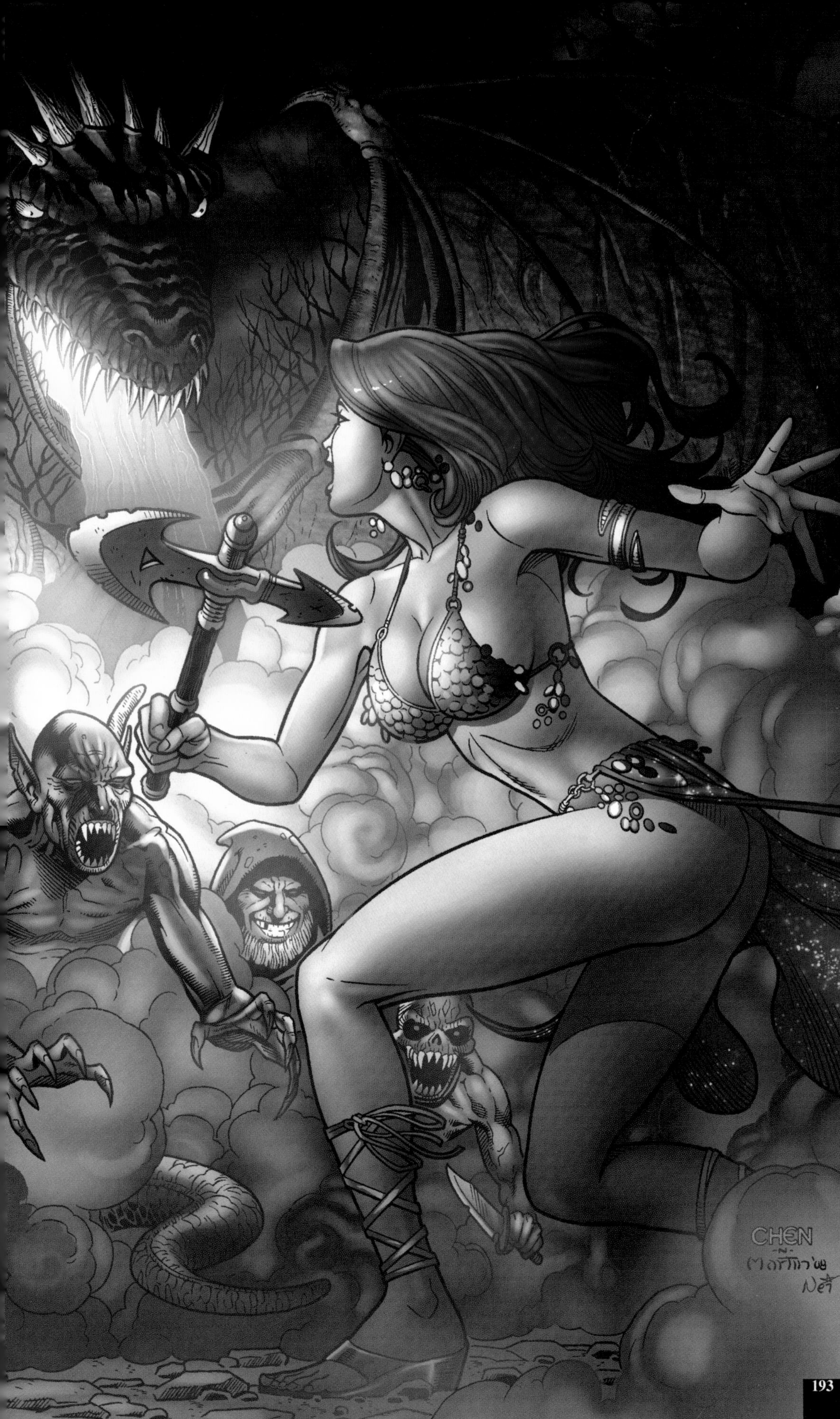
CHEN

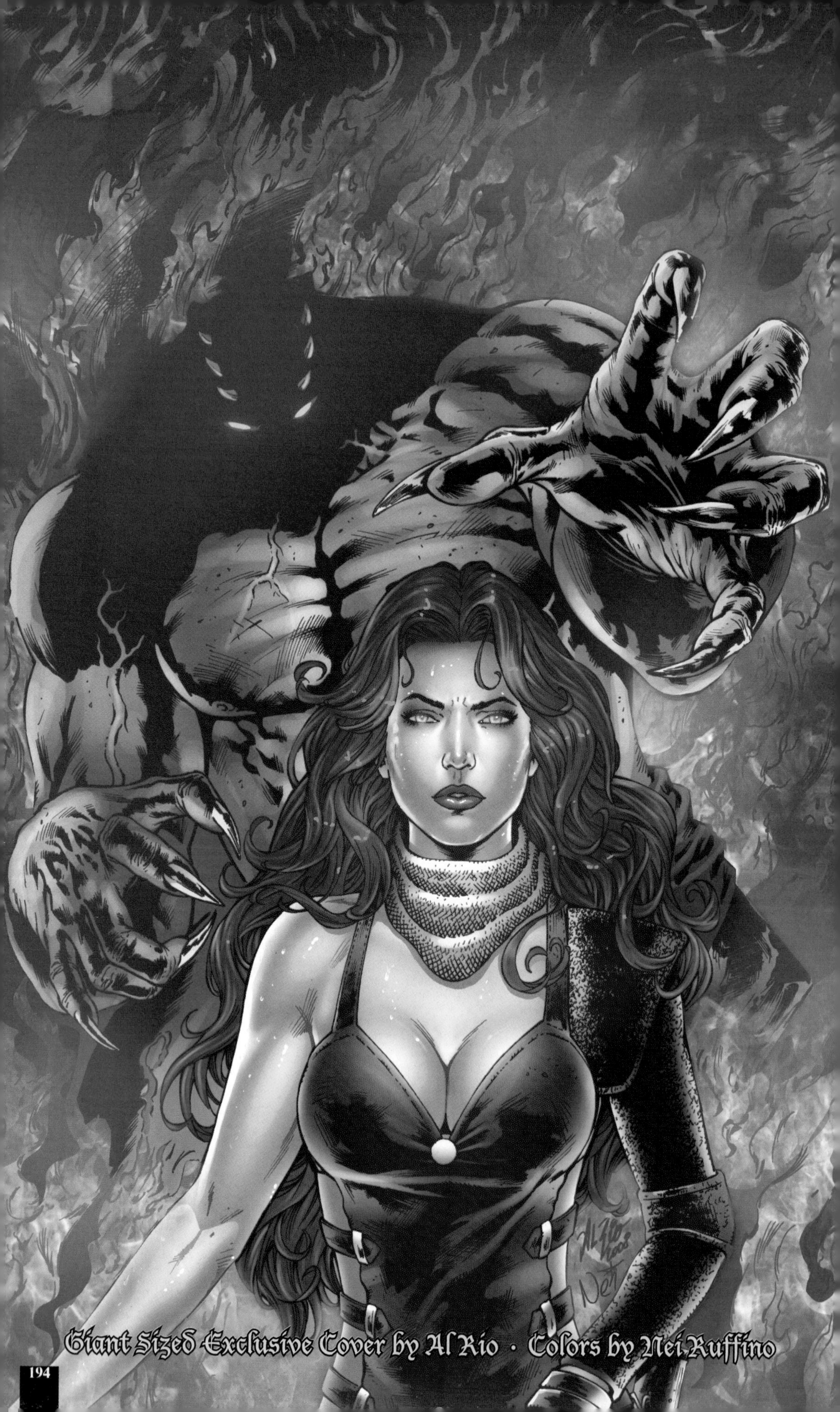

Giant Sized Exclusive Cover by Al Rio · Colors by Nei Ruffino

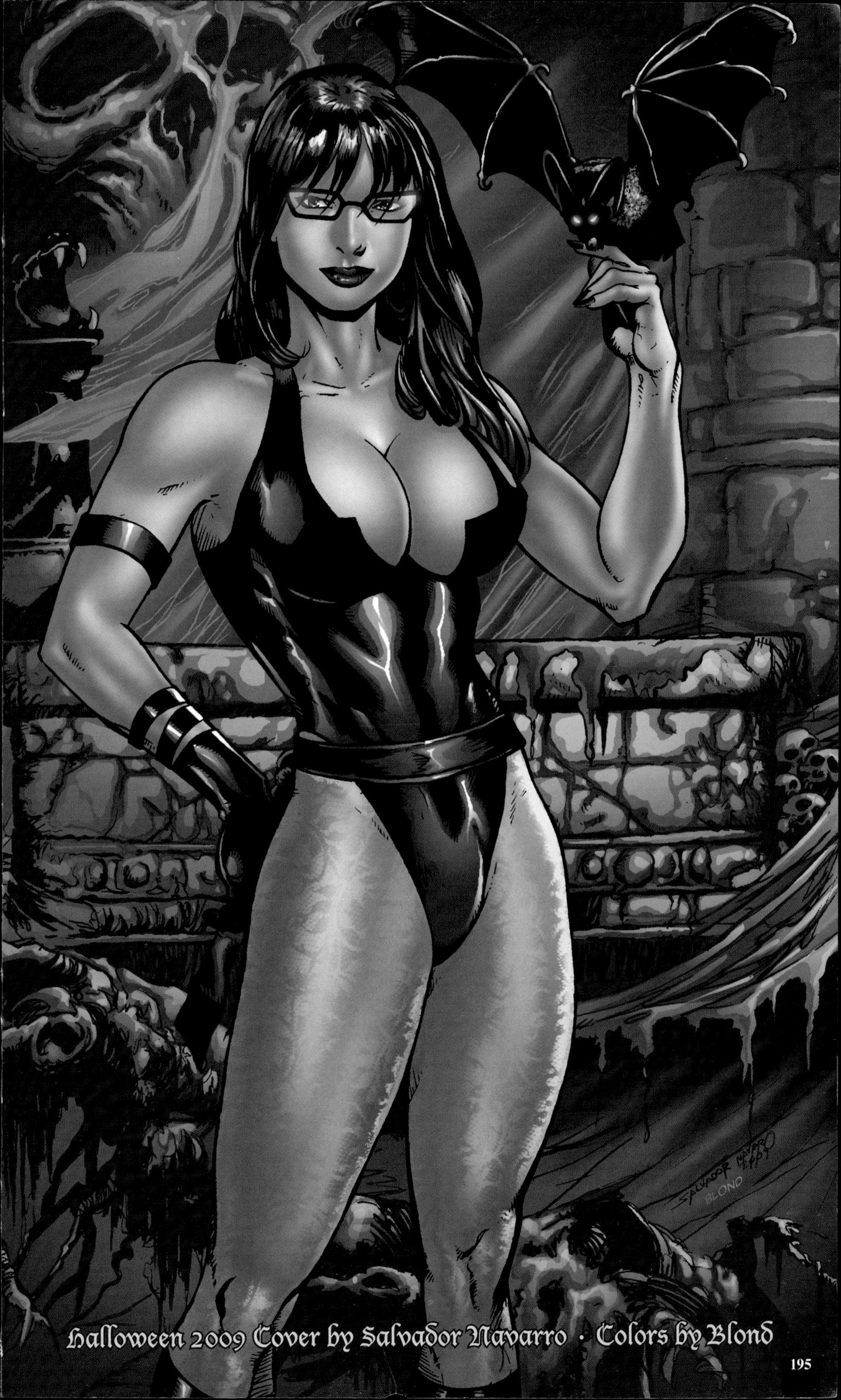
SALVADOR NAVARRO
BLOND

Halloween 2009 Cover by Salvador Navarro · Colors by Blond

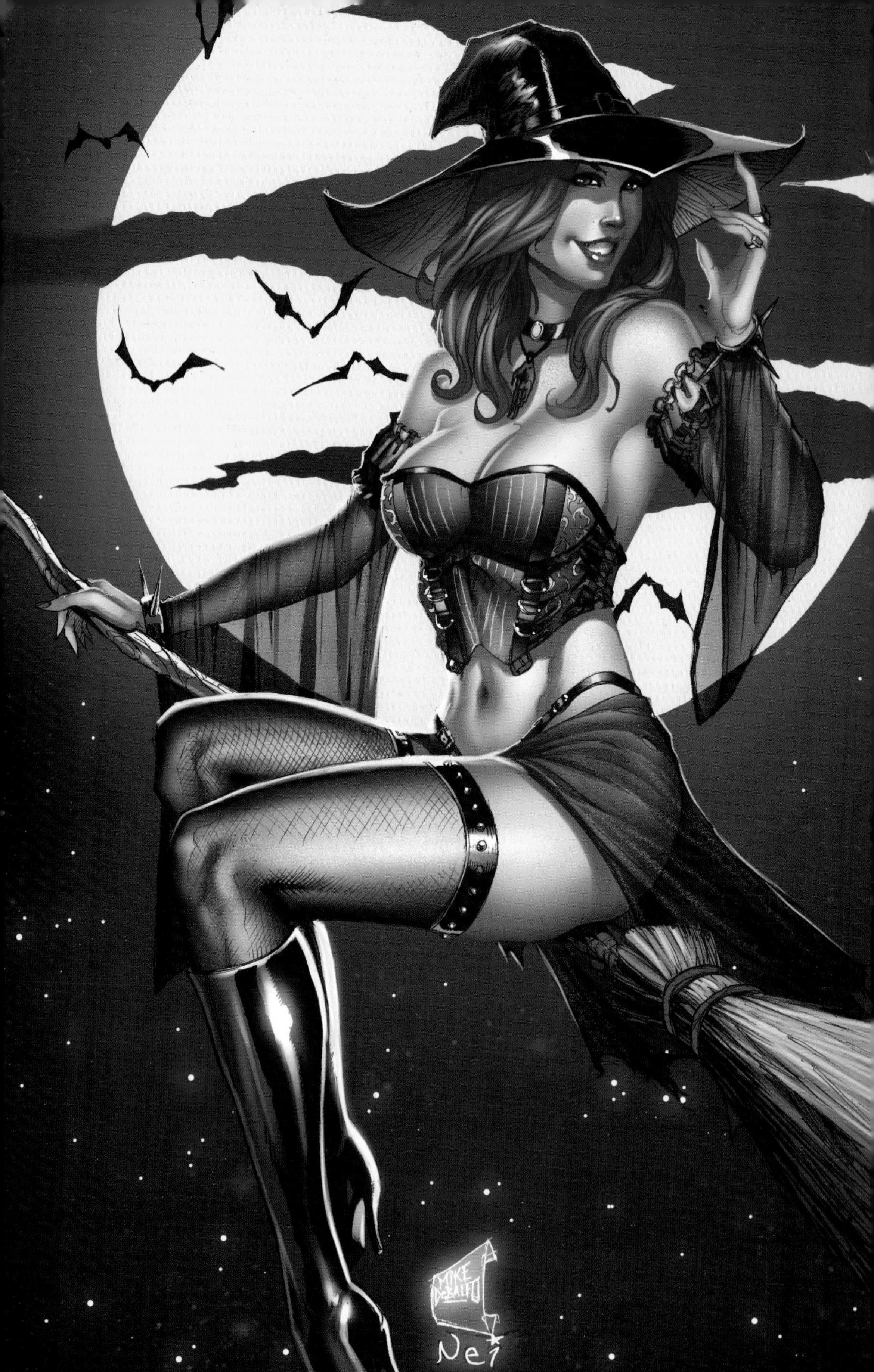
MIKE DEBALFO
Nei

Halloween 2009 Cover by Mike Debalfo · Colors by Nei Ruffino

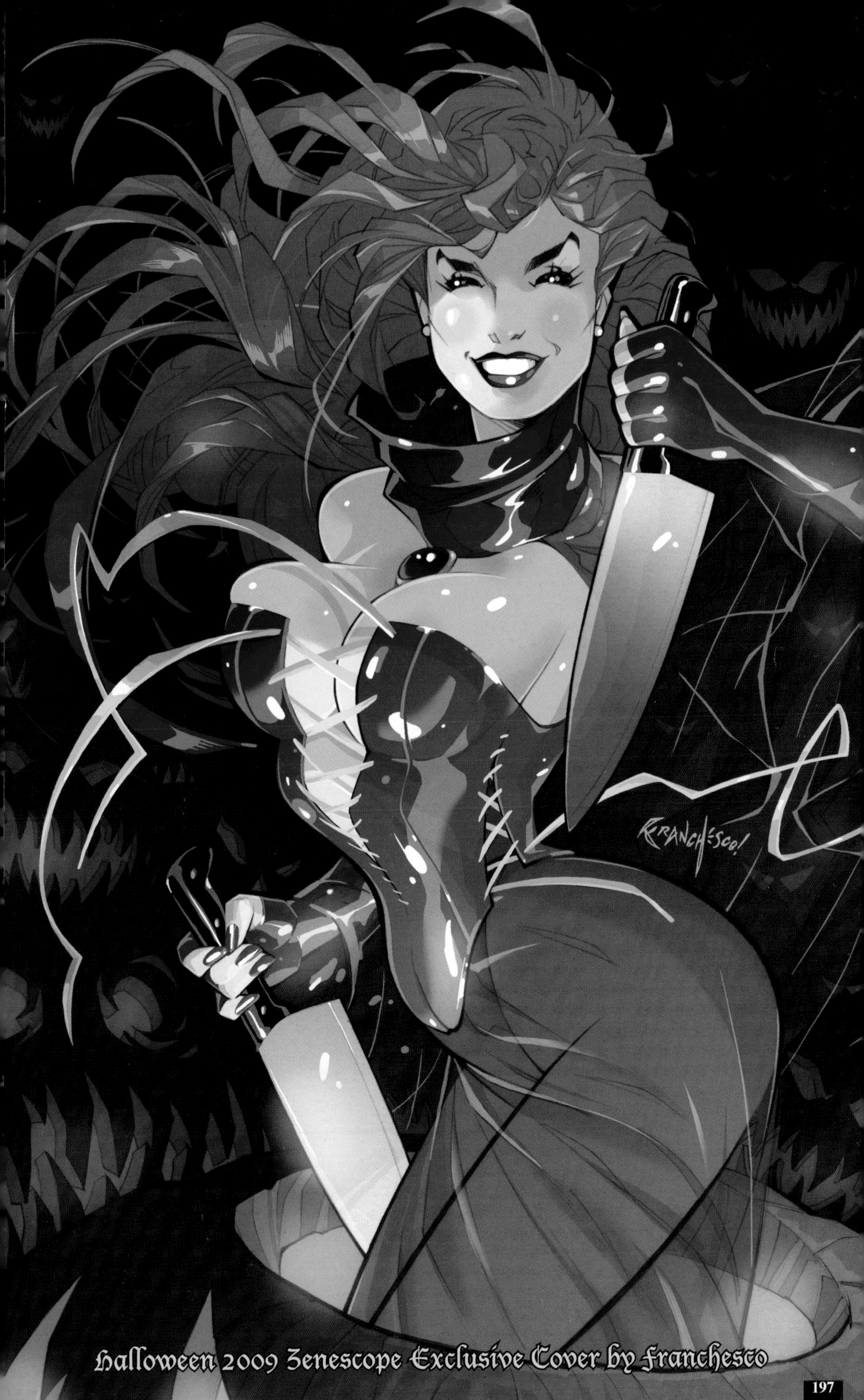
FRANCHESCO!

Halloween 2009 Zenescope Exclusive Cover by Franchesco

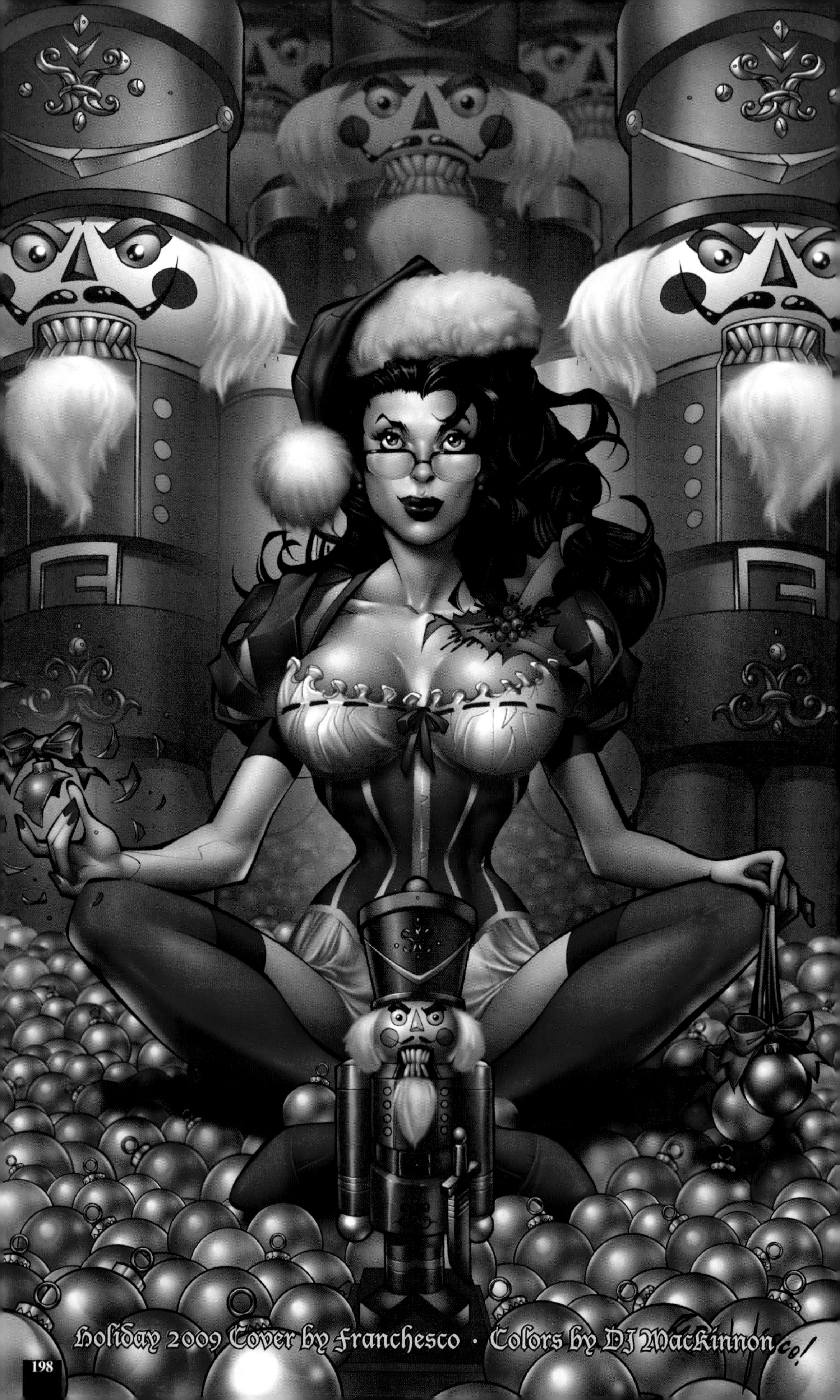

Holiday 2009 Cover by Franchesco · Colors by DJ MacKinnon

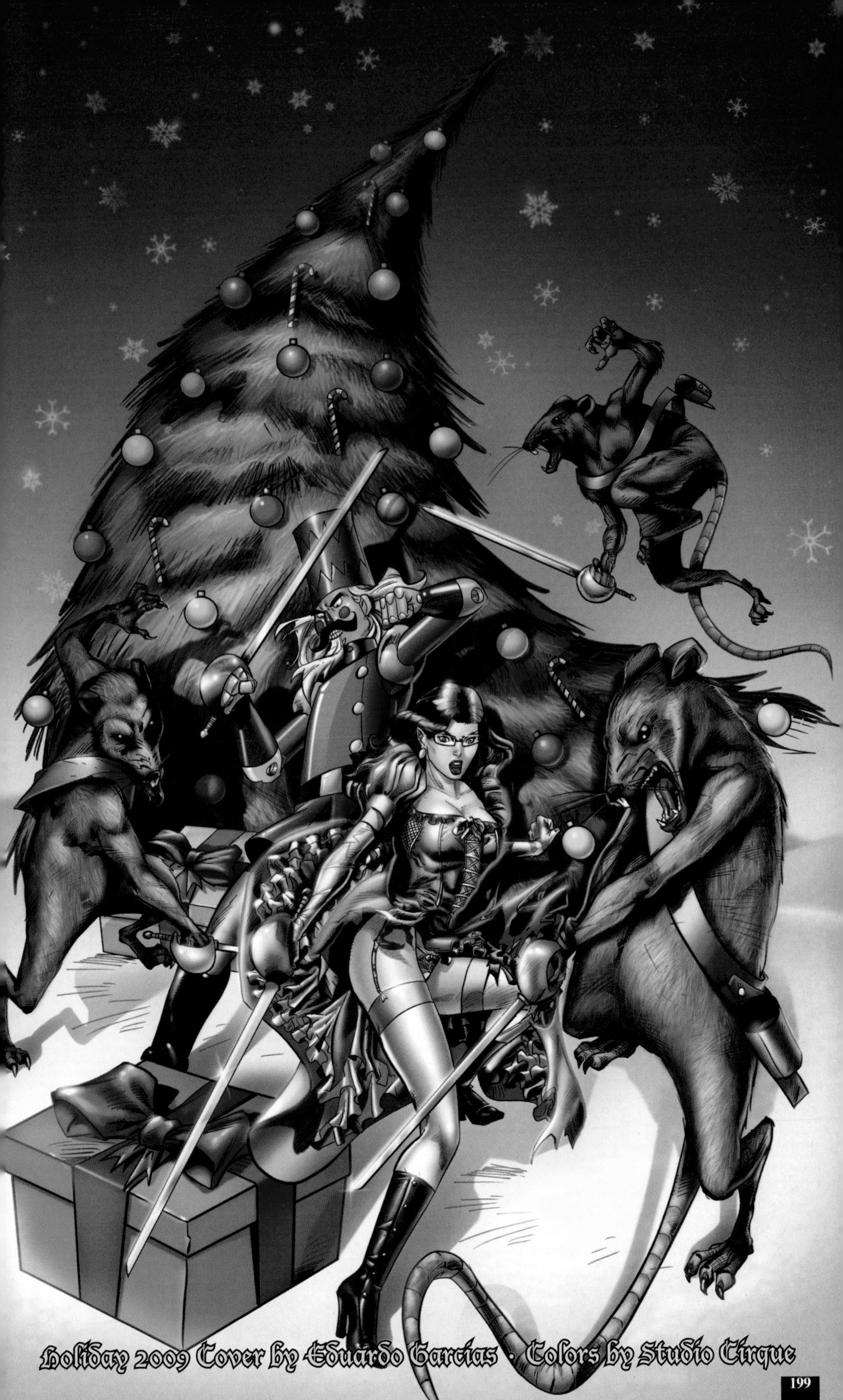

Holiday 2009 Cover by Eduardo Garcias · Colors by Studio Cirque

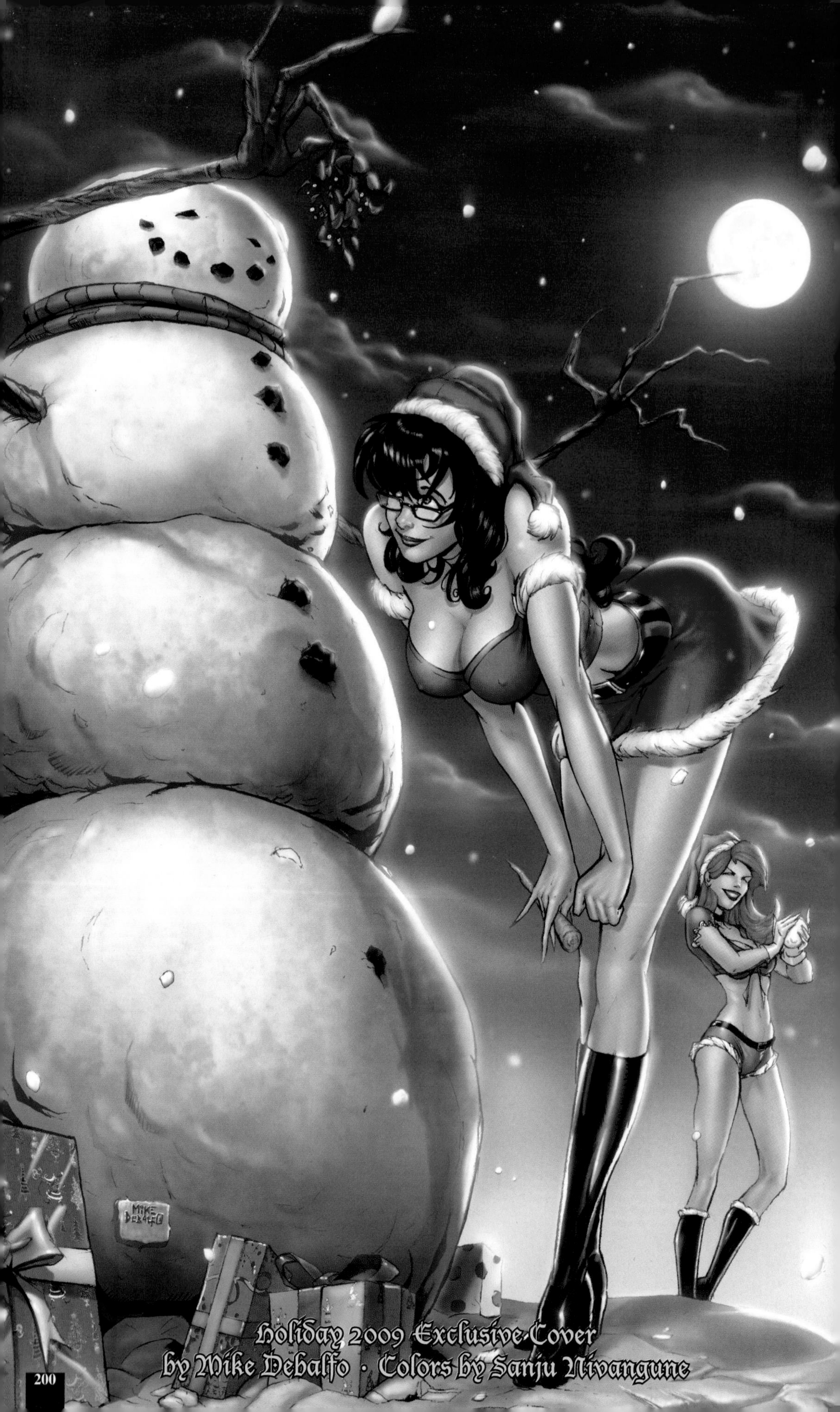
MIKE
DEBALFO

Holiday 2009 Exclusive Cover
by Mike Debalfo · Colors by Sanju Nivangune

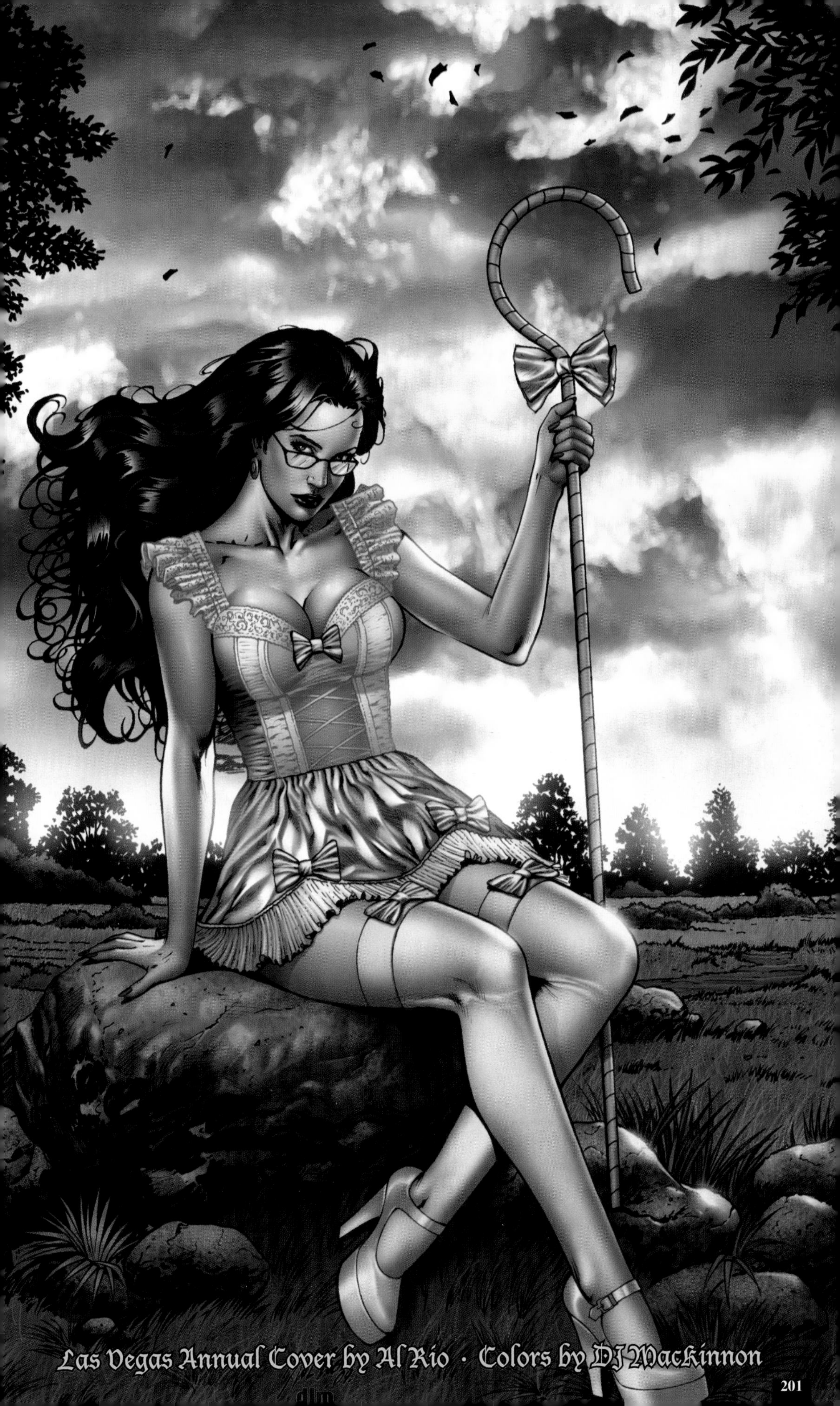

Las Vegas Annual Cover by Al Rio · Colors by DJ Mackinnon

Las Vegas Annual Cover by Facundo Percio - Colors by Annette Kwok

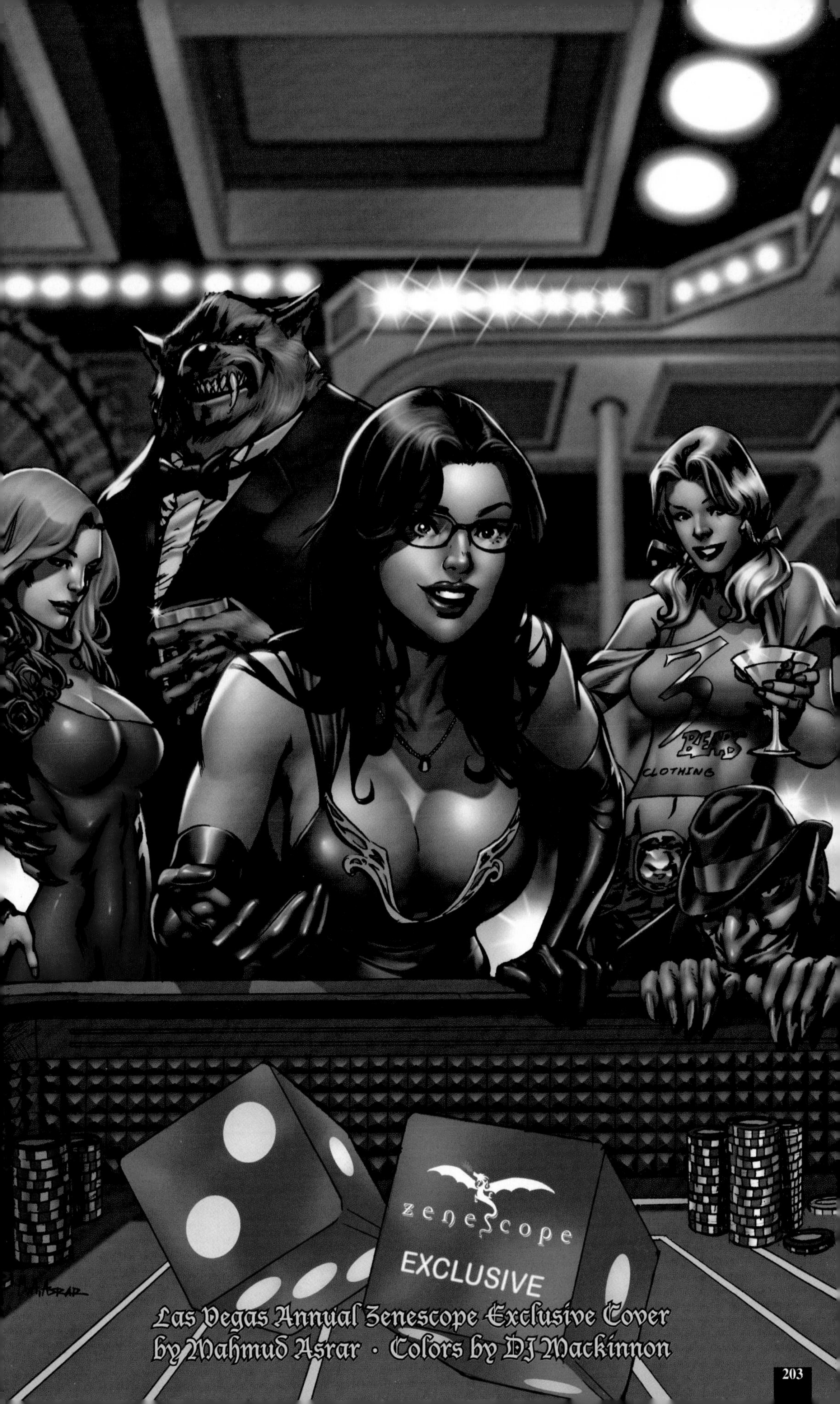
CLOTHING
zenescope
EXCLUSIVE

Las Vegas Annual Zenescope Exclusive Cover
by Mahmud Asrar · Colors by DJ Mackinnon

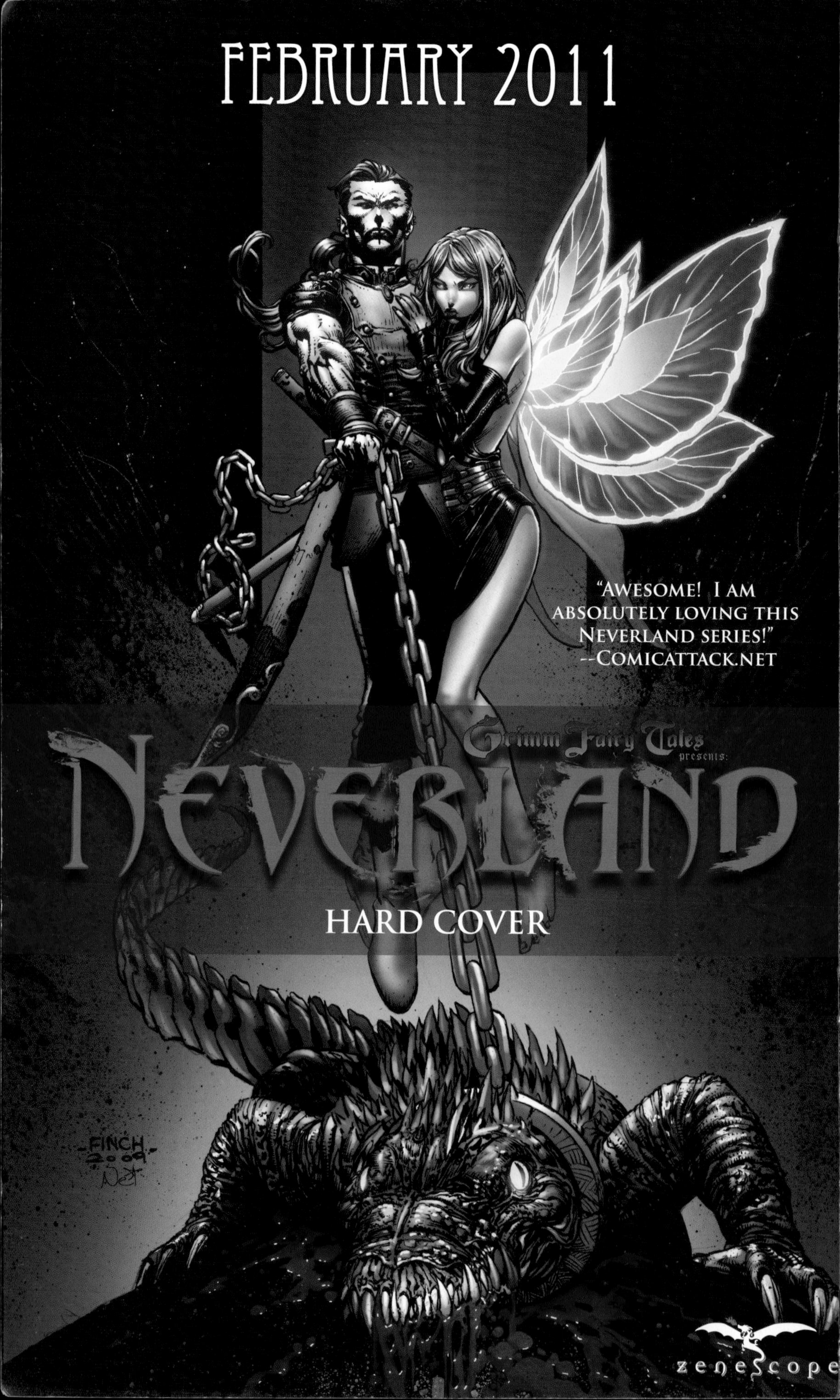
FEBRUARY 2011
"AWESOME! I AM ABSOLUTELY LOVING THIS NEVERLAND SERIES!"
--COMICATTACK.NET
Grimm Fairy Tales presents:
NEVERLAND
HARD COVER
FINCH 2009
zenescope

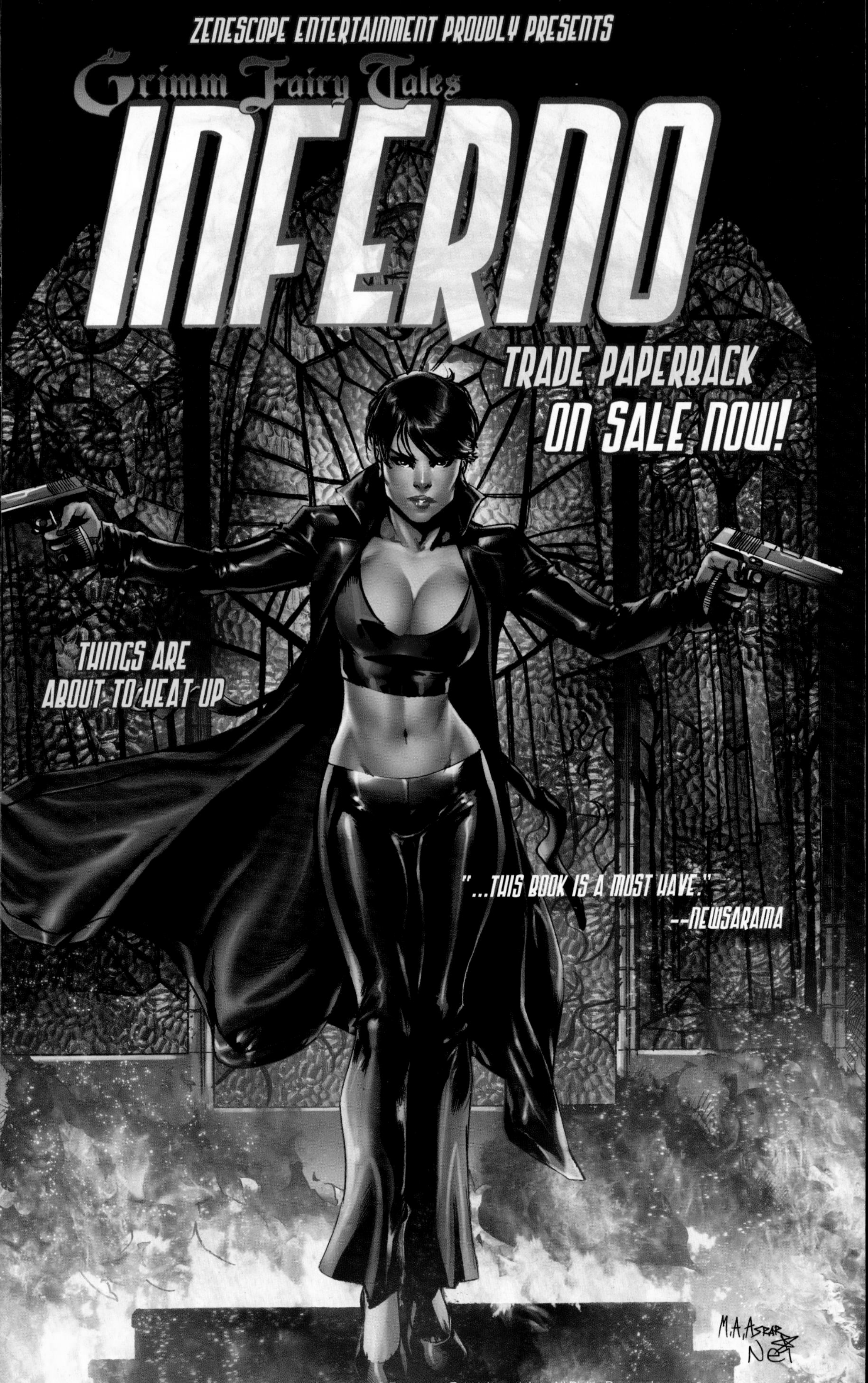
ZENESCOPE ENTERTAINMENT PROUDLY PRESENTS
Grimm Fairy Tales
INFERNO
TRADE PAPERBACK
ON SALE NOW!
THINGS ARE
ABOUT TO HEAT UP
"...THIS BOOK IS A MUST HAVE."
--NEWSARAMA
M.A. ASRAR

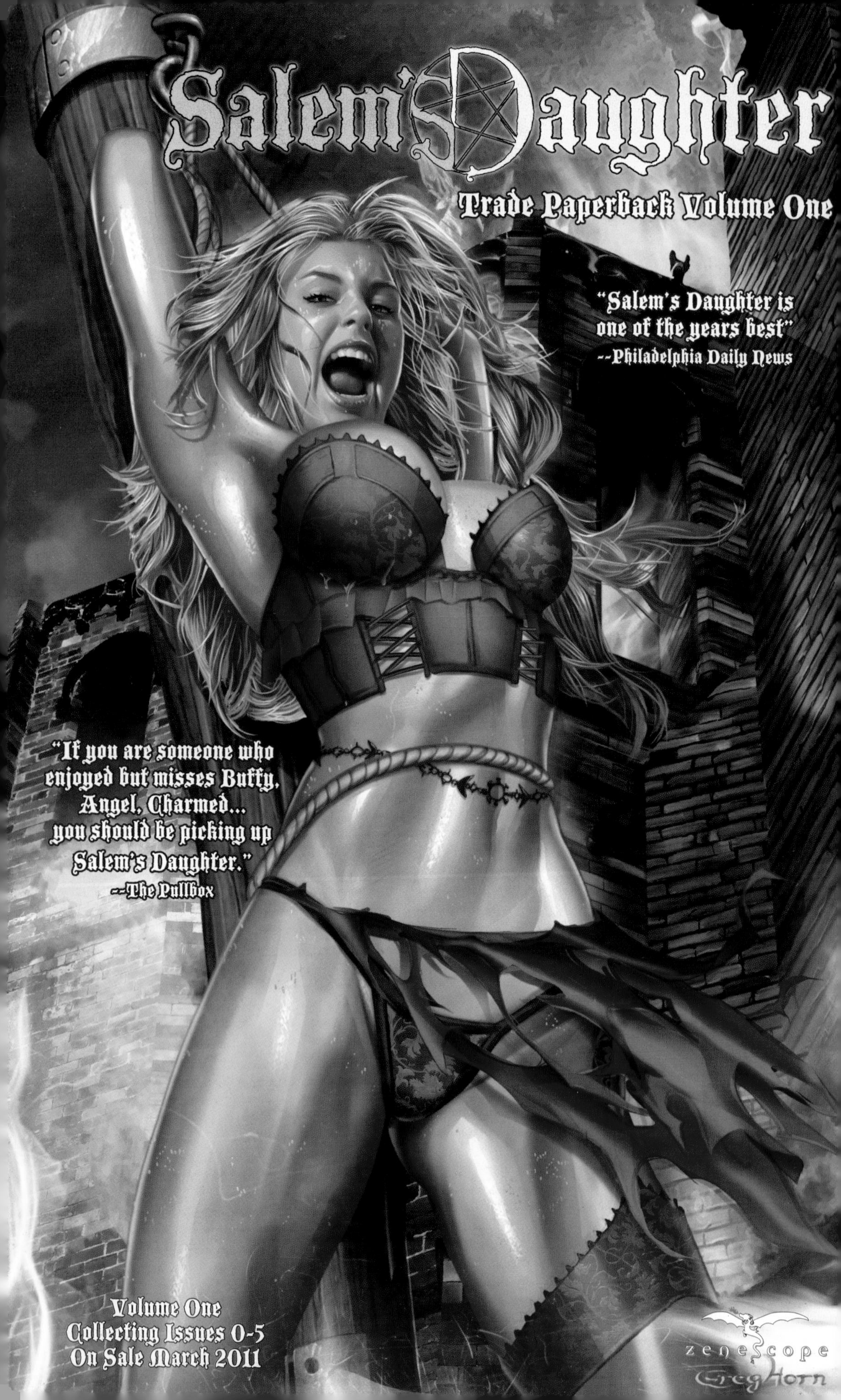

Salem's Daughter
Trade Paperback Volume One
"Salem's Daughter is one of the years best"
--Philadelphia Daily News
"If you are someone who enjoyed but misses Buffy, Angel, Charmed... you should be picking up Salem's Daughter."
--The Pullbox
Volume One
Collecting Issues 0-5
On Sale March 2011
zenescope
Greg Horn

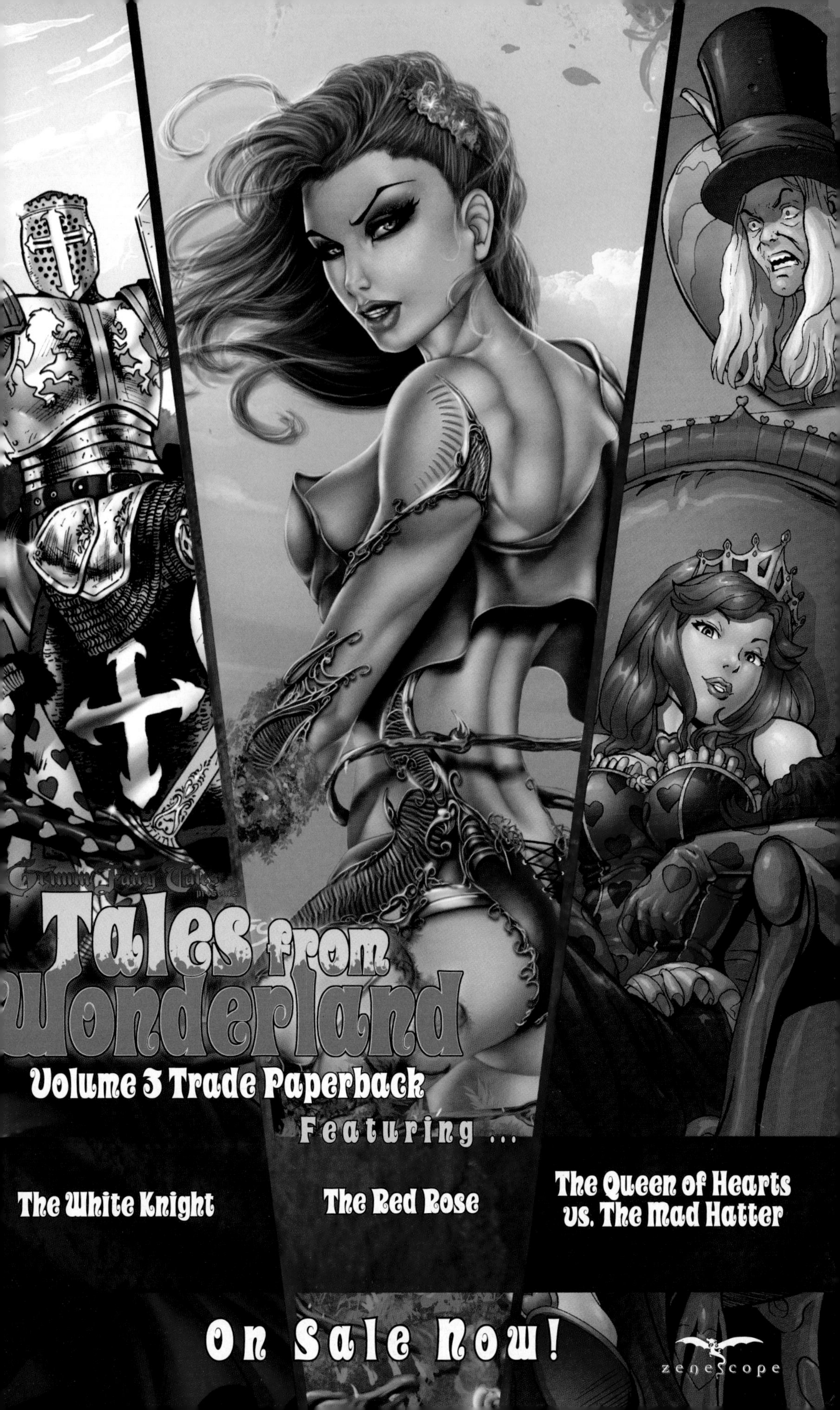

Grimm Fairy Tales presents
Tales from Wonderland
Volume 3 Trade Paperback
Featuring ...
The White Knight
The Red Rose
The Queen of Hearts vs. The Mad Hatter
On Sale Now!
zenescope

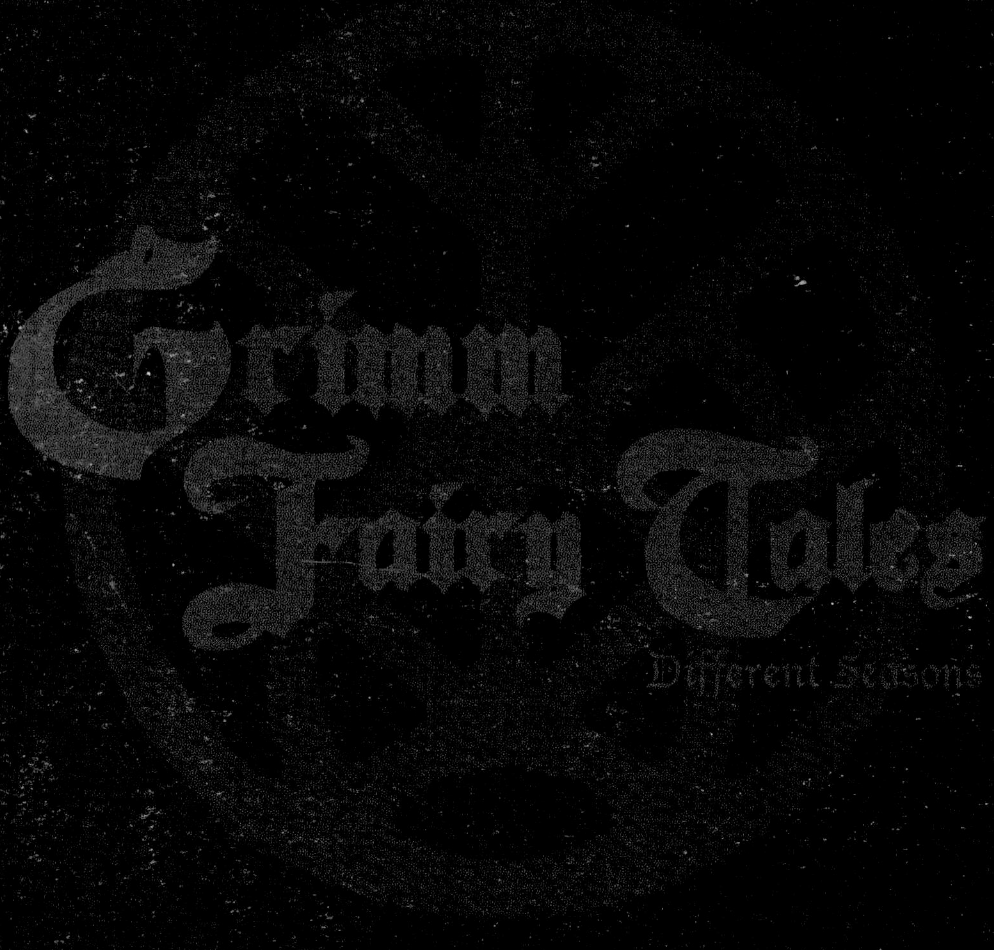
Grimm
Fairy Tales
Different Seasons